Praise for
ADAM & EVIE'S MATCHMAKING TOUR

"*Adam & Evie's Matchmaking Tour* is everything I wanted it to be—romantic, funny, tender, sexy, honest, and beautifully written. Let Nora Nguyen be your tour guide on the romantic trip of a lifetime."

—Meg Shaffer, nationally bestselling author
of *The Wishing Game*

"What a gorgeous love story—cinematic, spicy, and emotionally wise. Nora Nguyen has perfected the romance novel."

—Annabel Monaghan, nationally bestselling author
of *Summer Romance*

"Nguyen effortlessly guides readers through Evie and Adam's exhilarating romance, striking a perfect balance between tender moments and sparky banter. Romance lovers and armchair travelers alike are sure to be sucked in."

—*Publishers Weekly*

"Readers will be swept away by *Adam & Evie's Matchmaking Tour*, which brims with emotion, sparkling banter, and sexy romance. Set against the idyllic backdrop of Việt Nam, this is an immersive love story about taking leaps, following your heart, and seizing second chances in life. Nora Nguyen's talent shines on every page."

—Lauren Kung Jessen, author of *Lunar Love*

"A sexy tale that h̶   ̶ing."

—*Library Journal*

ADAM & EVIE'S
MATCHMAKING TOUR

ADAM & EVIE'S
MATCHMAKING TOUR

A Novel

NORA NGUYEN

AVON

An Imprint of HarperCollins*Publishers*

ADAM & EVIE'S MATCHMAKING TOUR. Copyright © 2024 by Thao Thai. All rights reserved. Printed in the United States of America. No part of this book may be used or reproduced in any manner whatsoever without written permission except in the case of brief quotations embodied in critical articles and reviews. For information, address HarperCollins Publishers, 195 Broadway, New York, NY 10007.

HarperCollins books may be purchased for educational, business, or sales promotional use. For information, please email the Special Markets Department at SPsales@harpercollins.com.

FIRST EDITION

Designed by Jackie Alvarado

Library of Congress Cataloging-in-Publication Data has been applied for.

ISBN 978-0-06-338150-6

24 25 26 27 28 LBC 5 4 3 2 1

To all the lost ones who wonder if they can ever return home

San Francisco

"Green is your color, Evie-pie."

Auntie Hảo removed the dangling jade earrings from the silk pouch and helped Evie secure the gold latches behind her ears. Evie swung her head gently, shaking the smooth circles onto her cheeks. In Auntie Hảo's enormous gilt mirror—bought at an estate sale of a minor Thai princess—Evie saw herself reflected. Gangly, too tall for her age, and eternally uncertain; uncool by anyone's standards, especially Queen Bee Tessa, who ruled the seventh grade with steely determination. But with the jade earrings, Evie felt different. Older, maybe. Definitely more sophisticated. They looked like they belonged.

"I love them," Evie said, touching her ears. "They make me feel more Vietnamese."

"Your father would have been proud," Auntie Hảo said, smoothing Evie's wayward hair from her forehead.

"Not my mother," Evie muttered. "She hates anything that reminds her of Việt Nam. And Dad."

Auntie Hảo avoided her niece's eyes. "Grace is still grieving."

Evie didn't say that Grace slept every moment that she wasn't at work. Once, Evie tiptoed into her mother's room and tried to wake her—it was dinnertime, and there was no food in the house—but Grace only flipped over and hugged the pillow tighter. "Why can't everyone leave me alone?"

she'd asked, her voice muffled. Evie wanted to scream, *Because you have a daughter! And someone has to keep this family together!* Was this how everyone grieved?

Evie's father, Danh Lang, had died the previous year, and neither his wife nor his daughter had recovered. Evie's brand of grief was channeled into mournful stanzas in her journal, while Grace's seemed to rise like a fog in the house, covering every inch, every formerly happy memory. The rooms, once full of voices and laughter, became dreadfully quiet. Empty.

Now all Evie had of her father was Auntie Hảo. And Grace didn't even want her to have that. She'd tried to stop Evie's summer trip to San Francisco to visit Auntie Hảo, but Evie's wheedling eventually worked. Maybe Grace needed a break from her melodramatic daughter too.

"I won't forgive her for not letting me go to Việt Nam with you," Evie said.

"It's a big trip. Your mother was right to put a stop to it; I should have talked to her before I invited you."

"It wouldn't have mattered," Evie said sullenly.

"It matters to her."

"Tell me about Việt Nam," Evie said, changing the subject.

Auntie Hảo enthusiastically launched into a description of all the places she'd visited—Hạ Long Bay with its green-furred mountains and crystal-clear water; bustling Hồ Chí Minh City; the night market in Hội An, lit under swinging lanterns, where Auntie Hảo bought the jade earrings Evie wore now. Evie had seen plenty of photos of her father's birthplace, but she never tired of hearing the stories of Auntie Hảo's travels. To her, these places were more than just beautiful sites to visit. Each new city represented an invitation. A window into a life ready to be lived.

Sighing, Evie said, "I wish I could have gone with you."

Auntie Hảo studied her. Evie could tell she was seeing her deceased brother in Evie's features. Her face took on a solemnity that muted some of the merriness in her eyes.

Eventually, she said, "I promise you, one day, I'll make sure you get to Việt Nam."

"We'll go together," Evie said, brightening.

"We'll light up that whole damn country, Pie."

Evie could picture it so clearly: stepping off the plane with her hand in Auntie Hảo's. Flopping on a hotel bed to plan their itinerary while they bit into pastries from the street stalls. A rare smile flickered across her face.

Then the moment ended. Auntie Hảo stood briskly and pulled Evie with her, brushing the fabric from her ample lap. "Come on. Away from the mirror now; we have a party to host."

It was one of those balmy nights when the Pacific breeze drifted slowly off the water onto the balcony of Auntie Hảo's magnificent row house, the envy of anyone who'd ever dreamed of owning property in the Bay Area. Auntie Hảo was rich. Not just normal San Francisco rich. She could travel every week of the year, eat at every five-star restaurant, buy up all the designer boutiques in Union Square, and still have enough to go around. And she was husbandless and childless, which meant that her generosity usually filtered down to her nieces and nephews. Not that it did Evie any good. Aside from that blissful three-month summer vacation in San Francisco, Grace refused any help from Hảo, claiming that they were not a charity case.

But Evie didn't care about any of that. She just wanted to be *here*, with her aunt, in this mess of noise and delightful smells and sparkling promise. Auntie Hảo's parties were legendary. There was something about her joie de vivre that drew in all the local characters and even some minor celebrities. In San Francisco, Evie lived a different, more glamorous life.

That night, the bar was stocked and the caterers were milling, putting the finishing touches on the chocolate fountain and rearranging tiny sausage rolls that Evie snuck off the trays. Soon, there was the sound of the door opening—Auntie Hảo never locked her door—and thundering footsteps. The party had arrived.

Priya, Auntie Hảo's best friend and sometime-nemesis, was the first to sweep Evie into a hug. She wore a midnight-blue caftan and a pair of yellow flats with rhinestones on the sides. "My sweet little girl! I missed you. When are you moving to San Francisco?"

Evie laughed through the cloud of Priya's rose perfume. "I missed you too, Auntie P."

Priya pinched Evie's cheek, then kissed it juicily, squeezing her tighter. "Oh, but you're going to be such a beauty one day. Then we will make you a match to end all matches."

"She's too young to be thinking of that," Auntie Hảo cut in.

Priya shrugged. "Maybe. But when the day comes, she will have an epic love story, mark my words. A girl like Evie won't settle for anything common. There will be melodrama! Misunderstanding! Spice!"

"Um, thank you?" Evie said, a little breathless now.

Auntie Hảo scowled, her dark eyebrows drawn like angry eels. "Unhand my niece, you menace. You're choking her."

Priya eyed the sausage roll in Evie's hand. "She's more likely to choke from that nasty excuse for food you serve."

"My caterer is *very* exclusive," Auntie Hảo said indignantly. "He was on the 'Restaurateurs to Watch' list in the *Chronicle*."

"Hmph. I told you time and time again I would help cook. I *am* the best samosa maker in town!"

"Did you give yourself that title?"

"You have always been jealous—"

"Of *what*, exactly, Priya? Your dry-ass rice pilaf? Your watery gazpacho?"

Priya's eyes blazed dangerously, but an undeterred Auntie Hảo stuck her hands on her hips, puffing her cheeks out like a gibbon establishing dominance.

Evie made a hasty escape from the brewing storm and soon found herself passed around the party like a tray of hors d'oeuvres. Liam, the semisuccessful playwright who always seemed to be in a state of crisis, moaned about his difficulty casting the lead character while sloshing his cocktail on Evie's new Laura Ashley dress. Paris, a gender-fluid clothing designer, tried to talk Evie into modeling for their next show. Samara, an art historian in a skintight black jumpsuit, pulled Evie aside to ask if she'd started her period yet, then proceeded to tell her about the miracle of menstruation, to Evie's abject mortification.

Even still, she loved Auntie Håo's friends. They filled her life with audacity and magic. In their example, she could believe that living outside the broad strokes of expectation could be something wonderful, instead of something to be feared, as Grace had believed. Evie always tried to position herself close to the writers, a morose bunch with cutting observations and tweedy good looks. Her dream was to become a writer someday, though she had no inkling of what she would have to write about. Everything in her life seemed so terribly predictable—and she worried that she was the most boring thing in it.

But Auntie Håo never made her feel that way. She was convinced that Evie would do something great, and even if Evie didn't believe it, basking in her aunt's confidence felt like chugging a soda—the bubbly joy went straight to her head.

As the party ended, she heard a commotion coming from the balcony. With surprising strength, a woman in a glittery silver dress shoved the chocolate fountain onto a handsome man with a pointy beard—a famous magician, Auntie Håo whispered, who had a reputation for kissing his assistants. Evie watched in horrified fascination as the chocolate exploded onto the man's white shirt, dripping all the way down to his shoes. To add insult to injury, the silver-dress woman shoved a hunk of pound cake into the magician's mouth, like an apple in a pig.

She shouted over her shoulder, "If you *ever* step out on me again, Phineas Ash, it'll be a boiling pot of oil I dump over your sorry head!"

Phineas stared after her for a moment, then chewed the cake thoughtfully. After a moment, he grinned a chocolatey grin and gave the crowd a bow. "And for my next act, I'll piss off another woman with the bad judgment to date me!"

They clapped as he plodded stickily toward the napkins.

"Never a dull moment," Auntie Håo said at Evie's side.

"Should we help Phineas?"

Auntie Håo gestured at the magician, now surrounded by at least four tutting, spectacularly beautiful women. "I think he'll be fine."

Phineas smirked as he licked the chocolate off his finger.

Auntie Hảo continued, "This is why we don't let ourselves get too entangled with men, Pie. They're useful for a good time, but ultimately disappointing."

"My dad wasn't like that," Evie said defensively.

"Of course not. He was one in a million. Our bloodline has always been exceptional. But Phineas, much as I love him, is sadly more representative of the general population."

"You've never met anyone worth marrying yourself?"

Evie had never heard a whisper of romance around Auntie Hảo. It confused her; lovable Auntie Hảo could have had a million admirers in her lifetime, yet she'd lived alone for decades. It wasn't even about Auntie Hảo's warm beauty—cute, peachy cheeks, twinkly black eyes, permed black curls—but her whole air of mischief, of expectation. That kind of delight was hard to find in life and would have surely drawn in many a man.

"Marriage is for the birds," Auntie Hảo announced. "One day, I'll tell you about the time my parents tried to force me to go to a matchmaker. You can imagine how *that* went. Anyway, I'm not saying you can't have fun with men, honey. But sometimes a woman only has herself to count on."

Evie thought of Grace, sleeping with her back toward the door, completely drowned in grief. Maybe Auntie Hảo was right. Who was to say if love was worth the heartbreak? Or the chocolate mess.

"I can count on *you*," Evie said, wrapping her arms around her aunt's waist.

"So you can, Pie. Forever and ever."

Above them, the moon shone with a milky luster. Summer would soon end, and Evie would go back to her life in that lonely house, trudging through her school days with kids who ignored her, bleakly marking holidays her mother refused to celebrate anymore. But then another summer would come, then another. Of all the promises already broken in her young life, she knew she could at least count on Auntie Hảo's. And maybe someday, she would live a life worth writing about.

EVIE

Midland, Ohio

Evie-pie!

I'm dead, it seems. That old witch Priya will take my place as the head of the gardening association, I suppose. What a mess she'll make of things—her tulips! If you lived in San Francisco, I'd tell you to spy on her for me. Maybe you can arrange some espionage anyway.

Instead, you're wasting away in Midland—but not for long. Dear one, I have a proposition. It's a big one. I always intended to leave you my house in San Francisco. After all, you were practically raised there. You can sell it or live in it or set up a crazy artists' commune (just please, no orgies on my crane tapestries). I wouldn't have it go to anyone else.

But, in my old age, I suppose I've become rather meddlesome. You see, I've decided to add a condition. It's a little one. Tiny. You may inherit my house if you agree to go on a matchmaking tour in Việt Nam. I've even chosen the matchmaking organization! Love Yêu (get it?!) is a brand-new feminist-run tour, perfect for a poetess like yourself. I reserved a spot for you as soon as I heard about it.

I know you'll think this out of character for me—after all, I spent years decrying the worth of men. While I don't think a partner is the only answer, I do think you're lonely. Don't talk to me about that Atlas fellow. He's Phineas in wire-framed glasses.

*You could use a shake-up. I'd like you to have a shot at love—
with a man or woman, Auntie doesn't judge—before you become
cynical. There are many ways to be brave, but I admit that I was
never brave in love. Forgive me for saying I see a lot of myself in you.
I suppose one's deathbed can make one morbid at times. Regretful,
even.*

*Why Việt Nam, you ask? Well, we are all a bit disconnected
from our heritage. Your father would have wanted you to visit the
homeland. And I promised. Two birds, one stone! Plus, I thought you
might get some inspiration for your poetry. Many of our people were
absolute fire—as the kids say—in the poetry department.*

*I've put aside some money for your fee for the tour. All you need
to do is contact my lawyers, and they will set it all up. Because I know
how you like to drag your pretty little feet, there are a few clauses. You
have three months from the receipt of this letter to complete the tour.
Photographic evidence of you in the motherland must be sent to the
lawyers. If you don't complete your mission, my most beloved, then
the house will be sold—probably to some soulless developer—and the
funds distributed among your grasping cousins. I know you know our
home (for I've always thought of it as ours) deserves a better fate.*

*But I'm no despot. You don't have to fall in love. You just have to
try. And once the tour is complete, even if you have found no Prince
Charming to shove in your suitcase, you'll get the deed to the house.
Win-win! What's a few weeks to a lifetime of promise?*

*Evie-pie, I love you so much that I think I might burst with it.
My hopes for you are myriad, and I believe that you will soon find
the path to your wildest dreams, even the ones you are too afraid to
speak aloud.*

—Auntie Hảo

Evie finds the letter no more sensible after the hundredth reading than after
her first shocked skim, a few days ago. She hasn't told anyone about Auntie

Hảo's deranged, posthumous wishes, save her cousin Lillian Lang-Peterson, who squealed with delight and immediately tried to book Evie on the first flight to Hồ Chí Minh City.

"Why the hell not?" Lillian had demanded, hands on her pregnant middle.

The reasons are many. First of all, can one go on a matchmaking tour if one already has a boyfriend? Not that Atlas ever registered to Auntie Hảo as a serious partner, despite the few times she met him. He'd turned up his charm, rushing to open doors and pick up the bill at the fancy restaurants he'd persuaded them to go to, but Auntie Hảo had only sniffed in his direction, as if to say, *You don't fool me.*

Aside from Atlas, there is Evie's job as an adjunct writing professor at Midland College, one that employs her through the summer months and keeps the cockroaches from skittering around in her bank account. And Việt Nam! Who picks up and hops on a flight halfway around the world with only a month's notice? But that was Auntie Hảo to a tee. Tempestuous, adventurous. The opposite of the person Evie has become at the ripe old age of thirty-two.

Evie shoves the letter back in her messenger bag and fumbles under the squat gnome where Atlas keeps his house key. Unlike her unkempt apartment, Atlas's house looks like it could grace the front of a real estate catalog. With the blue wooden shutters and actual landscaping in the form of bright poppies and leafy hostas, there's not a stone out of place.

She juggles her purse, along with a paper bag full of groceries from the gourmet store on Main Street, and lets herself in with the key. Even though they're technically not supposed to be dating, it's the worst kept secret in the whole English department, of which Atlas himself is the head. One too many faculty members (and students) have seen them leaving readings together or her hastily dashing from his house in the early morning wearing yesterday's teaching clothes.

Today is Atlas's forty-fifth birthday and a particularly melancholy one for reasons Evie cannot uncover. He's been moping over his Earl Grey for the past week, muttering something about mortality and life lessons. Evie, being the good secret girlfriend she is, has decided to cook his favorite meal—beef Wellington with a side of mashed parsnips. Along the way to the kitchen, she passes photos of Atlas at Oxford with his boxing pals, a black-and-white portrait of a walrus-'stached Thomas Hardy, and a small oil painting of Atlas's deceased hound, Doyle.

In the kitchen, she hums as she gets out the pots and pans, scrolling through the ingredients on her phone. While she cooks her way through a very complex dish she has no business attempting, she tries not to think about Auntie Hảo's letter and the promising little thrill it gives her. Of course, she can't just *go to Việt Nam*. She has a life here! And she's just learned that parsnips aren't as horrifying as she supposed they would be!

But then there's the row house in the heart of San Francisco. A real estate boon for anyone. Evie wouldn't live in it, but she could sell it, which would set her up for a long time. No more adjuncting on a pittance. No more random editing jobs from Upwork. She could finally not worry about money and *write*.

Turns out, poetry isn't exactly a get-rich scheme, though she *was* named the poet laureate of Midland by a portly mayor with faintly veiled literary aspirations.

Her debut book of poetry, *Auntie Hảo's Cabinet of Curiosities*, did moderately well, but once the early reception died down, there wasn't enough luster to carry her forward. Since then, she's missed out on numerous opportunities to attend hallowed residencies in the woods, where all the writers sing about their most burning aspirations over an open fire.

She's missed out on jobs too, especially ones promising permanency and the dangling carrot of a tenure-track life. Her agent nudges her monthly about a new manuscript, telling Evie unnecessarily, "The iron is no longer hot." Perhaps Evie has been in a bit of a creative funk since Auntie Hảo's death.

She's pondering this as the fire alarm goes off, blaring so loudly that she has to cover her ears with her oven mitts. Smoke billows from the oven. *Oh,*

God, she thinks, *475 degrees is definitely not the same as 375.* Last time she tries to cook while distracted. Last time she tries to cook at all.

Just as she's pulling the beef Wellington out of the oven, she hears the front door open. And there's Atlas pausing in the kitchen archway in a sky-blue button-down that somehow matches his eyes perfectly. He takes a dishcloth and, in one smooth movement, bats it toward the smoke alarm, appeasing it enough for the siren to dissipate. He opens a window, then the back door. Then, he stares, bemused by Evie's flour-streaked boots, the ragged mess of her hair, and the blackened blob on the baking sheet.

"Well, darling, this is a surprise," he says, with a faint British accent.

Atlas isn't British but has Anglophile aspirations that Evie has always found charming. The accent only disappears when he's been drinking. Then he has a slight drawl from Montana. A man of many accents.

She motions to the burnt top of the dish. "I don't think it's supposed to be that color. But it's your favorite."

"Kidney pie!"

"No," Evie says dejectedly. "Wellington. Beef."

"Chin up, Evie. The mashed potatoes look just the thing."

"Parsnips."

"Huh." Atlas pushes his glasses up on his nose.

"Happy birthday," she says, shrugging.

He laughs and opens his arms to her. She steps into them, thankful that he isn't scolding her for nearly burning down his house. Gently, he rests his chin on the crown of her head. There it is, that mind-numbing comfort that only Atlas can give. She wants to place her head on his shoulder and sleep forever and ever. Briefly, she wonders if this is really what you want to feel in a relationship. Comfort is a beautiful thing, but is there such a thing as too much of it?

He'd been the one to pursue her with a job offer, after her poetry collection started getting some minor awards. He told her that Midland needed a voice like hers on its literary scene. She had been bopping around a small town in Iowa before that, and she guessed Ohio might be a slightly different shade of the same, so she agreed. The dollar could stretch far in a place like this.

It had been natural to fall into bed with Atlas after a few months of teaching writing seminars and attending faculty meetings where he presided. Toward Evie, he's always been attentive and sincere, and seems to truly care about her work. Sure, he's sometimes a little pretentious, and he likes to flirt with other women much more than she enjoys watching him flirt with other women. And of course, they annoy each other after long periods of time together, as two introverts can. But surely he never deserved Auntie Hảo's raised eyebrows and unveiled disdain. If she could have conjured up a perfect, nerd-hot boyfriend, it would have been Atlas, right down to the argyle socks.

Even still, Evie finds herself wondering if she's missing something.

He drops a kiss on her lips and says, "Let me go change. I have the smell of undergraduate desperation on me."

"Ah. Eau de Can-You-Change-My-Grade?"

"What else? I suppose the smoke masks it now."

"I'm sorry."

"Let's order in pizza, love."

As Atlas bounds up the stairs to his room, Evie sighs and punches in an order for caprese pizza on her phone's restaurant delivery app. Then she spies the edge of Auntie Hảo's letter peeking from her messenger bag.

Evie scoffs at the name of the matchmaking service. Love Yêu—*yêu* meaning "love" in Vietnamese. Her countrymen sure love a good pun, judging from the names of the local restaurants: Phở Sho and Nguyening at Life. Evie flips open the laptop on Atlas's kitchen counter. Password: 060253. The late Queen Elizabeth II's coronation date.

She is about to type "Love Yêu" in the browser when she spies an open Google document on the screen. It's a job description. For . . . an adjunct creative writing professor. She peers closer. Reads through the requirements. It's *her* job. Same salary, same title, same parking benefits. Contact email: Atlas.Matthews@Midland.edu.

"Oh, dear."

Evie whirls to see Atlas in a gray polo, his face looking equally ashen. He's reaching toward her, but she flits out of his grasp.

"Are you interviewing people for *my* job?" she asks, her voice low and deadly.

"That is—" Atlas pushes a hand through his beautiful auburn locks. "It's just that—"

"For a man so eloquent, you are looking like an open-mouthed carp."

"Evie, please understand," he pleads. "Your student evaluations have not been . . . up to par. There have been complaints about your grading structure from the students."

"They don't try!" Evie cries, throwing her hands up. "They're entitled! And lazy!"

"Certainly, but their parents pay tuition and fund the department."

"And that's a reason to kowtow to them?"

"All I'm saying is that certain concessions must be made," he tells her tiredly. This is not the first time they've had this conversation. "We meet them halfway. And some of the subject matter you've covered seems unorthodox."

"Sad Dead Women?"

"Precisely."

Evie had assigned an influx of writings from early feminists who, unfortunately, usually came to dismal ends. Sylvia Plath and Virginia Woolf and Anne Sexton, beautiful voices that left their mark, long after their lives ended. She thought her curriculum was unique. That it said something about life and love and trauma and the creative life. She assumed her students would find resonance in the despair of the greats. Instead, there were reports that the college counselors had seen a marked uptick in sessions scheduled by students from *her* class, specifically.

Atlas asks, a touch of plaintiveness in his voice, "Did you *have* to call it that?"

"It was that or Head in the Oven."

He gestures expansively with his palms, as if to say, *See?*

She can respect that he needs to let her go. People have been fired before, perhaps even by those they were sleeping with. And she's not terribly invested in teaching at the moment, it's true. At least, not teaching this particular group of undergraduates. But to *hide* the firing from her and draft a job posting before she even knows that her professional days are numbered, before she even has a plan . . . well, that is another level of betrayal. Humiliation. More than that: it's cowardice, through and through.

Looking now at Atlas, his pained eyes landing everywhere but on her face, she realizes that she does not want to spend another minute at his home, pretending to be cheerful about his birthday while he slowly pulls her job out from under her. She's too mortified to be the good secret girlfriend today.

"I'm going now," she announces. "I hope you choke on your birthday pizza."

"Wait, Evie. Stay. This doesn't have to ruin everything between us."

"Call me when you have the balls to communicate like a human."

She snatches her bag, along with Auntie Hảo's letter, and flounces out of the room, with Atlas calling halfheartedly after her. On the porch, she sees a young freckled man in a dirty shirt, carrying a large pizza box as he squints at the door number.

"Large caprese?" he asks, blinking bewildered eyes at her.

"I'll take that," she says, snatching the pizza from him. And without missing a beat, she throws the box like a Frisbee into Atlas's prized garden, where it knocks over a gnome and splays across a hedge like a fallen banner.

The pizza deliveryman clears his throat. "Good aim. Hey, is that you, Professor Lang? It's Sage. From your Intro to Poetry class. I was wondering if I could get an extension on—"

"Yes!" Evie says over her shoulder, bounding to her car, pizza forgotten. "You can have an extension until the end of time! A's for everyone!"

"Whoa, really?"

As she starts her car, Evie begins to reconsider the turn her life has taken. No job. No summer plans. Nothing but time ahead of her. She holds Auntie Hảo's letter, then brings it to her chest, like a kind of talisman. A few weeks of sightseeing for a house that's worth several million dollars, plus some much-needed breathing room from her cowardly secret boyfriend. Who wouldn't take the offer?

Her heart beats a little faster, though at the moment, she doesn't know if it's due to the confrontation with Atlas, or excitement, or pedestrian hunger. Whatever she decides, though, she knows she has to do it soon. Open doors don't stay open forever.

ADAM

Hồ Chí Minh City, Việt Nam

By the time his sister, Ruby, arrives, Adam Quyền is already in a foul mood. He eyes her as she sweeps onto the plastic stool across from his with her dark sunglasses perched on her nose, though it's nearly nighttime in the overcrowded, beer-drenched District 1 in Hồ Chí Minh City. Around them, the cloud of pollution from commuter traffic has begun to dissipate, leaving a sticky film of humidity. There are throngs of tourists already inching toward the bars and indoor clubs, sweat mustaches peppering their upper lips.

A few women—Vietnamese and Anglo alike—eye Adam in his tailored navy slacks and white button-down. His sleeves are rolled up, which is basically a flashing lighthouse signal for lusty women everywhere. The slacks, though, are wet from the Tiger Beer someone just spilled on him. He's got his arms crossed, and his brow is thunderous. The picture of unapproachable.

He doesn't pay attention to any of the women, even though typically, he might have flirted with a few just for kicks. To keep in practice. Lord knows he's not looking for anything longer than one night of escape.

But he can't focus on the display of beautiful women in front of him at the moment. All he wants is a shower, then a long sleep after the day he had rushing around Ruby's matchmaking business, Love Yêu Tours, answering calls and setting up meetings with interested investors. Explaining Ruby's clever little pun to foreigners.

If it had been anyone else, Adam would be halfway to his high-rise by now. But Ruby summoned this meeting, and technically, she's his boss—although a highly haphazard one, as their whole staff might concur in the privacy of their offices. There are days when she disappears without warning, only to return with a spiraling list of impossible demands for everyone in the office, especially Adam.

"Why are you sulking now, Baby Bảo?" Ruby coos. She flags down a server for two Heinekens.

A muscle in his cheek twitches. No one calls him Bảo anymore but his parents. Adam is easier for a variety of reasons, not least of which is that he works with many American and Australian investors, for whom Adam is simpler to remember. It annoyed him at first, having to swap his name for the ease of foreigners, but in actuality, he's become Adam Quyền completely: impenetrable exterior, hard jaw, a force to be reckoned with in business. Ruby, too, changed her name from Thu when she began operating as a public figure after founding Love Yêu. But his sister's use of his Vietnamese diminutive is purposeful. She likes to remind him of his place as both her younger brother and employee.

Adam gestures toward his pants. "Drunken accident from some tourist on a post-college pleasure cruise. And the beer is warm here."

"It's Sài Gòn. The beer is warm everywhere. And *they* don't care," Ruby says, gesturing at a group of young men awash in sunburns and sputtering out loud jokes to every passing woman.

"I hate tourists."

"You hate *everyone*—well, except for pretty women who look like Ngô Thanh Vân. Besides, we need those tourists," Ruby says serenely. "They could be looking for gorgeous Vietnamese spouses too."

Ever the opportunist, his sister.

She orders a spicy green papaya salad and glistening skewers of nem nướng. As he serves them both, she looks down at her phone with a frown. He knows what she's reading. The press release on the first matchmaking tour is due to come out in the morning, and Adam sent her the draft right before he left their office—the last to leave, as usual.

"So what's wrong with it?" Adam asks, trying not to grit his teeth.

She bites her lip. "Well, BB. It's not exactly *terrible*."

"Come off it. I can take your feedback."

"This press release just feels a little soulless. You're talking about a great romantic tour at all the finest luxury hotels, with the most sumptuous food and once-in-a-lifetime experiences that only we can make happen."

"Has anyone ever told you that you're too understated, Ruby?"

She screws up her face, then lets it fall. "We *must* be the best, Adam. Do you know how much competition is out there? It's a bloodthirsty arena, the Vietnamese tourism industry. If we offer the romance without any of the seediness, the guests will understand we're onto something new. Something that transforms fleeting attraction into an epic love story."

"Do you even believe any of this yourself?"

"Do I need to?"

Ruby, ever practical and rigorously competitive, has never had compunction about whittling a situation to her desires, stripping away the emotion to reveal that thin, sturdy core that matters most to her: success. Sure, she can speak the language of romance when it serves her purposes, prettify any commercial transaction. That's what makes her so good at her job. She can talk about heritage and mountaintops and soulmates until she turns blue in the face. But at heart, she's a pragmatist. To her, there is a price on everything. Including love.

Even her own marriage to Thăng seems to run like an assembly line powered by their mutual ambition and utter lack of dependency on each other. Thăng spends most of his time traveling to Australia for work. Often, they seem less like lovers and more like allied soldiers in an invisible war, armored and loyal to the last.

Adam studies his sister as she raises her arms theatrically.

"These men and women will be making the memories of a lifetime while falling head over heels with someone who's experiencing all that right along with them."

"I said that in the release," he protests.

Ruby squints at her screen. "You did not. You wrote, and I quote, 'Love

Yêu aims for the most efficient results for our clients.' I know you worked at a bank before coming on to Love Yêu, but *could* you sound any colder?"

"I'm not a writer. You knew that."

"Well, perhaps we need to hire you a writer someday. After the tour. But for now, is this really the best you can do, BB?"

Adam drags a tanned hand through his hair. "I'll give it another shot, okay?"

"You know I can't give you any passes because you're my little brother."

"Yeah." He knows because Ruby tells him—and the whole staff of Love Yêu—at least once a day.

"I have faith in you."

He swigs his beer, biting back his words. He's *good* at his job, and Ruby knows it. Before signing on to work as the chief marketing officer for Ruby's fledgling company—which had somehow won funding from a couple of investors, in addition to their father—he was making more money than he could spend as a hedge fund manager for Hồ Chí Minh City's elite. Banks were clamoring to poach him. There was talk of him becoming the youngest VP in the company's history. And now he's reduced to being his sister's charity hire.

Sure, he's not the most poetic of the bunch. But he's good at maintaining professional relationships, and he's determined enough to wedge doors open for them. Ruby was the one who convinced him to leave his job, saying that she couldn't trust anyone else with her precious company, and their parents had urged him to do it, saying that it could become a family business. An empire. Ruby, to them, has always been a sure bet.

And after that mess with his former girlfriend of three years, Lana, he was ready to exit the world of high finance anyway. Start over, where no one knew about his humiliation. Though, in retrospect, is it really starting over if you're just hitching your wagon to your big sister's star?

Now Ruby's studying him with a mix of concern and speculation. The look that says she's plotting something. He wonders if she's remembering Lana too, and the failed marriage proposal that nearly all their friends and family witnessed firsthand. He can't shake the image of Lana staring back at him with wide, fearful eyes, pressing her lips tightly as she shook her head faster and faster. *No, no, no.* She didn't even have to say it. He knew before he finished speaking that they were over.

"BB, the truth is, you're not going to really *sell* Love Yêu unless you've experienced it firsthand. After all, have you ever heard of a chef serving a dish without tasting it first? You're just a bystander, not a true advocate for the brand. And, I'm sorry to say, it shows."

"Excuse me? *You're* not going on any matchmaking tours, Ruby."

"Well, I'm married."

Adam bites his tongue in order to avoid talking about Ruby's marriage. Last time Adam saw him, Thăng was sporting a tribal tattoo and a new earring, both marks of a midlife crisis if he'd ever seen one. Ruby said she liked the earring, but the telltale tic along her right eye revealed that she was lying.

She continues, "And as a matter of fact, I *am* going on the first matchmaking tour. Someone has to keep the ship aiming straight. And you're going with me."

"Like hell I am."

Ruby slips her sunglasses over her head, making a shiny black crown with them. To others, she might seem formidable. To Adam, she is still the annoying know-it-all who'll always be their family's only Golden Goose, no matter how much Adam tries to prove himself.

She purses her lips in her most imperious expression. "You are if you're going to stay CMO of Love Yêu. We've been preparing for this for so long. The stakes are unbelievably high."

"Ruby." The music from the club next door pounds into Adam's skull. "I'm not doing it."

"Listen, BB, I'm not saying you have to fall madly in love. In fact, maybe it's better if you don't. But you must know what it is we're all about. And you will never be able to tell just from testimonies or photos. You are in the perfect position to experience it yourself—young, handsome, successful. You're exactly the kind of client we want to attract."

"I'm not a client," he stutters. "I'm the CMO."

"Exactly. And we're a start-up. We all put in the hours—and yes, I know you work yourself to the bone here. So maybe you look at this tour as a kind of vacation. You just have to sit back and take notes. Enjoy the most luxurious accommodations our country has to offer. It isn't the *worst* torture."

"You're patronizing me."

"Only a little. Anyway, you're going, and that's it."

"Want to bet?"

Ruby is unbothered. "You'll see that I'm right someday. And see if you can work the word *unforgettable* into this dry little press release."

Adam throws a handful of bills on the table and shoots a glare back at his sister, who's already turned to spear a piece of papaya, chewing with the carefree equanimity of a Cheshire cat who's eaten all the canaries. Avoiding the winding groups of drunken revelers singing Việt ballads at the top of their lungs, Adam stalks back to his apartment in District 2.

He passes the Bến Thành Market, where vendors are preparing for the night market. His favorite fruit vendor waves a spiky bunch of rambutans in recognition. A few blocks later, he's in front of his apartment building, a boxy, futuristic high-rise with huge glass windows bolstered by shiny steel inlays. He usually takes pride in walking through the doors of the building, into the sumptuous lobby with its plush carpets and busy, well-heeled residents. It's a reminder of his accomplishments, even if they are tied tightly to those of his family.

"Mr. Quyền," the concierge greets. "Your father left this note."

The concierge slides a piece of paper across the counter. Why the elder Quyền can't leave voicemails like a normal overbearing father is beyond Adam's comprehension. But of course, with a voicemail, his father would miss the opportunity to drop in unannounced, dragging his imperious gaze over Adam's apartment while offering unsolicited business advice.

Adam unfolds the note and reads his father's brusque handwriting: *Dinner on Saturday. Don't be late.* He closes his eyes. Another family dinner where his parents fawn over Ruby and cast his own shortcomings on him. It's enough to make him want to disappear up the mountains on his motorbike. Stage his own death. How much would it cost to forge a new identity?

"Thank you," Adam says, crumpling up the paper.

"Have a good evening."

"You too," Adam says, trying for a smile.

As he opens the door to his modern, immaculate apartment, he understands that his privilege has always shadowed him, even in that brief time when he attended Stanford for his MBA, when he was just a sweatpants-clad student like everyone else. A blissful year of freedom. Yet nothing would have been possible without his father's money. *He* wouldn't exist the way he does without it. But that doesn't mean he's ever stopped wanting to prove that he's more than a rich kid.

In his apartment, he takes a long shower, then wraps himself up in a robe. He fingers the sash, remembering how he and Lana would sit in their matching robes on their deck, watching the stars come out above that blistered horizon as they talked about the future. They had such clear plans: Both would rise to great heights at their finance firms, then they would buy a big apartment in the heart of the city; a house by the beach too. They'd have three kids and take vacations to Thailand and France, where she'd show him around all the places where she'd studied as the expat daughter of a Vietnamese diplomat. When he thought of the later decades of his life, he saw himself with her.

But the dream died before it even began, with that very public and ill-fated proposal. After that night, he lost trust in women, yes, but more than that, he lost trust in his own instincts. Now all he has is a few hurried affairs that last a night, maybe a week at most. And work, always work. It's enough because it has to be.

He fires up the computer and logs in to the server where he keeps the marketing documents. He opens the press release, which is completely marked up by Ruby with comments like "Snooze!" and "But what are they supposed to *feel*?" With a sigh, he rolls his neck, then perches his fingers over the keyboard.

Love Yêu: the Unforgettable Matchmaking Tour.
Come join us . . . come aboard . . . come escape into . . .
For the first time in the history of . . . unforgettable shit
DELETE DELETE DELETE.

Since it's their inaugural tour, there are no candids, only stock photos that Ruby found, where gorgeous models stare, awed, into picturesque vistas of temples and beaches. Some hold hands, while others laugh, their heads inclined toward each other in intimate conversation. It's all meant to look romantic yet luxurious, a far cry from the traditional Vietnamese matchmaking tours, where paunchy white men in cargos plod onto overcrowded country buses in the hopes of finding subservient Vietnamese wives. Ruby was very clear on that. She did not want to be another stereotype, another advertisement for colonialist yellow fever.

And to Adam's credit, he understands that he's aced that part of the assignment. Due to his considerable branding efforts—including hiring a deluxe design firm that charged them an insane amount for a logo and website—and the safeguards they put in place, like background checks, sizable client fees, and a rigid vetting process, no one would confuse Love Yêu for a smarmy love tour where fetishists wax poetic about their desire for "an old-fashioned lady." If anything, Love Yêu is meant to attract a new generation of men and women: one determined to have both love *and* purpose.

On board, they have a team of matchmakers who consult for Love Yêu, along with behavioral psychologists, Zen practitioners, and couples therapists who will smooth the way for romance.

But the romance part remains opaque for him. How can he properly write about and sell the appeal of a matchmaking tour if he doesn't believe in lasting love himself? His cursor blinks at the end of the document, like a reminder of the romantic dead end he slammed into at that cursed dinner six months ago. The press release is, undeniably, a soulless advertisement for something that should be enveloped in glamour and, yes, romance.

He pounds his fist on his desk. "Damn."

He knows then that he will be going on the matchmaking tour. Ruby is right, as she so annoyingly often is. There's no way he will be able to excel at his job without understanding what intangible something makes the brand so special. Without witnessing the matches firsthand. It's one thing to hear Ruby talk about her vision. It's quite another to see it in action.

But Adam does not have the stomach for love. He vows that he will be an observer, nothing else. He'll prove to Ruby that he has fully earned his CMO title, that he can grow the company to the heights it deserves to reach. And, if anything else, this will put enough distance between him and Lana and the memories they made together in Hồ Chí Minh City.

EVIE

Midland, Ohio

Evie's never been fired before in her life. In her most logical moments, she can understand that there *is* a difference between being fired and not getting your contract renewed, but right now, it's just semantics to her. Either way, she's been *let go*. Rejected. Taken out like skunky, week-old trash. The icing on the humiliating cake is that everyone—including Atlas—knew exactly what was going on. Scatterbrained Evie, the last to know. The one left behind.

For days, she has holed up in her apartment, eating copious amounts of shrimp chips and avoiding the telephone, but tonight, she must finally peek out of her hidey-hole, like a shamefaced groundhog.

She's getting ready for a reading at the campus bookstore, Bookender's Game, with great, groaning reluctance. Before her firing, she agreed to introduce up-and-coming poet Lancaster Small, a young man with sad eyes and a voluptuous smile usually aimed toward the most attractive men in the creative writing department. Lancaster is good, she'll give him that. Writes a lot about axes and hunting in the woods with his father. But he has a solid handle on imagery, a great hand for a punchy closing line. And he's *producing*, which is more than Evie can say for herself.

As the chair of the department, Atlas is obligated to attend. He'll cast his magnanimity on budding writers intent on worshipping at his shrine. Evie can think of few things she'd like to do *less* than see Atlas, but she doesn't want to let down Lancaster, who took a workshop with her back when she was first starting out at Midland. Even then, he'd been prolific and talented.

So she takes the longest and hottest shower of her life, scalding her skin until it reminds her of the pink flush of a salmon fillet. Then she sits in front of her laptop in a robe. Her email is flooded with messages from students asking for recommendations or last-minute grade adjustments. But she supposes she won't have to worry about that anymore. She deletes most of the emails in one fell swoop.

Not her problem.

What *is* her problem? The lone email from her agent, amid all the Midland College addresses, hinting strongly that they would have to have a phone conversation soon. Evie *hates* a phone conversation. And she knows the agenda all too well. Her agent will ask what she's working on. Evie will bluster or change the topic to *Real Housewives of New York City*, fooling no one. Her agent will sigh and ask if she's considered a writing residency. Eventually, they will both hang up, feeling as crusty and deflated as Halloween pumpkins in November.

Each time they talk, Evie wonders: Is *this* the day I'll be cut? It had been an anomaly for a poet like her to get an agent in the first place—an opportunity she'd hoped might give her legitimacy with the traditional publishers. But she's managed to throw that out the window too.

There's also the fact that she hasn't written a poem in almost a year. At first, she blamed the marketing for her book—it took time to peddle her wares in near-empty bookstores, after all—but now it is deeper than that. Every time she takes out her notebook, she is met with blank, blank, and more blankness, her thoughts scattering like scared little chipmunks. She gazes at her wall of Mary Oliver, Adrienne Rich, Ocean Vuong, Maggie Smith. Each line of beauty taunting her. They were so easily moved by things, these poets. When was Evie last moved by *anything* other than the middle-aged drama between affluent influencers in the Big Apple?

Then there's a pounding on her door, a frantic and complex code-knocking that Evie would recognize anywhere.

"The knocking doesn't *mean* anything, you know," she shouts.

"That's because you refuse to learn Morse code."

Though she's in no mood for visitors, she flings the door open anyway, to see her cousin and Energizer Bunny of a corporate lawyer, Lillian Lang-Peterson, wearing a bespoke two-piece suit that hugs the slight curve of her pregnant middle. Lillian's hair is swept into a chic ponytail, but little tendrils escape, softening her perfectly made-up face. She swoops Evie into a hug and gives her a crushing kiss on the cheek, leaving a coral imprint that Evie tries to wipe away, to little success.

Lillian says, "I'm driving you to the reading. Graham just told me the news. I'm so sorry, honey. Why didn't you call?"

Lillian's husband, Graham, is the head of the School of Humanities, and Atlas's boss. The two get along swimmingly, which makes Evie certain that Graham knew about her impending firing long before he told Lillian.

"How could you know already?" Evie hears the indignant whine in her own voice.

Lillian pours Evie a glass of wine, shimmering to the tippy-top of the glass. "Well, Graham is part of the new hiring committee—"

"The *hiring committee*? That Ralph Fiennes–wannabe bastard moves fast!"

Lillian hands Evie a glass. "I know it's convenient to think that Atlas had a vendetta. But what's done is done, Evie. Let's focus on what's next for you."

Evie sinks into the couch. "What's next is a lifetime of peanut butter sandwiches until I die via a satanic raccoon cult—"

"Raccoons are more cunning than one would think," Lillian says speculatively. "One was even kept as a pet at the White House once!"

"A raccoon has achieved more than I have in one lifetime."

"Aren't we dramatic this evening."

Evie thinks it's a cruel thing for Lillian to say. Everything has come so easily for Lillian over the years. Even as a child biting on the ends of her hair, Lillian knew exactly what she wanted to do: wear great clothes, make a lot of money, and marry a handsome man. And it all *happened*.

Evie, on the other hand, never knew what to do with herself, especially after her father died. She had no road map. When she pictured her life, it was like looking at a crude picture through a pair of waterlogged diving goggles. She could see the shape of something, yet never make it out. When she found poetry, things became marginally clearer. But now how can she make a living this way? The dubious honorific of poet laureate of the township of Midland hardly comes with a salary.

"You'll pick yourself up, Evie," Lillian says, gently now. "You always do."

"I wish Auntie Hảo were here." The words escape before she can stop them.

"I know." Lillian clasps her hands. "Speaking of. Any decision on that matchmaking tour?"

"Love Yêu?" she groans.

"I've been to their website, Evie, and it's a hoot. I mean, in a good way."

Lillian shoves her phone into Evie's hand, and she glances down at the splashy homepage, with a gorgeous waterfall scene, featuring a silhouette of an entwined couple at the base. Large white magazine script plasters over the image: *An Unforgettable Love Story*. Upon scrolling, Evie sees that the first tour leaves from Hồ Chí Minh City in a little less than two weeks. There are six locations, spread over three weeks, each more gorgeous than the last. Too good to be true.

"Nope," Evie says emphatically. "I'm allergic to . . . all of this."

"To fun? Beauty? Adventure?"

"Yes, all that. Look at my arms—hives."

Lillian brushes Evie's arm away. "Why? It looks dreamy! Touring around Việt Nam, surrounded by beautiful and successful people? It's just what you need. And it's not like—"

"I have anything else going on?"

"Well." Lillian shrugs.

"There's the satanic raccoon cult."

"So conduct your rituals in a five-star hotel in Hồ Chí Minh City.

Auntie Håo would have wanted no less for you. For what it's worth, I think it could be life-changing."

"You think I'm going to fall in love with a guy who lives across the world, then *Eat Pray Love* myself into a new person?"

Lillian gives her a big squeeze. "I don't want you to become a new person, idiot. I like you the way you are. But what have you got to lose? And what will you gain? Selling that house will get you set up for a *long* time, Evie."

It isn't like she hasn't thought of the row house and the possibilities it opens. Financially, it would be the windfall of a lifetime. The pressure would be alleviated dramatically; she could take her time finding a new teaching position. Maybe even take a break to find out what she really wants to do.

But her heart fills with pressing sorrow when she thinks of cleaning out the house and putting it on the market. Watching anonymous Silicon Valley hotshots peering through the rooms, wrinkling their noses at Auntie Håo's collectibles, her wonderfully outdated finishes. *A gut job*, they'd think. They wouldn't see the layers of history, the whispered conversations on the balcony, the wild parties, the quiet mornings splayed on that circle of sunshine in the living room while Auntie Håo bickered on the landline with Priya. Comfort. Home. How do you put a price on something like that?

With a shake of her head, Evie finishes getting ready for the reading while Lillian flips on the news, giving unsolicited sartorial opinions on Evie's wardrobe. Evie lands on her favorite black dress, Audrey Hepburn style with the boatneck and A-line skirt, a leather jacket over it, along with a pair of spiky earrings that catch the light. Her notes are in her bag, praising Lancaster's immense potential, his command over language, the way his poetry transports . . . She yawns thinking about it. But she gets in Lillian's Mercedes and spackles a slightly deranged smile on her face.

At Bookender's Game, the crowd is dense. Everyone is milling around with ponderous looks, a book or a glass of wine in their hands. Evie recognizes her colleagues from the department, as well as some local mainstays of the literary scene. There's a studied shabbiness to their intellectual posturing, as if they understand the need to shroud their comparatively plush lifestyles to ward off resentment. Evie's always felt a little juvenile amid all this professorial style, but she swallows the intrusive thoughts, along with a canapé or five, all lubricated by the vodka tonic she's drinking.

When the bookshop owner calls her to the podium, she smiles weakly at the crowd.

"As soon as I read Lancaster Small's poem 'Ode to My Father's Rusted Hunting Knife' in an Intro to Poetry workshop, I knew an exceptional new literary voice had arrived."

She talks about his prizes and grants—ones she'd applied for unsuccessfully herself—and his newly released book of poetry. Evie doesn't know for certain, but as she scans the room, she thinks she spies several pitying looks aimed her way.

Lillian stands with Graham, her head resting on his shoulder, his arm loosely slung around her waist. Their casual comfort with one another makes Evie's stomach drop a little. When was the last time she was so content with another person?

Then her gaze catches on a pair of familiar blue-gray eyes. Atlas nods encouragingly. Somehow, that irritates her into fumbling with her notes, then abruptly closing her speech as Lancaster glides into the spotlight, a little confused, but ready to perform nonetheless.

After the reading, a crowd lines up for Lancaster's autograph. Evie, who hasn't bought the book herself, squeezes past them to find the crudité table. She's feeling hot and a bit faint, on the opposite side of "pleasantly buzzed," and she knows she needs something in her system before she throws up all over the place.

"You look well, Evie," Atlas says, his fingertips briefly touching her elbow. "Do you think we could chat somewhere? Outside?"

"Why now?"

"I regret how our last conversation went. It strikes me that I perhaps wasn't the most sensitive to your situation."

"Or honest," Evie says. "You've already formed a hiring committee, haven't you, old chap?"

Atlas has the grace to look downcast. "Listen, Evie. I have such little control over these things, and I was just trying to save you some grief."

"Don't you think I would have found out eventually?"

"Of course. But I thought you might have moved on by then."

There's that feeling again—one of being left behind. What Evie doesn't say to Atlas is that she's not at all good at moving on. She's still hung up on slights from high school, like when Mandy Knight told her that her left boob was bigger than her right, and she spent an entire year weighing each on a kitchen scale she'd squirreled into her room for that purpose. It is *really* hard to weigh B-cups on a kitchen scale.

What she wouldn't give for the carefree insouciance of another woman—heroine energy. And yet. Amid her self-pitying, Evie recognizes that, for all her faults, she's at least lived honestly with her feelings, which is more than one could say for *some* dandified chuffers.

Lillian skims past a cluster of students attending the reading for extra credit and then she's on them, with her arm firmly hooked through Evie's.

"Have you heard Evie's big news, Atlas?" Lillian's words are a little too big and bright. "She's going abroad!"

"Lillian—" Evie begins.

At the same time, Atlas asks, "Abroad?"

"She's traveling to Việt Nam for three entire weeks! On this grand, luxurious matchmaking tour! Isn't that just the biggest adventure? Imagine: our Evie meeting some devilishly handsome, successful man who will sweep her off her feet. Kelly Marie Tran will play her in the Hallmark Channel adaptation."

"Matchmaking tour?" Atlas repeats. His voice is a little flat. "But that doesn't sound at all like something Evie would do."

They're both staring at her, waiting for her to jump in. The thing that smarts is that Atlas is absolutely correct. Evie has always been an unabashed romantic in spirit—her poetry has the wild restlessness of Keats or

Shelley—but in action? She's as prosaic as they come. Her whole career has been an exercise in choosing the safest options—applying to colleges that she thinks she has a shot at, vying for the fellowships that colleagues recommend. She never wanted to disappoint Grace, who'd given up so much for her. It was only during those bygone summers with Auntie Hảo that she'd ever found a whisper of excitement in real life.

And maybe that's what Auntie Hảo is giving back to her: a shot at romance, at a time when she's lost faith in it. A chance to go on an unforgettable trip, at a time when she can hardly afford to pay her own rent. At first, Evie felt a little miffed by the condition—why not just give her the house? But now she's beginning to see it as an opportunity. Lillian is right: What does Evie have to lose? More important, what does she have to gain?

An image of waterfalls brushes into her mind, cinching her decision.

Evie lifts her chin and says, "Sure it does. Who would say no to a trip of a lifetime?"

Atlas blinks, then opens his mouth to say something.

But Lillian squeals and leads Evie away, rambling about all the most scenic locations from her own trip to Việt Nam two years ago, the new wardrobe they'll have to buy Evie, and the prospect of all the handsome men she'll meet. Despite herself, Evie feels a smile creeping across her face.

Việt Nam. Where no one will know about her failures or her grief over Auntie Hảo, that shadow that's followed her for much too long. She could be anyone at all. Someone brave and a little reckless, someone who can finally get over her writer's block and find her way back to her first love, that of words. Lillian may be daydreaming of handsome men for Evie, but Evie is thinking about how to clamber out of this stagnant creative pond she's floating in.

New country, new Evie.

5

ADAM

Hồ Chí Minh City, Việt Nam
two weeks later

It physically pains Adam to be late for anything. Lateness means that you lost control of time. That you swerved away from carefully laid plans into a terrain of chaos and melting watches, like one of those trippy Dalí landscapes. When he runs even a few minutes past an agreed-upon hour, he can feel the self-disappointment needling under his rib cage, sharp and punishing.

But today, the lateness can't be helped. The elder Quyền—Ba, to Adam and Ruby—calls just as he is leaving the LYT offices, as if he knows exactly which timing will inconvenience Adam most. The purpose of the call is the usual buffet of pleasantries: Ba berating the company's lack of investors, questioning Adam's financial projections, wondering if he will be attending his mother's sixty-fifth birthday gala in the fall, a monstrously extravagant event at which Lana and her fiancé will surely appear. In any case, Adam's input is reduced to a series of apologetic grunts.

Ba doesn't like to talk with his children; he likes to talk *at* them. Usually, the conversation would last an indeterminate amount of time, until Ba ran out of oxygen or tobacco for his pipe, but tonight is the night of the tour welcome festivities, so Adam hastily ends the call first, hearing an echo of belligerence down the line as he taps the phone off.

Ruby has been welcoming the guests all day at the hotel, but Adam, like a coward, hunkered down in his office with a giant coffee and a silenced cell phone until the very last minute. Social events aren't a draw for him unless there's a specific purpose for them. She'll have his head if he misses the welcome cocktail hour too.

He hasn't picked up his dry cleaning yet, but there's just enough time if traffic isn't too congested. The only thing worse than being late is being underdressed.

He pulls his leather driving jacket over his button-down, hops on his motorbike, and enters the long stream of cabs and motorbikes in District 2. He hopes that he can screech in front of the dry cleaners right before they close. The smog hangs low, a crepe sheet over the street, twining around the motorists and sedans. His helmet shield begins to fog from the humidity.

Just a few more blocks. The minutes are counting down. This dry cleaner never, *ever* stays open a moment past closing time.

He revs the engine, earning an obscene gesture from a granny with a flower cart, and starts to make a turn toward a back-alley shortcut.

At that moment, a woman in a hot-pink dress steps into the street, leaning down to scoop something into her arms. Adam slams on the brakes with a loud screech and a gust of putrid diesel, earning a surprised look as the woman glances up with a pair of uncommonly large, prolifically lashed brown eyes. Then, almost without thinking, Adam pivots his motorbike so it forms a fenced blockade around her bent body. Drivers and bikers honk past them, then wind back into formation, leaving Adam with a humming engine and a thunderous heart rate. But now he's stuck between the sidewalk and the ceaseless flow of traffic, consigned to watching the woman nonchalantly amble back onto the sidewalk with—what *is* that—a rooster?

She smiles—*grins*—and gives a little wrist-twiddling wave, the irate rooster squawking in her arms. "Xin lỗi, Chú."

Chú?

That's *the* last straw. This clueless woman used the honorific reserved for mole-speckled great-uncles with rheumy eyes and a penchant for dried tamarind. Adam considers himself at least a decade away from chú-dom.

He pulls the bike out of traffic, removes his helmet, and yells, "What the hell are you thinking?"

She frowns, patting the wriggling rooster in her arms. "This guy wandered onto the road."

Now that he's closer, he can see that she's youngish—his age—with dark hair and petal-pink lips and an impractical dress that rides up her distractingly long legs. But he won't be pulled in by her looks. He can spot her kind a mile away—a Việt Kiều, one of those loud, indecorous Vietnamese Americans who come looking for a cheap vacation without bothering to learn a single thing about the culture they left behind. Who else would interrupt traffic for an animal that had probably ambled off the chopping block to begin with, expecting people to part like the Red Sea for her? The idiocy. The entitlement.

He switches to English. "So you wandered in with him? Do you know how insane that is? This is Việt Nam. Any other motorist would have run you over."

"But the rooster—"

"Was going to be someone's dinner anyway."

She squints at the clucking mass in her arms. "He seems kind of scrawny for a meal."

"That's because he's not full of GMOs," Adam begins, then shakes his head. Why is he getting so distracted? Her eyes blink innocently at him. He returns to his tirade. "That's not the point! Why would you risk your life for something so stupid? My life, for that matter?"

Her face clouds, nonchalance finally broken. "Listen here, you leather-clad Lothario. There was plenty of clearance between me and the street."

"Centimeters," he retorts. "Inches, to you."

Why is he arguing with her? Maybe it's the adrenaline or the way she stands with a hip jutting out, that ridiculous bony rooster still in her arms, that furious look in her eyes. He *wants* to push her buttons, the way she pushed his. Anger puts the fire in his blood. He senses the same stubbornness in her that he has, and it lights him up inside. A challenge.

And she doesn't back down. "Anyone with eyeballs could see that it was going to be just fine. You were clearly overreacting."

"Excuse me? I saved your life."

"To save a life, it would have to be in danger in the first place. Look, Chú—"

He grits his teeth.

She continues, "I'll thank you for your unnecessary help, but now, why don't you hop back on your little bike"—here, she makes a dismissive gesture with her fingertips—"and go back to terrorizing people on the streets?"

"Little bike," he sputters. His Kawasaki is his pride and joy. He's put in many weekend hours cleaning and upgrading it with custom treatments and paint. It is the only one of its kind.

Then, before he can complete his thought, a vendor in a blood-splattered apron with a cleaver stalks onto the street, cornering them. The young woman in pink backs away, trying to offer the struggling rooster to the vendor, who shouts in a string of profanity-laced Vietnamese. The rooster's flapping sends up a flurry of red-gold feathers before it deflates, resigned to its fate.

The young woman stares down at the bird, now a limp mess of wing and scaly claw in her arms. Chagrined, she asks, "Is it playing dead?"

Again, another flurry of Vietnamese from the vendor, each syllable climbing in decibels so that curious pedestrians slow their stride to stare.

Adam suppresses his laughter. "She's saying you owe her sixty đồng for her rooster. Among other things."

"Sixty đồng?" Panic dances across her face.

He shrugs. "A bit high, you're right. You could always haggle the price down."

"But I don't *want* it. What am I going to do with a goddamn rooster?"

"Should have thought of that before you nearly killed yourself for it."

With one last glance at her seething expression, he smirks and hops back on his bike, returning her finger-waggling wave mockingly as she opens her mouth, fuming. By now, the traffic has cleared marginally, and he zips back into it, making his way down the side alley he was originally aiming for. A burble of laughter emerges in his throat. When was he last so irritated and amused at the same time?

Even as he rides farther and farther from the woman, he can't help but think of her furrowed brow, that *really* short pink dress, the damn rooster. Whoever she was, she at least kept his evening from complete, soul-crushing boredom.

Small mercies.

Minutes later, he squeezes into the dry-cleaning shop just as the owner gets up to change the sign. The little bell dings as he enters. It's nearly dinnertime, and he can see the children in the store hopping all over the shop owner, their mother or grandmother, ready to go home. Holding up his hands in a gesture of apology, Adam fumbles for his receipt. The owner, an older woman with a tight bun, appraises him in silence, eyeing his expensive watch, the foppish way his hair falls over one eyebrow.

"Payment?" she asks, her voice monotone.

He never feels more like a bumbling kid than when he falls under the gaze of a retail auntie, that terrifying mixture of sweet-faced pleasantry and blade-sharp negotiation. "For your trouble, Auntie," he says, handing over the money along with a large tip.

She gives a quick snort before handing him his freshly laundered and ironed shirts and slacks. "I wouldn't be troubled if you didn't come at closing time," she huffs.

Adam should be accustomed to this by now, the way the aunties and uncles eye him in disapproval, pegging him as a playboy before he's even spoken, but it still smarts, to be seen as a black sheep before you've even opened your mouth.

Sometimes it's easier to play into those beliefs. Don't let them have the chance to pierce that armor.

But nevertheless, Adam remembers his manners and says with a small bow, "Thank you, Auntie. And good evening."

He leans down to ruffle the hair of one of the young children at his feet, a boy who looks up with a beaming, hero-worshipping smile. One secret: Adam adores children, and they, for all his stony posturing, are drawn to him like moths to flame. He hopes Ruby and Thăng will have children soon, so he can spoil them, though he can't imagine Thăng as a father.

He flicks the kids each a coin. "Be good for your family."

The kids stare at their coins, then the boy holds his back up. "You keep it. You need this more than we do."

The shop owner smirks before inclining her head toward the door, a not-so-subtle reminder that he's interrupted her evening.

Adam doesn't know why he bothered dry-cleaning his clothes, since he'll only have to shove them into his suitcase for the tour, but it's like habit to him now, all these little things you do to get through life. Routine, order. Schedules he thrives on. You attend the family dinners, where your mother questions you relentlessly about your love life and your father grunts disapprovingly through each course. Grab a beer with your friend who finds your impending participation in a matchmaking tour both uproarious and unbelievable. Get the dry cleaning, because you're still the CMO of your sister's business and must make a good impression at tonight's welcome dinner, and every day thereafter on the matchmaking tour of your nightmares.

Inside the hotel lobby, the lights are dim and the music is quiet, elegant. It's a contrast to the roil of emotion in his stomach. He follows the signs for Love Yêu Tours, then enters a room with wall-to-wall carpeting decorated in whorls of gold and an immense crystal chandelier. There's a steady hum of conversation, polite yet bristling with built-up tension. As it should be before a matchmaking tour.

Already the crowd has separated into smaller groups, everyone evaluating each other, silently labeling viable candidates. He sees Ruby frowning at him, tapping on her watch face as she speaks to a woman with a shoulder-length bob. There are about twenty men and women in the room, evenly dispersed by gender, all wearing the same cocktail dresses and slacks, their smiles awkward but hopeful. They're all attractive and, Adam realizes, entirely forgettable.

Not that it matters. He's here on business, not on any sparkly quest for love.

Adam knows he should introduce himself and socialize, but instead, he veers right toward the bar.

He leans over to the young man pouring drinks and says in Vietnamese, "I'll have a gin and tonic. Extra limes. Extra cold."

"He will not," says an annoyed voice to his left, in Vietnamese as well.

The crowd here is composed of expats and native-born men and women, but the assumption is that all Love Yêu activities are conducted in English. Easiest for all involved, though the majority of the clients are bilingual, at least.

Standing next to him is a tall woman wearing the shortest, skimpiest dress he's ever seen. It's hot pink, made of some cheap spandex, and hugs her curves intimately, skimming her waist and cleavage plastered on display. With a start, he realizes—it's the rooster woman.

He doesn't know how he could have missed her in the room. Her long hair sweeps over one shoulder and toward her waist, curling slightly at her forehead from the damp weather. Begrudgingly, he makes note of her lush features, the soft flush spreading across her cheeks.

Ah, he thinks, trying to ignore the sizzle of attraction in his gut. *Of fucking course.*

"You cut me in line," she continues. "You can wait your damn turn. Or are you not accustomed to polite society?"

He blinks. She blinks back at him slowly, mockingly. Adam tries not to notice that her eyes are a gorgeous honey color, lit deeply from the inside and ringed by thick lashes. She has a tiny freckle below her left eye, offset like a cascading star. Without a doubt, the most beautiful woman he's ever seen.

And she probably knows it, he says to himself with a scowl.

"Where's your rooster?" he asks in English, watching recognition dawn in her eyes.

To her credit, she doesn't miss a beat as she switches languages. "Where's the chip on your shoulder?"

"Do you know who I am?" The words fly out of his mouth before he can stop them. What. An. Asshole.

"No clue," she says in a bored tone. She turns to the bartender with a dazzling smile that makes Adam's stomach clench, despite himself. "I'll take that glass of riesling now."

The baffled bartender hands over her wine, and she takes a large glug. A tiny drop lingers on her lips. Adam stares down at her, mesmerized and irritated at the same time.

"I'm the CMO of Love Yêu," he says haughtily.

"Am I supposed to be impressed by that?" she asks with an upward tick of her mouth.

"I don't like to wait."

"That makes two of us."

She drops a tip in the bartender's glass and turns on her heel—wearing a pair of rugged combat boots instead of the expected stilettos, Adam notes—melding into a group of women who seem to part for her, as if stunned by her too.

He feels a flicker of vexation in his stomach, mixed with something more puzzling. A sense of nerves? Anticipation? When he looks at her, he sees a woman accustomed to getting everything she wants. Judging from her accent—another spoiled American. A brat looking for another moneybags benefactor. Adam doesn't have patience for women like that. Never has.

And yet. He can't take his eyes off her.

The bartender asks, "Do you want that gin and tonic now?"

Adam nods, reaching for the cold glass, but his gaze bores into the mystery woman's back across the room. If his job is to make a good impression, Adam knows he's already failed. He's supposed to be charming and engaging. Instead? He's grimacing darkly at one of the well-paying Love Yêu clients, wishing he could corner her to give her a piece of his mind. He tries to ignore the thought of the things he'd do to her if they *did* make their way to that dark corner. First, he'd start with licking that drop of wine right off her smug lips. Then . . .

As if reading his thoughts, she turns and gives him a slow, maddening wink that renders him temporarily, unexpectedly breathless.

EVIE

Hồ Chí Minh City, Việt Nam

Well, she thinks, *that was a bust.* She peeks over her shoulder to see the glowering Vietnamese Adonis—CMO of Love Yêu, as he'll tell you himself—shooting daggers at her. Why does she have to resist the urge to stick her tongue out at him? He's just so self-satisfied. Domineering. That clenched jaw, cut with devastating precision, and those smoldering dark eyes, deep as a night sky. It should be criminal to be that gorgeous. And that annoying.

Even after she'd paid the full sixty đồng for the rooster, let it loose in a deserted alley with a niggling sense of guilt, and conducted the walk of shame back to the hotel, where she would wash the stench of livestock and humiliation off her, she couldn't stop thinking about him. The smirk. The leather jacket. The way he quickly, decisively shielded her body from the street—even though, she maintains, she did not need his help in the first place. She'd felt brief yet pronounced disappointment when he got back on his bike and rode away.

But now, she'll be spending three full weeks with him. She can't decide whether she is intrigued or dismayed.

She is thoroughly *distrigued* by him.

Evie tries to lean back into the conversation with the other guests on the matchmaking tour, but she can't help yawning. It was absolutely the wrong move to schedule her flight the day before the matchmaking tour takes off for their first destination—Đà Lạt, the mountainous City of Eternal Spring in the Central Highlands region. She could use at least twenty hours of extra sleep before stepping on that bus tomorrow.

Earlier, she'd landed in Hồ Chí Minh City in the wee hours, jet-lagged and stiff from hours of sitting on two planes and lying crookedly on the lounge chairs at the Seoul airport. Her bag is nowhere to be found, which she only learned after circling the Tân Sơn Nhất International Airport about twenty times and filling out as many forms.

But when she first saw the sunrise casting its purple light on the steely buildings over Hồ Chí Minh City, her heart began thrumming a little faster. The moment her feet landed on the pavement, officially a part of this complicated, beautiful country, she thought of her father and his longing for Việt Nam that never abated, even after decades in America. She thought of Auntie Hảo and her giant house full of mementos from her birth country, a shrine to the Việt Nam of her dreams. How many times had Evie wrapped herself in the scarves, hidden stones in the hand-carved jewelry boxes, doodled with Auntie Hảo's quill pens? And now here she is, in the midst of all the history and heartbreak of a country that she's never dared to claim for herself.

That morning, a stray breeze brushed up the back of her neck, and it felt like a kind of blessing. At that moment, Evie vowed to squeeze all the adventure out of this trip. For Auntie Hảo, and for herself. She doesn't know what will happen after these three weeks, but she promises herself that she'll be fully present for every second.

New country, new Evie.

Now she turns her attention back to the stage, where Ruby Quyền stands in a tailored black dress cut above her knees. Evie tugs her own hemline self-consciously. She bought it hastily at Bến Thành Market without trying it on, forgetting that she's about six inches taller than the average Vietnamese woman. So much for a first impression. No wonder Grumpy CMO looked down his haughty nose at her. In a room full of elegant penguins, she is a giant, flapping flamingo.

Ruby smiles grandly at the gathered tour guests. "I'm sure you've all had a chance to acquaint yourselves with one another, but this is just the start. We're in for a very memorable three weeks, all completely planned out for you. So your only job is to relax and enjoy one another's company. Our staff is here for your every need. If you find yourselves wanting to spend more time with a special someone—"

And here, several people titter, as if the whole point of this tour isn't to find a special someone.

"—then you only need to approach one of us, and we'll set up romantic one-on-one time just for you. I'm Ruby Quyền, the CEO of the company, and a great believer in the power of purposeful matchmaking. I met my own husband through a matchmaker, though I didn't have the advantage of a breathtaking tour around the country to help my own romance along."

There's something severe about Ruby, making her an ill fit for the romantic premise of the company. Evie is a little intimidated by her. She reminds Evie of one of those girls from high school, the well-coiffed, Harvard-bound overachievers who might be perfectly nice, but aren't, at heart, terribly kind.

"To my left are Đức and Cherie, tour guides well-versed in Vietnamese history, lore, and entertainments. Think of them as your personal concierges."

Đức, a young man with a fedora perched rakishly on his forehead, winks at the crowd. Cherie, a woman with thick-cut bangs and a timid expression, gives a tiny wave. They lean toward each other, as if twinned. Evie wonders if they're a couple.

Ruby continues, "And over here is my brother, Adam. He's—"

"The CMO," Evie says with a roll of her eyes. Then she claps a hand over her mouth as she sees everyone, including Ruby, turning to her. That came out louder than she'd intended. Adam stares at her with a dark, indiscernible expression.

Ruby pauses, considering Evie, then says, "Right. He's here to help as well. He'll be documenting the trip, as well as helping to coordinate. But he'll also be a guest, just like you. Eligible too."

As the guests chuckle, Evie sees a slight blush heating up Adam's neck. It really shouldn't be as adorable as it is.

Ruby asks everyone to introduce themselves, and it feels a little like the first day of school. Evie makes note of a red-haired owner of an Australian architecture firm named Connor; an American professor from Vanderbilt named Riley, a second-generation Vietnamese immigrant, like her; and a good-natured Vietnamese banker who calls himself Pin. There's also Talia, a poised and lovely Saigonese woman with a bob. And of course, the only bona fide celebrity of the tour—Fen, an actress from Shanghai whose bored expression rivals Adam's detached reserve.

The international nature of the tour surprises Evie, but then she realizes that this is a moneyed crowd with the means and desire to relocate for the right reasons. To them, the astronomical fee for the tour is not a lifetime investment; it's a bit of change for a summer adventure. The stakes are not high.

What are the stakes for her? Sure, she gets the San Francisco row house at the end of all this—not a small boon, by any means. But to what extent is she actually expected to participate? Who would know if she spent the entire three weeks bouncing from spa to spa, never once going on a date?

Even so, Evie isn't without honor. She knows she'll try her best to get into the spirit of things for Auntie Hảo, even if it means making herself a little ridiculous. Besides, Riley is pretty handsome with his tweedy, professorial look. He reminds her of Atlas, actually.

When it's her turn, the last in the group to speak, Evie clears her throat. "I'm Evie, and I'm from Midland, Ohio. I teach college kids how to write essays about dead authors, and sometimes write books myself."

"Anything we've heard of?" Riley calls.

"Probably not unless you've been digging in the bargain bin in my hometown bookstore," she deadpans, pulling out some good-natured laughs from the group. Talia, who identifies herself as a philanthropist, gives her a warm smile.

Out of the corner of her eye, she sees Adam studying her. He asks, unexpectedly, "And what are you looking for from this tour, Evie?"

The room goes quiet. No one else was probed about their romantic hopes and dreams, Evie notes with indignation. She also notices the emphasis he puts on her name. *Adam and Evie.* God, that's unfortunate. But she's not one to turn down a challenge. She stands taller in her boots.

She quotes, in her studied poet voice, "I'm looking for a love 'loved, in secret, between the shadow and the soul.'"

"Neruda," Riley says appreciatively. "Beautiful quote."

Talia agrees. "Beautiful wish."

Adam meets her gaze, then his eyes flicker away, unreadable.

Abruptly, Ruby ends the night by saying that they'll meet in the hotel lobby at eight a.m. the next morning. She disappears with another magnanimous smile, gesturing toward the gift bags. Her eyes glaze over Evie as she passes.

Evie says goodbye to the women around her and finds her room. At least she had the wherewithal to book a room at the same hotel as everyone else. It's got a lovely view over District 1. She reaches for the fluffy robe hanging on a hook, divesting herself of the cheap dress, then roots inside her gift bag. Inside are luxury skincare products, a mini bottle of champagne, some beautifully packaged chocolates, and new, state-of-the-art noise-canceling earbuds. There's also a silk scarf and a silver flask with Love Yêu's logo engraved tastefully on the front.

She pours herself a glass of champagne and calls the airport. Thankfully they've found her suitcase and promise to deliver it to the hotel within the hour. She checks her phone and sees messages from Lillian and Atlas.

Atlas, cryptically: Have a safe trip, Evie. Call me if you get bored?

Lillian, gleefully: Day one of the rest of your life! You better send me photos daily or I'll Liam Neeson myself to the homeland for you. Also, any cute millionaires?!

Evie leans into a plush armchair. She deletes Atlas's message, then writes to Lillian: This place is lousy with cute men! Why didn't I come sooner?

Lillian, eleven hours away, shoots back a near-instantaneous reply—a trio of fire emojis and a single eggplant that makes Evie giggle, then sigh. At home, she always had her friends and colleagues and students, along with Lillian and Atlas, even, filling every moment of her day. Here, no one knows her at all. This could be a good thing—a chance to reinvent—but right at this moment, it makes her feel quite alone.

She pours herself another glass of champagne. By the time the concierge calls her to say the bag has arrived, Evie is half-asleep on a riesling-and-champagne buzz and stored-up weariness from her flight. She zombie-walks downstairs, then signs for her bag and tips the concierge. Though it's a three-week tour, Evie only has one suitcase, packed to the brim with swimsuits, sweaters, dresses, and new athleisure she's sure that she'll never use. They were told to pack for a variety of climates and activities, and Lillian had insisted on charging half the things in the suitcase to Graham's credit card. "Under-the-table severance," she'd called it.

Evie drags her suitcase into the elevator, huffing from its weight and thanking her stars that she's only got one.

Right before the doors close, a tanned hand stops them. Adam Quyền strides in, pausing when he sees her panting from exertion in her robe. Will there ever be a time when Evie looks presentable in his presence?

"Are you all right?" he asks.

"Just fine," she breathes back. "The altitude has gotten to me, you know. I'm on the—what?—eleventh floor?"

He nods confusedly and opens his mouth to speak when the elevator suddenly fills with a family getting on. They're chatting boisterously as they take up every inch of the tiny space with their suitcases, jamming Adam closer to Evie.

She can feel his warmth through the fabric of her robe, see the way his gaze flicks down at her. It's then that she realizes the robe gapes a little in the front, revealing a shadowy vee of cleavage she hadn't intended to make quite so visible. She draws the robe closer, accidentally knocking their hips together.

A tingle. Some flustered blinking. She's so distriqued.

A ghost of a smile tugs his lips. It changes his serious, almost severe expression into something . . . charming? The family continues joking with one another, unconcerned with the simmering interaction behind them.

"Wardrobe malfunction?" he asks in a low voice. Is he *flirting* with her? He smells pleasantly, lightly, of whiskey. Why is she fighting the urge to lean closer to him?

She pulls away, as far as she can get in the crowded elevator, and hisses, "You wish."

He raises an eyebrow. "I meant, the dress from this evening. I saw your suitcase and figured you were a victim of Việt Nam's hulking bureaucracy and had to get a substitute outfit in a rush. Would explain some things."

Even though that's exactly the case, Evie doesn't want to give him the satisfaction. She asks, "And what was wrong with my outfit?"

The family exits the elevator in a great rush, leaving silence behind them. For just a floor, it's the two of them, deadlocked. Neither moves apart, though there's plenty of room now. She finds herself licking her lips, then hating herself for it. This man does not need the satisfaction of knowing he's stirring something confusingly delicious within her. Is it her imagination, or is he breathing a little heavier too?

His lids lower, and he drags his bottom lip under perfect white teeth. What. Is. Going. On? She hasn't felt this perturbed since her first viewing of Rose DeWitt Bukater's steamy handprint in that old jalopy on the doomed *Titanic* as an uncomfortably lusty preteen.

Oof, and there goes her wayward imagination. Adam, wearing suspenders, effusing about ice fishing in Wisconsin as her bosoms heave in a beaded Edwardian gown. Adam, sketching her like one of his French girls, his charcoal-stained fingers running across her bare flesh in the velvety candlelight. Oh, *geez*. She must be more jetlagged than she thought.

He cocks his head as if reading her thoughts. She tries clearing her throat, but it comes out as a kind of low-pitched bleat. What was she saying?

The elevator dings. He moves away from her. But then, in the door opening, he gives her a lazy look and says, as a parting shot, "The dress was fine. But I like the robe better."

The elevator closes before she can retort, but not before a telltale flush rises to her cheeks. She thinks, *I'm in trouble, Jack.*

ADAM

Đà Lạt, Việt Nam

Adam should be enjoying the sprawling views from the terrace of the Đà Lạt Palace Hotel, which looks onto the peaceful Hồ Xuân Hương, a lake with gently rippling waves. An orange dawn reflects in the water like a crushed carnation. Any other human would be thanking their personal gods for the chance to stay at the elite, impossible-to-book hotel, buffeted by a majestic slope of mountains in the distance.

At dinner last night, the guests had gushed about their rooms, marveling at the gilded mirrors and fireplaces, the framed landscapes. They said if these accommodations were a sign of things to come, Love Yêu Tours had already outdone themselves. Ruby smiled smugly into her wineglass, then subjected them to an expert panel discussion on zodiac compatibility that Evie had snored through. Not that Adam noticed her more than others. Not that he was *looking* for her every chance he got. Oh, no.

So what if he knows exactly where that freckle sits on her animated face? Or that he'd once caught a whiff of her perfume and stopped, nonsensically, to close his eyes, abruptly halting the line filtering through the hotel doors? Or that, after the elevator, he finds himself thinking of all the other tight spaces in which he could find himself with her?

This morning, Adam is oblivious to the beauty around him, absorbed instead in paging through the bursting file on the café table in front of him. It's crammed with dossiers of the tour participants, presented to the guests upon their arrival in Đà Lạt. Each page, accompanied by a full-color headshot, details the guest's degrees, job history, likes and dislikes, and even whether they have been married or not.

He'd questioned Ruby about the wisdom of handing the guests all the on-paper facts about their romantic prospects in one swoop, arguing that it removed the mystery of getting to know someone fresh, without expectations.

Ruby had only waved him off. "Do you think these guests are looking for charity cases? They are the best of the best—well, most of them."

She wrinkled her nose at this and continued. "And they want partners who can elevate their life. Add to it, not become a burden. All this stuff matters. Plus, we don't want them to think we'd just let *anyone* in."

Adam protested, "But where someone went to school hardly makes them a *burden*."

Ruby rolled her eyes. "Okay, Mr. Stanford. Save your romantic ideals for the marketing materials."

Despite his earlier resistance, he now flips through the pages with interest, noting the facts that jump out. That Talia was once named Miss Sài Gòn and now volunteers her time facilitating the delivery of solar panels to remote mountain villages. That Riley's book on Indochinese politics parked on the nonfiction *New York Times* bestseller list for three consecutive weeks, after which he'd been interviewed on *The Daily Show*. That Fen, the only child of a domestic aviation tycoon, has acted in a series of dramedies dubbed in six different languages.

But what he's really interested in—even if he can't admit it to himself—is the very brief dossier on Evie Lang. What *is* her deal? He tells himself it's just professional interest on his part. He's looking out for the company. Trying to eliminate the outliers, anyone who doesn't take the mission seriously.

But another part of him knows the truth—he's just compelled by *her*. It has been ages since anyone has made him want to take a closer look, even if for all the wrong reasons.

Peeking out from her dossier is a candid photo, unlike the glossy images from the other guests. In it, she's at the beach, laughing so hard that her eyes almost disappear, head tilted slightly back. He sees the tanned column of her throat, the hint of a tiny tattoo behind her ear. That wild mass of hair tossed by the wind.

She's a professor at a small liberal arts college in the Midwest. Her poetry collection won some minor praise. She's never been married. But that's it. The fields for likes and dislikes are totally blank. In a sea of too much information, Evie remains the one with the least to reveal. Adam hates to admit it, but that's precisely what makes her so interesting to him.

"This is stalker behavior, you know."

He starts when Evie plunks down across from him, holding an enormous café au lait and a flaky croissant. She gestures at her photo in front of him, which makes Adam redden. Her hair is swept up, and a pair of huge sunglasses rests on her nose. He's frustrated that he can't see her expression, but he guesses by her tone that it's somewhere between amusement and annoyance.

He shrugs and moves the papers to make more room for her. "It's research. For my job."

"And what was that again?" she asks sweetly. "You didn't say."

Catching his scowl, she laughs and says, "Well, I threw that whole file folder in the trash can. Would have tossed it into the fireplace if I knew how to work it."

"Why would you do that?"

A part of him is disappointed that she won't see his own résumé, full of accomplishments that would impress any woman. Then he despises himself for feeling that way. Why is he so intent on impressing this stranger?

She takes a big sip of coffee, and the foamed milk lingers on her lip. "Because I don't *care* about any of that. Your medical history is hardly going to interest me—except, I guess, if you have an STD I need to know about. But I suppose you wouldn't put that on an official questionnaire."

They pause awkwardly at the mention of sex. Adam slides his eyes away from her. He remembers feeling flirtatious and unguarded toward her last night in the elevator—a consequence of the extra whiskey he had before leaving the bar—but now, in the light of day, he stiffens again, reminding himself that she's just another Việt Kiều looking for a good time. No one to take seriously. No one to take *him* seriously. She's better off with one of those Americans who'll leave after the three weeks are over.

"Well, maybe some people like to know about the partners they get involved with," he says finally. "It helps protect them."

"From?" She raises one arched eyebrow.

"I don't know. Opportunists."

She scoffs. "This tour costs ten *thousand* dollars without travel expenses. Do you truly think anyone here is looking to entrap some rich spouse?"

He shrugs. "You never know."

Riley, the Vanderbilt professor, pulls up a chair. He's got a full breakfast plate of eggs, sausages, and thick brioche. His glasses slide down his nose.

"Who's looking to entrap a rich spouse?" he asks.

"According to Mr. CMO there, any one of us," Evie replies with a twinkle in her eye. "But honestly, if I were a person who wanted to marry a billionaire, I would probably look in America."

"Because no one in Việt Nam is worth your time?" Adam finds himself snapping.

"No, *Adam*," she says patiently. "Because I had to travel twenty-plus hours to get here. And my Vietnamese is kinda shitty."

"It's not bad," Adam mutters begrudgingly.

With his mouth full, Riley asks, "So why *did* you come?"

Adam is asking himself the same thing. He sees Evie falter, debating what to reveal. Is she a liar? Or is she just guarded like him?

Evie says, "Well, who's going to turn down a trip to a gorgeous country with all you beautiful people?"

Adam opens his mouth to call her out for evading the question, but then he shuts it when she turns to him, lifting her sunglasses to survey him.

"What are *you* looking for? Both of you. You put me on the spot last night, Adam," she says. "Thanks for that."

Riley laughs. "Yeah, he did. I think we're all going to answer the same thing, right? We want to find our partners. Someone to make us laugh, who gets our specific brand of weirdness. I live in America, but I'm willing to move for the right person. Or maybe she'll move for me."

Across the way, Talia is sitting with her tablet, ankles crossed as she flicks her delicate fingers on the screen. Pin, the banker, swoops in next to her, pointing over her shoulder at the tablet. Within moments, they sink into animated conversation. A frustrated Connor stands with his mouth agape, clearly annoyed that Pin has displaced him.

"Speaking of moving in." Riley grins.

Evie says, "Maybe we should tag people with a sticker to call dibs."

"I'll bet we can find a more civilized way to proceed."

"I wouldn't be so sure about that," Adam mutters. "People can be idiots when it comes to love."

Riley asks, "What about you, Quyền? Who's caught your eye?"

Adam coughs. "I'm just a spectator."

"Sure, sure," Riley tells him, waving a fork good-naturedly in his direction. "You keep telling yourself that. Go on enough of these romantic excursions, and you'll find yourself falling in love with a rock."

"Speaking of excursions, what's on the agenda today?" Evie asks.

"Don't you read *anything* we give to you?" Adam says, throwing up his hands.

She shrugs. "I've had enough of homework. I prefer . . . adventure."

"Chaos," Adam mutters. She glares.

Riley saves them by answering, "We get a choice. You can have a leisurely walk to Pongour Falls or join the daredevils riding the alpine coaster to Datanla Falls. Kind of a no-brainer for me. I love a good adventure."

Adam leans over to Evie. "Because I'm sure you didn't read the itinerary, alpining to the waterfalls just means sitting in a cart and wafting along through the wilderness on a track."

Riley looks skeptical. "I heard those carts can go pretty fast. And you're just in a dinky box in the middle of a forest, hundreds of kilometers from the ground."

"That's true," Adam says contemplatively. "Probably not the easiest, if you're not used to it."

Evie tosses her head. "What makes you think I need easy?"

Adam gestures at her outfit: white trousers and a silky top that accentuates the smooth gleam of her skin.

She says, "I'd change, of course. Surely *you're* not alpining in a three-piece suit. Or maybe you would. Heaven forbid you'd wear something without a tie."

"You've met me all of two days."

"You were reading a *dictionary* on the bus ride to Đà Lạt. While wearing a tie, no less, and ignoring every single one of us. Don't you get carsick like normal people?"

"It was not a dictionary," he mutters. "It was Pushkin."

"Ah, right, your typical pleasure reading. Anyway, I can't even see you enjoying some waterfall view. Here we are in a gorgeous place, and you're just looking through papers, like a sad, overworked businessman."

"And you're spending it needling *me* instead of enjoying the so-called gorgeous place," he retorts.

Riley's eyes ping-pong between them, a bemused expression on his face.

"I'm just saying." Evie shrugs. "We'll all be at the waterfalls, and you'll be holed up in your room like a cave dweller, grunting into your belly button about how many meetings you're missing. Mark my words."

"My *belly button*?"

"The point is: I bet you can't go even a day without checking your email."

He retorts, "Some of us have jobs."

If he weren't looking at her so closely, he wouldn't have noticed the change in Evie's expression, a sudden darkening of her eyes.

"You know what they say," she tells him. "Marrying your work is a sign of an underdeveloped emotional cortex. Overcompensation for a lack of personal connection."

"You're just making this up."

The truth is, he *is* worried about dropping the ball at work. Even though he's technically working on the tour—and getting paid for it—he constantly wonders if there's something he's forgetting back at the office. Some way in which he'll unwittingly bring disaster to the company and disappoint his family. Same crippling fear as usual.

Aloud, he only says, as a sort of challenge, "I'll see you at Datanla Falls, then?"

"Would not miss it for all the Pushkin in the world."

He gathers his file and stands. Riley waves at him while Evie pointedly glances away, refusing to acknowledge his departure.

Adam hears Riley sighing behind him, "*Ooo-kay*, then."

What is it about Evie Lang that makes him so irritated? Her absolute lack of seriousness, despite all the hours the staff put into making this tour a success? How she's willing to waste a fortune on what, to her, must be little more than a whim? Or maybe it's just the fact that she is so self-assured, so *American* and independent, something Adam has never been for a moment in his life. He wonders, briefly, what it would feel like to let go, the way she does. To just give up caring what other people think. But then he shakes his head. Appearances aren't everything, and no matter what she says, he has his doubts that she's really got as much bravado as she pretends to have.

In fact, he'd bet everything in his bank account that Evie Lang will make it nowhere near an alpine coaster today, or any day. And he'll be right there to remind her of that.

EVIE

Đà Lạt, Việt Nam

"Well, shit, that's a long way down," Evie says, a tug of trepidation in her voice. "Does it feel like they're going *really* fast?"

"Normal speed," the operator tells her, rolling his eyes ever so slightly up to the heavens. *God save me from neurotic tourists*, Evie imagines him thinking.

"What if they smack themselves against a tree trunk? Is it too soon to talk about Sonny Bono?"

Around her, blank stares and a thick green forest, through which the 2,400-meter alpine track winds like a silver snake. Trees stretch on either side of the track, skinny and gray-barked. Truth be told, it's more beautiful than menacing, but Evie isn't exactly a *sporty* human. Once, she managed to flip herself into a ditch while riding a visiting professor's unicycle on a dare, resulting in a very sheepish, muddy walk back to campus that no one ever let her live down. But Evie Lang has never stepped back from a dare, which might explain why she's standing here, watching a series of carts disappear through the forest.

She imagines herself falling off the track, plummeting into the impenetrable wilderness, though the operators assure her that the course runs on a thoroughly tested electromagnetic system that has proved perfectly safe for thousands of rides.

She can see the announcement now: *Beheaded before her first Wallace Stevens Award.* As if she'd ever be in the running for that.

"Can I see the blueprints on this system?" she jokes to the straight-faced operator.

There's a deep, taunting voice in her ear, equal parts sensual and irritating. "You aren't afraid, are you?"

There it is again. The heat that rises along her neck. That squirmy, all-too-attentive feeling somewhere below her stomach. It should be criminal for someone so annoying to be as attractive as he is.

"Please remove yourself and your cheesy aftershave from my immediate vicinity now," she retorts.

Stepping back, Adam says indignantly, "This cologne was custom-made."

"By some back-alley granny still using a vinegary old bottle of Red Door?"

The truth is, Adam smells great. A mixture of pine and laundry. Fresh, green, outdoorsy. And of course, he's dressed perfectly for the outing in a pair of joggers and a muscle tee, revealing his biceps and just a faint hint of pectorals. *He probably has insane abs too,* Evie finds herself thinking resentfully. She's glad now for the yoga pants and workout tops that Lillian packed, though the crop top is more revealing than she'd typically choose.

Riley gets in his cart. His hair flops boyishly over his eyes. "I'll come back for you if anything happens. Bon courage, ma belle."

"Why is he speaking French?" Adam grumbles.

"Some people have culture," Evie says.

Riley winks as he buckles himself up, and she has to admit, he's awfully cute in a mildly dorky way. A man without ego. Refreshing.

Then it's just her and Adam left.

The guide turns to them, visibly bored. "Together or separate?"

"Separate," Evie splutters, while Adam just raises his eyebrow. "As far apart as we can get, actually. Maybe he can go without a cart! His hard head will bounce him all the way down."

"You're sweet," Adam says.

The operator helps her in, and she buckles herself up, steadying her feet against the interior of the cart. It's completely open on all sides, which makes her feel a little vulnerable, though there are rails at least, farther down on the track. Before she takes off, the guide says something into his earpiece.

Then he announces, "The car behind us has broken down on the tracks."

"Seriously?" Adam grits. "When will it be fixed?"

"Could be a few minutes. Could be an hour." The operator shrugs.

Adam groans. "Typical Việt timeline. Well—how do I get down, then?"

"Taxi? Running on the track? That hard head I heard about?"

Adam gives the operator a death glare.

The operator continues, "Or you could hop in with *her*, I guess."

For a brief second, Evie considers zipping off without him. Leaving haughty Adam Quyền gaping in the dust. There's a measure of undeniable satisfaction in the image. But instead, she gestures at the open seat behind her in the coaster car.

"Hurry up, then."

After he's buckled in, she starts the cart at a very leisurely pace. At first, the rattling motion is unnerving, but then she gets used to it. It feels comfortable and breezy, and if she ignores her passenger, she can imagine she's alone in the woods. It's actually quite nice, she decides. Not scary at all.

But then she hears him sigh deeply. She's basically sitting between his legs, an awfully intimate position. If she leaned back just the littlest bit, she might feel his— Nope. She will not be thinking about that.

"You know a caterpillar just passed us?" he grumbles.

"Who cares? No one's behind us to complain."

"I care because I want to get to the waterfall before dark."

"What happens after dark? You turn into a werewolf?"

"Can you just take your hand off the brake, please? The little kids riding on this track are going twice as fast as we are. And keep the ride smooth. I don't want to wind up stuck in a treetop because of you."

"You don't want to mess up your *hair*."

"It's good hair, what can I say?"

"I'm driving Mr. Diva," she says to the treetops.

But she obliges, speeding up. The coaster slides through the trees, wind whooshing around them. Despite herself, she begins to laugh, whooping as they gain speed. It's like flying. When was the last time she had so much fun? Every time there's a slight drop, she leans back, jutting her elbows on Adam's knees to steady herself. Is it just her, or do they tighten just the tiniest bit? Protectively? No, just an instinct.

"Not so bad, is it?" he asks behind her. She looks back and spies a ghost of a smile on his lips.

"Not the *worst*, I guess. It reminds me of the coasters on Kings Island, though I've never been much of a coaster girl."

"Yeah, I don't like them either. Make me queasy."

"Adam Quyền, if you puke on me, I will make your sister add that to your dossier. 'Really suave but gets carsick like a toddler.'"

"You think I'm suave? Correction: 'really suave'?"

Evie doesn't give him the satisfaction of responding. They near Riley's car on the tracks, and she finally slows, coasting them to a reasonable pace the rest of the way down to the waterfall. At one point, they're so close to the edge of a drop that she holds her breath. But then she feels Adam's knee nudging her, and she relaxes. Some of the curves are abrupt, jostling them in the car, but she's grateful for the experience. She sends up a silent thanks to Auntie Hảo. *I never would have had a chance to see this without you.* Every minute she spends in Việt Nam feels like a small bit of reclamation. Her dad's heritage, hers again.

"So what's your deal, Evie Lang?" Adam asks, interrupting her reverie. "Why are you here? And don't try to talk your way out of it."

Somehow, on this quiet and scenic ride, she feels more inclined toward honesty. "It was a condition for an inheritance."

"Let me guess: Asian relative?" She hears a hint of amusement in his voice.

"Naturally. My Auntie Hảo said I had to go on this tour before I could get the deed to her house."

"Must be some house."

"It is. A row house in San Francisco. The kind of real estate you'd do anything for. Three stories. Victorian architecture. A real historic treasure in the middle of the Haight. Way too big for just me."

"What are you going to do with this historic treasure?"

"No idea."

But that's a lie. She might not have a clear plan, but she has visions that she can't chase away, despite their utter impracticality. She thinks of long nights under a moonlit sky, music threading through the breeze, the smell of samosas and sourdough starter, laughter rising and dying with the waning hours. She thinks of a desk near a window through which she can see the sprawl of Buena Vista Park. She thinks of words spilling onto the page. Inspiration and joy and purpose.

But no house can give her these things, she realizes, finally sinking back to earth. Her dreams, as always, feel just out of reach.

Adam asks brusquely, "So what, you marry some rich dude from the tour and live happily ever after in your row house?"

She wishes she could turn and look at him. "No way. Auntie Hảo wouldn't make me do that. She never married, and she probably thinks I will never marry either. I think this is just an experiment. Her beyond-the-grave dare. She was always challenging me. She thought I was meant for big things—*love bravely*, she liked to say."

"Oh." His voice softens. "Well, that doesn't seem so bad."

"Plus, I kinda got fired from my job. So I wasn't doing anything this summer anyway."

"That's rough," he says. Is she imagining it, or is that a faint hint of sympathy in his voice? "I'm sorry to hear it. Poetry professor?"

"Generally," she says. "I teach fiction too. Just a catch-all of literature to engage the young minds. What about you and your Pushkin? You a poetry lover too?"

"I was reading his short stories. I'm not really a poetry person."

"And what exactly is a 'poetry person'?"

He answers, "I don't know. Someone broody. Emotional—"

"Heaven forbid we show emotion."

"And maybe a bit unhinged?"

"Un*hinged*?"

She's in the midst of spluttering when the coaster car slides into the base of the waterfall depot. Adam leaps out with the grace of a panther and reaches over to help her out. His hands wrap her waist, and when he looks down at her, his eyes seem to take her in, a question lingering in them.

Do you trust me?

Of course she doesn't. He's no Leo. But she can't deny how good it feels to be lifted out of the cart by him. To have his hands linger on her waist. So close she can smell the faintest hint of coffee on his breath and the light whiff of sweat off him, a scent that does not bother her at all. It actually bothers her that she's unbothered by the deep humanness of his body. That she seems to lean into it, as if it were a homey fire in the midst of a Midwestern winter.

As soon as she's on firm ground, she tears herself away and scrambles toward the rest of the group. He stands with his hands still slightly lifted, as if in offering, staring inscrutably after her.

The rest of the guests are already at the foot of the falls, exploring and taking selfies. Evie stops short at the edge of the water.

Datanla Falls is not the biggest waterfall in Việt Nam, but it has a slow majesty, cascading through the leafy mountains into a cool sage-colored pond at its base. The surrounding rocks are rubbed smooth by the waves, black as onyx in some spots, earthy brown in others. She can hardly hear anything over the sound of the water. She snaps a selfie with her phone. Evidence for her aunt's lawyers—and for herself, as a reminder that she was once brave enough to chase this moment.

"Wow," she says to herself, breathing it in.

Close by, Riley gives her a convivial wave. As she moves away from the base of the falls and her hearing returns, he follows her. He's got a loping, confident gait and a lankiness she's always liked.

"That ride wasn't so bad, was it?" he asks.

"No," she confesses, shaking her hair out. "Though I did have to ride with Adam."

"Oh? How was that?"

"It was like having to chew rusty nails while listening to Chumbawamba's greatest hits."

Riley laughs. "A miracle you survived. So, you know the legend of this place?"

"Nope."

"They say that there once was a man who fell so madly in love with a beautiful woman that he was willing to fight ferocious animals for her. The fight was so intense that trees fell, forming the canyons at the base of the falls. But the cool thing about these waterfalls is that they're now known as a meeting place for lovers. It's supposed to be one of the most romantic spots in the region. There are seven waterfalls in all."

"You went a little history professor on me, Riley."

He smiles. "Well, I guess I have a tendency to do that. I have a huge interest in these landmarks. In fact, I was recently featured in *Publishers Weekly*. They called me 'the foremost expert in Vietnamese history.'"

"You agree with them?" Evie has to restrain the urge to roll her eyes.

But, for all her annoyance, there is a part of her that admires his unabashed display of credentials. There's something about the way a male academic pushes himself forward that makes her think, *Why don't I do that more?* Heaven knows, Atlas on his summer London fellowship is probably handing out galleys of his book left and right.

"I don't *disagree*," Riley says with a grin. Evie smiles back. She likes that he can make fun of himself. "You know a little about publishing yourself, right?"

He helps her onto a rock where they can see the rest of the group. Across the way, Adam grasps Talia by her arm as she tries to climb onto the bridge from the rocks. Evie snorts. Adam the chivalrous. Could he *be* any more predictable? Of course he'd be sweet and gentle to Talia, the tour's equivalent of a Disney princess. Evie would resent Talia if she also didn't like her so much. The woman seems completely guileless, as straightforward and authentic as her impressive dossier.

Evie says, "I published a book that did all right, but I've got nothing in the works now."

"Nothing?"

"The other day, I tried to turn my grocery list into a sestet."

"Oomph."

"Yeah, my agent's not happy about it. She's actually Asian American—Korean—and she guilt-trips me the way my mother never did. Next, she'll start sending me pointed clips from Harvard professors and asking why I couldn't muster that kind of dedication."

"So your mom wasn't a tiger mom?"

"I hate that term. No. She's also not Asian. She's a nice woman from the Midwest who makes amazing casseroles and hangs up the Buckeye flag every Sunday of football season. Don't get me wrong; she's not *thrilled* with my career choice. Thinks I'm crazy for pursuing poetry for a living. She keeps saying I need to hang up my adjuncting hat for something more stable, like nursing or teaching high school, like she did."

"How does she feel about you being on this tour?"

Evie tries not to think of her mother's last, disjointed email, sent a few days before she arrived in Việt Nam. Grace Lang had made it very clear that she thought this trip was a colossal waste of time and resources. She slid in a dig or two about Hảo's emotional manipulation. Evie had responded shortly, assuring her mother that she'd be safe. Nothing since then.

Aloud, she says, "My mother has many thoughts. Voices all of them too. She's the opposite of my father, who only strung together a sentence every blue moon. But they were important sentences. The only ones that mattered. It's a wonder that they found each other."

"How'd she meet your dad? Assuming he's Việt?"

"She's an ESL teacher. She was teaching classes at the community college in her hometown near Fort Wayne when she met Dad. Apparently he traded Tupperware containers of cơm tấm in exchange for private English lessons. His sister, my Auntie Hảo, told me that he spoke English perfectly well and that he saw her in the doorway of a classroom and just . . . followed her in."

"Wow. The long game."

"Yeah. Despite being a poet, I didn't really inherit much of his romantic streak."

"Maybe you'll find that you're more romantic than you believe. With the right man."

Evie has met men like Riley before: heavily credentialed, popular in their departments, and likely to flirt with students. In fact, she's dated men like Riley. Usually the relationship fizzles at some dive bar over too many drinks, after a few weeks of Evie failing to give enough adoration to the man in question. They're drawn to her because of typecasting. They think a female poet will be chaotic, simmering with passion. The wildcard, manic pixie dream girls of academia. And, maybe Evie does have some of those characteristics. But she's also got a deeply laconic side that resists any kind of overly serious navel-gazing. The trick has always been to find a man who wants to connect with every part of her, without trying to assign some sort of trope to her personality.

Her eye is drawn across the way, where Adam stands on the bridge next to the falls. He stares out into the water with a straight back, his hands clenched on the rails. When he glances back at her, she looks away quickly, which makes her stumble into Riley. As she disentangles herself, she senses Adam's hot stare beaming onto her. She's afraid to admit to herself how much she likes the feeling.

ADAM

Đà Lạt, Việt Nam

"Here we are," Ruby says brightly, standing up in the tour bus. "We'll spend a couple of hours at Bảo Đại's summer palace, then we'll sample some of the famous Đà Lạt pizza. I hope you've come hungry. If you choose to stay at the palace longer, let us know, and we'll send a taxi back for you. Then Đức, Cherie, and I will be conducting the first round of satisfaction surveys to gauge initial compatibilities and interests."

Adam fixes a crick in his neck and cranes his head to see where everyone's ended up on the bus. Of course, Evie's plunked down next to Riley, nodding as he asks her something. Adam doesn't know why this annoys him so much, but there's a small—tiny—part of him that'd love to dunk Professor Riley into the nearest waterfall. Too bad that outing's come and gone.

As Cherie and Đức lead the group down the steps, Riley speaks up. "Bảo Đại was the last king of Việt Nam. His palace was used as a retreat from the affairs of state. But in the French-Việt War of the 1950s—"

Fen interrupts. "Can it, Professor. There are tour guides inside."

Adam sees Evie hiding a smile. Since the previous day at the falls, Riley has hooked himself tightly to her at group meals and on the bus rides. He pours her wine solicitously, places his hand on the small of her back—something that inexplicably makes Adam clench his jaw—and has more or less staked his claim with fierce dedication. None of the other men approach her, except for Connor the architect, who is oblivious to all social cues.

Once or twice, Adam has seen Evie looking away from Riley with a glazed expression, tapping her fingers absently against her wrist. What is she thinking? On paper, she and Riley seem perfect together. Same industry, same country. Adam has no idea what she's looking for, but if she wants some successful American guy from her world, she's not going to get any closer than Riley—at least, not on this tour.

He glances at his own seatmate, Talia. They've been having a perfectly lovely conversation about the climate of Việt Nam and the best coffee to order (she enjoys cà phê trứng; he prefers a simple Americano), and her numerous charity causes. Right now, she's devoted to stray animal rescue efforts in Hồ Chí Minh City, in addition to the solar panels.

She laughs self-consciously. "I can really go on about these things. Tell me about where you grew up."

She fixes her attention completely on him, and he can't deny that it's pleasant to be around a person who is determined to see the best in everyone. He didn't grow up believing that others had pure intentions, and it's refreshing to witness someone whose goodness hasn't been dampened by the world. Sort of like looking into the eyes of one of those newborn kittens on posters that teenage girls love to plaster on their walls.

But a newborn kitten doesn't exactly inspire feelings of attraction.

She reminds him, in some ways, of his mother. Effortlessly mannered, patient, conventionally stylish. An asset to every social situation. He's about to deflect Talia's curiosity by asking her about her travels as Miss Sài Gòn when he catches Ruby grinning at them. She gives him a small thumbs-up.

Okay, that was odd.

It's only been a few days, but most of the tour guests are more or less clear on whom they want to pursue. Some are keeping their options open, talking to multiple candidates, while others are firmly devoted to one person, going so far as to hold hands like high schoolers testing their first attempts at PDA. It's surprising and endearing to see how quickly these pairings happen.

Some of the older folks gather in the evenings, partnering for hands of tiến lên, while they discuss how disappointing their grandchildren are. A couple in their sixties was even seen entering the same hotel room together, unabashedly fueling the stereotype about older adults with voracious sexual appetites.

Now the older adults are the first to stream onto the palace drive. The landmark is a two-story, marigold-colored monstrosity, its exterior painted in a white grid pattern. Vivid flowers and foliage surround the palace in neat rows.

Behind Adam, Evie muses, "They really loved that nineteen-seventies bathroom tile look, huh?"

Adam turns and grins at her, earning a bright smile in return. "My parents haven't quite moved away from that look themselves. I think they call it Bidet Chic."

But then Riley puts in, "Actually, it's the Art Deco style, which was very popular at the time in Việt Nam. Did you know that this is the most visited of the emperor's three summer palaces—"

"*Three* summer palaces?" Evie says. "I have *one* apartment, and it's not even properly air-conditioned. Well, I suppose it was initially. But a bird made a nest inside the unit a few months ago."

"And you . . . didn't think to get rid of the nest?" Adam asks, puzzled.

"I mean, no." She blushes. "They seemed pretty happy there. What's a few months of extra heat?"

Talia observes, gently sympathetic, "That sounds uncomfortable."

"Just another excuse to wander around my apartment naked," Evie says blithely.

Riley's frowning at her, lecturing about how important it is to put wildlife in its proper place, but Adam can't help the flush that creeps up his neck. The image of Evie lounging naked around her house, leaning to retrieve a mug from a high shelf as her hair floats down her back, touching the swell of her ass—well, it's an image that'll be lodged in his head for a while. He tears his eyes away from her lips, the sight of a bare shoulder jutting from the one-strapped shirt she's wearing, and clears his throat.

"You all right?" Talia asks.

"Just fine," he says tightly.

Inside the mansion are twenty-six rooms. The royals' personal quarters are on the second floor, while a spacious reception area and the king's own office space take up the first floor. The lacquered furniture sits in grand rooms with carved archways and detailed ceiling work. The palace carries a kind of solemnity that could leave anyone awestruck.

"It's not exactly Versailles," Riley says. "But here, you'll note the European tilework—"

"Can it, Professor," Adam shoots back, earning a sly grin from Fen.

Adam studies the engraved glass map of Việt Nam. Such a narrow country to have summoned so much avarice and corruption in others. He's grown up memorizing the history of the last king of Việt Nam, the handsome playboy and last scion of royalty in a long and complicated legacy, but he's never truly considered what it might be like to tour these sites, to breathe in the past himself. He's never been a person who hungered to visit tourist spots, though in truth, this is a piece of his own homeland. It belongs to him too. He kicks himself for not taking more time from his studies and work to try to understand the spirit of his people. In that, perhaps he's as bad as any Việt Kiều.

"Bảo," Ruby calls. "This is the home of your namesake."

Talia smiles at him, while Evie gives him a questioning look. "Oh, your name isn't Adam?"

"It *is*," he says. "But my given name is Bảo. That's what my parents call me."

"It means 'treasure,'" Ruby puts in.

"Oh, I like it," Evie says. Her eyes soften. "You must mean a lot to your parents, for them to give you such a name."

There's a pause as he takes this in. Adam knows that if there's any treasure in the family, it'd be Ruby, not him. Somehow it bugs him to have everyone know his given name, like he's letting them in on a secret, even though it really *isn't* a secret at all. He's just grateful that Ruby doesn't call him Baby Bảo, as she usually does.

He nods to Evie, a little coldly, then turns to Talia and asks if she wants to see the library.

Adam and Talia pass a stand full of dress-up clothing, noticing that Đức has already pulled out his wallet and begun gesturing toward a costume. The king's garments, of course; no mere soldier apparel for Đức. He struggles to pull on a yellow robe, then the towering headpiece, shoving his baseball cap into Cherie's hands. A bored-looking Fen takes pictures of him posing in front of the doorway. He's trying to pull Evie into the costumery, but she's laughing and shaking her head. Her laugh is like bubbling champagne, golden and airy. There's a part of Adam that wants to coax that laugh out of her more often. Instead, he looks down at Talia, who's examining the books.

"So do you like history?" Adam asks Talia.

She nods. "I do, quite a bit. When I was young, I was often sick, so I would read a lot of my father's books. He was an amateur historian. I've visited all of King Bảo Đại's palaces."

"How does this one compare?" Adam asks.

She grins. "It's no Bidet Chic."

Impulsively, trying to go beyond her polished exterior, he asks, "If you could live anywhere, where would you live?"

"Honestly? I love Hồ Chí Minh City. It's energetic and diverse and always keeps me on my toes. Plus, it's where I can do the most work for the people who need it."

What had he expected her to say—Uzbekistan? Her answer is honest and admirable, of course, and should be exactly the one he wants to hear, but it leaves him feeling a bit wooden. Talia's greatest charm is her predictability. She's a warm bowl of cháo, a wool-knit sweater. She makes so much sense.

And yet—he doesn't long for the comfort of cháo as much as he should. He longs for the spice of Thai chilis, the startling sweetness of rock sugar. The unexpected.

"Where would you live?" she asks.

Somewhere in the next room, Adam can hear Riley going on about how Charles de Gaulle once stayed at the palace. He turns, expecting to see Evie pressed to Riley's side, but Riley is surrounded by a group of the older aunties and uncles, nodding emphatically at everything he has to say, while a bemused tour guide tries to correct some of Riley's more colorful elaborations.

"There's no evidence of that . . ." the guide adds faintly, only to be interrupted by Riley again.

Talia gets swept up in conversation with Ruby about the ceremonial fashions of the time, and Adam, moving toward the windows, sees something flit out of the corner of his eye. A flash of a bare shoulder. Long hair rippling behind her as she runs through the palace gardens.

Unable to help himself, Adam absentmindedly gives an excuse to the group and stalks out the back doors to follow her.

EVIE

Đà Lạt, Việt Nam

The breeze in Đà Lạt soothes Evie; it's a welcome break from the close air of the tour buses and her brief stint in Hồ Chí Minh City, where the humidity reduced her to a damp mess. For the first time in too long, it's just her, alone with her thoughts out in the world. As nice as Riley is, he's not exactly attuned to her need for occasional moments of silence. He's not attuned to much in the way of emotional intelligence if she's being frank. But she can't deny the attention is nice. A balm to her recently broken heart.

But *was* it broken? Humiliation aside, she hasn't thought very much about Atlas since she landed in Việt Nam. In fact, she's not sure she's ever loved anyone enough to be broken by them. Is she just a superficial human? Her MFA colleagues wrote blistering, wounded poems about their great loves, but the only great love Evie has ever had was her father. No other man has come close.

It was the cautionary tale she learned from Grace, before she even had the chance to date—love faithfully, if you must, but only let them in so far. Otherwise, the loss might crush you, the way Grace was crushed by Evie's father's death. Grace would be just as happy for Evie to remain alone forever, as long as she led a financially stable, relatively unscathed life. Her motto couldn't be further from Auntie Hảo's. Instead of *love bravely*, she might as well have stitched the words *love sedately* into her embroidered pillows.

The truth is, on this trip Evie hasn't had the time or inclination to do anything other than live in the present. Just that morning, she sat at the desk and tried to write. Nothing resembling a poem came out, but she saw images forming in her mind. The trees careening past her at Datanla Falls. The blushing cord of sunrise above the mountain silhouettes. A pair of strong hands wrapped around her waist.

Nope. She will *not* think of that. Especially since he's currently wooing perfect Talia while Evie walks the gardens alone. She refocuses on the sights around her, describing them in her head as if she were transcribing the visual into words.

Bảo Đại's garden is immaculately manicured, with closely set paving stones winding around the trees and plants. The mansion sits atop a hill amid the Love Forest—again, only the most romantic of settings for this tour. Evie has to admit how well organized these excursions have been. The weather has also been pristine so far; sunny and mild in the highlands, kissed by a bit of breeze. Maybe Ruby has some connection to the love gods. Knowing her, she's probably sacrificed a whole herd of oxen to ensure these idyllic conditions.

And it works! Evie can't help noticing how many people are already coupled up. She tries to be happy for the couples, shuttle her cynical self back to its mildewy cave, but mostly, she's mired in self-pity, thinking how impossible a true match seems to her.

That morning before breakfast—another rich meal of pastries and French-style hot chocolate—Atlas had texted her from London. It was seven a.m. her time; one a.m. his.

Thinking of you. I'm in my hotel room in London. It's like coming home.

Evie thought, *I bet it is.* England is Mecca for him; she'd once suspected he had a shrine to the king somewhere in his house, though no one—not even Atlas—could find much to admire in that prickly monarch. She was afraid Atlas would try his hand at international sexting, a practice neither of them was particularly suited for even when they lived in the same zip code.

When she didn't respond, he continued, I'm going to the British Library tomorrow. You'd like it.

The bummer is that of *course* she would like it. Libraries were her only escape during those long years of a lonely childhood. But the British Library? As unlikely as her ending up on a luxury tour in Việt Nam.

Evie never had the same opportunities to travel as Atlas. He comes from old money, the kind that often goes to Europe on summer breaks—or "holiday," as Atlas is wont to say. His (repressed) father is an economist, his (anxiety-crippled) mother a well-respected CEO of a literacy foundation. Evie has never met them, and for that she is glad; they seem to be the type of people specifically created to summon feelings of ineptitude in mere mortals.

Atlas himself speaks four languages, not including English, and can talk to anyone about where they are from with eerie specificity. He has a reference point for nearly anything, from obscure Russian ballet to the regional cuisine of ancient Persia. That erudition intimidated, then enraptured Evie, who could never be accused of being encyclopedic in anything but the best way to piss off academic autocrats.

She comes from a working-class family that was proudly careful with their dollars and took exactly one vacation a year, to a lake in Michigan with a borrowed time-share. She put her head down in school, never looking twice at the flyers for study abroad, knowing she couldn't afford even a road trip to the nearest big city. Auntie Hảo had offered to fund her travel, plenty of times, but Grace had insisted that they didn't need Auntie Hảo's charity. She was too proud to take money from her dead husband's sister, even if it was for her only daughter. Evie also suspected that her mother was jealous of her relationship with Auntie Hảo.

But those summers in San Francisco were her only glimpse of a world wider than the one she lived in, with strip malls and the same three movies playing at the theater, the same kids in every grade in school, all of whom ignored her.

So maybe being with Atlas was about more than the orgasms or the wide selection of Earl Grey teas in his pantry. He is sophisticated and adventurous and confident—qualities Evie wishes for in herself. But whenever she talked about a country she wanted to travel to, or a historical site she itched to see, he always found a way to mention, with an almost imperceptible hint of boredom, that he'd spent time there before. It made her feel so small. Evie wonders what it would be like to experience something new with someone *together*.

Out of loneliness or weakness, she had texted back to Atlas: Send photos of all the books. I expect a full catalog by day's end.

With me in front of them? ☺

Only if you're wearing a Shakespearean wig.

They'd texted for a few minutes longer, and for a brief time, it felt like they'd slipped into their usual flow. The same jokes, that ease of knowing how the other would respond. But of course, it was just an illusion. He's halfway across the world. *And* he lied to her. Something Evie is learning is that you can move forward, but it's nearly impossible to slide back.

Now she leans to smell one of the amaryllis blooms in the late emperor's garden. In the short time she's been in Việt Nam, she's seen more species of plants and animals than she has in years. It makes a part of her ache, knowing how temporary this sensation of discovery will be. In time, she'll be back in America, contemplating her life anew.

A bee emerges from the heart of a flower and begins swooping around her head. She yelps. She bats it away with her hands. It only gets more aggressively loopy.

"You demonic bastard insect!" she cries.

Behind her, a deep laugh, a hand on her elbow. Adam's touch calms her more than it should.

"You're not supposed to bother the native fauna, you know," he says.

Evie is indignant. "He bothered *me*."

"I think he was just flying."

"*You* also bothered me, for the record."

He carefully steers her away from the irate bee, who begins to slow his frantic circling once Evie stops waving her arms.

"This is an apt metaphor," she sighs.

"For what?"

"You know. The human condition. We're doomed to seek beauty—and then be rebuffed by it."

"More accurately, you're probably not supposed to freak out at the first sign of an insect. Are you allergic or something?"

"I *could be*!"

She tosses her hair over her shoulder and begins to make her way to the palace. Then, she pauses and looks back at Adam. He's smiling at her in a lightly mocking way, his head cocked to one side. Handsome in a pair of navy trousers and a white collared shirt. Does this man ever wear casual clothes? And why does he manage to look so irritatingly *hot* in everything?

"Go on," he says. "I know you're anxious to reunite with Riley."

She begins to protest and then, catching sight of his raised eyebrow, dissolves into laughter. "He means *so* well."

"Do you think Trevor Noah hates him?"

"What do you know about Trevor Noah?"

Adam frowns. "You think we're totally devoid of access to American culture over here? That we're all pulling water from wells and gaping at computers like they're shuttles from outer space? That I can't log on to You-Tube when I want?"

"Honestly? I just didn't think you had a sense of humor."

She winks. At that, Adam pauses, then throws his head back and laughs. She can't help but smile, knowing she pried something resembling human emotion from him. She's never even seen him laugh before. It's warm, and just a little goofy, like a kid who's been caught doing something he shouldn't. Maybe there's a little more to the Grumpy CMO than his tight-ass exterior.

"I have jokes," he protests.

"Aside from your wardrobe?"

"This is *bespoke*."

They walk back to the palace together, trading insults along the way, but once they arrive and look around, there's no sign of the Love Yêu group. Just a few tourists wandering, a small child who gives them a shy grin. They exchange a look and rush back to the entrance of Bảo Đại's palace. No tour bus. No sign that anyone waited for them.

"Those mutinous assholes," Evie gasps.

"We're not on a boat. I'm sure there's an explanation."

Adam checks his phone then and shows it to Evie. Five text messages from Ruby, warning him about missing the bus. Then a final, irate one, telling him to take a taxi back by himself. *No one texted me*, Evie thinks. Then she remembers that she left her phone back at the hotel anyway, so she wouldn't be tempted to keep messaging with Atlas. Whoops.

"Well, there's nothing to do about it now," he says, annoyed. "Let's grab a cab back to the hotel."

They slide into the back of a cab, and Adam begins to give the address of their hotel. Then Evie's stomach lets out a loud churning noise that sounds like the snore of an ancient sea dragon. Adam hides a grin.

"Are you hungry?" he asks innocently.

She really is. Those croissants are much too light to sustain her.

She says, "Well, those mutinous assholes are going to eat delicious Đà Lạt pizza. Let's go get some food."

The cabdriver, a man with a wide grin and high cheekbones, turns back and says, "Đà Lạt pizza? That's just a gimmick. You want some real Đà Lạt cuisine? You go for bánh mì xíu mại."

"Vietnamese meatballs with baguette," Adam translates.

Her stomach rumbles again. "What the heck are we waiting for?"

The driver takes them into town and drops them off in front of a simple stand. There are just a few plastic tables under a tarp, and a basket stacked high with golden baguettes the size of their forearms. Nothing like the grand dining rooms and endless champagne they've been plied with on the trip. But Evie doesn't care. She sinks into a table, sniffing the air like a hound. She smells tomatoes and garlic, and a deep meaty scent. Her stomach devours itself as Adam orders for them.

"Can you toss me a breadcrumb while I wait?" she asks the server pathetically.

Nearby, there are shops with similar setups: soy milk vendors and coffee stands, a fabric store with brilliantly colored fabrics. A woman sitting next to a pile of knitted sweaters, each more intricately designed than the last. Evie makes a note to buy one for Lillian.

"Here," Adam says. He reaches over to another table and snags a shallow bowl of boiled peanuts. "These will tide you over."

She bites into a salty, creamy peanut and immediately starts shelling the rest. "Open your mouth."

"I will not."

"I have fantastic aim. I played in a junior basketball league."

"You've never said anything more unbelievable in your life."

"Come on, Bảo," she croons.

With a beleaguered sigh, he unhinges his jaw an inch, like a child refusing to eat his peas. Evie aims a peanut into the tiny opening between his lips, but it instead bounces off his eyebrow and slides down his shirt. She cackles as he fishes it out and tosses it back at her. When she ducks, the wayward peanut sails past her, hitting a man behind them in the back of the head. He glances over to find both Adam and Evie staring back in wide-eyed innocence.

"You are a menace," Adam mutters once the man has torn his glare away from them.

She furrows her brow. "Vietnamese peanuts have a different density than American ones. That must be it."

"And a tireless bullshitter. So where is your dad from?" Adam asks.

He leans back in his chair, so far that Evie thinks he'll fall into the dirt. But he doesn't. Just crosses his arms in that charming way, raising an eyebrow.

"Can Tho," she says between mouthfuls. "You know, the floating markets? He and his siblings—including my Auntie Hảo—used to talk about waking up at dawn as kids to watch the vendors with fruit stacked up on their boats, each so full it looked like they were going to capsize. Auntie Hảo would bat her eyelashes until someone threw her a misshapen orange or something, and they'd all make off with their treasure. I think that's part of the reason why Auntie Hảo sent me on this trip; thought it'd be good for me to see the homeland."

"She was right. I can't picture what it's like to live so far from your origins. Your Auntie Hảo is the one your book is named after?"

"You looked up my book."

"The dossier," he says. "I looked everyone up."

Adam's words are measured, and Evie checks to see if he's poking at her, but he seems to be waiting for her answer.

She says, "Total stalker."

He rolls his eyes.

A second later, the meatballs arrive, swimming in a savory tomato sauce, accompanied by halved baguettes. Adam turns his meatballs into a sandwich—a sub loaded with jalapenos and cilantro, like all Vietnamese sandwiches—while Evie breaks off pieces of her bread and drags them in the sauce. She stops to sigh, enraptured by the dance of flavors.

"I'm gonna have babies with this meatball. We're going to have a gigantic meatball pram filled with juicy little meatballettes named Cassidy and Fudrucker."

"That good?" he asks, amused.

"*Amazing.* God, I'm so glad we made the detour." Evie takes another bite. "So, yeah, Auntie Hảo was this huge figure in my life. Just so bold and wide-open, nothing like a traditional Vietnamese stereotype of a conservative spinster. Everything was bigger, brighter with her. She embraced life; and she taught me to do it too, whenever I visited her in San Francisco."

"What does embracing life look like to you?"

She stops chewing. "That's a good question. I can't say I've figured it out yet. Auntie Hảo is dead, but in some ways, she's still here. I think about her constantly. We never did travel together, which I regret more than any-thing else."

"I'm sorry to hear about your aunt."

"Thanks. She treated people like they *mattered*, regardless of how old they were, or how much money they had, or what they had accomplished. Her friends were these famous, bohemian people who'd been all over the world, and she included me in their conversations as if I had something new to contribute. She had this way of extending community through example. Do you know what I mean?"

"I can't say I do."

"Well, it's a rare trait, I guess. There was this time, when I was a teen-ager, when I was writing all these angsty poems. It drove my mother nuts—I don't blame her, truthfully. But instead of making me feel juvenile like any-one else would have done, Auntie Hảo took me to poetry readings and set up mentoring sessions with poet friends of hers. She had no creative aspi-rations herself, but she believed in the value of creative work. She believed in *me*."

"As she should have."

Evie gives a dry laugh. "I don't know. I haven't amounted to much."

"She would disagree, I think."

He looks sincere, his eyes soft and patient. His sympathy makes her want to tell him more about Auntie Hảo. It's been so long since she truly wanted to talk about her grief with anyone. But she can't linger in that space. Not with him. It's too close to intimacy. So Evie does what she does best. Deflect and make things weird.

"She would have loved Fudrucker and Cassidy like her own," she in-tones. Adam frowns, seeing through her nonchalance. She turns the ques-tion around on him. "What does embracing life look like for you? More bespoke suits?"

His expression turns stormy as he pivots away from her. At first, Evie's worried that she's destroyed their tentative truce. That he'll shut her down and insist they go straight back to the hotel.

But eventually he says, "I thought it was following this road map that my parents had laid out for me. Making a lot of money, living in their neighborhood, maybe getting a summer home somewhere like they did. I was supposed to go to medical school like my dad. When I decided to pursue business, he was lukewarm. If anything, his expectations got higher, like I had even more to prove because I set off on my own. Still, I was on track for the rest of the future they had planned for me."

"But?"

"There was a woman. It ended—"

"Like a train wreck?"

"Like Mount Vesuvius."

Evie ignores the jolt of jealousy that seizes her. "Ah."

"It wasn't just her, though months ago, I would have said she was the one who ruined my life. I'm not so sure that the future I'd once planned would make me happy anymore. Being on this trip, seeing all these sights. This is the first time I've felt alive in a while. Like shedding skin, you know? Or taking flight." He laughs awkwardly. "Cheesy, right?"

"Not at all. I got this tattoo in honor of Auntie Hảo when she died, but also as a reminder to be braver. To allow myself to fly."

She tucks her hair behind her ear to show him the small tattoo there. It looks like a wing. The dip of the feathers grazes her hairline slightly. Like a kiss. He reaches across the table as if to touch it. She arches her neck to allow him access. His fingertip is warm and so gentle that it makes her shiver.

Seeing her tremble, he leans closer. Now he's staring at her with a darkness that isn't annoyance, but something more unreadable. Under the heat of his gaze, she forgets about the meal in front of her, the dozens of people going about their business. The rest of the scene becomes a blur that makes way for his eyes, his lips.

She leans forward too. This whole day has led to *this* moment of assuaging her curiosity. Driving past the layers of reserve to his molten core. What makes him conflicted. What makes him undone.

"I love it," he says. But he's saying something else, another message underneath that hushed voice. He's saying he sees her desires. That he's not afraid of them. That, despite their rough start, they are more alike than she'd ever imagined.

"You do?" Where has her breath gone? It's hitched up along his tentative smile. It sails across the table, already landing in the cave of his mouth, tangled with his breath.

In a second, their lips will touch. Her hunger now has nothing to do with food, and everything to do with the man in front of her. The one who proves himself, again and again, an enigma she needs to explore.

But right before they can offer themselves to each other, there's a dripping along her arms and shoulders. The sky is opening. A sudden summer storm arrives hard and fast, drenching them in rain, making the dirt soggy around their feet.

"The baguettes," Evie whispers despairingly.

"My shoes."

Adam's leather loafers are ruined. She braces herself for some kind of fit—the kind Atlas would have had, if any of his carefully chosen clothing were marred by the elements.

But instead, Adam's lips twitch, and a second later, he's laughing in that goofy, gulping way. She can't help joining him, their laughter lighting up the alleyway, neither of them making a move to huddle closer to the shelter of the restaurant. They just extend their arms, letting the rain wash down on them.

"It's like running through sprinklers," Evie says, delighted.

"Getting hosed down by an irate nanny after filling her pockets with pudding while she napped."

"You have experience with that, Quyền?" She likes the thought of a tiny, mischievous Adam running around with his spoonfuls of pudding.

"No comment."

"Putting it in the dossier."

The storm soon passes, and there's the faintest outline of a rainbow left behind, a new humidity in the air. Evie knows her hair is a puffed-up mess, with the ringlets around her forehead that appear after the rain, and that her clothes are clinging to her, but she doesn't care. The storm is so unexpected, so refreshing, that they both forget about the near-kiss they would have surely regretted.

Then Evie sees Adam's dancing eyes. He reaches for her hand. And her eyes slide to his lips, still quirking in amusement.

Almost. The kiss is almost forgotten.

ADAM

Nha Trang, Việt Nam

They are all waiting on Evie Lang. Adam sneaks a glance at Ruby. She's getting visibly irritated, drumming her nails against the leather tops of the seats, staring pointedly at her watch, though it's only been five minutes since they were supposed to depart for the boat cruise around Nha Trang Bay. Ruby's inflexibility bothers Adam, though just a few days ago, he would have had the same reaction. Now he wants to say, *We're on a vacation. This is supposed to be fun.*

When was the last time he thought about *fun*? It surely has nothing to do with a long-haired, boot-wearing woman with a devastatingly adorable freckle below her left eye. Nope.

No one else has noticed Evie's absence; they're too preoccupied in their excitement over being so close to the most beautiful beaches in Việt Nam. Pin is offering everyone on the bus squirts of his industrial-sized bottle of hand sanitizer while Riley is explaining how he can juggle six balls without dropping a single one. Fen makes an inappropriate ball joke that causes the aunties on the bus to scowl.

Meanwhile, Adam tries not to think about his almost-kiss with Evie a couple days ago in Đà Lạt. He definitely does not want to linger on how he stays awake remembering the tattoo behind her ear, the unbearable sexiness of her running to the hotel with him in a wet dress, tendrils of hair clinging to her face.

Finally, at ten past the hour, noticing that Ruby is approaching near-combustion at the very minor deviance from her tour schedule, Adam announces, "I'll go see what's keeping Evie."

Ruby says, "She's not answering my texts or Zalo messages."

Adam says dryly, "Somehow I don't think Evie Lang has downloaded Zalo. She hardly remembers she has a phone."

Ruby continues grumbling. "Why are Americans always late to everything?"

There's a chorus of good-natured protest from the Americans on the tour, including Riley, who insists, "I was the first one on this bus."

"You don't get bonus points for being a kiss-ass," Fen hisses.

"I'll be right back," Adam mumbles.

As he slides past Ruby, she gives him a level gaze. He avoids her eyes. Ever since Đà Lạt, she's been pacing like a caged animal, jumping on him for everything under the sun. He tried to ask what was wrong, but she shut down immediately. He can't help thinking that whatever is bothering her is deeper than the stress of running the perfect matchmaking tour.

But what could she have to be anxious about? She and Thăng have just bought a vacation home in Australia, one with a breathtaking view of the Tasman Sea. Everything is going exactly the way it should at LYT. Their social media page is bursting with heart eyes and wistful comments, along with some pledges to sign up for the next tour. Yet Ruby can't seem to settle; it's like spikes are poking her under the skin, stirring her toward perpetual irritation.

When he asked her if Thăng was proud of her success, a certain malice entered her laugh. A bitterness. She walked away without answering the question, which is unlike Ruby. She always likes to have the last word.

He shakes his head, clearing the thoughts. Of everyone, he will never have to worry about Ruby. She can handle herself in any circumstance. She was bred for domination.

He knocks loudly, rudely, on the door to Evie's beach hut.

In Nha Trang, they have fabulous accommodations on one of the private beaches, each in a small hut decorated with sumptuous furniture. Their decks overlook the water, where a salty wind blows up in the morning. Breakfast is delivered promptly, along with steaming carafes of strong coffee. He'd woken up and poured himself a cup, watching the slow pull of the waves and wondering why he ever thought he'd be able to settle in boisterous Hồ Chí Minh City. That's the thing about an unforgettable vacation like this; it can make you pretty discontented with your real life.

"I'm *coming*!"

Evie flings the door open, jumping on one leg as she pulls on a sandal. She's wearing cutoff jeans that show off her tanned legs and a T-shirt that hangs loosely off one shoulder. Her hair is wrapped in a loose bun, small strands brushing against her jawline. Why does the sight of her always leave him a little breathless?

"Ruby's having a fit," he tells her, more to cover up his discomfort than to chide her.

She tugs the door closed behind her. "I know, I know! I'm sorry. My cousin Lillian called and then there was a problem with my shower and—well, let's book it before your sister buys me a flight back to Ohio."

"Not tired of Việt Nam yet?"

"Never," she tells him, right before she takes off at a run. "The fun is just getting started."

As they make their way toward the bus, Adam can't help thinking that Evie is pure temptation. Chaos. She could create a storm in even the most carefully planned situation, often through no true fault of her own. She just invites the messy, the spontaneous, as if a part of her is always magnetized toward the hidden adventure. Her lack of conformity fascinates him—even as he knows it has historically repelled him. After all, what drew him to Lana was her utter predictability. There was no surprise in their relationship—until, of course, there was.

But Evie is a thunderbolt to her core. She electrifies the system. Someone like him could only be a wet blanket, muffling all her instincts.

Before she skips onto the bus, she turns around and tells him, "I like your shorts."

He glances down at his board shorts, light turquoise with white piping, then flushes for the good part of the bus ride to the bay. He tries to make normal conversation with Talia, who's enthusiastic about snorkeling and suntanning, but his eye is drawn toward Evie more often than he'd care to admit.

When they arrive at the beach, Adam is eager to step onto the pale sand, so soft that you can walk barefoot for miles without tripping on a shell. He helps Talia down from the bus and is rewarded with a warm smile. Out of the corner of his eye, he sees Riley doing the same for Evie and tries not to grit his teeth.

The bay opens in front of them, a gleaming blue expanse with rippling mountains in the distance. The trees cast pockets of shade around the beach, while colorful stalls dot the sand. Vendors sell everything from fresh coconut juice to string bikinis that would make a nun flush. Though it's early, there are already groups of sunbathers lying belly-down on the sand. Some stretch their feet into the shallows of the bay. It's paradise, or the closest thing to it.

Ruby claps her hands once, her usual habit, and says, "Welcome to Nha Trang. We'll be staying here for three days, so make the most of it. Today, you'll have your choice of sunbathing in luxury in our private, fully serviced cabanas or going on a boat ride to the surrounding islands, where you can snorkel and swim to your heart's content. We'll leave for the resort at nightfall, though of course, feel free to take a taxi to your beach hut if you prefer to depart earlier. *Please* don't separate from the group without telling us where you are going."

He ignores his sister's pointed admonition and sneaks a look at Evie. She's radiant in wide-eyed delight, the first to throw off her shoes and scramble toward the water. Ruby has arranged giant tents with comfortable chairs for them, along with waterside cocktails and food service. A few of the couples are already settling in with drinks or sliding into a comatose state with the crash of the waves as their soundtrack.

Adam, Evie, Ruby, and a few others decide to go on the boat ride, while the rest stay onshore. Fen, wearing a siren-red *Baywatch*-style suit, looks a little green as she lurches onto the boat. He fishes some antinausea medication out of his pocket and hands it to her.

"This'll be great," Adam says with what he hopes is a comforting smile. "Once you get your bearings."

She fists the pills and swallows them without water. "So you say. I'm not a fan of boats. All that tumbling. But the zodiac consultant said that those born in the Year of the Ox are prone to staying too set in our ways. So this is my attempt at a shake-up."

"Good for you."

"I was skeptical. But let's just say—some things resonated. Part of the workshop was about the qualities of your sign that impede you from growing in your relationships."

Adam had missed the workshop, busy as he was fielding calls from his father and remotely managing the day-to-day marketing tasks with his team in Hồ Chí Minh City.

He muses, "I wonder what the consultant would say about those born in the Year of the Dragon."

Fen slides him a look. "Arrogance. Dragons are arrogant."

"Sounds like that consultant is a quack."

Fen indicates Evie with her head, cackling. "Evie said the same thing. Her sign is a tiger, and the consultant called her reckless. She didn't enjoy that. In fact, she might have spent a good twenty minutes arguing about it. Girl doesn't like to be contradicted."

Adam snorts. "I take it back. Maybe that consultant is legitimate after all."

"I'm pretty close to someone who was born in the Year of the Tiger, and let's just say—Evie reminds me of her." Fen smiles to herself. "Sometimes dramatic. Confident to a fault."

"That's one way of putting it," he grumbles.

"But here's a thing about tigers. They give off this cocky, devil-may-care attitude. But no one cares more than them." Fen's voice gets soft as she tugs the ends of her hair pensively. "They're sensitive, always questioning themselves. They can be the loneliest sign of the zodiac. Yet faultlessly loyal in relationships. Tigers fall fast, and they fall hard. Tigers are *special.*"

"It sounds like you *are* pretty close with this tiger in your life," he teased. "Maybe you should be with her, instead of on this boat."

"If only."

A small flush grows on her cheeks as her mouth twists into a private smile. One meant for just her and her memories. He contemplates the enigma that is Fen—a woman with a story hidden under those layers of glamour and toughness. If she already has love, though—and she seems to, judging from her moony expression—why is she on this tour? It must be a colossal waste of time. Before he can say anything more, her face shutters and the carefree, teasing actress is back.

She pins him with a smirk. "Here's another fun fact about tigers. Guess which zodiac sign they're most compatible with?"

Adam shrugs, though he thinks he might already know, if the gleam in her eye is any indication.

"Dragons, of course," she confirms.

Before he can protest, she's stumbling off again, grasping her stomach as the waves slosh around them. He's left with the distinct and regrettable urge to look up everything he can on zodiac compatibility, though just two minutes ago, he couldn't have cared less about any of it.

Once the boat moves at a steady clip, the guests shuck their outer layers. Evie tosses her shirt off and Adam tries (unsuccessfully) not to stare at her bathing suit, a black halter-style bikini top with the tiniest pair of bottoms he's ever seen. She starts slathering her skin with sunscreen. Riley, seeing his chance, shoots up to offer to help with her back, but Adam intercepts him, smoothly taking the bottle from Evie as she turns to look at him in surprise. Riley plunks back down on the bench with a furrow of petulance.

Her skin is sun-warmed under his hands. He tries not to linger, though the feel of her is sinfully delicious. He slides the lotion over her shoulders, down onto the small of her back.

"Is this okay?" he whispers in her ear.

She smells like coconut, salt, and something floral. Heady. He wants to *bathe* in that scent.

"It's perfect. Thank you," she says over her shoulder, a little breathlessly.

When he steps away, he has to catch his own breath for a second.

Tigers. Dragons and tigers. His mind fills with images of her in that tiny bikini, sprawled on the forest floor, her hair shaken into the grass, a mess of beautiful abandon. Her wide eyes staring up into his. Her hand reaching for his neck, pulling him lower, closer. The sunscreen bottle drops out of his hands.

No. *Nope.* He blames Fen for all this animal talk.

Brusquely, to cover his distraction, he says, "Good thing I showed up. You look like you'd burn like a crab in five seconds flat."

She frowns, then shoots back, "And *you* look like you haven't seen the sun since Nosferatu last emerged."

His mouth twitches. "I'm told vampires are trendy."

"Maybe if you're a teenage girl with Robert Pattinson posters on your wall."

"That's not you?"

"I much prefer therianthrope werewolves," she says, as haughtily as one can when admitting a comprehensive knowledge of Stephenie Meyer's greatest hits.

"That's a big word."

"Find *that* in your Pushkin."

And then, like a cool breeze, their laughter releases the tension from the conversation. *Laughing* together. He likes it—the trill of hers overlaid onto his own, like the sweetest melody. He thought it was fun to needle Evie Lang. Turns out, it's far more gratifying to make her smile in that sudden, unguarded way.

File that under unexpected discoveries on this trip.

His laughter slowly dies once he feels his sister's eyes on them. Contemplating. Judging. He turns from Evie and tries to make conversation with the rest of the group. Donning the CMO hat instead of the one he really wants to wear. The intrigued-by-an-infuriating-poet hat.

They continue to sail around the bay on peaceful waves, stopping for the guides to point out famous landmarks like Monkey Island, inhabited by thousands of carousing primates, and the coral reefs flocked by schools of tiger fish. After an hour, they finally dock near Hòn Miễu Island, a remote and rocky beach dotted with fishermen casting their lines.

While everyone gears up for snorkeling, Adam dives into the water. Thanks to all those lessons his parents made him take at the local gymnasium, he's a strong swimmer, even for someone who hasn't been near the water in a decade.

His arms slice through the water, pushing and pulling the warm waves around him. Above, the sky is a brilliant blue, the color of a robin's eggshell, and the sun remains unblemished by clouds. He hasn't felt this relaxed in years. It's as if someone tugged on a string in his body, loosening him up day by day. It feels good, if terrifying. In the back of his mind, he asks, *What if I loosen up so much that everything comes undone?*

If just the echoing strains of Evie's laughter make him rethink his life—his purpose on the tour—what would it do to him if he gave in to his attraction? Told her what he really thought of her?

This question makes him swim harder and faster, until his brain clears of everything except the exhaustion of driving his body to its limits.

Riley calls, "Hey, Michael Phelps. Leave some water for the rest of us."

"He's not a *whale*, dummy," Fen returns. "It's not like he's drinking it."

Adam ignores the laughter and keeps going until he can't anymore.

After his swim, he hauls himself onto the beach and onto one of the shaded lounge chairs. Out in the water, he can see the snorkelers occasionally surfacing for air. Evie emerges from the water like a dolphin, shaking the water off her body. Next to her, Riley surfaces a second later, and she gives him a big splash that makes him sputter in annoyance. Evie catches Adam's eye and waves to him on the shore. He gives a small wave back, unable to suppress his smile.

"She's beautiful, isn't she? In an unpolished kind of way."

Ruby sits in the chair next to him, and Adam tries to shake his annoyance. He doesn't want to talk to anyone about Evie, least of all his sister, who's staring at him with a piercing kind of concentration that lets him know she's got something on her mind. Her gaze slides to Evie, who is jumping onto a wave in her halter bikini. Adam can't help seeing Evie through his sister's eyes. Chaotic, unpredictable. Unlike any of the other careful tour guests.

He has an urge to defend Evie. Where Ruby would call her unpolished, he would opt for wild, untamed, irresistible. But he can't say that to his sister. She's a shark looking for blood.

"Evie Lang? She's okay," Adam says, trying for nonchalance.

"You were swimming fast out there. Like you had something to prove."

"Just exercising."

"Here, BB. Eat this."

Ruby hands him a plate of bánh căn with seafood and quail eggs. Each rice pancake is crispy on the outside and soft on the inside, melding perfectly with the seafood and the dash of nước chấm. The dish smells so good, and he was swimming for so long, that he can't resist shoveling mouthful after mouthful.

"Where'd you get this?"

"Stand up the beach."

"Thanks, Chị." He rarely calls her by her Vietnamese honorific, but today, it comes out. Probably, there's always going to be a part of him chasing her footsteps, wondering how he can possibly emerge from her shadow.

Ruby's face softens as she watches him eat. "Remember how often we'd steal bánh căn from the banquet tables as kids? Or chả giò? Anything that could fit in the palm of your hand was fair game."

He laughs, cheeks still full. "Mẹ got so mad at me once that she made me eat a whole plate of chả giò in one sitting. She said that if I was going to behave like a common thief, she'd punish me like one."

"Pretty sure criminals aren't made to gorge themselves on homemade chả giò. That sounds more like a Japanese game show. Or an American one."

"I was so sick from it that I couldn't eat chả giò for months! Even now, they make me queasy."

"Yeah," Ruby says, picking at a spot on the knee of her linen trousers. "We didn't have the most empathetic of parenting models, I suppose. Maybe that's why I'm hesitant to have kids myself."

Adam pauses for her to continue. It's rare that Ruby confides in him, especially about her marriage and family prospects, which have always been so opaque to him. He doesn't want to spoil this space between them, tremulous with things they never say aloud. Regrets about their childhood. Uncertainties about their future. Adam and Ruby had been raised to show no weakness—especially Adam. He was meant to be stoic and purposeful, like his father, a man leading the family without hesitation, without fear. But now, seeing Ruby questioning her ability to raise children, Adam wonders if they both have some unlearning to do.

"I think you'd be a great mom," he says gently. And it's true. She's tough, but fiercely protective. Behind all that rationality and ambition lies the young girl he remembers looking up to. The one who brings him lunch from a stand. Who looks out for others, even if they don't ask for help. The one who demands he lead a whole department at her company, trusting him day in and day out to bring her vision to life. Somewhere in that filing cabinet of a heart, there's a woman who believes in underdogs. "You could loosen up a bit more, though."

"Coming from you, that's pretty rich."

"Fair." They laugh briefly, before he sobers. "Seriously, Ruby. Are you happy? I know you're under a lot of pressure, but . . . I don't know. You seem even more miserable than usual. You're on a love tour and treating it like an executioner's march."

Anger flashes in her eyes, but then, just as quickly, it dies. She sighs. "What's happy? Just a temporary emotion. I'd rather have stability than happiness."

"Is Thăng stable?" The question flies out before he can stop it.

He thinks she'll shut him down with one of her patented older-sister glares, but instead her shoulders lower and she seems to deflate.

"Thăng is Thăng."

"What does that mean?"

He has the sense that he's treading on thin ice. He means the question sincerely, as an invitation to talk, but she hears his question as a challenge. Perhaps it shouldn't be surprising. They've spent the majority of their lives picking at each other's weaknesses. Pushing each other further, yes. But historically, they haven't exactly been pillars of support.

"He has his life. His hobbies. Now that we don't have to worry as much about money, he wants to travel all over. Get more tattoos, probably. In his dream scenario, we'd be in Australia, hanging ten all day by the beach. Or maybe he'd just be there on his own. In either case, babies don't figure into his plans."

"People have babies in Australia."

"They do. But you also have to spend time together to make babies."

"Gross, Ruby."

"Ah, right. I forgot that the nanny's facts of life talk skipped you entirely."

"Have you talked to Thăng about any of this?"

She swallows. "No. Why should I? We're both doing fine. We work together; we understand each other. Ba and Mẹ love him. Our families are close. Children aren't a dealbreaker to me. The path has been set."

Was that what marriage was to her? What a depressing thought. But, if Adam was really honest, he'd have to admit that many of the preoccupations keeping her tied to Thăng were the same ones that had kept him tied to Lana. Common sense winning out over unpredictable passions. A family trait, apparently.

"We're not frozen into our paths, Ruby," he says. "You can change your life in whatever way you want."

As if waking from a dream, she shakes her head, hard. She forces out a laugh. "And what? Abandon this Love Yêu empire? Look around you, BB. We're living the life so many people dream of. What a fool I would be to give this up for a chance to wipe a baby's bottom."

"If you say so. I don't think they're mutually exclusive, for what it's worth."

She turns her gaze to him. "The truth is, BB, we might not be frozen, but we've both been building our futures for as long as we've been alive. Even when we were toddlers. Everything leads to the life we're meant to have."

"According to who, though?"

She continues as if he hadn't spoken. "I know Lana was a setback, but that doesn't mean you're destined to be alone. Far from it."

"I don't want to talk about—" Lana is a humiliating topic and, as far as Adam is concerned, an irrelevant one.

"I'll tell you something: I may have had ulterior motives in inviting you on the tour. I looked at the list of candidates, and when I saw Talia's dossier, I just *knew*. In fact, one might say I handpicked her for *you*. It is, after all, my job. And trust me—I had the matchmaking consultants weigh in, and we all agree: she is an impeccable match."

"Talia," he says, a little woodenly. He shouldn't be surprised by Ruby's machinations.

"She's gorgeous and accomplished, not to mention kind and selfless. Just look at all the causes she's uplifted. All the people who admire her— and not for what she brings to them, but for who she really is. Half the men on this tour are completely in love with her."

"Your point?"

"Really, she's the ideal partner for anyone, but especially you, who work so hard and need a wife that can support your career. Someone polished. And haven't you been drawn to her?"

Perhaps, a few years ago, he would have pursued Talia with the same single-mindedness that he devoted to his relationship with Lana. She's someone who might slide perfectly into his life. A missing puzzle piece.

She's educated and sophisticated, warm and discreet. There's no contradiction with her, no surprise. His days would be easier with someone like Talia.

He doesn't *not* like her, of course. But does she stir anything more in him than a gentle sort of admiration? Furthermore, does he need to be led into a relationship by his older sister? It's not as if he can't manage his own affairs, family interference to the contrary.

And just like that, the earlier intimacy with Ruby disappears. What's left is the usual stance of defensiveness and irritation.

He shoots back, "So you're saying that you want me to start dating Talia?"

"That *is* the point of this whole thing, BB," she says calmly. "I'm just saying that you need to think with more than just your lust—"

"*Ruby.*"

"Look, I know Evie's appealing. We've *all* noticed how often you look at her. How often you two run off together."

"It was just the once, and it wasn't on purpose."

"But say you want to take a chance on this relationship that would never work. Then what? You move to America? She moves here? She hardly speaks the language. She doesn't know anyone, has no career prospects or friends. It doesn't make sense."

"Why did you allow Americans on the tour, then?"

"A numbers game." She shrugs. "We needed their fees and the character they each provided. And I could see some of them moving to Việt Nam or perhaps engaging themselves with partners who might consider moving to America. Not Evie, though. The moment I saw her, I knew that she wasn't meant to live in Việt Nam. She's too . . . set in her ways."

"She's not some cranky octogenarian, Ruby."

"Frankly, I thought she and Riley would hit it off. I matched *them* together."

He grunts. "This would be easier if you'd just give everyone a heads-up about your master plans from the start."

"They aren't doing too badly, you see."

She gestures at Riley standing across from Evie, both waist-deep in the water. Riley's smiling as he helps Evie take her snorkeling gear off. She's tilting her head to beam at him, water dripping from her hair back into the sea. To any bystander, they look like a happy couple on their honeymoon. Adam dismisses a hot rush of jealousy.

"Just say what it is you want to say, Ruby."

"I'm saying that you need to think ahead. We're going to Mẹ and Ba's estate in Hội An soon. They've agreed to host our whole tour group. Just think about the woman you want on your arm when you see them again. The haphazard American? Or calm, accomplished, *perfect* Talia?"

"Evie isn't haphazard, Ruby," Adam says angrily. "Just because you don't understand her behavior doesn't mean there's anything wrong with it. I happen to admire her freedom. It's refreshing."

"Sure, admire it all you want. But think about my question."

"I don't make my romantic decisions based on our parents' desires."

Ruby shrugs. "Don't you? I did. Ultimately, each relationship we form is not just an extension of ourselves, but an offering that we bring to our families. A way to expand the legacy that our parents and grandparents have worked so hard to build. I married someone who fits into that legacy. Will you?"

At that, she takes his empty plate from him and saunters toward the snorkelers, ready to play the consummate tour host, as if their conversation hadn't happened at all.

He can't help replaying Ruby's words, though he tries not to. They have both been raised in extreme privilege for so long, but there is no question that there is also a cost on the other side of things. Upholding the Quyền family traditions of success and discretion. To exist in the lofty world they inhabit, there are unspoken rules that they each must face—or risk ostracism from it all.

Adam has always known after Lana that he would not risk himself again. Why is he considering it for a woman he's just met?

Yes, he said that he admired Evie's freedom. But what cost comes with that freedom? Would she abandon him, the way Lana did, once something more impressive came along? Or perhaps her sheer unpredictability would become grating over time. More likely, she'd become frustrated by his lifestyle of routine and order. How could someone like her possibly settle for someone like him?

When he looks up from the sand, where he's been focusing his attention, he sees Evie walking toward him. The sun is against her back, so she's just a shapely silhouette. Her steps are light. Even the way she walks radiates abandon.

He can't deny being attracted to her. But is attraction enough, within this world he's so deeply mired in?

Before she reaches him, Adam stands and walks away, cutting off whatever she wants to say.

He doesn't see it, but over his shoulder, he feels Evie's confusion. The way her steps lag, then stop in the sand behind him. It takes everything in him not to turn around, to meet her wide smile with one of his own. But he doesn't. He keeps walking.

EVIE

Nha Trang, Việt Nam

Evie hasn't been clubbing in over six years. The last time, she was dragged to a neon eighties-style discotheque by Lillian, who plied her with an endless train of syrupy shots bearing nondescriptive names like Virgin Daydream and GlitterPuss. Evie had taken about four before making an ass of herself on the dance floor by dancing with someone else's boyfriend. The girlfriend was irate at first, but after seeing Evie's flailing dance moves and her own boyfriend's slightly petrified confusion, she'd pityingly led Evie to the ladies' room. There, Evie proceeded to start a fight with her own reflection, much to Lillian's chagrin.

This was before she achieved any level of public reputation, and before every embarrassment was filmed for public amusement on TikTok. But still, when Evie woke in the apartment she shared with four roommates the next day, her arm wet from her own drool, with actual *bangs* she didn't remember cutting, she vowed that her partying days were over for good. And she meant it.

All or Nothing Evie, that's what Lillian called her. No wonder Evie is a recluse in Midland; she no longer trusts herself to have a good time without blowing it in some colossal way. As mind-numbingly dull as the academic events are, at least there are nearly *zero* chances of bangs, literal and otherwise. Atlas aside.

But now the consequence of her self-imposed monastic life is that Evie has no idea how to outfit herself for a night on the town. She holds up the pink dress she hastily bought in Hồ Chí Minh City, then throws it back on her bed. Everyone else will be dressed impeccably: sexy, but suitable. No spandex allowed. For once, she wants to fit in and let loose—appropriately.

Nha Trang is known for a raucous nightlife that draws thousands of tourists and locals, with rooftop bars that stream darts of multicolored lights into the sky, and underground clubs featuring the most coveted DJs, mostly white dudes with mesh tank tops and ironic 'staches. She'd seen several wandering the beach with huge Focal headphones, bopping their heads to inaudible thumping, sometimes brushing shoulders in greeting, as if they were part of a secret, subterranean hive.

She texts Lillian: SOS. Why did you not pack clubbing clothes for me?

Lillian's reply is immediate: Because we're not nineteen. And because I didn't think you would risk it after The Night That Won't Be Mentioned. You can't even glance at bangs without shuddering.

I have nothing to wear.

Can't you go buy something?

No time.

Aren't there like a ton of rich women on this tour? Go ask one of them for help. Let nothing stand between you and that throbbing D.

WTF, Lillian. WHOSE throbbing D?

That's up to you to uncover, grasshopper. (I mean uncover literally because of the D?)

Great. Now her cousin has become the sensei of sexual innuendo. Pregnancy has made Lillian even raunchier than usual.

Evie types: This phone is disconnected. Its owner unreachable, especially to family members who have clearly been watching too much Skinemax.

It hasn't been *that* long since she had sex, has it? Well, maybe longer than she'd like. At this point, she'd take a tiny orgasm. Even a meaningful brush on the side boob. A prolonged stare at her ankles? Is that too much to ask?

In the past few days, one-on-one dates have begun sprouting on the Love Yêu tour, like hopeful shoots of young bamboo. Tour guests are starting to find their matches or, at least, try their hands at dating in earnest. A few have even scheduled virtual appointments with the on-call matchmakers. Whether it is the heady scent of suntan oil or the sight of *so much* flesh splayed enticingly on the white sand, love wafts insistently through Nha Trang.

One tour guest, a woman from Huế, went on a romantic boat ride with a man from Hồ Chí Minh City and came back with her arms full of roses, like Lady Bountiful. An older Chinese merchant took a wealthy socialite out to dine at a famous starred sushi restaurant where a prime minister once took his favorite mistress. Even Pin managed to ask Talia for a sunset walk, complete with two tiny bottles of champagne and crystal glasses perched on a table in the sand.

Evie's tried to be a good sport, but with all the romance around her, she's finding it difficult not to feel just a little left out. Maybe that's why she can't stop stealing glances at Adam Quyền. It's not lust—it's desperation. FOMO. At least that's what she tells herself. But it doesn't really matter, because Adam hasn't given her a second glance since the boat.

One moment, he was slathering sunscreen on her back with buttery temptation; the next, he acted like she was invisible. He's been practically glued to Talia's side, except for that hour or so when Pin gallantly pulled Talia onto the sunset walk. It's not hard to see Talia's appeal, to be sure. She is living, breathing perfection. Who *wouldn't* want to bask in the glow of that seraphic presence? Evie is honestly half in love with Talia herself.

Evie glances at her watch. "Shitballs."

Only fifteen minutes to get ready, and she's wasted half of it contemplating everyone else's relationship. Evie pokes her head out of the hut and glances over at the tiny porch next to hers, where Fen sits with her legs crossed, smoking a cigarette as she frowns out onto the water. She's wearing a pair of leather pants and a one-shouldered silver top cropped to show a daring-yet-demure inch of creamy skin. Tiny diamonds dangle from her ears. God, that woman knows how to dress.

Evie hesitates, then, driven by pure desperation, calls out, "Uh, Fen? Any chance you have a spare outfit you can lend me for tonight?"

Fen shoots her an amused glance from under her thick red bangs. "You don't have anything for a snail shack?"

Before going to Karaoke Luxury, a venue with sumptuous private rooms and VIP service, some of the group will be enjoying one of Việt Nam's greatest pastimes: *ăn ốc*, translated to "eating snails." In many of the major cities are streetside stands with short plastic awnings advertising buckets of snails and shellfish—clams, blood cockles, mussels—all prepared exactly the way each diner prefers. Fueled by an endless amount of Tiger and Heineken, the ốc celebrations can often last well into the night.

For those who are not shellfish-inclined, Ruby has planned an elegant, multicourse French dinner at a four-star hotel. The choice was a no-brainer for Evie.

"It's the *after* I'm concerned about," Evie says, gesturing down at her robe. "I didn't pack very well, I'm afraid, for a karaoke club. I thought maybe you'd be the person to ask."

"For a makeover?"

"A light touch?" Evie says timidly.

Fen grins, then stubs her cigarette. "Come into my house of horrors."

Evie thought *her* hut was a mess, but Fen's is absolutely catastrophic. Every surface is covered in lingerie, used coffee mugs and champagne flutes, and pots of expensive Korean makeup. There's a pair of strappy sandals dangling from the doorknob.

"Okay, babe," Fen says, stepping back to look at Evie critically. "What's your vibe?"

"Dark academia? A little Goth? Like Madame Báthory meets Noam Chomsky?"

"I don't know who those people are."

"Fair enough," Evie says. "How about you just do whatever you want and I give you my undying gratitude if you somehow make me *not* late for once? It won't matter what I'm wearing to Ruby if I hold up the bus again."

Fen pushes Evie's chagrin aside. "It takes as long as it takes. Women like Ruby *need* something to be pissy about; it helps keep their minds off their dismal failure of a relationship."

"You know something we don't?" Evie asks, her interest sparked. Ruby never talks about her marriage, which is odd, especially for someone whose whole empire rests on the gushing promises of happily ever after.

Fen sits Evie down and whisks brushes from her overflowing makeup bag. Soon she's inches from Evie's face, skating powder across her cheekbones with expert confidence. Evie has a niggling suspicion that there's way too much highlighter involved—and are those *false eyelashes* she's applying?—but she listens without comment as Fen describes the phone conversation she overheard between Ruby and her husband.

"She told him that if he didn't get 'his sorry ass' to the Hội An family estate, he could find somewhere else to live."

"Hội An?"

"Yeah, didn't you know? Apparently Ruby and Adam's parents have some kind of villa compound and will be hosting us there. They're very fancy and very traditional, so I'm sure it'll be up to the usual tour standards. If they're anything like my father, I'm sure they insist on black tie attire just to use the toilet."

"Oh, great," Evie mutters. "More tight-asses who'll hate me. Must be hereditary."

Fen shoots her a look. "Right. Like you and Quyền the Younger haven't been tearing each other's clothes off with your eyes. Maybe with more than your eyes."

"Definitely not," Evie says glumly. "His eyes only seem to be focused on Talia these days. Not that I care."

"Hm. I don't see it." Fen ushers her into the bathroom with a dress hanging from a hanger. "Put that on. No questions."

"I don't really wear red—" Evie says before Fen slams the door on her.

With a sigh, Evie pulls on the dress. It's made from a smooth satin that hugs her hips, then flares out just slightly near the knee. The straps are thin, sparkling rhinestones, so iridescent that they almost look invisible in certain lights. It's a knockout of a dress. But is it really *her*? This isn't something she would normally pick out. It's bright, it's flashy, it demands to be seen. And Evie Lang is no wallflower, but she's no starlet either, not like Fen.

In the mirror, her eyes look huge with the false lashes, while her cheeks are a perfect combination of dewy and luminous from the highlighter. There are about five pounds of clear lip gloss on her mouth, making her lips gleam with the luster of a baby's freshly oiled butt.

"I look like a porn star," Evie calls.

"Fantastic. Get your ass out here."

When she walks out of the bathroom, Fen whistles and helps her spin with one hand. "You're going to go home with *somebody* tonight. Maybe two someones, if you're lucky."

Evie flushes at the thought, though it's not exactly an unpleasant one. She darts into her hut for her signature leather jacket, draping it over her shoulders. There. Now she feels more like herself.

As they walk toward the tour bus, she says, "Thanks, Fen. You saved me."

Fen waves her hand. "Don't mention it. We'll go shopping tomorrow for a real Vietnamese wardrobe. We have some of the greatest designers in the world. You might *think* you're into this whole combat-boot-tweedy thing, but I know you have a secret siren in there."

"I *like* my combat boots. Helps me crush the hearts of misogynists everywhere."

"Uh-huh. I'm not saying that you shouldn't be yourself. Keep the boots if you must. I'm just saying that maybe 'yourself' is someone you haven't gotten to know yet. Fashion is about so much more than *covering* yourself.

Or in your case, hiding. Look at how confident the women around us are. You think they care about making themselves less for anyone?"

"They are *so* chic."

"They are," Fen says with a smile. "I want to take half of them home myself."

Evie blinks. "Oh, I didn't realize."

"That I'm pansexual? I guess it didn't make it into that dossier. Doesn't exactly fly in this hetero circle-jerk the Quyèns are selling. Truth is, I just love the person, not the gender. It's an easier way to live, especially since most men are absolute pricks. I avoid them when I can, romantically."

"Show me your ways."

"Well, it only works if you're attracted to women."

"No dice," Evie says morosely, thinking of Adam's strong arms cutting through the ocean. The way the sea droplets clung to the cords in his neck. How his muscles jumped as he hoisted himself back onto the boat. Power and grace and devastatingly good looks—plus, she thinks with a scowl, a personality as consistent as an oven with a broken temperature gauge.

Fen interrupts her thoughts. "But the thing is, I'm already sort of in love, so I'm not on the market for anyone, no matter how amazing their abs are."

Evie cocks her head. "So why are you . . ."

"On this sham of a tour?" Fen finishes. "Babe, it's a long story and we're almost in the clutches of Chairman Quyèn, so I'll be quick—I kinda fell for my father's secretary, Mei. She's this sexy librarian type; a little like you, without the rampant anxiety."

"That is my chief personality trait, thank you very much."

"I can tell. Mei would never take my shit, even when I was trying to piss her off every time I went to see my father. Every time I pushed her, she pushed back, but harder. She's *smart*, in a totally not-normal, alien way. She actually scares me sometimes, which is hard to do."

"Is that . . . what you want in a partner?" Evie asks doubtfully.

"Listen: if your relationship doesn't at least teeter on the knife-edge of fear, are you really in love?"

Evie is beginning to question the wisdom of taking advice from Fen.

Fen continues, "The first time I tried to ask her on a date, she gave me the most intimidating dressing-down of my life. Said I was a spoiled brat. Wondered if I could find it in me to tear myself away from the mirror long enough to make conversation with another person. And the weird part is—I liked it. I really liked it. You know how sometimes when someone you admire tells you the hard truths about yourself, you just kinda—"

"Feel seen?"

"Exactly. No one had ever dared to talk to me like that. My agent, my friends—all a bunch of yes-men. I could have launched an unprovoked attack on an island of baby koalas, and they would have just . . . let me. Mei was right. I was spoiled."

"Until she came along."

"Until she came along. Wasn't easy, but I won her over eventually. Proved that I was more than a gorgeous face with really good legs and a smile that could light up any room and—"

"I get it," Evie groans.

"Long story short, one thing led to another and another, and then one day my father found us in flagrante on his desk."

"On. His. Desk," Evie enunciates. She's biting back a grin, trying to decide whether to be shocked or amused. Both.

"He was *supposed* to be in Shanghai at the time," Fen says indignantly, as if her father were the one with the audacity to unlock the door to his own office in the middle of a workday. "Anyway, he was furious about it, not because I'm pansexual or anything, but because he thought I'd ruin things with Mei, who's the most competent secretary he's ever had. I think she puts cocaine in his morning tea, personally. He was worried she'd end up quitting and he'd have to hire his dimwit cousin, who's been angling for the job for years. Plus, he had to get a new desk."

"Naturally."

"So then he said that I had to go on this tour and 'take a breather' from Mei, or he'd cut off my inheritance. I'm not usually inclined to obey, but, well—the acting gigs have dried up, and this look is expensive to maintain.

Besides, Mei and I will just get together after I come back and go on a luxury tour of our own, paid for by my father."

"A fuck-Yêu tour?"

Fen throws her head back and laughs. "I *like* you."

Though they are the last to arrive, Fen and Evie make it onto the bus with at least thirty seconds to spare. Seeing Evie, Riley shoots up with a huge grin, running his eyes down her dress until he reaches the silvery sandals on her feet. She knows she doesn't look completely like herself, and rather than that making her uncomfortable, she's feeling confident and capable, as if she's wearing a kind of armor. Who doesn't like to be lightly and curiously ogled? She slides the jacket down one shoulder and tilts her head up, allowing just a quick bat of her lashes.

"You've got something in your eye," says a voice near her elbow.

Adam, with a lifted brow, an impenetrable expression.

She leans close to his ear and whispers, "And *you've* got something up your ass."

Evie can tell he's fighting a grin. She plunks herself down on an empty seat with a smile of her own. The beach whizzes by as they drive into town, a blue sea line leading their way. The sun is slinking into the horizon, casting a flush of neon pink over the city. Leaning palms silhouette in the light, a postcard come to life.

Once again, Evie thinks of Auntie Hảo, wishing she were here. Wishing she could meet Fen and Riley and even Ruby. Adam. What would she have to say about this motley crew?

There's a home for all the weirdos.

Again, that image of the San Francisco row house rises, unbidden. A bonfire, surrounded by friends holding cups of spiked cider, sharing their stories. Their larger-than-life personalities. A kind of safe house for the creative, the idiosyncratic. Folk musicians strumming guitars into the night, dancers with their impromptu performances on tabletops. A poet taking blurry, ill-lit photographs. Marking the memories of a time when they were all young and wildly inspired.

She'd never been there—at that bonfire, among those raised voices—

but she feels as if she had. An eerie sense of déjà vu overtakes her. Not a memory, then, but a premonition? A wish?

But the row house is meant to be sold, inflating her pathetic bank account with more zeros than she's ever seen in her life.

Right?

She catches Adam's eyes lingering on her hemline from across the aisle, then sliding quickly away. She hears Auntie Hảo's voice in her ear, like a mischievous whisper. *A little repressed, but if anyone could loosen him up, it's you, my Evie-pie.*

Like that, Evie is seized with a longing for her aunt that is so pure, so deeply rooted in grief, that she gazes into her lap to avoid meeting anyone's eye. A small tear wets the crimson fabric of her dress.

Then a tissue, appearing at her elbow. Talia doesn't say anything, but smiles at her kindly, without expectation. Not for the first time tonight, Evie finds herself grateful for the unexpected kinship around her. Perhaps she *has* been shut off to people for a while. Perhaps it's time to change that. It must mean something that her most beloved fantasies circle around community, something she's never really had, except in brief, stolen snatches. To belong, you have to be present. Vulnerable. She can learn to do that—or fall on her face trying.

ADAM

Nha Trang, Việt Nam

The tour group leaves piles of clam and snail shells on the ground like peanut shells in a roadhouse. There's a smell of smoke and brine. The heat from the fires keeps away the mosquitoes dancing in frantic formations just outside the light. Families sit at the long wooden tables, kids poking sticks at the discarded shells, holding them above their heads like hinged maracas. An older gentleman burps loudly, a symphonic end to their dinner.

"Really!" his wife yells, slapping him. "We're not at home, old man!"

He guffaws. "Damn right we're not! Because the food here is actually good."

His wife throws a cockle at his head, which he dodges with ease. He tries to pull her close for a kiss, but she brandishes a pair of chopsticks, conjured from the ether of the night, and pinches his lips with them, eliciting a yelp of pain.

"This is what you have to look forward to if you get married," Adam murmurs to the group.

"Maybe they should see one of the Love Yêu couples therapists," Riley offers.

"Side business: Hate Yêu Counseling," Evie quips.

The group groans in unison and Evie chuckles at her own joke, taking one last sip of her salted lemonade. She says, "I'll be here all night, folks. Riding this pun."

"As long as that's not all you're riding," Fen adds.

What does *that* mean? Adam glares at Fen, who shoots him an innocent, if amused, look from under her lashes.

A little girl, about seven or eight, sidles up to Evie and reaches up to touch the rhinestone straps of her dress, each strap glinting in the dim streetlights. So thin it would take *nothing* to tear them off. Just a light pull of the teeth. Adam groans internally, then shunts those thoughts from his mind. He takes a deep swallow of his Tiger Beer, trying to ignore the interaction in front of him, which has grown uncomfortably adorable.

"Hey, sweetie," Evie says to the girl in Vietnamese, her voice lowering a few octaves, soft and confidential.

"Xin chào, Cô," the girl whispers.

"How many snails did you eat tonight? Ten? Twenty?"

The girl grins. She's missing a tooth in the front and one on the bottom. "I *hate* snails. I only eat cake."

Evie nods solemnly. "Of course. Like a princess."

"*You're* a princess," says the girl worshipfully.

"But I'm not the one with the sparkling shoes," Evie says, pointing to the girl's jelly sandals flecked with tiny gold stars.

"Watch me twirl in them!"

Evie reaches out a hand and spins the girl around. She laughs giddily, bumping into Riley, who tries to hide his annoyance.

"Cute kid," Riley grits.

"Come back here, Lan," the girl's mother calls.

She trips away, waving at Evie, whose grin is so brilliant that it washes her whole face in light. Đức and Cherie settle the tab, while the rest of them clean their hands and faces with scented wet wipes.

Unwillingly, Adam pivots to Evie, standing just a few feet from him, that dress glowing red like an alarm. It softened him to see her interacting with the little girl. It's as if her restlessness momentarily stilled into peace, or something like it. She's never been tender around him, and somehow that little glimpse of her hidden heart feels as rewarding as finding a pearl inside an oyster.

They wait for the private cars that will take them to Karaoke Luxury—no hulking tour bus for their entrance tonight. The other dinner group, the one Talia was part of, with the fancy cocktails and charcuterie plates, has probably already arrived at the karaoke club. Adam's group has a minor setback when Connor wanders off on a mysterious shopping expedition and keeps them waiting for at least twenty minutes on the street.

There's a shuffle nearby, and Adam turns to see what's going on. Lan, the little girl from dinner, careens toward them, arms outstretched for one last hug from Evie. At the last second, she trips on a purse on the ground and goes flying into the street, her arms lifted like wings. At that exact moment, a moped tears down the alley from the opposite direction.

Adam can see it happening so quickly, yet for him, time is frozen. He imagines the worst-case scenario.

"Stop!" he shouts. "*Stop!*"

Without thinking, he lurches forward. He has a brief moment of déjà vu, thinking of how he stopped traffic for Evie and her stupid rooster. The panic, the fear. The adrenaline.

From the corner of his eye, he sees Evie moving ahead. Stretching her arms as far as they will go, she pulls Lan from the street, lightning-quick, so they land in a crumpled heap together. Adam steps between Evie and the moped, diverting it in another direction. A loud screech shatters the air, and they choke in the sudden dust kick-up from the driver's swerve. The driver shoots an obscene gesture their way but disappears without incident.

"Fucking crazy drivers," he says. Turns to Evie and asks, strangled, "Are you okay?"

"I think we're fine," she says shakily.

Evie picks herself and Lan up. Adam walks them back to safety, his hand resting on the small of Evie's back. Despite the adrenaline pumping between his ears, and probably hers too, they act as a coordinated team, as if they've saved hundreds of children on the streets of Nha Trang together. He wants to pick *her* up, the way she did the child, scooping her onto his lap protectively, shielding her from anyone who could hurt her.

He's seized with an unwelcome, all-too-vivid image of her lying in the street. Broken. He closes his eyes and swallows hard. *Nope.* Some things are off-limits. Like the thought of her ever getting hurt on his watch.

"Wow," Riley breathes. "That could have been bad."

Adam turns to Evie, who's still cradling Lan, whispering something in her ear. The girl's face is pale, shocked, as she belatedly grasps how close she came to disaster. She nods at whatever Evie's saying and clings to her neck. Lan's parents rush up, taking her from Evie's arms. Apologizing for taking their eyes off their child. They shoot a grateful look at Adam too, then jog away, murmuring comfort into Lan's ear.

As soon as the child is gone, he's next to Evie in a flash, running his hands up and down her arms. He bends to look into her wide eyes.

"Did you get hurt when you fell?"

"Not much."

Adam can see Evie beginning to shake. He pulls her to him, whispering, "It's okay. You're okay, sweetheart. You were so brave."

Sweetheart? Where did that come from?

He can't deny that the word, tender and intimate and full of unsaid feelings, slides easily off his tongue. He's never used endearments toward other women. But she pulls it out of him as easily as a snake out of a charmer's basket.

She nods against his chest. There's a kind of blooming there, an opening where her head is touching his heart. He's stroking her hair, not caring that everyone can see his tenderness toward her. In fact, he's feeling downright feral about her. Let anyone get in between them now.

What other woman would have thrown herself so readily into danger for a stranger? Impetuous, determined, *breathtaking* Evie.

Only after she steps away from him does he release her, though his arms feel empty without her weight, the feel of her featherlight touch. He wants to pick her up and carry her straight to his hut, where he'll lay her down on the bed and inspect every inch of her. Running his lips over any purpling bruise, any jagged scratch, until she forgets everything except the feeling of his tongue soothing all the tender, waiting parts of her.

"Nicely done," Fen says, interrupting his thoughts. "You both deserve a stiff drink."

The private cars pull up, sleek and dark. Adam helps Evie into one of them, then props her shins up on his knees to examine them. He loves the weight of those long legs on him. How he has them trapped under his arms. She protests, but he continues looking. Just a few scrapes on her ankles, but no blood. Fen squeezes Evie's hand from the other side of the car.

"Okay, Dr. Dreamy," Fen says, angling her eyebrows at him. "Now that you've made sure your girl's as flawless as ever, can we go get shit-faced and forget about homicidal Việt motorists?"

Your girl. Adam grunts, releasing Evie's ankle, trying not to let anyone see how much the words grab him. How nice they sound. He turns to the window with a fierce frown.

She's *not* a forever partner, he reminds himself. Ruby isn't always right, but she's right about that. Sure, Evie Lang is gorgeous and compelling. Sure, she's always interesting, always surprising. *Sure*, he wants to tear her clothes off every time she steps into a room and worship every single inch of her stupidly soft skin. But she's going to leave the damn country in less than two weeks. There's no future in that.

Plus, it's not like she's gone out of her way to make *her* interest clear. So it's a moot point. Isn't it? She shoots a tentative smile his way, which dissipates all the thoughts from his head except the ardent wish that every single person in the car would disappear, leaving them completely, dangerously alone.

As soon as they arrive in the lobby of Karaoke Luxury, they locate the rest of the tour group milling inside. Echoes of music waft from the rooms, strains of familiar Vietnamese and American songs, along with a chorus of off-key singing. Some of the older folks had decided to go back to the hotel, so it's mostly guests in their thirties and forties left, calling out their favorite karaoke tunes. Celine Dion is a favorite with this crowd. The air carries a slightly floral scent, taut with promise.

Adam spots Talia near the entrance in a navy dress cut conservatively to her knee. She gives him a smile as he makes his way over.

"How were the clams?" she asks.

"Plentiful. Slimy. Delicious," he says.

"That's a lot of adjectives!"

"How was the French food?"

"Cheesy. Rich. Incredible," she answers. "France has always been a bucket list item of mine, and now it's soared up the list."

"I hope you'll get there eventually."

"What's on your to-visit list?" she asks.

"Portugal. Chile. The Arctic Circle."

"Oh! Slightly more exotic than my list." She laughs in self-deprecation. "I think you'll get to those places too, Adam. You seem like a resourceful human."

Talia makes him feel like he's sitting near a warm fire. Comfortable. She's kind and smart, not to mention lovely. So why hasn't he asked her on a date? Tonight, he tells himself. It's the only way to get to know her better. After all, Pin went on a date with her, and now he's glowing every time he glances her way. *This romance thing can't be all that hard*, Adam thinks. He wonders, though, why he's not feeling even a hint of jealousy at the thought of Talia going on a date with someone else. If anything, he's glad for them. An unlikely, yet strangely rootable pairing.

Ruby leads them to the private room she's booked. It's a large and flashy space with three long leather sofas lining the walls. Gold carvings run up to a recessed ceiling painted like a night sky, complete with rosy-cheeked cherubs with bare butt cheeks. There's a big television on one wall, resting on a shiny, tufted leather backing. Filigreed sconces cast a warm light.

It's gaudy and opulent and the very *definition* of nouveau riche. Hugh Hefner meets someone's fevered interpretation of a rococo painting. Adam's parents would have had a conniption in this room. But he finds himself admiring the decor anyway, not for its innate style, but for its sheer give-no-fucks nature. Someone picked these furnishings because they *liked* everything, not because some interior design aficionado was telling them what to buy.

Everyone makes their way to a sofa of their choice, kicking off their shoes, sprawling cozily on top of each other. A server makes his way around, taking their drink orders, while Ruby orders bar snacks for the group.

"Hey," Connor whispers at Adam's elbow. "Want some of this?"

He inclines a little vial toward Adam, gesturing for him to pour it into his newly acquired cocktail.

"What *is* that, man? Is it illegal?"

The drug laws are stringent in Việt Nam, so it's hard to get anything into the country. It's also not something that you get a light slap on the wrist for. There is literally a death penalty for drug trafficking. Adam wonders how Connor could have possibly found himself a dealer so quickly, when savvy local residents can hardly penetrate the sophisticated—and highly secretive—underground network of illegal substances.

Connor snorts, pushing his glasses up. "No way. I don't fuck with that. This is bison semen mixed with caffeine."

"Come again?"

Connor nods, a little smugly. "Exactly. It's supposed to improve virility. Got it from this man at a stall in the market. Actually, it might not have been a stall. He was just kinda standing there and pulled this from his pocket. Said it'll *change your life*. It better. It cost me a fortune."

Adam studies the vial dubiously. "I'm pretty sure that's just rice water."

"Mixed with cornstarch," Fen adds, overhearing them.

Connor shrugs and dumps the whole thing into his drink. "Suit yourself. I'll be flying high while the rest of you are wondering how you wasted your youth."

He sips, then coughs. "Uh. It's kinda *warm* still? Tastes—"

"Like a great Friday night," Fen completes with a wink.

Evie, overhearing this, has her hand clamped over her mouth, trying not to laugh. Adam crooks his head, as if to ask, *Is this real life?* She shrugs and raises a glass of sticky rice wine in a toast. The reddish-brown liquid sloshes slightly as she takes the shot, clenching her eyes shut. Everyone cheers her on.

"A hero in more ways than one!" Fen toasts.

She hands them all shots. What the hell. He swigs the rice wine back. It's the first of many rounds for all of them.

The night is a blur of terrible singing, strobe lights, and at one point, an impromptu strip show from Đức that Ruby quickly interrupts with gritted teeth.

Adam sits next to Talia, and she's a great sport, clapping at even the worst singers. She takes a shot or two, but remains in perfect control, again revealing herself to be one of the most appropriate adults on this whole tour. She sings a shaky yet earnest rendition of "Endless Love" that does nothing to stir him into anything more than warm admiration.

Then it's Evie's turn to take to the stage, after a small push from Fen and Riley. Her cheeks are flushed, and there's a languor to her eyes, a mischievous tilt of her lip as she picks out her song.

Onstage, she juts out her hip and says, "This one's for the Love Yêu romantics out there."

His heart gives an annoying, irrational jump. She's pure starlight, eclipsing every other person in the room, so that all he can see is her, glowing in that ridiculously sexy red dress, her shoulders shimmying with the frenzy of a cabaret dancer.

Free. That's the word for her.

Seconds later, the jaunty strains of "Summer Nights" from *Grease* come on over the sound system. The crowd starts to whistle.

"Get it, babe!" Fen shouts.

Most everyone's seen the film phenomenon, or at least they recognize the happy-go-lucky song with not-so-subtle innuendos. Evie beams in the spotlight. She flips her hair as she begins to walk the stage and belt at the top of her lungs.

"Summer lovin', happened so fa-a-a-ast. Met a girl . . . Shit, guys, this is a duet! Help!"

Connor hops onstage with her, driven by the bison semen, or the lure of Evie's smile. "Crazy for me-e-e . . ."

Soon, everyone who knows any bit of the song, and even those who don't, call out the lyrics flashing across the television screen.

Meanwhile, Evie is laughing and gulping out lyrics while twirling with Connor around the stage. The lights bounce off her hair, catching the glint in her eye. She's a dervish of fun. Adam has seen a few versions of Evie tonight, but this one—this one is intoxicating.

He can't hide the smile spreading across his face. He whistles long and loud between his fingers.

"She's a pretty good singer, huh?" Talia says, studying him closely.

"She's okay, I guess. A little flat."

Truth is, Evie is no secret pop star, not like Fen, who'd commanded the stage earlier with her belting rendition of a Mariah Carey song that left them all breathless. But there is something about Evie that no one can tear their eyes from.

"She's captivating." Talia corrects him with a gentle smile. "I never took you for a liar."

Adam is about to answer when Connor begins heaving on the stage, in the middle of a chorus. Evie jumps back just in time to avoid a pile of pale-colored vomit on her sandals. Suddenly everyone rushes up onstage, patting Connor on the back, grabbing him bottles of water, a fistful of napkins. The music is forgotten.

"Oh, crap," Ruby says, staring down at the vomit and a hunched-over Connor. "Are you okay?"

He lifts his head, a little wan, but mostly just sheepish.

He turns to Ruby with a hiccup. "I have some advice for you."

"Okay," she says, wrinkling her nose in a mixture of disgust and consternation as he dry-heaves again.

"Never—and I mean *never*—buy any back-alley substances from strange men," he manages to get out, wiping his face.

"You did *what*?" Ruby asks, nearly combusting.

Đức and Cherie grab a staff member to clean up the mess, while Ruby ushers Connor out of the room, against his ringing protests.

"Stay if you want," she calls to the group over her shoulder. "I'm taking him back to the huts."

"Wait up," Talia says, standing. "I'm going to call it a night too."

A few of the tour guests filter out with them, including Pin, Talia's constant shadow. Adam begins to stand but pauses. He doesn't really want to go.

The music starts up again. One of the quieter tour guests, a venture capitalist from Boston with an affinity for pinstripes and lukewarm tea, grabs the mic and throws down such an on-beat version of Outkast's "Hey Ya!" that the group goes wild, pounding fists and flinging coasters on the freshly cleaned stage with loud hoots. At some point, Fen tosses her strapless bra at the venture capitalist, who catches it with one hand and lassos it over his head.

It's a night for the books.

Afterward, when the singing has died down and they're lingering over their last drinks, Adam sneaks a glance at Evie sitting across the way, hair slicked to her neck in sweat-damp waves. She's moved on to glasses of iced water, but there's still that buzzy, tense air around her. Her eyes are closed as she sways gently to the last of the ambient music, her lips moving just a little. When she opens her eyes and sees him, she gives him such a beaming, open, *joyous* smile that his breath catches. It's sunshine and sweetness, reminding him of the thrill of riding his motorcycle fast down a country road. Mystery and abandon and sex, all in one smile. He can't tear his gaze away.

This woman.

"Hey! Before we call it a night. One last parlor game!" Fen calls.

"What do you have in mind?" Riley asks, yawning.

Fen looks around and catches sight of an empty champagne bottle. She dangles it in front of them and says, with a challenging lift of her chin, "Spin. The. Bottle."

EVIE

Nha Trang, Việt Nam

First, Riley kisses Đức on the top of the head. Cherie plants a chaste kiss on Adam's cheek. The venture capitalist blushes scarlet as Fen sticks her tongue down his throat, then tells him loudly that he can keep her bra. *For the memories.* The kisses range from sultry to playful, but high on drinks and the excitement of the night, everyone is game. There's a kind of innocence to it all, like they really are thirteen and at a basement party again.

When it's Evie's turn to spin, the last of the group, she grabs the champagne bottle and gives it a forceful, flourishing twist of the wrist. She's the only one who hasn't been kissed.

Riley makes a crooking motion toward the spinning bottle. "Let's end on a high note."

It continues to whoosh with a mind of its own. The group, excluding a broody-looking Adam, hoots gamely. But then the bottle stops, as if jerked to a pause, right in front of Adam himself. Evie meets his gaze. The tightening of his jaw. A sharp intake of breath.

Is her heart racing faster? Or is it just the adrenaline of the night, settling now into a place that feels decidedly *un*-innocent?

Everyone claps, oblivious to their discomfort. She feels as if she's in an arena, fighting for her life. But it's not her life—it's just a kiss. Right?

"Make it good, babe," Fen tells her.

Could she refuse? Why would she? It doesn't even have to be on the lips. *Not* kissing him would make it a bigger deal. She's trying not to lick her lips. Not to blush. Definitely not imagining the rest of the room disappearing, so it's just him and her, surrounded by plush couches in the darkness, faraway strains of "My Heart Will Go On" egging her fantasies.

"We're not getting any younger," Riley says crossly.

"Is it her first kiss?" someone whispers within earshot, much to Evie's indignation.

"It is not! I am a champion kisser, thank you very much!" she protests.

Fen crosses her arms. "Prove it, hotshot."

Evie crawls across the rug toward Adam. Why isn't he budging? Does she have to do all the work here? Finally, she's facing him, riveted on his lips. She leans over, glad for that mint she'd snuck after the last cocktail. His eyes catch hers, sending a flipping motion through her belly. It's just a kiss. One little, measly, *meaningless* kiss.

One measly kiss that makes her lower belly tingle as if someone had released a net of pheromone-addled butterflies into it. Totally normal, right?

And then, at the last minute, just before her lips touch his, he turns his head, leaving a column of cold air where his face was. He stands, nearly toppling her. Her mouth meets floor instead. Carpet fuzz instead of sweet softness.

"Ugh!" she cries, wiping her lips. "Let a girl down gently, Quyền."

At the same time, he announces, "This is ridiculous. It's time to go back to the hotel."

The rest of the group exchanges puzzled looks as Fen mutters, "Killjoy."

But they gather their things and follow him to the front of the karaoke bar, where the cars are waiting. The mortification seeps into Evie's veins. Stupid, stupid. Was her breath *awful*? Or was the prospect of locking lips with her just that repellent? It had seemed he was going to kiss her at the bánh mì xíu mại stand. What had changed in a matter of days?

With a sinking feeling, she wonders if Adam has fallen for Talia. After all, he's been attached to her side like a fanny pack on an octogenarian bingo player. Despite that rigid, emotionless exterior, he seems like a man with honor. Loyalty. So why didn't he just . . . not play? Why humiliate her like that? She slides into one of the cars without checking to see who's in there.

But of course, she nearly bumps into a glowering Adam on the seat, with Cherie and Đức on the seats facing them. His hand rests an inch from hers in the tight quarters, his tall body folded over, and it's hard not to touch. But somehow they manage, though she feels the heat between their fingertips, the nearness of him. She avoids his gaze, sure that he's doing the same.

Luckily, Đức babbles on for the entirety of the ride back to the huts. He's detailing their upcoming flight to Huế, the imperial seat of the Nguyễn dynasty, known for its deep-rooted history and sweeping landscapes. If Evie weren't so flustered, she'd be listening. She's been waiting for a brush with history like that. But at the moment, she's mostly trying to keep herself from bolting from the car into the banks of the ocean from the sheer awkwardness of her proximity to a near-catatonic Adam.

Soon, the city lights give way to the dim stretch of the private beach where they're staying. Đức and Cherie are lodging closer to the north end of the beach—in separate quarters, Evie notes—so they get dropped off first. Đức waves a newsboy cap at them before shutting the door. Then it's just Adam and Evie, staring out opposite windows.

He breaks the silence. "I still can't figure out if they're siblings or lovers."

Evie giggles. "I'm voting for siblings. Cherie can do better."

"But his hats!"

Their laughter, sudden and so very welcome, cuts through the thick wedge of awkwardness between them. Why can't it always be this easy with him?

The driver pulls up to their row of huts, and Adam slides a tip over the seat rest. He grips Evie's hand tightly as he helps her out of the car. The pitch-dark night is studded with hazy clouds that obscure the stars and moon. Even the cabin lights seem sparse and muted. There are few reflections on the water, and the air is still, almost as if it's braced for a storm.

Something about being alone in the dark with Adam sends a thrill up Evie's spine. His nearness draws her closer, even as she tries to slide away. She feels like she has to actively restrain her hand from reaching for his again. After just a few steps on the uneven ground, Evie manages to trip on a piece of kelp.

"Rude," she mutters, kicking it with her sandal.

"Hey," Adam protests, picking the stringy vegetation off his pants. "You threw seaweed at me. Talk about rude."

"Sorry." She doesn't sound a bit sorry. "At least it wasn't a hermit crab."

"Small mercies."

"Shoot, watch out for that dip in the sand. You'd think they would have motion-sensing lights or something. This is a hazard."

"Let me walk you back to your hut." She begins to protest, but then he says firmly, "Your shoes are ridiculous."

"They are Louboutins," she says haughtily at first. Then uncertainly, "Is that the one with the red soles? Fen let me borrow them."

"Yep, that's the one." Is that a hint of a smile on his shadowed face?

"Regardless, I can walk myself the few feet to my hut. I have a great sense of direction. Well, except for that time I confused Indiana with Iowa and ended up on a very unexpected road trip to Muncie."

"What did you find in Muncie?" Now he's definitely smiling.

"A cheese shop that served olive-flavored Havarti."

"Sounds delicious."

"It *was*! And there was this streetside troubadour who tried to hitchhike with me."

"The beginning of a great love story?"

"Would have been, had he not been tempted by the all-you-can-eat mayonnaise festival one town over. I did make it to Iowa . . . eventually."

"And that was in your home country. Here you'll probably wander into Thailand, which would *really* screw up the tour schedule."

"As ever, a gentleman," she says sarcastically.

In the faint light, she can see him stretching his hand to her. She starts to protest, but then his palm is flush against hers, fingers intertwined. Did he just *rub* her thumb with his? There's an electric tingling in her hand now. Like the start of a fire, hot and wispy. A sensation that makes you pay attention.

More, she wants to insist.

Though her hut isn't far, the walk is slow going. He leads her along capably, and she just barely resists melting into the solid strength of his body, his purposeful gait. He's like the pied piper of clumsy, semi-inebriated women—only less creepy.

Stop it, Evie, she thinks sternly. *You are not thirteen. You do not need to make out with just any Tom, Dick, or Adam.*

"I'm not just *any* Adam," he puts in, his voice tinged with amusement and just a touch of umbrage.

Evie clasps a hand to her mouth. Not again. She can't seem to resist voicing whatever is on her mind around him. At first, it was because she'd wanted to needle him. But now? He makes her comfortable enough to unleash even her strangest thoughts. Somewhere in her mind, she hears Auntie Hảo's mirth-filled chuckle.

He goes on. "Though maybe I need to hear more about this making-out thing."

They've arrived at her hut, eyes searching for each other in the dark. She snatches her hand away, remembering the way he humiliated her at the karaoke bar. He couldn't even give her a demure peck without literally running from the room. And now, when no one's watching, he's flirting with her like she's going to fall all over him at the first flash of that (devastating) smile? Cocky son of a weasel.

"No, you clearly do not want to hear about making out with me," she says in a whispered hiss, trying not to disturb the other guests staying nearby.

"I don't?" There's something behind his words now. Hot and sensuous, like a breath evaporating down her neck.

She snorts, ignoring the effect he has on her. "Don't use that cheesy

Leonard Cohen voice on me. You couldn't get away fast enough in the karaoke bar."

"That wasn't—"

"It was just a game! I wasn't expecting us to reenact that smooch from *The Notebook* or anything."

"Good scene," he says, sounding a bit distracted now. "If you're a bird, I'm a bird."

Did he just step closer to her? She steps pointedly away. "Not that I care, but I saw that look on your face. You were disgusted. It's very clear you have no interest at all in—"

In an instant, his lips are on hers, interrupting her words, and it's then that she really *does* melt. His kiss starts off tentative, exploratory, a kind of consent-taking. *Are his lips really this soft?* she thinks absently. He could be sponsored by ChapStick.

More. More of this.

He leans away, leaving just enough space to say, "I wasn't disgusted. I just didn't want to kiss you like *this* in front of a whole room. I didn't want anyone but you to witness this. To see how much I wanted it."

"Why not?" she asks in a small voice.

He growls. "If I started kissing you, I wouldn't be able to fucking stop, Evie Lang."

And he's back, pulling lightly on her lower lip with his teeth, running his tongue across the seam of her lips. When she pulls his head closer, pressing their faces together, the whole tempo of the kiss changes, like an ocean suddenly turned stormy. He roughly backs her against the side of the hut. She can feel the knot of the wood, the press of his body. His lips are hot, breath tasting just faintly of mint and sea breeze. Every inch of him, though she can't see any of it, feels firm and muscled. He just feels *right*.

Without thinking, she slides her tongue into his mouth, tangles it with his. It makes her breathless. They can't stop touching, kissing, letting their fingers explore the contours of each other's face.

"Goddammit, Evie," Adam rasps.

His hands tangle in her hair, pulling gently so her head falls back slightly, and her neck is exposed to him. With slow and deliberate movements, he runs his lips down the column of her throat, licking a trail of salt and sweetness that makes her belly clench.

"You taste so good," he murmurs. "I want to lick you all over."

She makes a sound somewhere between a sigh and a mew, and when she does, he presses her harder into the wall. She lifts one leg, curling it around his hip, which makes him growl again in the most primal, intoxicating way.

"Yes," she sighs, not realizing she'd said anything until it comes out. "Don't stop."

Don't stop kissing, touching, making those animal sounds that melt every ounce of control she has left. *Don't stop holding me*, she wants to say.

One of his hands presses flush against the side of the hut, next to her ear, while the other roves down to her hemline, where the crimson dress rides up her curves. With an impatient movement, he lifts the hem of the skirt above her butt and begins tracing the line of her thong, from its near-nonexistent back to the front, into the apex of her thighs. His fingers are *so* close to the molten wetness inside of her that her legs open involuntarily. Welcomingly. She's panting for the release of his touch. All he has to do is just slip his finger a little to the left, past the thin fabric of her underwear . . . One tiny centimeter between this desperate moment and the release that only he can give.

He mutters, "I knew it would be like this. From the second I saw you, I knew that you would destroy every single ion of control inside of me. I can't get enough of you, Evie Lang."

A surge of hot lust beats against her thighs. She hisses, half as a challenge and half as a plea, "Then take me. Take as much as you want."

He groans again, louder this time. She's wild with wanting, each inch of her pleading for more. Her body feels like it's taken flight, and his touch is the only thing centering her, even as it frees her. He shifts and rips the fabric of her thong, and then—

"Hey, watch out!" a distant voice calls.

A few feet down, there's a slamming door. Loud noises fill the air suddenly, like a party is just letting out, a cacophony diffusing into the night. There's the clang of shattered glass, followed by laughter and shouting.

The spell breaks.

All at once, Evie and Adam look around them, finally taking note of where they are. The night is dark, but their eyes have adjusted and they can see silhouettes of trees, lights flickering from other huts where guests are moving from room to room. Anyone could have come out. Anyone could have witnessed them making out. And more. Abashed at the thought, they pull apart.

Evie can't help the feeling of loss once his body heat separates from hers. It's more primal than blocked lust. It's as if she's lost a part of herself.

He backs away. His eyes shut down, turning from hers. "I'm sorry. I shouldn't have done that."

"Oh."

"You can get the rest of the way on your own?"

"I can?" She stares up at him with lust-fogged eyes.

"Home, I mean."

What the hell? That's it? How can he go from a smoldering demigod of dirty talk and unexpected tenderness to this cold, businesslike robot? It's like a switch has flipped and the world has changed around her.

Not trusting herself to speak, Evie nods slowly.

He clears his throat and gives her one last, unreadable look. "I'll see you tomorrow, then."

In a few long strides, he stalks away, his hands now clenched tightly at the sides of his body, his back rigid. He doesn't look back at her.

Evie fixes her dress. Gathers her torn underwear. Her heart won't stop thudding. It's so loud that she hardly hears anything else as she walks into her hut and falls onto the bed, thinking of nothing but Adam's hot breath, his tongue on hers. How far they could have gone together. How far she *still* wants to go.

And for a second, it had seemed as if he felt the same. *I can't get enough of you, Evie Lang.*

That lasted for all of a minute before he was running. Again. A wave of embarrassment makes her cover her face, even though she's alone.

Why should she be lusting after a damn coward? Unfortunately, her hormones haven't gotten the we-hate-Adam-again memo. They're still singing with frustration, primed for release. Too bad that he seems entirely unequal to the job.

With a groan, she pulls a pillow across her face and wills her breath to slow down. But she's afraid she can't fight this feeling anymore. The desperate, maddening *wanting* of him.

ADAM

Huế, Việt Nam

Two sleepless, sheet-rustling nights and as many mornings of awkward eye avoidance later, Adam finds himself walking across the Meridian Gate to the Imperial City of Huế. He lags behind the group to take in the majestic sprawl of the Citadel in its full glory. His breath catches in his throat as he scans the palaces and shrines, the tucked-in villas for the mandarins of yore.

Modeled after Beijing's Forbidden City, the Imperial City looks onto the Perfume River, where the royals once surveyed their vast riches, the forested mountains situated just beyond. The river flows into the moat surrounding the palace complex, clear and still in the morning. Though the Imperial City was burned and destroyed during the many conflicts of the latter half of the twentieth century, it rises still with a dignified grandeur that can make a Vietnamese national's heart ache. Including Adam's own.

Why has it taken him so long to see this? He has all the money he could want. Surely he could have carved out the time for a glimpse of his homeland. But he's been too busy chasing other things. Wishing he were elsewhere on the ladder of success. So many wasted years.

He looks around, hoping for a shared glance with Evie, but she's far ahead, walking arm in arm with Fen and Talia. But *why* does he want to share this with her? What is it about her—besides the simmering lust she seems to evoke—that makes him want to follow her around like a lovesick puppy? Adam feels a rush of antipathy at that word: *lovesick*. He doesn't *do* lovesick. Romance is for the weak and easily influenced. And he's always understood that love isn't meant to be a great burst of fireworks. Nausea or roiling emotions, bad choices in the dim hours of night. It's supposed to be slow and steady and *safe*. A rational, determined partnership above all else. Like what his parents have. Like what he thought he had with Lana.

In the rush of the crowd, he must run to catch up. Most everyone is dressed conservatively, since entry to some sites in the Imperial City requires covered shoulders and knees. Fen keeps trying to roll up the cuffs of her knee-length shorts—bought at the last minute for this excursion—though a glare from Ruby usually quells her attempt for at least a minute or two.

Adam feels a rush of affection as he sees the small groups chatting. The tour is halfway over, and it seems to be working like a dream. Couples are sneaking kisses or holding hands, shy and hopeful in the first flush of affection. He's taken many candid photos, considering the best ways to market this tour with video interviews and testimonies afterward.

Despite his earlier skepticism, he can admit that Ruby was right. She and the matchmakers know what they're doing. They are creating the circumstances for some truly epic love stories—or at least, the beginnings of something more exciting than what each guest might have lucked into on their own. It's not a perfect formula, but it's one worth investing in. He's proud to have been a part of Ruby's vision.

And beyond the newly emerging relationships, there are fast, if surprising, friendships forming. Evie is helping Talia drape a shawl around her shoulders, flinging it with rakish verve.

"Now you're ready to wed an emperor," Evie says.

Talia laughs. "I don't think I'll be marrying into royalty anytime soon. *You*, however. Aren't you dating some English duke?"

Adam stops in his tracks, halting the line of traffic behind him. What's wrong with his eyes? He only sees red. His line of vision narrows on her, and her alone. She's *dating* someone? A fucking duke? And she's got the audacity to go on a matchmaking tour?

Evie quickly corrects her friend. "No, girl. I said he *thinks* he's an English duke. He's a literature professor at the college where I taught."

"Dreamy."

"And I'm definitely not dating him."

Adam's blood pressure goes down. Then shoots back up when Fen teases Evie, "Sure you're not. That's why he's blowing up your text messages even when he's on the other side of the world and it's midnight his time? With photos of his lordly penis?"

Adam bites back his scowl. The thought of another man filling her phone with lewd photos makes him want to throw it into the Perfume River, like some hulking caveman.

"They're all library pictures!" Evie swears, lifting her arms with a laugh.

Library pictures. Some English professor who apparently has zero boundaries when it comes to text messaging. Adam is so annoyed that he can barely speak as he brushes past the women at the arched gates. He doesn't even apologize when he knocks into Fen's elbow.

"Excuse you," Evie says.

He gives her a withering glare. "*Some* of us are here to see the sights, not gossip all day long."

"What's up his ass?" Fen mutters behind him.

He doesn't stop to listen to the rest as he catches up to the tour guide, who describes the thoughtful layout of the palace, designed to align with the Five Cardinal Points, Five Elements, and Five Colors. There's a soothing symmetry and rationality to all this beauty that cools Adam's rising blood. He likes knowing exactly what to expect.

Ruby stands by herself, staring down at her phone with a frown. Even with the turmoil that Evie's kiss (and that tiny, silken thong) summoned in him, he notices that his sister isn't her usual cat-ate-the-cream self. In fact, she's been decidedly *unengaged* in the tour, which isn't at all like her.

"You should be proud," he tells his sister.

They stride to the pagodas, perfectly in step as usual. Like soldiers. *Or robots*, he thinks.

She tucks her phone away and blinks out into the crowd. Connor, who's finally pivoted his attention from the kind-but-aloof Talia, has his arm slung around the shoulders of a socialite from Hồ Chí Minh City named Veronica. She's staring up at him with a mixture of awe and adoration. Adam sees the beginnings of a new couple. Another success story for the pamphlets.

Ruby offers a small smile. "I *am* proud. I didn't know for sure what would happen. But there's something in this formula that works. Taking someone out of their usual context. Introducing them to people they might never have met."

"The luxury accommodations and staggering five-star meals don't hurt," Adam says wryly.

She laughs. "Nope. Not with this crowd."

Adam shakes the thought of how his most memorable moments on the trip—the meatball stand, the ride down the alpine track—all happened *away* from the crowd, when he was most grimy and undone. And, coincidentally, when he was with Evie.

"Ever the savvy entrepreneur."

"Can't apologize for seeing an opportunity and running with it."

He asks, "But why matchmaking? Why not just . . . a regular tour? Wouldn't have been so niche. Would have made you more money."

"You sound like Ba now," Ruby says. "He's always sending me business advice."

"Ba advises *you*? I thought I was the only one with that dubious honor."

She stares. "Are you kidding me? I'm the firstborn *and* a woman. I have been under his thumb my entire life. He was trying to enroll me in business classes when I was seven. That man gave me a monogrammed *briefcase* for my twelfth birthday. Do you know what a girl wants when she's twelve? *Not a briefcase.*"

"I got mine when I was ten. And it was filled with spreadsheets! It may have just been discarded by some poor sap Ba fired who never picked up his belongings."

"He would have fired me many times over if he could have."

Though they laugh together, Adam hears the pain in her voice, shadowed by his own. He's always assumed that he gets the brunt of his parents' ire, but maybe that isn't true at all. Maybe Ruby just does a better job of hiding her hurt. Though she shouldn't have to. They're siblings, after all. Who can understand their world of privilege and shrouded disappointment better than the two of them?

Ruby muses, "It's going to be strange to see them again. In this new way, with all these new people."

"You don't think they'll be happy to have us?"

The siblings make their way past a bridge crowded with koi, orange mouths puckered open for food, then past a series of massive bronze cannons.

She's cautious as she answers. "They will welcome us. But they won't be able to turn off that part of their brains that criticizes everything. There'll be *something*."

Adam knows that anxiety. He's felt it coming on for days. This dread of anticipating a storm without proper shelter or equipment. It makes him feel flayed open, childlike, to imagine Ba's rigid stance, Mẹ's restless gaze. Sometimes Adam wonders if his parents see him at all, or if they instead see a hologram version. Pixelated, unformed. Needing intervention.

The Quyèns have always wanted the best for their children. It's in their blood, a love so fierce that it often manifests in a need to control, to push the world (and their children) into something resembling order. This type of symmetry can represent security—or a cage, depending on your perspective. Most days, Adam hardly blames them; they've lived through more in their lifetimes than many can even conceive. Despite their wealth, they were never fully protected from the horrors of war or unrest. It's natural for them to crave peace now.

Yet, looking at his sister, he sees something tremulous in her. A weariness that he instinctively wants to pull from her body into his, like when they were children racing, and he purposefully slowed down so she could catch up. So she could win, as was her right as the older sister.

His voice softens as he says, "Ruby, you know you can talk about whatever's going on."

She raises an eyebrow at him. "You looking to be my therapist, BB?"

"No, Chị. I just want you to understand you don't have to do it alone. That's why you have a team. That's why you have a *brother*."

They stand in a long red hall with open corridors and a recessed ceiling. Delicately carved doors swing open to let in the slightest breath of air skimming down the Perfume River, carrying the fragrance of flowers that fall from trees onto the banks and into the water.

For a second, Ruby and Adam are two sides of a coin. Two still statues, considering their lives and their relationship to one another.

Then Ruby seems to shake herself. "What could possibly be wrong? I have everything I ever wanted. I have no right to complain."

"You can always ask for more."

"No. I should learn to be content with what I have. I just need to discard my melancholy, BB. It does absolutely no good."

Once, Adam would have said the same thing. He'd have tucked his emotion someplace safe—a monogrammed briefcase crowded with spreadsheets, perhaps—and gone on with his life. But now he doesn't feel the usual urge to hide. This trip has changed him. Made him more willing to confront messy things. Messy people.

And maybe a part of him can now admit to his own messiness. Embrace it, even.

Across the way, running along the bridge with a fistful of koi food, there's a swish of long hair. A smile that sparkles more insistently than the sunshine in the highest hills of the central region. His heart skips.

Dulling his emotions would mean dulling the strange, growing sensation inside him. Something more than lust, more than affection, even. It's a feeling as magical as a single flower petal stolen from the surface of a winding river outside an Imperial City.

EVIE

Huế, Việt Nam

Evie had forgotten about that spike of anxiety she gets every time she receives an email from Grace Lang. Her mother, unlike most Boomers, is a consummate avoider of phones. Even back when Evie was in college, then graduate school in Iowa at a prestigious workshop she never quite lived up to, Grace preferred meandering emails over phone calls or, heaven forbid, face-to-face contact. Midland was no New York or Los Angeles, but it terrified Grace to imagine leaving her hometown. As a consequence, Evie only saw her mother on the rare occasions when Evie returned home. And even those visits continued to dwindle after college.

Evie skims Grace's mostly unpunctuated, vaguely E. E. Cummings–like lines, with a dash of Emily Dickinson for good measure. While teaching, Grace had been a rigid adherent of proper grammar, but now, loosened by retirement or general giving-zero-fucks, her words weave in fascinating (if infuriating) directions. In another life, perhaps Grace herself might have become a poet, had she not been crushed by an unholy fear of bucking convention.

> A letter came—I opened it, by mistake, thinking it for me
> yet it was for you. And it spoke of termination
> and extending benefits though what benefits are there to find
> in being fired

do you remember when you tried to drop out of your master's degree

and I told you that nursing paid beautifully

such talent you had for tending the vulnerable—

like when you volunteered with the cats at the humane society

what am I—your mother—to think when such things fall onto my doorstep like mice droppings

can't help but wonder what you are doing in Việt Nam as your career falls apart

You were always a dreamer

lost like your aunt

the horizon taunts you.

Think hard on where this adventure has gotten you—is it too much to ask

that you be safe in the storms

of life

Evie groans and archives the email, though stops short of deleting it entirely. After all, in its own way, it is a baffling work of art.

The horizon taunts you.

Isn't that the truth?

And this is just what she needs: her guilt-tripping mother tugging on her heart from across the world, reminding her of all her failures, past and present.

Once, she remembered Grace differently. Grace always had a love for the dramatic—confined as it was to her husband and child—but she'd also been a relatively cheerful human, taking Evie to pumpkin patches on the first weekend of October, helping her affix iron-on patches to her denim jacket that she insisted all the other girls were wearing. Grace had been social and energetic, always willing to volunteer in what little spare time she had after teaching. She'd loved meeting her friends at the salon, emerging hours later in a puff of light brown curls, dancing in her husband's arms in the kitchen as he admired her new hairstyle.

Her mother was there. *Fully* there, until—

And here Evie bites back the memory of her late father, one of the precious few she has. Danh Lang, extraordinary perhaps only to the people who knew him, was a quiet wood-carver who worked in a small shop off a country road. He customized cribs with fantastical animals or ten-foot wedding arches that distracted brides and grooms into forgetting their own vows. It was true that he didn't have a *flourishing* business, in the traditional sense. He put in much more effort than his fees demanded, often working late into the night in the workshop to add that last charming detail for his delighted customers. Those same customers remained loyal through all the phases of their lives, often making excuses to consign a toy chest or jewelry box they didn't need, just to show their support. Though perhaps it had been difficult to win the trust of their insular community at first, especially as one of the only Asian Americans living there in the mid-eighties, Danh and his woodshop became a beloved part of their town until the day he died.

And Grace never pressured him to handle his business differently, though they could have made efficiencies aplenty. She loved him too much to change a vocation that gave him so much joy. What was important was that he was happy, and they had enough to get by.

Evie adored the time she spent with her father in the workshop, sweeping up the sawdust, trying her hand at carvings when she got older. Sometimes she just sat in the corner and read her stacks of books—*The Giver*, *James and the Giant Peach*, and her favorite, *A Light in the Attic*—until the late hours when the chill descended and the sky began to purple. They drove home with the windows open, even in winter, talking quietly about all the little inconsequential things Evie regrets not being able to remember now. In some ways, her summers with Auntie Hảo were like that too. Comfortable, yet utterly magical in their unrushed rhythms.

Danh was diagnosed with colon cancer when Evie was eleven years old, and their small world shook forever. Danh and Grace spent many weeks in Cleveland seeking treatment from the best doctors, or in California researching experimental treatments. Evie, worried and dealing with some of her own adolescent struggles, was left at home with Grace's parents, who were kind enough, if remote. Grace emptied out their savings in the last few months of Danh's life, trying to buy him just a little more time. Evie's parents refused to take any money from Auntie Hảo. They sold the workshop at a pittance, which tore Evie's heart apart. She could see it devastated her father, but he was too caught up in Grace's stormy determination to save his life.

When that didn't work, after Danh was cremated and his ashes scattered over the rolling fields near their home, they found themselves swimming in medical debt. Grace begged for loans from the bank, sitting through countless meetings to no avail. Finally, she accepted money from Auntie Hảo, who'd convinced her that it would have gone to Danh anyway. It humiliated Grace to do it, but the alternative was bankruptcy, perhaps even the loss of their home. She worried that Evie would go hungry or have to tuck away her dreams of college. Their household absorbed their shared grief, then Grace's spiraling anxiety.

It took years, but Grace finally paid everything back, though now she's haunted by the thought of debts unpaid, creditors calling at all hours. She would do anything to avoid living a life where a lack of money could dismantle everything she has built.

So on an intellectual level, Evie understands all this about her mother. She shares some of the fear of disaster and the need to protect oneself from heartbreak. One does not live through a hurricane without enduring some wreckage, after all. But she also possesses her father's relentless idealism, his conviction that if you can find a way to do what you love, the rest will follow.

Many days, she feels like there are two forces tugging at her. One, spearheaded by Danh and Auntie Hảo, telling her to reach wildly, to live as if each day is her last. But on the other side, there's Grace, cautioning her against loving with abandon and trusting that the world will catch your fall. The reality is, for many women, the world is not built to catch them at all. Life isn't a net. It's a funnel, swirling you ever faster to the narrow, uncertain end.

As an antidote to her mother's email, Evie glances through a text from Lillian. They're interviewing for your job right now and Graham is at his wits' end. Everyone coming in is either a pretentious prick or a near-teenager, barely out of the classroom themselves. It's a shitshow.

Plus a dancing emoji.

Evie writes back: You do know that you're rooting against your own husband now, don't you?

Lillian's response: I'll stick it to the man any day for you, cousin.

Loyal Lill. Evie had known that her department would be interviewing soon, but it hurts nonetheless to hear about it. Sure, she's never been a natural at teaching at the college level, but she wasn't terrible at her job. Back in high school, she tutored young kids, and she *loved* the playfulness of those lessons. Incorporating music and art and pop culture. Finding a way to bring words to life for them.

At Midland, it was about following a strict paradigm of composition lessons, plus a splash of classic poetry for "culture." The admins looked askance at lessons like hers, and honestly, the students seemed bemused as well, uncertain of how to perform when there was so much freedom in the curriculum. In one ill-advised lesson plan, Evie brought in miniature tubs of Play-Doh and asked them each to sculpt their concept of death. At least two students dropped out after that class. Evie reflects that perhaps her classes could have benefited from a *little* more structure.

Meanwhile, nothing from Atlas in days. It doesn't bother her, exactly, this rhythm of unpredictable texting. After all, when he was wooing her, there was a similar pattern of push and pull. She'd found it exciting then. But she's not thinking of Atlas in that way anymore. She's thinking of a certain gorgeous man with impossibly soft lips, a hard jawline, and hands that seem to know *exactly* what to do with her body.

She groans.

"Five minutes, babe!" Fen yells, pounding on the door.

Her footsteps fade before Evie can respond. Fen has taken to this aggressive, unsolicited reminder for Evie nearly every morning, though Evie assures her that she *can* be on time when needed. But it always makes her smile to hear Fen at the door.

Evie throws a pair of shorts over her bathing suit and adds a loose linen shirt. At the last minute, she plops a straw hat on her head. Some of the tour guests are taking a boat cruise down the Perfume River to the better-preserved of the seven imperial tombs in Huế. Others, declining the roasting heat, are going to a spa at the Azerai La Residence, trying out traditional Vietnamese cupping methods, as well as something puzzlingly referred to as "bamboo leg therapy."

Once Evie and the rest of the boat guests arrive at the dock, she sighs, thinking of the serene spa day she passed on. No Adam in sight. Evie tries not to think about where he is. Surely he's not a spa guy. The man doesn't have a relaxed bone in that (incredibly muscled) body. Since the night outside her hut in Nha Trang, she's been seized with *very vivid* fantasies of that body. She tosses and turns most nights, wondering if it would be completely insane to show up on his doorstep, banging loudly the way Fen does for her every morning. Asking for . . . what? Release from this blue-balled hell?

Every time they meet each other's eyes, he is either extremely smoldering or extremely avoidant. No consistency at all. It gives a girl whiplash.

Evie tosses him out of her mind, like a moldy piece of cheese. She's been looking forward to seeing Emperor Tự Đức's tomb. The artistic ruler's tomb is a uniquely picturesque spot, with stately gardens and organic landscaping, all centered by a pond where the emperor himself liked to spend his afternoons reading and writing poetry dedicated to his many mistresses.

On the boat, she snaps photos of Fen and Talia, along with the other guests. Their long barge is painted with yellow scales, and the front is shaped like a dragon head with sharp, carved teeth. She hesitates for a second, then sends a handful of photos to Adam. She lied when she said she threw the dossier out. She saved it just for the contact information.

No answer. She sits in the covered interior of the boat and fiddles with her bag, then opens her notebook, pen poised. A poem on demand is unreasonable to expect, but maybe just a quick note? Anything?

Don't rush it, Evie-pie, says Auntie Hảo's disembodied voice in her mind.

But all that comes to her is an everlasting blank, as white and unblemished as a snowy field. Had there ever been a time when she scoffed at writer's block, producing with the verve and passion of a young poet? A time when she'd been bloated with confidence and expectation, the world fluttering open in front of her like the leaves of a book?

Those days seem very, very far away.

She sighs and snaps the notebook shut again, tucking the pen into her hair in a bun. Takes a big swig of water. Dehydration will cause strange and unseemly visions, she's been told. Maybe she should welcome a hallucinatory trip. She'll take any writing fodder at this point.

"You all right there?" Talia asks, settling in next to her.

"My inspiration has dried up," she answers. "Like sands through the hourglass."

"Poetic."

"And one hundred percent plagiarized," she says glumly. "Is it me, or is it hot as Satan's armpits today?"

"That's Việt Nam for you. You sure that's all?"

Nope, not by a long shot.

Talia continues, "My mother used to tell me that being near the water made people more pensive. I know I've been thinking through things."

She gives Evie a warm smile, and something about the other woman reminds Evie of the gentleness of her father, working steadily in his workshop. That calming way of listening, as if her words matter. She feels a sudden rush to confide in Talia—but what would she even say? How can she explain her simmer of emotions?

Finally, Evie admits, "I'm grateful to be here, but I'm worried about what I'm leaving behind, back home. This is an escapist trip, you know? Everything is just so gorgeous and luxurious. But it isn't real life."

"Are you worried that you won't find someone you connect with?"

Evie laughs shortly. "No; that's the least of my worries. I just think I might be procrastinating about my future. I know this will come as a devastating shock to you, Talia, but I'm not exactly at the top of my career. Not like the rest of you. I'm no award-winning philanthropist."

Talia shrugs. "That's only one part of life. I like what I do for a living, but I struggle in other ways. I'd give it all up today for the right person."

Her eye slides to Pin, who is pointing to the shore at a giant ibis with a lightly curved beak. Evie crooks her head, glancing between the two. Beautiful Talia and shy Pin. Could it work?

Talia says lightly, "We all struggle. It's the human condition. We're all looking for something, otherwise we wouldn't be here."

"What are you struggling with?" Evie tries to hide her incredulity. Talia seems to have absolutely everything.

"I've had some difficult relationships. Men who want me to be an accessory for them or, simply, a silent companion. Dating is hard when you're known as a commodity—Miss Sài Gòn—rather than a living, breathing, flawed human."

Evie thinks guiltily about her own preconceptions of Talia. Wasn't the point of the tour to get to know people outside of their first impressions? Wayward poet, pristine beauty queen—Grumpy CMO? None of these quick categorizations are nearly as interesting as the humans themselves, complex and ever-changing.

"I'm sorry, Talia. You're so much more than some sash you wear."

"I'm learning that," she says softly. "I got so small after those relationships. A lesser, more frightened version of myself. My sister urged me to consider this trip, to welcome what the unknown could bring, even if it means a shake-up to my world order. She says that bravery is not an inherent trait but a practice, a series of decisions you make every day, big and small."

"My Auntie Hảo said the same. In fact, those were pretty much her last words to me. Before—you know."

"I'm sorry for your loss."

"Thanks. Grief is a funny thing. It feels like I can't be happy without the sorrow finding a way to jut through. Like stepping on a shard of leftover glass when you're just trying to walk down a hallway in your home."

"Take it from someone who's lost both parents: that mixture of emotions is the price of a life fully lived. I'll take the grief if it means I don't have to miss out on any of the love that precedes it."

Evie reaches over to squeeze the other woman's hand. "You're a very wise lady. I can't even be jealous of how wonderful you are because I like you so much. Pin is lucky to have you."

Talia blushes. Evie watches her sidle next to Pin, asking a question about the ibis. For them, love seems to be a slow creep, a warm blanket thrown over a sleeping body. Comfort. Evie's heart aches for them. And maybe, just a little, for herself.

Then, a buzz in her pocket. Adam. You forgot the selfie.

She snaps one of her grinning at the camera, then sends it off, along with a caption. Try not to obsess over me too much.

A few seconds later, his reply arrives. Too late. Already made it my phone wallpaper.

Replacing your vampire glamshot?!

Pssht, he writes, vampires are so yesterday. It's all about therianthrope werewolves now.

She can't stop smiling and wishing he were *here*. But then, her smile fades. Next time she sees him, which Adam will she get? The playful, smoldering one who flirts over text? Or the cold CMO who looks at her as if she were a bothersome disturbance in his perfectly planned day? How much whiplash can a person withstand before throwing in the towel?

Evie is a woman of determination, but even she has her limits.

ADAM

Huế, Việt Nam

Adam is covered in a fine layer of yellow dust as he pulls up to Emperor Tự Đức's tomb in the late morning. While everyone else took the boats, he rented a motorbike to visit the tombs. He'd wanted to see them far more than he wanted a kelp massage at the spa, but he needed time alone to process. Some space in the Huế countryside to collect himself.

And it is a balm for him, riding fast and unfettered down the narrow roads, pulled by the imposing green mountains, the dense acacia forests with leaves that shudder gently as he passes. On his bike, he doesn't have time to overanalyze every scenario; run comparables and put together multipage RFPs. He just has to react to the landscape in front of him—the winding roads, the crowding trees. It's simpler and, somehow, more essential to drive by instinct.

At the tomb, he rides across the bridge, past the short stone statues of mandarins flanking the path, and through the ceramic-tiled entrance. There's no sign of Evie, and Adam tries not to dwell on the fact that he had most definitely been hoping for a glimpse of her. More than a glimpse. He'd been so surprised by her text message that he pulled over to the side of the road to respond. He grinned stupidly when her selfie came in, then proceeded to save it on his phone.

"Emperor Tự Đức was the longest-reigning emperor of the Nguyễn dynasty at thirty-six years. He was known to be an excessive and cruel man, though an indubitable patron of the arts. At least, of his own artistic practices."

The guide lectures about the emperor's 104 wives (and unnumbered concubines), along with the bloody coup that sprang up during the construction of this very tomb. He points to a theater meant to host performances for the emperor and his considerable family.

"And you can also wander to the Hoa Khiêm Temple, where the emperor's family worshipped, or the beautiful Xung Khiêm Pavilion, where he liked to compose poetry."

Bingo. Where to find a poet, except in a place built for an emperor poet?

The pavilion surrounding the tomb is a large, shaded wooden structure overlooking a golden-green lake dotted with lily pads. When Adam strides in, his eyes immediately land on Evie, sitting on one of the steps leading into the water. She has her notebook open on her lap as she looks out onto the rippling lake.

A flash of sunlight, and all at once, her dreamy expression changes. It brightens with sharp delight, eyes widening, lips falling slightly open.

Inspiration, Adam thinks.

Her fingers reach up for the pen holding her bun upright. As she bends over her notebook, her freed hair dances along her shoulders and down her back. He's mesmerized by her. Unable to stop himself, he takes a photo. For the marketing materials, of course.

Adam slowly tries to withdraw, but as he does, she glances back and sees him. She shuts her notebook and tucks the pen behind her ear. Soon, she's next to him, leaning on the rail.

"I didn't mean to interrupt you," he says.

"I was done," she says, waving her hand. "Did you know that poets across every country and every age are bona fide assholes? It is known."

"You mean Tự Đức's hundred and four wives? Or the coup that he inspired by working his servants so hard they refused to lift another brick for him?"

"I mean the fact that this buffoon arranged to have himself—and his vast treasure—buried somewhere else. As in, *not* in this tomb that took so much time and labor to produce. And before he died he ordered that all two hundred servants who buried him be executed so that his treasure would never be found by grave robbers."

"Couldn't they just have . . . not done it? He was dead, after all. Who would have blamed them?"

She lifts her shoulder in a shrug. "Maybe they were afraid he'd haunt them beyond the grave."

"I'd take that chance."

"Me too. So where were you, anyway? Did you swim here underwater?"

"In that filth!"

She wrinkles her nose and looks at him pointedly. "Speaking of *filth*. Did you ride here on a mule?"

"Motorcycle. And I smell like a damn perfume river."

She leans forward, inches from his face, and takes a playful sniff. Adam braces himself against the rail so he doesn't pull her forward, covering her mouth once again with his. He thanks his stars for expensive cologne and twenty-four-hour antiperspirant. Even as she's sniffing him, he can smell *her*, a light orchid scent, mixed with something a little muskier. Her sweat and specific blend of body chemistry.

"You'll do," she admits with a smile, tucking her notebook back into her bag. "Let's catch up to the rest of them before ol' Tự Đức's ghost pulls you into the lake."

Then she's flounced off, practically skipping forward so that he has to run to catch up to her. It annoys him, this chasing act. Why can't this woman just stand still?

"So what were you working on?" he asks.

"Poetry stuff."

". . . Like?"

"Images. Feelings. Line breaks."

He shoots her a deadpan look. "Yeah, I can see why you're the poet laureate of Midland. So good with words."

Her mouth falls open as she turns to him. Whoops. He revealed more than he meant to. "You were *looking me up*, Adam Quyền. What's the Vietnamese equivalent of Google?"

"Cốc Cốc. And I *wasn't* looking you up," he fibs, with zero conviction.

During one of the sleepless nights since he kissed her outside her hut, he bought a digital copy of her book, read it (loved it, truth be told), then searched through everything he could find, like a stalker. Never, not even with Lana, had he bothered to do so much due diligence on a woman. But it is *her* fault, he thinks irritably, for not thoroughly filling out the dossier like the rest of the tour guests. He'll die before he admits how deep of a dive he really took. He even found a charming little poem about a one-legged pigeon that she wrote for a kids' literary magazine.

But she notices his flush right away and smirks. It would normally annoy him, but he's distracted by the way her freckle seems to dance when that animated face is moving. How she tucks a piece of her lower lip behind her teeth as if repressing her laugh.

"So what *does* being a poet laureate entail?" he demands.

"Of Midland? Well, it's a very prestigious role that I take seriously. I visit the senior center once a year and recite poetry while the octogenarians either tell me that nothing that isn't in iambic pentameter is worth reading or try to set me up with their grandsons."

"You could have taken them up on it and avoided this tour altogether."

"Unfortunately for me, their grandsons are still Boomer-adjacent."

"What does that mean?"

"Mostly that they lecture me on quiet quitting and my stubborn lack of home ownership. One of them told me it was pointless to become a writer, since we were all going to be replaced by AI in the next five years."

Adam's brow furrows. "Boomer-adjacent sounds like dimwit-adjacent."

"Exactly!" Evie says brightly. "Anyway, as the poet laureate, I also once almost cut a ribbon at a bookstore for the unveiling of their poetry section."

He shakes with laughter. "How does one almost cut a ribbon?"

"It turns out that some kid got impatient and hacked the ribbon apart before I could, so I just had to pose with the scissors like I did. I don't think I fooled anyone," she replies morosely. "Oh, and when that frozen yogurt place opened up, they put a signed copy of my book by their best pint of vegan cherry swirl."

"Wow. Those are . . . a lot of honors. Should I get your autograph now or later?"

"Probably never. My term as poet laureate is at an end. I'm sure they'll pick Lancaster Small as the next one. You can ask for *his* autograph, if you fight a line of young swains for it."

"Did you just make up that name?"

"Sadly, no," she says, a shadow of a smile in her voice. "Though I suspect he did. He's my former student. Student-turned-way-more-accomplished-poet. I'm the unemployed has-been struggling for her next big break. Doesn't fit on a business card, though. Ugh; sorry about this dumping. I'm in one of those career spirals. Have you ever been in one?"

Adam thinks. He supposes when he quit the bank that there was some relief in leaving that world behind. But he'd been satisfied enough with the work. It appealed to his sense of order. Now working on marketing for Love Yêu Tours is uncharted territory. He understands what he's doing in the *abstract* but hasn't gained enough confidence to know if he's dropping something important. It's like staring at a recipe, without any inkling of how to combine the ingredients.

"I guess I sometimes doubt that I'll be able to be everything my team needs. A good leader, a good coworker. I'm adept at some of it, sure. I like messing with the data. But marketing is a lot more creative than what I've done in the past, and I'm not naturally a creative person."

"I don't buy that."

"It's true. I tried to add a pie chart to the website, but Ruby made me cut it."

"So why're you doing it?" she asks curiously. "The marketing stuff?"

He shrugs. "I'm learning new things, and I like that. Plus, my sister asked."

"If she jumped off a bridge—" she murmurs.

"What?"

"Huh?"

"You said 'if she jumped off a bridge . . .'"

"American idiom. It's what mothers say to their foolish kids who follow the crowd to peril. The saying goes: If your friends jumped off a bridge, would you follow?"

"Are you calling me foolish?"

She winks. "If the shoe fits. Speaking of—do you know my shoe size? Did you find *that* in all your online stalking?"

"No." He reddens.

"I'm just saying that you're allowed to exist separately from your family. If you want. Many of us feel indebted to our parents, but the truth is, parenthood is a choice *they* made. We can't dedicate our lives to pleasing others. Love isn't transactional like that."

"That's very American of you."

Evie tosses her hair. "I think you mean, That's very wise of you, Evie Nichole Lang, my new life coach and mentor."

"Nichole's your middle name?"

She scoffs. "As if you didn't already know."

"I'll take the advice into consideration."

Watching him closely, the way his eyes narrow just slightly, she changes the topic. "Anyway, you've found out a lot about *me*. You probably discovered that time I got voted Most Likely to Get Lost in a Corn Maze in high school. It's only fair that you tell me something about *you*."

"What's a corn maze?"

"A Midwestern abomination that forces people to wander aimlessly around miles of corn for the sake of dubious leisure. Torture, but sometimes you get apple cider at the end of it. Tick-tock, pal."

She puts a hand on her waist, cocking her head expectantly.

"Okay! My real name is Bảo, as you know. My sister calls me Baby Bảo, which I hate."

"*That's* where the BB comes from. I like it—Bảo, that is."

"After an emperor, I'll remind you."

She smirks. "As if you needed any more air in that head of yours, Bảo."

Truth be told, he doesn't *hate* the way the name sounds in her mouth, her lips creating a tiny circle at the end of the vowel, like she's forming a whistle. Or puckering up for a kiss. When Ruby calls him Bảo, her tone makes it clear that she's establishing a power dynamic. There's an intimacy to the way Evie says his name that makes him blink down at her appraisingly.

She goes on. "But it's kinda weird, right? You're a man in his forties—"

"Thirties," he grits.

"And your sister treats you like either a baby brother or an employee. What's *with* that?"

"Your guess is as good as mine," he says.

By now, it's afternoon, and they're facing the emperor's twenty-ton stone stele lodged in a giant brick building. The huge tablet is partially a confessional, carved with almost five thousand characters detailing all the emperor's own mistakes and regrets throughout his reign. To look at the imposing stele is to be transported back in time. Evie and Adam crane their heads to take it all in.

"That is a *lot* of regret," she says.

And suddenly, Adam doesn't want to be surrounded by regret for a second longer. He wants to be on his bike again, coursing through the countryside, taking in all the beauty around him without thinking about Ruby or his parents or his job. And he wants to do it with *her*. Infuriating, unexpected, madcap Evie.

"Want to go for a ride?" he asks, holding out his hand.

She blinks. He can see her calculating the choice, and for a moment, he regrets saying anything. But a second later, her hand is in his. Her eyes, trusting and excited. A new feeling swells inside him, bubbles and warmth, and he lets himself savor it, like a perfect sip of champagne.

"If you harm a hair on this poet laureate's head, the mayor of Midland will hunt you down," she warns, fluffing the bottom of her hair for emphasis.

"I would expect no less."

"Oh, who am I kidding. They have Lancaster Small on speed dial."

On the bike, she tucks her body behind him, resting her helmeted head on his back. Her knees squeeze against his hips, and he can feel her fingertips clenched against his stomach in a death grip. He's about to call her out on it, but then the words die on his lips. He *likes* her clinging to him like this. He starts the motor and lets them fly.

Adam wouldn't have necessarily chosen to spend the day with Evie at a series of tombs, but sometimes, you take what you can get. Honestly, he likes that she's prone to wandering away from the crowd. It speaks to her rampant curiosity, so oversized and insistent that even Ruby's rigid tour structure can't contain her. He wouldn't have predicted it, but he enjoys wandering too. The world has opened in a way that feels utterly thrilling and confusing. For once, he's asking himself what he actually wants, digging through the layers of expectation to find his way to a tentative—and true—answer.

What he wants is more of *this*. Adventure. Being near Evie. Forgetting the rest of the world.

The Imperial Tomb of Đồng Khánh, their next stop, is only three kilometers away by the road hugging the Perfume River, but Adam stretches the trip, taking dips and turns where he can. He points out the open-air coffee shops with drop ceilings of woven grass, porches lined with bright, dangling lanterns and handwritten signs on slabs of wood. Thin lines of trees snake toward the river, which is now a golden thread in the distance, warmed by the afternoon sun. They can't speak much over the roar of the bike, but Adam feels Evie squeeze her fingers in excitement, wriggling behind him in that *thoroughly* distracting way.

"Stop it," he says through clenched teeth.

She doesn't, only wiggles *more* forcibly, causing the blood to rush to places it really shouldn't while he's driving. She says, a laugh deep in her voice, "Just pay attention to the road, Chú."

He growls. "If you call me that again, I will drop you off in the nearest corn maze and let you fend for yourself."

She releases an outraged sound behind him. "That was *not* meant to be ammunition. Ah, well, at least I didn't internet stalk you like a damn creepo."

He only shakes his head, unable to deny it. The smirk ticks up the corners of his mouth anyway. The Evie effect. Confusing. Stimulating. More distracting than any beautiful scenery in the Vietnamese countryside.

When they approach Vọng Cảnh Hill, a summit known for its epic views, Adam idles the engine. Once used as a strategic military site, the forty-three-meter-high hill is now a favorite gathering place for families and lovers. Everything shines green, like the heart of an emerald. It's enough to make anyone stop in their tracks.

"Can we go to the top?" Evie shouts, already slinging her leg out from behind him, lifting her helmet off her head. He mourns the loss of her warmth.

He's about to scowl at her for descending from the bike without waiting for him to fully stop, but as he watches her shake out her hair, glancing back at him with that mischievous, slightly daring smile, he doesn't say a word. He just follows.

I'm so fucking lost, he tells himself. He doesn't mean the path, of course. She leads him to places without a clear destination, and he is helpless to resist. A student of her whims. He can't decide how he feels about this.

They walk the steady slope of the road to the top of the hill. Looking out between the pines, they can see the vista stretching for miles and miles, revealing the languid flow of the river, the shadowy crests of mountains. Above them, sparse clouds dot the clear blue sky, like dandelion puffs that they can reach up and grab.

"This is a prime make-out spot," Evie says.

Adam turns to her, marking the way her smile flashes, brighter than the summer sun, and how she leans lazily against a tree. She's not batting her eyelashes, exactly, but there's definitely some significant blinking. A teasing air around her, a kind of invitation. He steps forward, ready to say—do—something. Ready to accept the invitation she's extending.

He feels himself tensing, reaching for her. Can he do it? Talk to her like a human, revealing everything he really feels about her, without all the jokes, all the carefully laid booby traps? He could release the barriers and find her somewhere on the other side of the stone walls. He could ask for a chance.

And if he's brave enough to ask for what he wants, maybe he can get it this time. The glimmer in her eye makes him think that anything is possible.

But then his phone buzzes. He tries to ignore it, but there it is again and again. Ruby.

BB—come back to the hotel.

I mean it. NOW.

The police are here.

EVIE

Huế, Việt Nam

When Adam and Evie rush into the hotel, there's a clamoring scene in the lobby, one that has drawn a crowd of people, some of whom are completely unrelated to the tour. Connor lies flat on the floor, splayed out with his eyes open, holding a cold compress to his nose, while Đức stands, handcuffed, beside two extremely unamused policemen in green uniforms. Cherie sobs next to him. Ruby has her eyes closed, fingers pressed to her temples.

"What's going on here?" Adam demands.

Around them, sitting at the edge of their seats on the chintz furniture like gladiator spectators, are Vietnamese aunties and grandmothers pointing at Connor and Đức alternately. They try to explain to Adam the situation with a series of wild speculations worthy of any Việt-dubbed Korean soap opera. It's a cacophony that makes Evie's head ache, even as she runs to Connor and kneels by his side.

"Are you okay? What do you need?" she demands, lifting the cold compress to check his nose, bleeding and bent at a slight angle. She can't remember if it was always that way.

Connor sounds nasally as he dabs at his nostrils. "I need a plastic surgeon. That fucker over there *punched* me."

"Why did he do that?" Evie glances over her shoulder at Đức, who looks decidedly unrepentant.

"Apparently, he's been sleeping with Veronica."

"Who?"

He gestures to a tall, thin woman calmly grabbing a drink at the bar. Ah, yes. Veronica the socialite from Hồ Chí Minh City. Evie has been so preoccupied she forgot that Connor and Veronica are a sort-of item now.

She helps Connor up, but before she can lead him away, Connor shrugs out of her hands and lunges toward Đức. Or, more accurately, toward the newsboy cap affixed on his head, as if it were his secret kryptonite. Đức screeches and holds up his fists, defending his headwear, while a policeman shouts them both down. Adam steps in and pulls Connor back firmly, muttering something under his breath that makes Connor stop struggling.

There's a resigned sigh around the room and a disapproving series of clucks from the aunties, both of which clue Evie in on the fact that this particular performance has been repeated quite a few times in a short span.

Cherie sobs, "Đức *can't* go to jail! He'd never make it in there."

Indignantly, Đức says, "Of course I can."

Connor hisses, "There are no *women to steal* in Chin Ham."

"No one's going to Chin Ham," Evie tries to put in. "What is Chin Ham?"

An auntie shouts helpfully, "It's a prison! We call it Hell on Earth!"

"Stop it right now," Adam shouts, his voice ringing with authority. "There's a man who's been severely hurt, by the looks of it, and you're all acting like it's a game show. You should be *ashamed*."

One of the aunties sniffs and says, "If you misbehave in public, you get a public judgment."

Another, perched on an ottoman, lifts a stack of bills in her hand. "I had my money on the scrawny one with the hat. Fights like an alley cat."

At that, Đức shoots her a wink, to which she adds doubtfully, "Not sure what that Veronica woman sees in him, though."

An octogenarian in an absurdly bright chartreuse áo dài huffs and points at Connor. "Ah, you're crazy! Look at that red hair! You think the gingerbread man doesn't have some fire in him?"

Đức's face falls while Connor smirks.

At that, Evie starts to giggle, which makes Adam glare at her. *You're not helping*, he seems to say with his eyes. She stares at her feet penitently, a ghost of a smile still playing on her lips. She thinks that if Connor is well enough to smirk, then the situation can't be so dire. But then she catches sight of the uniformed officers and resigns herself to silence.

Adam continues, "All right, everyone, that is enough. Cherie, please arrange to take Connor to the hospital to be examined. Ruby will go with you. I will talk to these officers. Everyone else, *please* disperse yourselves."

Why, exactly, is his authoritative tone *so* attractive right now? The twitch of his jaw makes parts of *her* twitchy.

A chorus of light groans and some pointed scowling emerges from the aunties, but Adam's voice carries a note of threat, and they comply. Evie is impressed that he's able to command a room so capably, though she does wonder why he feels the need to manage everything himself. It has to be a lot of pressure, she thinks.

"I'll see you later?" he mouths.

Nodding, Evie takes herself to the bar for a glass of sugarcane juice, cloudy with muddled mint and spiked with just a *little* gin. She gets out her notebook and poises her pen over the page. She finds that she has so much to say.

Despite the fistfight—or aftermath of it—Evie isn't thinking about the tour group. Her mind is on the slope of hills, the sight of the emperor's stele of regret. The flow of the Perfume River, a site made mythic by the people who flock to it, hoping for their own dash of romance.

It's not a lot, but a few lines come to her. Snatches of something new. Even as the bar crowd shuffles and turns over once, twice, she continues to scribble, head bent, biting the tip of her pen every so often.

She thinks about home and the myriad definitions of the word. Wasn't she writing about a kind of homecoming in *Auntie Hảo's Cabinet of Curiosities*? And isn't she writing about home now—home, laced with grief and gratitude and so many shades of longing? What would her father have made of all this? He'd never had a chance to return to Việt Nam after emigrating, but he'd kept the traditions in his own ways. Teaching Evie how to speak Vietnamese. Making sure they always had a plastic jar of đồ chua in the fridge. Observing Tết and the seasonal festivals. She pictures him standing at the stern of a boat—young, healthy—with his hair blowing in the sea breeze, admiring the wood carvings that she'd seen that day.

In another life. Another timeline.

A tear drips onto her notebook, but she doesn't move to wipe it away. It's part of this story too. Home has never been just a location for her; not Midland, not Việt Nam, not even San Francisco. It's the people. The rituals. That sense of safety, knowing that you can be as strange and messy as you need to, and still, there will be a place for you.

She writes until her hand cramps and her stomach grumbles. Doubtless, the rest of the group will be sitting down to the formal dinner, but she doesn't want to leave yet. She orders a crispy seafood bánh khoái, with a starfruit-studded salad on the side. As she's about to put a bite of the pancake in her mouth, Riley sits next to her with a grin. She'd expected to see him at the tombs, but he surprised everyone by going to the spa instead.

"Up for sharing?" he asks.

Reluctantly, she puts some on a plate for him. He orders himself a beer. She notices that he's glowing, face pink and dewy from the spa treatment. He really is an attractive man. A bit shiny at the moment, but no one's perfect.

"You're luminous," she comments.

He pats his face. "Thanks. I figure, how often is it that I get to do a full-service spa treatment at the most luxurious hotel in Huế?"

"You're making me regret the tombs," she laughs, not meaning it.

"I bet they were something. Is it true that Emperor Tự Đức isn't even buried in his own tombs?"

"Yes! *And* the asshole's remains have never been found."

"Imagine walking through a garden and tripping on an emperor's shin-bone poking through the soil."

Evie shudders. "Thanks, but no."

"It's been a while since we've talked. I almost wondered if you were avoiding me."

"Oh! Not at all."

Truly, Evie hasn't much thought of Riley in a few days. Among her mother's email, her emerging friendships, and a certain dark-eyed, firm-jawed CMO, she hasn't had much time.

He smiles. "Well, I don't think I've made my interest unclear, right?"

"Noo-o-o," she says, drawing out the word. She blinks into his attentive gaze. He's been perfectly clear. She's the one who's unclear about what she wants.

"So, would you want to go on a date with me?"

"A date."

"Yes, you know. The *point* of this tour? I'd like to take you to the garden houses. Maybe hunt for the emperor's corpse. I'm sure Ruby will be able to arrange something in a jiff."

"Oh, I wouldn't be too sure about that." Briefly, Evie describes what happened in the lobby, leaving out the way her breath quickened at the sight of Adam taking charge. "Anyway, I saw Connor going back up the stairs earlier, so I think everything's okay with his nose."

"Ha! I guess that explains why I saw Đức's bags outside the hotel. Poor guy. Kicked off the island in infamy."

Evie will miss Đức. She'd admired the way he'd seized the experience—perhaps too much, in retrospect—and made the most out of every excursion. He was never afraid to say what he wanted, and in the process had likely inspired others to live more boldly (if ridiculously) too. That was the whole point, right?

Still, you can't exactly uppercut a tour guest as a paid employee and get off without consequences.

Riley clears his throat. "Well, anyway. Public fisticuffs aside, what do you say? You're the only woman here I'm interested in. We have so much in common, and I want to keep talking to you as much as I can in the time we have left. I'd hand you a rose, but all I have is this flame flower I picked."

He sets the red bloom in front of her. It touches Evie, that he thought to do this. She considers him. Riley is attractive, sweet, interesting—and interested in her. Wasn't this what Auntie Hảo intended when she arranged this posthumous little bargain? What had she said—*love bravely*. What would it hurt to be a little more adventurous?

Her mind falls on Adam, as it frequently does these days. There are so many *almosts* between them. Will they ever get the chance to finish anything together?

Then she shakes the thought of him away. They have no commitments to each other. If anything, he swings hot and cold depending on the day. They kiss (or almost-kiss)—then he disappears. It's the pattern of a commitment-phobe, and Evie knows something about *those* from her illustrious dating career. Maybe going on a date with Riley won't lead to anything. But he's there and he's willing to go all-in on her. That isn't something to throw away without some consideration.

Evie tucks the flower behind her ear. "I'd be honored to go corpse-digging with you, Riley."

Breakfast the next morning is a stilted, almost funereal affair. Ruby is wan and lackluster, struggling to pin her usual strident good cheer onto her face. From what Evie can tell, Đức was evicted late last night, and Connor, though just a little battered, is pouting in his room, refusing to come out. Cherie can hardly keep herself from sobbing into her bowl of hủ tiếu. And Adam—well, Adam is shooting death-daggers at her and Riley, who's talking animatedly next to her.

"The ancient garden houses are a testament to feudal architecture—living history that you can walk around in," Riley says expansively, gesturing with his coffee mug in emphasis.

"You mean, like all of Việt Nam?" Adam mutters.

Ruby says, "I've arranged for a private musical performance at the An Hiên garden house for you two. Followed by a European-style picnic on the grounds. Your car should be out front any moment now."

Riley beams at Evie, then holds out his hand. Awkwardly, she rises to join him. Now Adam is outright glowering, the frown on his face so stern that it reminds her of storm clouds passing on an otherwise sunny day. Threatening. Why does a part of her *like* that he's looking that way? If anything, it shows that he cares.

As Evie follows Riley out, she feels a hand on her elbow. Hears a voice in her ear.

Adam whispers gruffly, yet so low that only she can hear, "We're not done, Evie Nichole."

Her insides clench in the most pleasurable, addictive way. *More.* Her betraying heart skips, on high alert as always, when he is near. All she wants is to face him, to hear what it is he has in mind, but there's a crowd, and Riley waiting expectantly for her. She draws away from Adam, hoping that her gulp isn't an audible one. But when she looks back, Adam gives her a slow, sensuous smile. A promise.

So much trouble, she thinks.

That day, the hours seem to draw out like unspooling thread. She and Riley explore the lush gardens with their stone walkways and arching greenery. The musical performance in the pavilion is achingly beautiful, that unique and transportive brand of ballads that Việt Nam is known for. And later, as they enjoy the picnic with tiny rounds of brie and jars of fig jam on a blanket overlooking a pond, Evie thinks of how lucky she is to be able to experience such a thing. By all measures, it's a perfectly romantic day, full of good conversation and incredible sights.

"I wish I could stay here forever," she says.

Riley agrees, "That would be just a dream. But you'd like Nashville. It's full of history too. I want to show you around, Evie. I want you to meet my friends. You're the first woman who's interested me like this. The first one that I can really see fitting into my life."

She makes a noncommittal noise, shoving a piece of baguette into her mouth.

He says, "Unless you don't want that."

He studies her before his face falls. She hates hurting him like this. But the whole day has been completely, one hundred percent platonic. That's not what a great love affair should feel like. She'd made a vow to be honest with herself on this trip. And she honestly can't make herself feel anything more than friendly affection for Riley.

He leans forward, asking simply, "Could you see yourself with me back in the States?"

And Evie tries to imagine it. Moving to Nashville. Dating Riley—and possibly more. She *knows* his world. How easy it would be to slide herself into it, possibly get a job at Vanderbilt or a nearby college. Going to those readings again, making conversation with people who regularly quote Derrida (Derr-i-*dah*). It would be a seamless fit, making a life with Riley.

Yet all she can imagine is Adam's hot breath on her cheek. The way he makes her feel flushed from the inside out, as if there's a fire stoking in the pit of her belly. How she thinks of him constantly, even on this date, wishing that he were next to her. Longing for his banter, the way his laugh can make her so giddy, as if she's earned a great treasure. Wanting to speed up every moment they're apart until they can be in the same room, touching again. Isn't *that* what love should feel like? Maybe it's just lust.

But even still, for all of Riley's many wonderful qualities, something inside of her turns away from what he offers.

Loving bravely also means knowing to let go of an option, especially when there's something else out there you want more. Even if that something scares the daylights out of you.

"Listen," she begins.

Riley draws back.

"Ah," he says, a little sadly. "I see."

"Riley—"

He swallows and manages a smile. "Don't worry, Evie. I'm not heartbroken. And I don't regret meeting you or anything."

"Me either."

"Some things aren't meant to be. It's nice to be with another academic whom I don't find to be a total asshole."

"You can change your mind about me at any time," Evie says miserably.

He gives her a peck on the cheek. "Hope not. Friends?"

"Friends," she says, adding a fervent and hopeful emphasis to the word.

As he gets up to brush the crumbs from his lap, he looks down at her once more. There's a crook to his lips as he says, "I hope he treats you well."

"Hm?" she says, feigning ignorance.

He ignores her. "But I have my doubts. Take it from me: Adam Quyền is not the type of man who will ever settle down. He's not looking for anything serious. Not after his ex."

"His ex?" Adam hasn't talked about her in great detail.

"He proposed to her. It ended badly. I heard Ruby and Adam talking about her—Lana, I think it was. I don't think Adam is over her."

Then Evie is left in the garden among the fragrant blooms, the gentle ruffle of the wind, with Riley's words in her ears. *Not the type of man who will ever settle down.* Does she want to settle down? There's a vision, then, of Adam in bed next to her, his hair mussed from sleep. He's leaning on one arm, staring down at her with those gorgeous dark eyes, tracing her lips with one finger.

I don't think Adam is over her. Evie doesn't have any reason to be jealous, but the thought of Adam proposing to someone else, making a life with a faceless-but-likely-stunning woman, makes her feel slightly nauseated. No wonder he's so hot and cold. He doesn't know what he wants either.

They are two lost people finding comfort in one another for a brief time.

Is this spiky, electric thing between them just a fleeting fantasy, something summoned by the outrageously romantic circumstances of this tour? Where would they go, in real life? To Midland? She can't imagine him there. Would she stay in Hồ Chí Minh City? He'd get bored of her ambling around in his space, never fitting in with his well-heeled friends.

What if Riley is right, and she is just a diversion for Adam, a way to pass these three weeks, an ego boost after his breakup? After all, he wasn't exactly clamoring for love at the beginning of the tour. What if he was trying to tell her how he felt all along, and she was just too infatuated to hear it?

Not for the first time, doubts begin to crowd her thoughts, jumbling her so much that she finds herself unable to trace her way back to her own emotions.

ADAM

Huế, Việt Nam

Connor doesn't emerge from his room until a quarter past six. Adam knows this, because he's been holed up with Connor for the better part of the day, trying to convince him to rejoin the tour, despite Veronica's cruel, two-timing heart and the slap-punch heard around Huế.

Connor spends most of the hours ranting about suing Đức and Love Yêu Tours, though Adam takes neither declaration seriously. And while Connor's dramatics—throwing pillows across the room, wailing into his own reflection—are undeniably tiresome, Adam understands where he's coming from. Betrayal is a bitch. It was, after all, what prevented Adam from ever thinking about a woman with serious intentions. Until now.

The whole time Adam is coaxing Connor down, he can't stop imagining Evie and Riley on their date. Would they be strolling hand-in-hand? Would Riley try to kiss her under an archway of blooms? Would Evie *let* him? The thought makes Adam clench his fists. He knows he has no right to be possessive, but the notion of *anyone* touching Evie fills him with a fury he's never felt. It's primal to want someone like this. Uncomfortable.

But he can't help himself. All he wants is to grab her as soon as she comes back, take her to his room, and finish what they've started—again and again. Kissing her lips until she's forgotten her name. Licking down every inch of bare skin until she shudders into him—

"You coming to dinner?" Connor asks, his hand on the doorjamb, all prior melodramatics forgotten at the thought of a hot meal.

Adam shakes his head tightly. He's in no mood to see anyone. And if he meets Riley, he's afraid he'll try to punch him or something equally steeped in unnecessary machismo. Two physical assaults on one tour. Doesn't seem like the best advertising. Instead, Adam stalks to his room and takes a very cold shower, trying (and failing) not to think about Evie.

The next day, Riley, Fen, Adam, and Evie are due to go on an overnight expedition to the massive caves near the village of Phong Nha while the rest of the group visits the Museum of Royal Antiquities. There's a slow, gray drizzle outside, and most everyone prefers the warmth of the museum—or better yet, a cozy day at the hotel, enjoying all the amenities and playing card games in their robes while drinking thick, French-style hot chocolate. This is what he finds the tour's older contingent doing, all while heckling the younger folks for venturing out in the rain like fools.

But Adam is anxious to see the much-lauded caves, known as some of the largest in the world. The four guests will get private access to the campgrounds, situated right at the mouth of one of the openings, a rare perk that few will ever experience. Early in the morning, Adam sets out to buy a plastic poncho for himself from a shop near the hotel—and on second thought, gets ponchos for the rest of the group. They'll stay dry once they're inside the caves, but the hike there will be wet. He shoves the ponchos into his backpack, then adds a change of clothes, nuts and dried fruit from the Dong Ba Market, and plenty of water.

Downstairs in the lobby, the first tour group is leaving for the museum. Just before Fen joins them, she slips something in Evie's hand that makes Evie redden tremendously, fumbling to push Fen's gift into her pocket before anyone can see. Cackling, Fen blows Evie a kiss, to which Evie responds with a lift of her middle finger.

"The universal gesture of conviviality," Adam says.

Evie turns, still a little red. He likes seeing her flustered, unsure for once, though he would prefer to be the cause of it. Today she wears a pair of skintight leggings that hug every curve, sending a jolt of arousal through him. Her crop top reveals a few inches of tanned skin, on top of which hangs an unzipped, slightly oversized hoodie. Her hair is swept into a bun on her head with one of those ridiculous pens of hers that constantly fall out, clattering on the ground as her unruly strands release.

"Why are you looking at me like that?" she demands. She runs her tongue over her teeth. "Do I have watercress in my teeth?"

He clears his throat. "Isn't Fen coming?"

"No." She rolls her eyes. "She changed her mind at the last minute. Said that if she sprained her ankle in a wet cave, her agent would have her head. Then she proceeded to explain to me how every inch of her body is insured and would I want to be the cause of such a loss to the world?"

"The cinematic gods would never forgive us. What'd she give you just now?"

"None of your business," she snaps.

Again, that poppy-red flush. The embarrassed bite of her lip. Adam swallows a groan. How is she so damn sexy when she's just *standing* there in tennis shoes and a messy bun?

"Okay," he says with amusement. "Keep your secret. We just waiting for Riley?"

"Erm, no," she mumbles. She picks up her backpack—a tiny thing that likely holds little more than a water bottle and that notebook she's always carrying around—and makes for the lobby doors. "He said he had indigestion. Or something."

"*Or something*," Adam repeats. He hides a smile as he trots next to her. "Does that mean your romantic date didn't go well?"

"Again, none of your business, Curious George."

"What happened? Did he bore you to death? Try to get you to read his new manuscript?"

"So what if he did? *Some* of us like to consume literature more current than Tolstoy."

"*Dusted annals driven to a shelf—hieroglyphs of a broken heart—*"

He hadn't meant to say that aloud. But the words are inside of him now, memorized as if they were a part of his own history.

She stops suddenly, making him crash into her. Her eyes widen. "You read my poems?"

"Your whole book."

"And you hated it." She raises her eyebrows, arms crossed, a defensive pose meant to field criticism. Yet somewhere on her scowling face is a raw vulnerability she's trying to hide. She cares about what he thinks, even if she believes he doesn't like her work. It hurts him to see her like this. Why would she think anyone could hate her words? He'd devoured every single poem, each describing the yearning of the diaspora, the weight of history. Longing threads across each line. Her imagery is precise, her language at turns lyric and then shockingly brusque. An echo of her soul, he likes to think. Honest and complicated and worthy of many rereadings.

But he doesn't say this. He just takes an extra poncho out of his bag and drapes it on her body. He pulls up the hood so it covers her head. There's a tenderness to the gesture that makes his heart thud a little louder. It feels *right*. He's happy just being around her, protecting her, listening to her. This quiet joy is different but related to the arousal he feels every time she makes her way across his sight line.

What is this thing between them? It's not love. It's much, much too soon for that. It took him years to tell Lana he loved her. But Adam has to admit that it's more than lust with Evie. Lust-plus.

In her ear, he whispers, "I loved every fucking word."

The surprised gratitude on her face is almost enough to make him melt.

Later, their guide, Hải, drives them to the paths leading to Hang Én, one of the largest caves in the world, and the place where they will be spending the night. Through the car window, Adam watches the slow fall of the rain, the way the threads crisscross and waver, a thousand pearls clinging to the windshield. The guide describes underground rivers where they can swim and passages leading to the jungles. Tenth-century religious altars can still be found in the depths of the caves. Adam watches Evie's eyes widen at Hải's descriptions, her wonder bubbling to the surface.

"I can't wait," she breathes.

"Not a nice day to hike," Hải says, glancing back at them in the rear-view mirror.

"Good day to swim in a cave, though," Adam says. Not that he brought a swimsuit. It's the one thing he forgot.

"You want to turn back?"

Adam gives Evie a questioning look, but she shakes her head firmly. "Not on your life."

They trek for hours through a jungle, grateful for the ponchos as they huddle under whatever available tree cover they can find. The rain starts and stops, punctuated by bright bursts of sunlight that don't seem to last more than a few minutes. Evie doesn't complain even a little, though Adam can hear her breath start to quicken as the uphill climbs get steeper. He slows his pace so they can walk side by side.

Hải leads the way with a humongous backpack jammed with supplies. They stop for lunch at the Ban Doong village, where the Bru-Van Kieu, an ethnic minority of Việt Nam, lives. Over fish soup and bowls of rice, villagers talk about their ancestors' escape from the great flood, and how their small school emerged to serve the community. Adam and Evie listen, rapt.

Afterward, Evie plays with the children, who gravitate to her like she's their personal jungle gym. They hang off her, braiding her hair, offering her bites of food. Her clear laugh lights up the huts. She dances a little cloth doll around one girl's forearm, making her giggle. Another child tries to feed her a piece of banana.

"Your wife wants children, yes?" Hải asks Adam in a low voice.

Adam starts. "No, she's not—"

"Take it from me, my children are the treasures of my life. They require time, they require money, but you won't regret them. You give her babies. Lots of babies. My wife is pregnant right now!"

Unbidden, the image of Evie with a child in her arms rises in Adam's mind. Rocking slowly in a nursery glider while he stands in the doorway, beaming. He shakes the thought violently away.

"I hardly know that woman," he tells Hải, his voice gruff even to his own ears. "We met a couple weeks ago."

"No?"

"Yes."

"Your hearts have met long before that, I think," the other man says. "You remind me of my wife and me. Twinned souls. This is a rare thing— and rarer still when those souls are so at odds."

At that point, Evie finally, laughingly sheds her fan club of children and makes her way to them. "We're losing light, gentlemen. Chop-chop."

"Is that another inane Americanism?" Adam mutters.

Evie fluffs her hair and leads the way back onto the trail.

Sweaty but invigorated by the sudden spot of sunshine in Ban Doong, the three of them slosh through a damp valley on limestone paths and soon arrive at a cave entrance—the most remote one—shaped like a wide, gaping eye. Water dimples the surface of the silt-colored water. Because of the rain, which had picked up after they left the village, they are the only ones at Hang Én that day. The guide tells them that they are likely to be the only people around for the next day or so due to the unexpected storms.

"I don't mind," Evie says.

"Turn around," Adam tells her.

Though she is facing the interior of the cave, staring at the rough patterns on the walls, she obliges, pivoting her gaze back toward the jungle, which now reveals a cinematic vista of the towering trees and the streaming water. The scene looks utterly untouched, especially without the crowds, and Evie gasps at the sight, so unlike anything either of them has seen. They could have been in another era entirely.

She reaches for his hand and squeezes. His heart flips.

"Is this real life?" she whispers.

"I'm not sure. It could be a dream. Primordial."

"Magical."

The paths are muddy and slippery, but Evie presses on, leading them into the interior of the cave. Around them, the light buzzing of insects, settling in for the evening.

"Maybe she should be the guide," Hải says.

Adam shoots him a wry smile. "I think she would prefer that."

Once inside, they set their things as far from the opening as they can to avoid the wet splatter of rain, coming down ever faster now. Hải builds a small fire and tells them to explore while he sets up the tents. He urges them to swim in the water, cooled by the shade. A perfect antidote to the humid jungle heat.

Evie whispers to Adam, "I probably shouldn't tell him I intend on skinny-dipping when his back is turned. I forgot my bathing suit."

Adam grits his teeth at the image.

Inside the cave, there's a palpable feeling of crystallized awe, a settled solemnity earned from centuries of formation and repose. Timeless, yet constantly shifting. The light refracts and diffuses in a golden stream, grazing the surface of the rocks, the soft yellow sand. There's an almost animal-like musk in the air, something sensuous and questing.

Soon they arrive at the opening of a dark, narrow tunnel. There's too little room, so they crowd against each other, hip to hip. It would take next to nothing for Adam to place his hand on her waist, tug her in front of him, where she would feel the hardness of his desire for her. But he doesn't. He backs away.

"We should get headlamps if we go any further," he says. "Let's return."

Back at the campsite, Hải kneels before the fire, peering at his satellite phone with concern. When he sees them, he brushes the dirt from his knees.

"I'm so sorry to do this," he says. "My wife is giving birth. The baby is coming early—too early. I have to return to her."

"Of course you do," Evie says. She puts a hand on his arm. "What can we do?"

"Nothing; I just need to go now, so I'll make it back."

"It's not too dark?" Adam asks. The dusk is settling in, and it will likely be an hour or two tops before the sun disappears completely.

"I'll have my lantern. I'm used to this. But you—" Here, Hải glances around the cave, at the display of tents. "You'll come with me?"

"I think that'd just slow you down," Evie says, frowning. "Besides, I'd like to see the caves. Stay the night like we planned. I think we'll be fine. It's just one night."

She throws a questioning glance at Adam, who nods firmly. "Yes, we will be."

"I can send another guide in the morning to get you home," Hải says, a bit uncertainly. "You're sure you'll be all right by yourselves for the night?"

Adam says, "Completely. I won't leave her side."

Evie says indignantly, "Hey. I'm not some helpless damsel in a cave. Maybe you're the one that needs me not to leave *your* side."

"But what about the tigers?" Adam teases.

Evie narrows her eyes, then turns to the guide. "Just go take care of your family, Hải."

The other man nods, too distracted by the thought of his wife to protest. He deposits most of the food and supplies for them, as well as an extra satellite phone. His backpack thus lightened, he begins to make his way back through the entrance. He waves, disappearing into the trees, now fleet-footed without two extra hikers dragging him down. The rain has almost stopped, save an occasional flicker of wetness from the shaking branches.

And then it's just the two of them. Evie and Adam, stuck in a remote cave, miles and miles from civilization. Alone. It'll be a miracle if they survive the night without murdering each other, Adam thinks. It's that or screwing one another senseless. With her, there's absolutely no in-between.

EVIE

Huế, Việt Nam

They're quiet for a moment, huddled next to the fire, listening to the dying sounds of the day.

Then, in a small voice, Evie asks, "Are there really tigers?"

"Well, yes, but not many in the wild anymore. Unfortunately. But even if there were, they won't get close to the caves."

"How do you know?"

"They're not exactly eager to meet humans, and these caves are tourist destinations."

"Not today," Evie says, gesturing around. "I can hear my own heart thudding out here. And your annoying voice."

"You *love* my annoying voice."

"In small—very small—doses."

He grins at her lukewarm admission. "I'll take it. So, what do you want to do?"

It's Evie's turn to tease. "Quote each other's poetry?"

Adam flushes. Evie takes the opportunity to drink in his handsome features, lit by the flicker of the fire. Those beautiful, lush lips. The way his forearms clench and thicken as he busies himself, adjusting tents and lanterns around the campsite. Not meeting her gaze.

But she knows his secret now. He researched her. He read her *poetry*. This is more than many of her actual boyfriends have done. It thrills her, this sudden realization. And all she wants to do is shake him up. *Make* him pay attention to her. For days, whatever is between them has been simmering away. All she wants is to find that release. To lay it all out on the table.

With that thought, while his back is turned, she shucks off her hoodie, then her tank top. The leggings and underwear go flying soon after. She whoops and runs. By the time he's twisted toward the sound, she's already neck-deep in the small pool in the heart of the cave, near the dark tunnel they didn't enter. She splutters in the cold water. It's silk on her skin. A lover's caress. Adam's eyes widen as he takes in her bare shoulders, the slight swell along the top of her breasts.

"I told you I forgot my suit," she yells.

His face reflects indecision. There's a moment of choice. She sees it happening in front of her, that relentless mind weighing the costs. But just this once, she wants him to stop thinking.

"Come in," she calls. Then, more softly, "Please."

"I don't think you want me to do that," he rasps.

"I don't think you *know* what I want," she says, fluttering her lashes. "In fact, I think you might be a little scared of what I want."

Something glimmers in his eyes, just for a second, like a hot spark hitting dry hay. Challenge, answering hers. He begins peeling off his clothes. Even though she knows she should give him privacy, she can't take her eyes off him. And she nearly comes undone when he holds her gaze as he lifts his shirt, then steps out of his pants and boxers. She gasps at the sight of him, shadowed by the fading sunlight. His perfect abs leading down to a dip next to his hipbone and then the solid length of him, every inch of his body muscled, taut. Waiting for something. Waiting for her.

Then he's in the water, silently gliding closer. She thinks there's something panther-like about him, this air of power and danger. His arms loosely encircle her body, but he leaves some space between them. Leaving it up to her.

"So what do you want, sweetheart?" he asks.

She shivers. It takes her no time at all to surge up toward his body, wrapping her legs around his waist. His breath quickens, fast and hot on her face. She feels his hard length underneath her.

"Fuck, Evie," he mumbles.

She leans over and whispers in his ear, "It was a condom. Fen gave me a condom."

Adam makes a noise from deep in his throat, something like a growl, pure animal, pure want, and slams his lips on hers. This time, there's no hesitation. He takes the kiss from her roughly, parting her mouth with his tongue, drawing out the quiet mews as she sags under the headiness of his kiss. Her fingers entwine in his hair. And his fingers . . . God, his fingers are everywhere. In the dip of her back. Molding down her body, thumbs rubbing over her erect nipples, palming her abdomen. The water swishes around them.

"Don't stop," she murmurs.

"Are you sure, baby?" he asks, his voice low and gravelly with desire. She shudders at the endearment. "Because once I start, a goddamn earthquake would not stop me."

When she nods, unable to speak, caught up in the waves of pleasure he's wringing from her body, his fingers travel lower, until they find the slick heat of her. He's stroking softly at first, but then, once he finds the most sensitive parts of her, he rubs with insistency, sending her mind reeling. But it's not thoughts that run through her mind—she sees colors, hears the sound of the lapping water, of his heavy breath. She *feels*.

Then he slips a finger inside her. She nearly comes apart then, but he continues to push her past the limits of pleasure, stroking as his fingers— two now—enter and exit her in a slow, punishing rhythm that makes her writhe against him. He hits *every* nerve ending.

"Yes," she gasps. "Faster."

"You're so ready for me," he says. "Show me how you come, sweetheart."

The universe expands and contracts at his words. She's so close to her pleasure. So close to him. His fingers dance in and out of her, excavating the wetness inside her.

"Adam," she says, voice catching. "Please—"

He captures her mouth just as she comes in shuddering breaths that leave her body feeling like seaweed, loose and untethered from the world. He kisses her back to earth with slow and tender little touches that make her feel like she's floating. She is floating. He holds her up, breathing into her neck. As he removes his fingers, she's conscious of the way she's clinging to him, resting her head against his chest.

That was, by far, the hottest experience of her life. She could sleep for a thousand years in the aftermath of her pleasure.

But, underneath her, he's still thick and throbbing. She wants to give him the same pleasure he gave her.

With Herculean effort, she unwinds her legs. He makes a gesture of protest as if to cradle her back to him, but then she swims away from him to the edge of the pond. Slowly, feeling her power, she allows him to watch her as she sashays out of the water, landing at the edge of the tarp near their campsite. She sits, wet and naked, arms placed behind her body so that it's thrust out, like an offering for him.

"Come here," she commands.

In a second, he's out of the water too, and his body is poised on top of hers. With one deft, unusually athletic movement, she switches their bodies so she's on top of him. She takes his lips, tugging on his bottom lip lightly with her teeth. He curses under his breath, which makes her smile and take her time winding her way down his body, kissing languidly, until she can take his throbbing length fully into her mouth.

"Oh, my God," he says. "This is—you are—"

She continues to suck and stroke, touching his inner thighs, all the secret places of his. She feels no shame in her exploration. She thinks, *Whatever is between us, that's all there is.* Tension builds in her own thighs and all she wants is to get on top of him. To join him. All she wants is *more*.

"More, huh?" he asks roughly.

She hadn't realized she said it aloud, but now she reaches for the condom from the depths of her backpack and rips it open. She drapes it on him.

"More everything," she breathes.

Then, never losing eye contact, she lowers herself on top of him. His mouth drops open as he enters her. She lifts herself off his body, then rapidly descends, wringing a surprised, ecstatic grunt from him. The way they fit is like nothing she's ever experienced. Heat and wetness and friction that builds, like a flood, sending shivers of sensation up her legs, into her senseless brain that is lit up with nothing but pure bliss.

She leans over to kiss him, and he's grabbing her ass, directing her where he wants to go. Never losing control, even when she's on top. They're going faster and harder and now, there's no turning back for her. The stars get close again.

She bites her lip, moaning as he hits the parts of her that no one else has managed to, sparking something teasing, something immeasurably sweet inside her.

He says, with a kind of fierce savagery dragged from deep inside, "Baby, it's just us. Scream as loud as you want."

And she does. She screams his name again and again as he switches position, pounding harder into her every time, until it feels like they are inseparable. She wraps her legs around his waist and he gives one final, heady thrust as they both come undone together, exploding into a heap of spent pleasure and delicious, thrilling sensation.

They lie still, with his head on her shoulder, her legs still wrapped around him. Their breaths are perfectly in tune. To Adam and Evie, at this moment, there's no cave. There's no pond, no prowling tigers or looming forests. It's just the two of them, lost in an incandescent world of their own making.

ADAM

Huế, Việt Nam

Hours later, Adam finds himself watching Evie doze, her hand curled under her head like a pillow. He's draped a poncho over her, but there's no hiding the lines of her body, the sheer beauty of her sleeping form. A small, satisfied smile peeks from her face, the unconscious signal of joy, of trust. A smile *he* helped summon.

This knowledge wrings something precious out of him, a sensation a shade too close to . . . what is it? *Adoration.*

He wants to cover her body with his own—to make love to her again and again, yes, but it's more than that. He just wants to watch her sleep, every night, preferably in the crook of his arm, her warm body pressed to his. He just wants more of *her*. The thought fills him with panic so gripping that he turns to busy himself with dinner preparation, away from her, so as not to give in to it.

Night has fully descended. There's a smattering of stars shining through the opening of the cave. But the quiet does nothing for his racing thoughts. He's in deep. And what will he do when she leaves to go back to America, to her friends and family? He can't follow; there's nothing for him there. But why would she stay in Việt Nam? Their future is tenuous at best—and impossible at worst. Yet the thought of losing her is like a brick thrown at his heart.

After he's done reheating the cơm tấm packed into thermoses over the portable stove, she begins to stir, awakened by the smell of pork chops and scallion-flecked rice.

"I hope I'm not dreaming this," she says, eyeing the stove.

"You dream of dank caves in the middle of nowhere?"

"Judge not, for ye might be in those dreams," she intones with a wink.

"Hungry?" he asks, holding out a thermos.

"As a tiger."

She reaches for her hoodie and zips it over herself, then crawls onto the sand and takes the thermos from him. After her first bite, she makes a noise that's a shade from rapture. Adam notes amusedly: *Got it. Don't let her get hungry.*

They eat in silence, watching the flicker of the fire, sparks rising to meet the dark night. There's a nervous tension between them, an unwillingness to speak and spoil this spellbound night. Adam sees it in the way she avoids his eyes. The shy way she reaches over him for the metal cup. Once they're finished with dinner, she finally turns to him.

"I don't think I've ever been so hungry before."

"We worked up an appetite."

"The hike?" She blinks innocently.

He tucks a strand of hair behind her ear. Her eyes widen, and it guts him, her surprise. Is tenderness such a foreign concept to her? With a sigh, he leans over and takes her lips, gently, with a slow rhythm that nevertheless builds the heat inside him. For a sweet second, she returns the kiss, nipping at his bottom lip. Running her fingertips up the column of his neck. They dance closer and closer to the edge of their desire.

"It was good, right?" she asks.

He says, truthfully, "I haven't felt this good in so long."

At his words, she seems to withdraw slightly. She stares up at the walls of the cave, as if she might find an answer there. What did he say? The silence that grows between them feels cold and uncertain. Typically, he might withdraw too, giving her space. But he doesn't feel like doing things the old way. If she's uncertain or sad or scared, he wants to know. He wants to be the one to banish the worries from her constantly active brain.

"What is it?" he asks. He reaches for her hand.

She shifts, then meets his eyes. "Tell me about Lana."

"Lana." He feels his face clearing of emotion. That's the effect his ex has on him. Sterilizing.

She blurts, "I know you probably don't want to talk about her, especially to me. I mean, you don't owe me anything. And it's not like we're giving background information on our dating history. Heaven knows you don't want to hear about that time I accidentally flashed a Jonas brother at the airport. But Riley mentioned her, and it seemed really serious, and—okay, forget I said anything."

He sighs but doesn't drop her hand. "Gossiping is a national pastime here in Việt Nam, so I guess I'm not surprised that my business is out there."

"You don't have to talk about it," she says in a small voice.

"If you're asking, I want to talk about it," he says firmly. "I want you to know."

An image of Lana rises in his mind. Her face was once so vivid to him, but now he finds that he can only remember the broadest of strokes. Lana was—is—impeccable, with rounded, serene features and a soothing presence that belies her unquenchable ambition. She was great at tennis and always wanted one of those annoying bichon frise dogs. Incredible at her job. Good with his family and friends. In so many ways, a perfect fit.

"We both worked in finance. Her parents had known mine, so growing up, there was this kind of foregone conclusion that we'd eventually date. The world we grew up in—it was tight. Small. Protective. But for a long time, Lana was a safe port in all the machinations. She was kind and thoughtful and liked the same things I liked. She felt . . . transparent. Understandable."

Evie nods encouragingly, but he thinks he can see a flash of something in her eyes. A question? But she remains silent, her hand steady in his.

He continues, "Up until the dinner when I proposed to Lana, when I saw the panic in her eyes, the way she began shaking her head before I even stopped speaking. It turned out that she had been having an affair with my father's sixty-year-old colleague, a cardiologist with a yacht."

Her jaw drops open. "Oh, my God."

"A man that had given me red envelopes stuffed with money for Tết as a child."

"That's—psychotic," she sputters. "I have no words. No, wait, that's not true. I have all the words."

He grins. Of course she does. "Let's hear them."

She explodes. "How could anyone do that to a person they love? I know you cared about her, but damn if she isn't due to sit in some circle of hell with her moldy old cardiologist. I hope rabid chipmunks peel their hangnails until the end of time and they have eternal insomnia and the only thing they have to watch on TV is the last season of *Game of Thrones*. I hope they get force-fed candy corn until their poop runs orange and their teeth rot. I hope—"

Adam lets out a surprised laugh, gratified to hear her outrage on his behalf. He hadn't realized it, but for so long, he was hoping someone would take his side. See how he hurt. Ruby was sympathetic but distant, claiming she'd never liked Lana much to begin with—too much competition between the two. His parents found a way to blame him for it, telling him he should have known better before subjecting their family to such public humiliation. And maybe a part of him blamed himself for not paying more attention to the demise of his own relationship.

Their friends and families just wanted to move past the unpleasantness as quickly as possible, shoving everything into a dark corner. His pain had been an inconvenience to the charade.

"And you were heartbroken?" she asks, more softly now that she's gotten all the curses out of her.

"My ego was shattered," he admits. "But my heart? I don't know. I'm all right. Embarrassed, but not heartbroken. Maybe I'm just heartless."

"Adam Quyền, you are not heartless. *She* was heartless. Her cardiologist was heartless. You, however: you saved me and a hapless rooster from the homicidal motorists of Hồ Chí Minh City. You keep this company running. And you put up with every single one of us on the tour with so much kindness and patience that I truly think you deserve to be sainted."

"So you admit you needed saving that first day."

She groans. "I admit that you usually have decent intentions, no matter how misguided."

"My intentions a few hours ago weren't so decent."

She flushes, then smirks, pulling him by the belt loops so he's kneeling in front of her. Right where he wants to be. "Mine either."

"It was amazing, right?" he asks in a low voice. "Life-changing? Earth-shattering?"

She pretends to think. "I don't know. Could have been a fluke."

He growls, then leans down to kiss her, wringing pleasure from her lips until she's breathless, mewing softly. His hands move to her waist, and lower, cupping her backside like a hammock as he lifts her flush against his body.

He hears her gasp and moves his lips to her earlobe, licking the sensitive spot that makes her shiver. He discovered it last time and has no intention of bypassing an opportunity to make her shiver again.

He whispers, "Does that feel like a fluke to you? I can feel your thighs shake, you know."

She sighs. "You make a convincing argument, Quyền. Too bad we used that one condom already. We could build up our appetite for breakfast."

"Don't worry. I've got more," Adam tells her. He reaches into his knapsack and fans out a handful of metallic-wrapped squares.

Her jaw drops for the second time.

"Where did you get those?"

He says, deadpan, "The aunties on the tour."

They burst out laughing.

He continues, "They also offered me a vial of expired mint oil, rechargeable batteries without a charger, and what appeared to be a Hello Kitty–shaped lighter."

"What if it was a Hello Kitty–shaped vibrator?"

Adam gasps. "Sacrilege. I love that big-headed cat."

Evie takes one of the condoms and peers at it. A *large* size. Her eyes widen again, but this time, for a different reason entirely.

"They're walking drugstores," Evie says, her eyes drifting to his pants. "Aunties' Insane Apothecary."

"The title of your next book."

"Instant bestseller. I'm surprised they didn't hand you a bottle of lube."

"Baby, we don't need it."

Adam hears the gruff pull of his own voice, but at the same time, Evie hooks her arms behind his neck. She pulls him closer. Her eyes are sparkling with mischief. Promises. Then they are again lost in each other, in the quiet dark of the cave. And Adam does not want to be found, not now, not ever.

The next morning, after they've eaten and reluctantly dressed, they don their headlamps and move into the tunnels of the cave. Now that there's daylight beyond, the interior darkness doesn't feel quite as oppressive. Adam reaches behind for Evie's hand and feels an unmistakable pleasure when she squeezes it.

"Every time I think I've seen the most beautiful thing in Việt Nam, I come across something like this," he tells her. "These caves were just wrecked during the war. But they couldn't be destroyed."

"What's it like to live someplace like this? With such history?"

"You don't always remember the history. In Hồ Chí Minh City, I'm just living my normal life. Going to the office. Eating at a food cart. It's just normal life to me."

"Yeah. It's not like Romans are gawking at the Coliseum every day they pass it. And *I'm* certainly not bowing down every time I see the Piggly Wiggly in Midland."

"Is that an important landmark, then?"

"Yes," she insists, feigning indignation. "Once a visiting author streaked naked through the canned beans section on a dare. People got so offended that there were actual boycotts on campus in front of the English building. They held up signs that said 'Beans, not butts!'"

Adam bursts out laughing. "That's not true."

Evie raises her chin haughtily. "Don't mock our history, sir."

"America has real history, though! I hiked through the Muir Woods in college and never thought I'd see anything as magnificent as those redwoods."

"You were in California? We weren't far apart, then. At least, not during the summers I spent in San Francisco with Auntie Hảo."

"Yeah, though I didn't really make much of my American travels either. Seems like a trend with me."

"Let me guess," she says playfully. "You had your head sunk in business books the whole time."

"Something like that."

In reality, Adam's parents had pressured him to finish his MBA program in a year, instead of two. They'd wanted him back in Việt Nam, even though he'd have liked to explore his new home and maybe even make a friend or two. But there was no time for that *and* the fast-tracked course load. So he'd sped through the program, working double time to make sure he didn't disappoint anyone, even if it meant avoiding the mixers and rejecting the party invitations. He tried to bury his resentment. His father had paid completely for the program—an astronomical sum, given that he was also living abroad, in an expensive country where the đồng didn't stretch as far—so to Adam, it made sense that he would dictate the terms of such an investment.

And that's all Adam had ever been to them. An investment. Not a son with feelings or flaws. Certainly not one who wanted a path of his own.

"Would you ever go back to America?" Evie asks, pressing herself against the cave wall.

There's a rattling of hope inside him. A brief image of walking down the streets of San Francisco with Evie. Dipping into a bookstore together. Watching her read a poem in front of a crowd while he stands proudly in the background. Knowing he'll be the one to walk home with her. To *their* home. Then, just as quickly, he shuts the vision down with a hard, decisive thud, like slamming a door.

That can't be reality. It's just a dream. A stupid, too-hopeful dream.

As much as he enjoys her company, *craves* it—he knows he can't risk it all again for another woman. Even one who distracts him every hour of every day.

"No," he says, more shortly than he intends. "I have a company I'm building here. In Việt Nam."

She seems taken aback, her face withdrawn in the dim light. Her hand flutters from his, and he wants to grab it back, but he resists. She says lightly, "I get it. No one would expect you to uproot your life."

Between them, the unspoken words: *for a woman you just met.*

"Would you move to Việt Nam?" he asks, surprising himself with the question.

"I never thought about it," she admits.

His mind stalls. She never *thought* about it. Even though he'd said essentially the same thing, it pains him to hear it from her. That she too feels the impossibility of a future together.

She goes on. "This was supposed to be a brief blip. Just one last Auntie Hảo adventure."

"Ah."

"But," she says, her voice softening, "I do feel closer to her and my father here. When I see the mountains or a stream, I think—my father and his siblings could have walked along one just like this as children. I know why they had to emigrate. The war broke their family into pieces. My father never wanted to return. But I wish I'd had a chance to experience this with him."

The sadness in her voice makes him want to gather her close. "It seems like you've had a lot of loss in your life. I read it in your book too. It moved me, to see how you made art out of your grief. Not many people can do that."

"Let's just hope I've gotten all of the loss out of the way early." She shakes her hair from her face. By now, they're nearing the other end of the tunnel. They stand on a large boulder, staring at the steep incline below.

"I don't think it works like that."

"Anyway," she says, pivoting back and leading them toward the campsite again. "I sometimes look at how close you and Ruby are, and I feel slightly envious. I never had a sibling to experience things like this with. You must be looking forward to seeing your parents in Hội An."

"Sure."

"That was convincing."

"My parents aren't really the warm and fuzzy type. Especially my dad. He's not the type of person people get excited to see. I try to avoid him as much as possible, actually."

Now that they're nearing the light at the entrance of the cave, he can see her face squinch up in puzzlement. "But it's so generous of him to host us. He sent us an email yesterday, telling us how honored he is to meet us all. It seemed sincere."

"Sure, he can say the right things on paper. Anyone can. It's all part of how he maintains his image. But this whole charade is also a way for him to show off his wealth, and to weigh in on what Ruby and I are building. Which, by the way, *won't* live up to his exacting standards. This visit is another one of his elaborate tests."

She frowns. "I don't know, Adam. That seems like a lot of trouble to go to just to make a point."

"You don't know Loc Quyền."

"When I lost my father, I remember thinking that I would give anything for just one more conversation with him. I'm sure yours is a pain in the ass sometimes. But surely there's a way for you to understand each other. With a conversation? An honest one."

He almost laughs then. What conversation with his father has ever been anything more than a one-sided diatribe? A mountain of unsolicited advice? It's clear that Evie's father was a different kind of man.

"You know nothing about Vietnamese parents," Adam says, bitterness coating his words.

As soon as he hears himself, he understands his mistake. She's walking away from him, shaking her head. "Wait, Evie. I'm sorry—"

He puts a hand on her arm, but she shrugs it off and says, "I know I didn't get as much time with my father, but you have no right to act like I have no connection at all to him."

"I know—"

Then, a voice from the beach, "Hey? I'm the guide that Hải sent? I think we should probably head back?"

Evie jogs ahead of Adam. It makes him miserable to see her go, but he can't do anything except follow her, where their new guide is waiting with a beaming smile that feels like the polar opposite of how Adam feels. Why is he always saying and doing the wrong things with Evie?

And now he's in too deep. He cares for her in a way he's never cared for anyone before. He wants to protect her from everything that would hurt her. Including himself. The impossibility of his wildest wishes.

Though he's aching to pull her back in his arms, to plant kisses along her jawline and tell her how hard he's fallen for her, he doesn't. He begins packing his backpack, preparing to exit the fantasy, and move into the glaring light of the new day.

EVIE

Hội An, Việt Nam

"Is it just me, or has the sun grown twice in size today?" Fen mutters, lifting the folds of her silk shirt to air herself out.

"Like the Grinch's heart," Evie adds. "Or was that three sizes?"

Fen shoots her a dirty look. "Don't even *mention* anything covered in fur. My balls are sweating."

"You don't have balls," Evie says distractedly.

"Metaphorical ones. My metaphorical balls are the biggest ones here, and today, they are the hottest."

Evie laughs. "No one's going to argue with you on that."

"And why are *you* not drowning in sweat like the rest of us?"

Evie teases, "Maybe I'm just a better traveler than some pampered actresses we know."

"Who am I to refuse the life of luxury I'm so richly owed? Anyway, I don't know how you convinced me to skip the pool at the Quyềns' to go cook . . . hot noodles? Whose brilliant idea was that?"

"I think we're remembering the story differently."

The bus had dropped her, Fen, Pin, and Talia off in Hội An to see the sights, while the rest of the group and their luggage traveled to the Quyền estate to settle in. The exploration group would convene with the others for dinner.

Evie had initially longed for a cold shower and a nap in her room after the six-hour (luxury) bus ride, but Fen had insisted that they not waste a minute of the trip, which began with a famous cooking class in the heart of the city. Evie reluctantly agreed, sliding a glance toward Adam brooding in the front seat of the bus.

Things had been awkward on the hike from the caves. Adam barely spoke to her, though every time she lagged behind, he was right next to her, offering his arm or a bottle of water. The guide had chattered happily about the history of the caves, Hải's newborn baby, and American politics at large. ("Why," he'd wondered, "are American politicians so *ancient*?") Evie was glad for the distraction. Later, after they went their separate ways in the hotel, she felt a pit in her stomach, growing ever wider by the second.

Had he regretted their time together? She certainly hadn't. It was the best sex she'd ever enjoyed. But more than that—they had just *fit*. She couldn't get enough of him: the touches, the conversations, the silences. Sleeping in the cave beside him, even on that bumpy ground on a damp tarp, had given her the best rest she'd ever had in her life. She felt . . . safe.

But then there was that awkward conversation about their fathers. Whether either of them would move. Layers and layers of unsaid things. Hurts simmering beneath the surface.

And now he is withdrawing from her again. The constant push and pull. It's enough to make her scream.

Fen loops her arm through Evie's. They're walking across the covered Japanese bridge in Hội An, on their way to the cooking class. The bridge offers plentiful shade, a welcome boon in the heat, and they can see the river below with its clusters of water blooms and smattering of narrow boats, shaped like minnows floating slowly through the channel. Around them are colonial-style buildings with balconies and thatched roofs, each painted in marigold and sunset pink. Lanterns hang from the eaves, still in the windless summer day.

"So-o-o," Fen says, shoving an elbow into Evie's waist. "Did you use that condom I gave you or what?"

Evie shushes her, glancing back toward Pin and Talia, who linger by the temple entrance built into the bridge. They aren't paying attention at all, gesturing instead toward the carvings and statuary. Pin listens to Talia intently, blinking in time with her words, and Evie feels a clench in her gut. They make it look so *easy* to connect. Shouldn't it be easy?

Well, at least the physical part was easy with Adam.

Her mind wanders to his fingers entering her in the cool water of the cave pool. The way he knew exactly how to stroke her, how to bring her to the very edge before letting her come apart in his arms. How fucking *hot* it was to ride him on the sand, knowing that it was just them for miles and miles. *Scream as loud as you want, baby.* She fidgets at the memory of those words.

Fen crows, "You're *blushing*, you little sex goddess! I knew it. Everyone knew it. Was it good?"

Evie sighs. "It was spectacular."

Fen claps. "I'm the spicy fairy godmother! Raining condoms instead of fairy dust! Should have given you *more*."

"Oh, we had plenty."

"The aunties?" Fen asks knowingly.

Evie giggles and nods. "MVPs."

"So are you going to stay with him in his room tonight? Sneak into his childhood bed like the depraved minx you are?"

"His parents will probably be down the hall. Gross."

"Meeting the parents—a big moment across all cultures."

"Well, I'm not sure it's like that," Evie says glumly. "The sex might be phenomenal . . ."

"Say more."

"*But* Adam is all kinds of buttoned up. And not in a romantic, stoic businessman way. Though, yeah, he has that too. Trust me: he has zero desire to introduce me to his parents, no matter how good the sex is."

"Because?"

"I live in America. He lives here. He holds himself back. I'm a mess. We don't fit."

Fen leans her head briefly on Evie's shoulder. "Honey, maybe the outward circumstances of your lives don't fit. That doesn't mean your *souls* don't. That your hearts don't."

"You're a secret romantic," Evie says incredulously.

"It's not a secret at all. I have seen every single Meg Ryan movie ever bootlegged."

"Even *City of Angels*?"

"Even that one. Do I think Mei and I are going to ride smoothly into the sunset together? Hell no. But does that mean I'm not going try my damnedest to get her on that horse with me?"

"That's a lot of cowboy metaphors."

"You Americans aren't the only ones who like Westerns. Evie, you talk about fitting, but there's no such thing as a perfect fit. Love isn't perfect, because *life* isn't perfect. There's no secret architect making it all happen for you. Sometimes it's about chipping away at the circumstances of your life to *make* the fit."

Evie thinks about her father in his woodshop, the smell of pine and sawdust rising around them. How many hours had she spent watching him bent over a piece of wood, lovingly sanding it until the surface became smooth? Maybe love could be like sanding a piece of wood until its grooves fit perfectly into the joints. But where is the line between compromise and codependency?

"You are wiser than your years, young Fen," Evie says at last, planting a kiss on Fen's cheek.

The other woman raises an eyebrow. "Obviously."

A long line snakes from the cooking class entrance, full of tourists eager to learn from the chef. Pin and Talia have caught up to them now. All four eye the slow-moving line and the cramped, stove-fired interior of the building. A bead of sweat drips down Evie's neck. Fen stares for a second longer and then promptly grabs her arm.

"Yeah, no," Fen says. "This fresh hell is not happening today. I'm taking you to my favorite tailor in Hội An. They make the most gorgeous custom gowns."

"I don't know—" Evie begins.

"I promised to take you shopping. Plus, there's air-conditioning in the shop."

A few minutes later, they've said goodbye to Pin and Talia—both of whom opt to wait for the cooking class, like the good sports they are—and make their way down the historic streets of Hội An Ancient Town. Each balcony is loaded down with profusions of flowers, dripping off the rails onto the facades of the buildings. Canopies of rainbow lanterns hang over streets teeming with small wooden shophouses.

Fen's tailoring shop, The Silken Peacock, is on the second floor of a yellow building. The women sag in relief at the icy-cold blast of air-conditioning that greets them, both reaching eagerly for the coupes of champagne on a silver tray. Fen's tailor, Jade, ushers her in, immediately stripping her to get a more accurate measurement. As she jots down the numbers, Fen reaches to point to bolts of gorgeous fabrics, parading in her underwear through the shop with the dignity of a queen. Thankfully, there's no one there except for Fen and Evie.

Meanwhile, Evie sits on a velour ottoman and scrolls through her messages. Atlas sent a photo of the Tower of London, making a joke about the Plantagenet ghosts—an obscure reference to the War of the Roses and the young princes who disappeared in the tower. Classic Atlas. Just that right mix of dorky and brilliant and a little creepy.

She types back: It'll be like The Shining but with doublets.

You get me.

Maybe I just get archaic true crime.

Same difference.

Evie grins. Things are *easy* with Atlas. Or they were before they ended their relationship. And despite the fact that he was technically her boss. In the long list of Evie's great mistakes, Atlas was truly one of the more innocuous ones.

"Are you sexting with Quyền?" Fen demands, now half-clad in a pair of floor-grazing trousers with a bra on top.

"Just a friend back home."

"All right, your turn," Fen says, pulling her up from her seat. She hands her over to Jade, who appraises Evie from top to bottom.

"Pretty girl. Dresses like shit," Jade says.

Fen nods. "I know. She's determined to hide herself under layers of depressing black. Don't get me started on her footwear."

"Hey," Evie speaks up. "Standing right here. And I *like* my boots."

"She needs a new dress. By tomorrow," Fen says. "There's going to be a big, fancy dinner at the Quyền estate—"

"Oh, the beachfront villas?" Jade asks, curiosity piqued. "They combined *three* to make that estate of theirs."

"That's the one," Fen answers.

"Three?" Evie squeaks.

"They're richer than kings. That beach the villas are on is *private*. They own half the real estate in this town—and five others. Dr. Quyền is like a god around here; everyone is terrified of crossing him. He's a real dragon. You're going to *his* estate?"

Though Fen only nods in confirmation, Evie's mouth drops. She had no idea. Of course, she understood that Adam came from wealth. But this sounds like a staggering echelon. No wonder he was so tense about the visit.

"Okay," Jade says, looking up at the ceiling in concentration. "You need a Cinderella moment. This is a rush order."

"Price is no object," Fen says airily.

"Uh—it's a little bit of an object?" Evie puts in.

"Charge it to my father's account! He won't notice."

"You don't need to do this—" Evie begins.

"Yes, she does," Jade puts in, giving Evie a severe glare.

As Evie protests, Fen only crooks her head smugly, as if to say, *You have no idea*. An hour and three glasses of champagne later, the two women exit the shop with the promise of new dresses by the next afternoon.

"I need a nap," Fen says.

"Let's go back early," Evie suggests, her eyes drooping just the tiniest bit. She could sleep some of the bubbles off too.

Slightly tipsy, they hail a cab to take them to the estate. Unfortunately, they've ended up with a driver who thinks he's in a NASCAR video game. More than once, Evie reaches over to clutch a laughing Fen as they squeeze through the narrow streets at such twisting speed that she feels herself trying not to retch. Once they emerge from the city, they whizz past large almond trees tipping with flowers. Coconuts and papayas cluster in the branches as the congestion makes way for the resorts and beaches.

When they pull in front of the gated Quyền estate, Evie's heart begins to slow. Then, when she sees the buildings in front of her, she swallows. Hard. There are indeed three villas lined up, like triplet sentries. The largest one stands tall in the center, with its marbled columns and hotel-like entrance. Potted plants line the paved walkways, along with stately palms that lean toward the villas. Fitting with the theme of the city, a string of red lanterns hangs from each porch. There's a quiet elegance to the estate that Evie feels immediately drawn to. Even if her head *is* still spinning.

"They really should warn us before we go to a place like this," Evie mutters.

"You'll be fine, honey. Just hold your nose up and pretend you're unimpressed. Works like a charm with these people."

"Easy for you to say. You're a literal movie star."

Fen casts her gaze around, gesturing to a stone elephant resting at the steps of the main villa. "No wonder Adam's wound tighter than a bowstring. With this kind of money, they must expect him to marry a Thai princess."

Definitely not an unemployed, extremely broke poet from America who still can't tell the difference between a stock and a bond. Evie tries not to think of any gorgeous Thai princesses as she stumbles out of the car. The champagne *might* have gone to her head a little, especially since they ne-glected to eat lunch. She thinks briefly but longingly of the noodle cooking class, before setting one booted foot slowly in front of the other.

"Why is the earth moving so fast?" she asks.

"Slow and steady, girl," Fen murmurs. "Right behind you."

But it's too much—the heat of the day, the bubbles, the *slight* nausea from the Việt Vin Diesel's driving—Evie catches her foot on a broken cob-blestone and goes flying, like a yelping, inelegant seagull skimming the wa-ter for her supper. At the last minute, she awkwardly lifts her arms to break her fall, but winds up sprawled flat on her face anyway. Eye-to-eye with a pair of shiny black Jimmy Choo slingbacks.

"Cool buckle," she says.

The person attached to the Jimmy Choos clears her throat. "Are you all right, child?"

Looking up, Evie sees an imperious woman in her late fifties wearing a pair of eggplant trousers and enough diamonds to sink a barge to the bot-tom of the ocean. She resembles Ruby, with her high cheekbones and thick masses of dark hair. Adam's mother. *Of course.* And behind her is Adam's father, wearing a three-piece suit and an expression of grave and unmistak-able disapproval. It's all Evie can do not to tuck her head back onto the cobblestones and bawl.

ADAM

Hội An, Việt Nam

When he spies Evie on the ground, he rushes outside to help her, grabbing her arm so that she's held up on either side by him and Fen. Evie's trying to laugh, but he can see she's embarrassed. And who wouldn't be, with his mother and father standing silently before them, squinting at her as if she were an insect who just crawled onto their perfect lawn. He feels a rush of annoyance toward them.

"Ba, Mẹ," he says stiffly, "this is Evie Lang and Fen Li. They're part of the tour group as well."

"Ah," his father says in a dry voice. "The adventurers."

Evie smiles brightly. "Thanks for having us! I bet you never thought you'd host twenty people in your home. Don't worry—we'll stay on our very best behavior. Well, I will. I can't say the same about the rest of them!"

Adam finds her chatter endearing, a sign of her nerves and desire to make a good impression, but he can tell that his parents don't. His father has that constipated look on his face, the one he wears when he must bear an interaction he'd rather not prolong.

Evie holds out a hand. Awkwardly, his father takes it and gives a small shake. By contrast, Fen bobs a slight bow, the more traditional greeting for elders in Việt Nam. Adam watches as Evie notices her mistake, her face falling slightly. It crushes him, her discomfort. He's irrationally angry at his parents for being who they've always been: overly formal, domineering presences with zero humor. It's just who they *are*.

So why does he want to gather Evie up and spirit her far away? Preferably somewhere dark and quiet. Like a cave.

"Pleased to meet you," Mrs. Quyền replies faintly.

Mr. Quyền nods once and gestures to their housekeeper. "Welcome. Please follow Bông. She'll lead you to your quarters in the Blue Villa."

"Do you need some ice?" Mrs. Quyền asks, leaning toward Evie.

"No, I'm fine," she blusters.

Adam resists the urge to tuck a stray strand of hair behind her ear. To fuss over her ankle, which she seems to favor just slightly. There's a warm flush on her cheeks. She's wearing torn denim shorts that skim her thighs and her usual black boots, laced up to midcalf. The unbearably sexy combination of the shorts and the boots makes him groan inside. Despite his parents being next to them. Despite the fact that they hardly exchanged a word after the caves. This woman will be the death of him.

As Bông disappears with the two women, his father remarks, a faint note of derision in his voice, "What an interesting young woman."

It doesn't take a genius to know which young woman his father is mocking.

That night at dinner, a casual one on the beach with shaded tables perched on the sand, the tour guests mill around the chef-prepared dishes. They fill their plates with the usual street food favorites, like miniature bánh mì sandwiches, white rose dumplings, and crispy wonton wrappers topped with shrimp and a sweet tomato-pineapple sauce. Everyone hums appreciatively, snagging bites as they walk down the line.

Adam finds himself next to Evie in the food line. She's changed out of her shorts into a floral sundress with puckered sleeves and a tie in the front, showing just a small keyhole of skin. She's barefoot, and he can see the thin gold of an ankle band, glinting against the dying sun. Though it's still hot, clouds are starting to fill the sky, creating some extra shade around them. It's a perfect evening.

"Cao lầu!" she cries excitedly, picking up a pair of tongs to serve herself a portion of the thick noodles.

"Do you like this dish?" he asks.

"As long as she doesn't have to cook it," Fen quips.

When he gives them a questioning look, they fill him in on the day. The escape from the cao lầu cooking class to their afternoon at the tailor. The glasses of champagne and subsequent booze-induced naps.

"Good to get that fortification in early," he says. "My parents don't drink."

"That explains a lot," Fen mutters.

Adam laughs. "I agree, for what it's worth. My childhood would have been a different experence if they'd had a way to loosen up."

Growing up he doesn't remember his parents ever enjoying a cocktail together or even sitting down to a cup of coffee before the rush of the day. His father had work, and his mother busied herself with a thousand commitments and renovations around their houses. Adam and Ruby, in between getting shuttled off to school, were left in one of the homes with a nanny and told to entertain themselves however they wanted as long as they didn't get in trouble.

At night, his father would come home to brief his mother on his day, then go up to his home office again. Perhaps that was the model Adam had once imagined of marriage—separate yet bound by the same goals. Now he isn't so sure that his parents' marriage is anything to aspire to. After all, Ruby created a life modeled after theirs, and lately, she is the very picture of misery.

Fen wanders off to find Connor to tease him about his black eye, which has only deepened in color, making him look like a pirate with an eye patch. Evie and Adam are left alone at the table closest to the beach.

"Well." He clears his throat.

"This place—" she begins.

At that moment, his father and mother join them, to Adam's great surprise. They usually hover around Ruby, peppering her with questions. But now, come to think of it, Ruby is missing from dinner. She wasn't around this afternoon either, after the initial introductions. He feels a smidge of concern for his sister. She's hiding something; he's sure of it.

His father snaps a linen napkin onto his lap, then reaches over to adjust the flowers on the table, so they sit dead center, rather than an inch too far to the right. Only he would have noticed such a discrepancy. Adam feels his body seizing up. He's already pulling out his table manners though it's only a casual dinner, sitting a little more upright now, with one hand on his knee. Playing the dutiful son. He glances down at his clothing—a button-up shirt and chinos—and feels the urge to straighten a tie he's not wearing. His parents just have that effect on him.

Evie, by contrast, offers them a warm smile. She lifts her hand toward the ocean. "This is spectacular! How do you keep yourself from spending all your time out here? I would never leave."

"I work in Hồ Chí Minh City," Mr. Quyền tells her, picking up a piece of seared tuna with his chopsticks, peering closely at it as if it could twitch back to life. Adam remembers his distaste for sushi or anything even remotely undercooked. His father enjoys knowing that his food is fully, irrevocably dead. "My work doesn't allow much time for leisure. Not like my children."

Here, Mr. Quyền shoots Adam a small frown. Love Yêu hasn't gotten the number of investors their father would like, and he's been emailing Adam almost daily about their progress in wooing more. Adam has been working late nights, cold-emailing and applying to VC funds around the world, but it's never enough.

"You must not get lazy!" Mr. Quyền says, over and over again. No one but Adam's own father would ever accuse him of laziness.

Mr. Quyền believes Adam's time is better used in the office, rather than on the tour. Once, Adam would have agreed with him. But now? He can't be sorry for this taste of living, away from the constant grind of the city, the fluorescent lights and endless traffic. The tour has taught him a new way to live. A slower, more deliberate way. And he's not sure he wants to go back to the old life.

Before he can say anything, Evie's hand squeezes his knee. How does her touch manage to excite him *and* lower his blood pressure at the same time? Because she's magic. A magical, addictive little sprite who tastes like honey and salt and orchids after the rain.

"Oh, I wouldn't say that," Evie says lightly, in response to his father. "I think your children are pretty hardworking. They put together an entire business, after all. I doubt Adam and Ruby take much time for themselves."

Not accustomed to contradiction, Mr. Quyền drags his sharp gaze onto her. "Well, they've been gallivanting around the country for weeks."

"It's a matchmaking *tour*, Ba," Adam says, irritated. "The whole point is the traveling part."

"Matchmaking. What do you know about matchmaking!" he snorts.

Adam's mother carefully picks out all the toppings in her seafood salad until all that's left is lettuce, sitting limply on the plate. She sighs. "I could have taken you to the finest matchmaker, Bảo. That mess with Lana could have been avoided entirely."

Never mind that she pushed them together in the first place. Picked out the wedding flowers before they were teenagers. How easy it is to re-write history when you have no accountability, only fingers ready to point in blame.

Again, Evie speaks up. "I think you'll agree that he can hardly be blamed for *her* mistakes, Mrs. Quyền. LYT has made excellent matches already in just these two and a half weeks. Most of the guests are paired up and madly in love. What other tour could boast such results?"

As if in confirmation, guests mill in pairs around them, smiling blissfully into one another's faces. Some are holding hands. Others feed their partners playfully, feet touching under the table. Adam feels an unexpected swell of pride, from both Evie's defense of him and the sight of what Ruby has accomplished. What *they* have accomplished together. These couples may not be guaranteed forever partnerships leading to marriage and kids and golden anniversaries, but they're happy *now*. That's more joy in the world than before the tour began, and that's nothing to scoff at.

For the first time in his life, Adam finds himself valuing present happiness over a notion of future prosperity. He turns to smile at Evie, but before he can, his father's voice cuts through his thoughts, like a dagger through silk.

"Results like police threatening to press charges against a guest?" Mr. Quyền asks caustically. "Oh, yes. I heard about that from Ruby. She was hysterical. I knew this would be too much for you."

Adam flushes. "It's been handled."

"With *my* money."

"You are one of the company investors," Adam reminds him.

"Perhaps I'm beginning to second-guess that decision, Bảo."

Evie's eyes widen and ping-pong between them. He can almost hear her thoughts: *What have I gotten myself into?* She'll do what Lana did every time Mr. Quyền laid into his children. What Ruby's husband did. What Adam's own mother did. They ducked their heads and waited until it was over. No one was a match for Mr. Quyền's diatribes, so they didn't even try. It was a kind of abandonment, even if they were all physically sitting in the same place.

Adam hates to admit it, but tuning out the poison has become second nature to him as well, even if it costs him something every time. Like stepping out of your body. Letting yourself be stung by the wasp because it would take too much effort to run.

But he should have expected the unexpected from Evie. Because Evie is Evie, she doesn't sit back or cast her eyes to her plate like the others would. Instead, she places her chopsticks down with the confidence of a knight throwing down the gauntlet.

She says, "With all due respect, you shouldn't second-guess anything, Mr. Quyền."

"Excuse me?"

"Love Yêu is an extraordinary experience. Ruby is one of the few women who work in this space, and she's created something so unusual, so compelling, that people from other countries have spent thousands of dollars for a chance to participate. And Adam is the backbone of the organization. No one can doubt how much he does behind the scenes. The two of them will guard your investment. They'll surprise you, make no mistake."

Adam places his hand over Evie's on his knee and rubs a thumb over her knuckles. *This woman.*

Mr. Quyền demands, "And what do you know about business, young lady, to be advising *me*? Tell me: What do you do for a living?"

"I'm—a poet." There's a slight deflation of her zeal. Adam hates seeing her confidence wither.

He speaks up. "She's a fantastic, award-winning poet. She's the poet laureate of her hometown. Only a few people are successful in the way that Evie is."

"Ah." Somehow his dad manages to put a lifetime of superciliousness into that one tiny syllable.

Adam clenches his fists. *If he says anything to hurt Evie . . .*

Mr. Quyền continues, "So given your area of . . . expertise, Miss Lang, perhaps you might stick to advising on literature, instead of matters you don't fully understand."

"Ba," Adam begins, his voice shaking in anger. "You are a surgeon. You know less about business than me. Admit that, even if it'll kill you to do it."

"And who paid for all that business experience, Bảo?" Mr. Quyền asks, piercing him with an intensely disapproving gaze.

"Does anyone want dessert?" Mrs. Quyền asks, shifting in her chair.

There are two large, rose-colored splotches on Evie's cheeks now. She says, head held high, "I might not have an MBA, Mr. Quyền, but I'm offering my perspective as a guest on this tour. As a person with firsthand experience, and one who has taken the time to get to know your children. Take it or leave it. Actually, I think you'll probably leave it. But know that you're missing out."

Mr. Quyền narrows his eyes at her and wads up a napkin in one hand as if to throw it. But she cuts him off.

"Now, I think Pin is getting attacked by the birds, so I will just go and rescue him. Good night, Mr. and Mrs. Quyền. Bảo."

She slides him a small smile.

His heart nearly bursts as he watches her leave the table, tripping lightly in the sand. He wants to clap for her. Few people have ever dared to stand up against Mr. Quyền, much less walk away from him in the heat of confrontation. Usually, they batten down and take it, like sailors sitting through a storm.

Adam can tell it enrages his father to be thus dismissed. But he doesn't care. Something gathers in Adam's chest. Hope—and a deeper emotion. *Love?* The word, bubbling up in his mind, renders him temporarily speechless. Giddy, even.

Across the table, his father's expression darkens. Timid fear begins to emerge in his mother's, like she's bracing herself for unpleasantness. His father chews on a bite of noodle, dragging out the silence. Bending their attention, as always, toward his will.

"And this is why we would do well not to associate with Americans," Mr. Quyền says finally. "They will never understand our values."

Mrs. Quyền nods. "She seems very outspoken."

Adam snarls, "I think Evie understands values just fine, Ba. Maybe *you* are the one who focuses on all the wrong ones. Perhaps if you spent less time criticizing your children, you could invest some of that effort into self-improvement."

As he stalks away, he hears his mother gasping. His father's fist, pounding once on the table. Shaking in anger, calling Adam's name. But this time, Adam doesn't look back. He joins the rest of the tour group, laughing as they run through the flock of birds like children, Evie in the midst of it all with her arms outstretched, her head lifted toward the sky. Without hesitating, he runs with them.

EVIE

Hội An, Việt Nam

She's held it in as long as she can, but now it's two a.m., she desperately has to pee, and she's staring down the hallway of a *very* dark villa belonging to a couple who absolutely despise her. Glancing back into the room, she hears Fen's light snores. There weren't enough rooms for everyone to have a single, so most were paired up. The night is silent and darker than sin, with no moonlight streaming through the windows, no friendly twinkle of stars. And no night-light. What kind of sociopath doesn't keep a night-light in a hallway?

As she slowly makes her way down the corridor, feeling the walls and trying to remember which door leads to the bathroom, she can't help thinking about her outburst at dinner. What had come over her? It wasn't even her fight—well, until beaver-faced Quyền got personal—but it physically pained her to hear Adam's father speaking that way about him. For all Adam's faults, no one can criticize him for his lack of devotion to the company. Many times, returning after a late night on the tour, she has seen Adam working on his laptop at the bar, nursing a whiskey as he taps away, oblivious to all around him.

Now she thinks she understands why Adam withdrew in the caves when talking about his father. He was sharing something with her, something deeply painful, from the looks of it. And she rebuffed him, unable to practice enough patience to *listen* for once, instead of just reacting blindly.

And now she's done it again, creating tension and alienating herself from his parents, who are, after all, her hosts.

Where the hell *is* that bathroom? At that moment, she walks straight into a door.

"Ow." She grimaces.

She gives a quiet knock and, hearing silence, turns the knob slowly. With a sigh of relief, she takes in the tiled floor under her feet, the faint outline of a standing shower. A flick of the light reveals the interior of the bathroom, complete with a toilet. That blessed toilet.

After washing her hands, Evie tiptoes into the dark. A cinch now that she knows the way. She's thinking about the best way to get back into the Quyêns' graces—lavish flowers? Extravagant chocolates? Maybe just a simple apology. Ugh.

When she pushes open the door to her room, she stumbles inside . . . and walks right into a warm body. She opens her mouth to scream, but then there's a hand clamped over her lips. A warm breath in her ear.

"Shh," Adam says, tickling her neck with his breath. "It's just me."

"What the hell are you doing in the dark?" she demands.

He turns on a small lamp. "Working. But I was just leaving, actually. And then you invaded *my* space and stormed into *me* like a battering ram."

She hears the hint of a smile in his voice, and it's enough to melt her. Now that the darkness is at bay, Evie can see that the room is a small library lined with books from wall to wall. More a closet than an actual room. There's just enough space for a leather armchair in the corner and a table with a lamp. Unlike the rest of the house, which is spacious and elegantly designed, this room feels almost cramped, but not unpleasantly so. It has a cozy, lived-in quality.

"Sorry about that," she mutters. "I was trying to find my way back to my room."

"Two doors to the left."

The planes of his face are highlighted by the dim lamplight. A strong jaw. Lush lips. That disheveled hair, as if he's been running his hand through it as he read. He knows where her room is. The thought makes her tingly.

"Is this a library?"

"Sort of. It's just a space where I go when I'm here. Mẹ thought it was too small for anything, even a maid's room. I had the shelves built, and when I can't sleep—"

Evie touches the books. "Russian novels?"

"No," he says indignantly. "There are some British ones too."

"Atlas would be pleased," she says absently, sitting on the corner of his desk with a book in her lap. Paging through it.

"Who is Atlas?"

Evie looks up then. Is that a hint of annoyance in his voice?

"My ex. He's an Anglophile. Probably communing with Chaucer's ghost in Westminster Abbey at the moment."

"Ah," he says. His eyes flicker with something deeper.

She places the book back on the shelf behind her. "What is with the Quyền men and that word? You realize that being monosyllabic isn't as charming as you would lead us to believe?"

"I doubt my father's goal is 'charming,'" he says dryly.

"Really? He works so hard at it."

He chuckles, a surprising sound that makes her heart skip. Then he gets closer, so he's standing in front of her. She tries to scoot back, not because she doesn't want his proximity, but because she's afraid of what might happen if they get too close. There's nowhere to go, so she leans on her palms. Only then does she realize she's basically thrusting her scantily clad chest up at him. His gaze dips down to the small bit of lace in the vee of her camisole, then rises again to hers. Darkening with intent.

"I see now what you meant in the caves," she tells him. "Your father isn't at all like mine, and I shouldn't have assumed that we had the same experience, Adam. I'm sorry."

He shrugs. "You didn't know. But I'm grateful to you for defending me at dinner. No one has ever done that before. I mean, ever."

She can tell he means it, and that devastates her. The thought of Adam living his life in this lonely way, fielding criticism while never letting anyone stand by his side. That doesn't excuse her rash words toward his father, though. When she leans forward, one of her camisole straps falls onto her arm. Adam's eyes pivot to the strap and slowly, ever so slowly, he glides it back onto her shoulder with one finger. He doesn't lift the finger, only lets it remain, like a brand.

Her voice comes out too shaky. "It was nothing. Honestly, I was probably too harsh with your dad. Was actually planning on apologizing to him tomorrow. Smooth things over?"

"The hell you will," he swears, suddenly savage. "That fool needed to hear it. And not just from you. From all of us. Evie, do you know how it made me feel when you spoke up for me?"

"Lightly annoyed?" she asks in a small voice.

"So fucking turned on," he growls.

She feels her eyes widening, her legs turning weak under his gaze. *Adam.* His throat working down emotion as he plants a hand on each side of her. Invading her space, her air. Exactly where she needs him. Without thinking, her knees open for him, and she utters a sound like a surprised animal. A sound of longing.

He curses and slips into the opening between her legs, with only a couple of layers of fabric separating them. She uses the inside of her thighs to graze his hips.

He continues, "I wanted to take you far away from everyone and fuck you senseless on the sand. In the water. Everywhere. Every which way. On your back. Against a wall. Against this desk."

"Oh," she breathes. He's so close that she can smell pine and laundry detergent. And a hint of mint. A deliciously male scent that makes her irrationally angry at anyone who's ever gotten a chance to smell him up close like this before her.

He lifts one hand from the desk and runs it up to her jawline, using his thumb to stroke the heat into her face, until it travels down to the very center of her. Her eyes flutter closed.

He purrs, "How does that make you feel, baby? Knowing that every second of the day, I think of all the creative ways to make you come?"

Instead of answering, she wraps her legs around him and uses her hands to drag his face down to hers. Roughly this time, like she's starving and he's the very last meal on earth. When their lips meet, it's at a frantic, devouring pace, his lips crushing hers, his tongue traveling everywhere at once, drawing hers out in a tangle of sweetness and sensation. Then his lips are on her shoulders, his teeth tugging lightly at her straps.

"These tiny strings, holding up this tiny shirt," he groans. "I don't want to rip it. And I do. I'm afraid to get too rough with you."

Her mind circling in dizzy, pleasure-soaked circles, she faintly registers his words. And she realizes she wants it that way too. She can't pull the camisole over her head fast enough. "Get rough, Adam."

"You sure, baby?"

"Yes," she breathes, looking into his eyes, so he knows how certain she is. "I want all of you."

Without another word, his mouth is on her breast, sucking on her nipple, holding her against his body so there's no space between them at all. No air or sound, except for her moans of pleasure. While one hand kneads her other breast, his other travels down to the folds between her thighs, finding her wetness. His fingers slide around until they find the center of her pleasure. Then she sees stars. There's nothing in her brain but the feeling of his tongue circling her nipple while his thumb brushes again and again against her clit. Her head falls back, so the column of her throat is exposed, and then he's there, kissing and licking the tender skin.

"You taste so good," he murmurs. "But I want to taste you everywhere."

When she nods, unable to do anything else, her body a tense, packed ball of sensation, of heat and aching need, he gently places his hand on her chest and lowers her so she's flat on the desk, her legs splayed open before him. He removes her silk shorts, under which she wears no underwear. Seeing that, he groans and she smiles, knowing that she makes him feel just as undone as he makes her.

He kisses up her thighs, gently at first, almost like nipping, and then rougher, the way she wants him. He teases around her mound, licking the sensitive spots, but, frustrated, she moves her legs, drawing him closer to her. As close as he can get.

"So eager," he murmurs.

He chuckles, and then, before she can reply indignantly, he gives her what she wants, placing his mouth on her completely. He licks around her sensitive nub until her breath comes fast and hard, pressing and drawing circles around it. How does he know exactly how to wring pleasure from her? It's as if he's reading her mind, so in sync that they barely have to talk.

Then he slides a finger inside of her, and she loses all notion of where she is, what she's doing. She's panting fast as he licks and suckles, crooking his finger to find that perfect, sacred spot. And then her thighs tighten and she bursts apart, in a shower of pleasure and complete satisfaction. He draws away briefly, then comes back, as if to give her more pleasure. His breath hot on her.

"You taste so fucking sweet, baby," he murmurs into her thighs. "I could lick you all night long. The only dessert I need."

She sits up a little and shakes her head. "That's not enough. I want *you*. Inside of me."

She pushes him gently away and helps him out of his sweatpants. She drags her hand up his legs and strokes the length of him. Takes it into her mouth and sucks hard, licks with rough, short movements. Drives him to the edge, the way he did her. She cups his ass, drawing him closer, taking in another inch, then two.

"Come here," he growls.

When she gives another protesting lick, he pulls her up with two hands, as if she's nothing more than a rag doll, and pushes her onto the desk, so that her cheek is pressed against the cool wood. He uses his knees to open her legs wider. From her position, she can't see what he's doing, or read the expression in his eyes, which makes it all the hotter. Knowing that he will take her in exactly the way he wants. She hears the foil of a condom, then the feeling of his body settling behind hers. *Yes.*

"You ready for me, baby?" He uses his middle finger to feel inside the center of her. "You still feel wet as hell. Wet for me."

As an answer, she reaches behind her and pulls his body closer. Then the tip of him is at her entrance and he thrusts in a swift, heady movement that makes her gasp aloud. From this angle, behind her, he's reaching new places, new sensations. And he's not taking it slow this time. He's pounding into her, faster and faster, and all she can hear is the sound of flesh on flesh, his grunts of pleasure, and her own sighing moans.

She's trying to stay quiet, but all she wants to do is scream. Especially when he takes that finger of his and begins playing with her clit as he thrusts, activating every single sensation in her body. Lighting up the ions as she climbs closer and closer to her peak. And then she's there, falling fast, falling with delicious tingling sensations that shake her whole body. But she still wants more. More of him. More of *them* together.

"You are so tight," he gasps. "I can't stop. Evie, I'm going to come. I can't—"

As an answer, she pushes her ass back on his cock, shoving herself as hard and fast as him, meeting his thrusts with her own movements. Then, when he can't take any more, he grips her hips tightly and lets out his own release in a long, shuddering breath.

Moments later, he withdraws slowly from her and removes the condom. He pulls her onto the armchair, on his lap, and begins stroking her arms. Gently this time. Adoringly.

"Are you all right?" he asks in a quiet voice, kissing her shoulder. "Was that too much?"

She leans against his chest, curling up into his protective grasp. It feels like exactly where she should be. "I'm great. Better than great."

"Are you sure?"

There's a ragged tone to his voice. *That better not be regret*, she thinks. She pivots and reaches up to kiss him on the lips. Their kiss now has something new to it, not just the frantic need they summon in one another, but something more tender. A kind of intimacy that feels just as satisfying as what came before.

Evie allows herself to imagine it, just for a second. Coming home to him, settling her head on his shoulder as they talk about their days. Feeding him bites of ice cream, and then taking him to bed. Again and again. A lifetime of this. Her heart wrenches in a longing she's never felt before. The desire to keep him.

She says, meaning it completely, "Adam, I have never felt better in my entire life."

He gathers her closer, his arms surrounding her body like a blanket. When she cranes her head to look at him, she sees a smile growing across his face. Tentative, yet hopeful. Full of all the emerging feelings inside her. Lust and delight and the beginnings of familiarity. She wants to know everything about him, to always stand up for him against others, to hear his teasing and give it right back.

She knows they'll have to untangle themselves soon. It wouldn't do for them to be found naked, alone together in his parents' home. But she feels drowsy and sated and *so* very comfortable in his arms. Just for a second, she allows her eyes to droop. For her body to melt into his, like butter on toast. His breath slows to a steady rhythm that matches hers. She can't remember feeling this safe.

That's her last thought before she falls deeply, happily into sleep, with Adam nestled close behind her.

ADAM

Hội An, Việt Nam

"Adam." A light slap on the cheek. "Adam Quyền."

He mumbles and turns in his sleep. It doesn't feel like his bed, but he's very, very comfortable. As in, he could sleep for at least another day. Why would he leave this place?

He grumbles, "Not yet."

"Bảo. You have morning wood, and your father is here."

At that his eyes finally fly open. They dart around the room, taking in the shelves, the faint crack of daylight under the door, a semi-dressed Evie with laughing eyes, hands on her hips as she watches him struggle to sit up in the *very* comfortable armchair that he is now glad he bought.

"Liar," he says, his voice groggy.

"A little bit. But people *will* be waking soon, and we have to get back to our rooms before they see us."

In a few strides, he's next to her, pulling on her wrist so she swirls back into his arms. He plants a kiss on her lips, watching her eyes widen in surprise, then close to meet his kiss. So she feels it too. This thing between them has changed. And he likes it. His hand cups the back of her neck and she leans her head into it, blinking into his face. So beautiful.

"Who cares?" he murmurs into her lips.

She laughs. "Well, not me. But I think it *might* be better for us to maintain some decorum. In public at least."

"We're not going out in public again," he says, a little imperiously. "We're just going to stay right here and get our meals delivered and make love until the world ends. That okay with you?"

She melts for a second, and then gathers herself. "I've got to go, you Neanderthal. I have a roommate with questions. You have a tour group to host."

"More lies."

"I will see *you* later today."

She blows a kiss and sashays out the door. He groans as he pulls on his clothes and attempts to straighten his hair. Tries not to think of the mind-blowing sex from last night. The sight of her ass, offered up to him. Her lips on his cock. The sweet, addictive taste of her. Damn, his hard-on is growing again.

There's a knock on his door and, fully dressed but happily aroused, he opens it with a grin. "Coming back for—"

But it's not Evie at all. Bông, the family housekeeper who's been around for decades, gazes around the room with suspicion. Eyes him like he has something to hide. For all he knows, she could have one of those tiny sur-veillance cameras in her uptight bun.

"I saw Miss Lang come out. Is everything all right, Bảo?" she asks.

He clears his throat. "I was just . . . discussing the tour with her. She had a complaint we needed to resolve."

"At six in the morning?" she asks doubtfully.

Goddammit. He tightens his mouth and says, "Customer service is what we're all about. Can I help you with anything else?"

She shakes her head suspiciously as he gives a small bow and exits the room. Great, just great. Bông has always been in his father's pocket. When he was a kid, she'd report back to his father about any minor infraction, glowering in the corner as he or Ruby got punished. They joked that Bông got a bonus every time she uncovered some new mischief from the siblings. Of all people to find him and Evie, he would not have chosen *her*.

But as he stalks to his room, he puts it out of his head. After all, what can he do now? Furthermore, what can anyone do about his relationship with Evie? He's an adult. If he wants to be with her—in any way they choose—he will. No one would dare say a damn word.

"Ba wants to see you in his office," Ruby says, just as Adam is about to put a bite of breakfast into his mouth.

She's casting a shadow on his table, where he's drinking a cà phê and eyeing his plate of xôi mặn—the cook's sticky rice specialty, threaded with egg ribbons and jeweled cubes of Chinese-style sausage. Turns out: midnight lovemaking works up an appetite. He's ravenous. Adam has gone back for seconds and thirds on the breakfast buffet spread, surreptitiously eyeing the dining room entrance for signs of Evie.

"What are you, a messenger pigeon? Tell him to come see me himself." His own words shock him. One does not typically ignore a summons from the elder Quyền. Not if they choose to remain under his roof and in his good graces.

"He looks *very annoyed*, BB."

"Just another day in his sad life, then."

Ruby sits heavily across from him. "I would give anything for a cigarette."

"What's stopping you?"

She doesn't answer, but there's a bleakness to her expression. She picks up his coffee cup and takes a long sip. He doesn't protest. Today, she's wearing a pin-striped vest on top of black trousers, but her hair is askew. And she's not wearing makeup. On any other woman, none of these things would signal anything. But for Ruby, it means that her mind is occupied. Unsettled.

"Everything okay, Chị?" he asks, careful not to meet her eye. Ruby does not do well with confrontation or even the perception of it.

She drums a nail on the table. "Do you ever think we've wasted our whole lives? It feels like I'm on a speeding train, and I have no idea where it's going. I just hopped on because it was moving and because I thought I should be moving with it. And now . . ."

"Yeah?"

"Now I think it's far too late to get off."

Adam puzzles over this. Does Ruby mean the company? Her marriage? Their family? Theirs was not a relationship where metaphor substituted for logic. Her pensiveness is new and troubling. A disruption in his sister's usually sturdy stronghold—one he'd relied on.

"Well, why can't you?" He tries for gentleness. "If you're unhappy, I support you in any change you want to make."

"It's easy for you to say, BB. You receive half the pressure I do."

"Half? Really?" Bitterness coats his words. It's impossible for them just to be together in something. Ruby always insists hers is the greater burden. How to create a relationship with someone who's playing the trauma competition game?

Her gaze snaps to him, and suddenly, her expression shutters. "Go on. Ba gets angrier the longer he seethes. Might as well get it over with."

His father's office—the site of many a scolding, many a session of unsolicited advice—is on the top floor of the main house. Inside, the polished wood gleams. Instead of books on shelves, rows of filing cabinets line the room, all organized pristinely. Ba's desk takes up most of the width of the room. And Ba himself sits in a high-backed swiveling chair, his fingertips steepled above his lips.

"You asked for me?" Adam says.

Usually, his father prefers his guests to stand until invited to sit, but Adam isn't having any of it. He settles onto the vastly more uncomfortable chair on the opposite side of the desk, picking up a glass paperweight of Việt Nam on the desk. He spins it around. The major provinces are etched in silver. He traces his fingertip from Hội An down to Hồ Chí Minh City, then back again. How much has changed in a matter of weeks, a matter of miles.

He smiles at the thought of their upcoming cruise in Hạ Long Bay, imagining how he will stand on the boat next to Evie, watching the wonder cascade over her face. Clasping her close to him at night. Adam isn't a man who believes in fairy tales, but the hope gusting through him is fresh and keen, a breath of sweet sea air in a stuffy room.

"Việt Nam," his father murmurs. "The land of history. Of legacy. Do you know that of all the lessons I have ever tried to teach you, this is the one that matters most to me?"

"Even more than the one about how we only fly first class?" Adam tries to joke.

Mr. Quyền's expression is severe. "And it seems that very few lessons have penetrated you, my son. You are not young anymore. It's been time for you to settle down for years. Start a new branch of the tree. Of course, there were the strings of women in Hồ Chí Minh City. Don't think I don't know about them. But I was willing to dismiss those. And we'd hoped Lana might be the one, but of course, that was a disaster. All those wasted years."

"Yeah, I was there," Adam grinds out.

Mr. Quyền goes on, "And now it seems that you are determined to continue wasting your life."

"What does that mean, Ba?" Adam hears the acid in his own voice. His fists clench around the glass paperweight so hard that it might break apart with one forceful squeeze.

"It means that it has escaped no one's notice how besotted you've become with the American—"

"Evie."

"Miss Lang. Your sister has been updating me on your adventures. It seems that you've become close. Closer than appropriate."

"She *spied* on me?" Adam is incredulous—and, if he's being honest, a little hurt. He and Ruby haven't always been aligned, especially when it comes to the ways they should conduct their activities, but they've never *reported* back to their parents. That's crossing a line. It dismantles an honor code he thought was clear to them both.

"Miss Lang is not one of us, Adam. I don't mean just in terms of her mixed race."

"Careful, Ba."

Mr. Quyền gives his son an amused look, as if he can't believe Adam has the audacity to caution him about anything. "She is American, through and through. Despite how well she speaks Vietnamese, she is brash, like all the Americans. Her clothes, unacceptable. Not to mention her profession, her outspokenness."

"That's *enough*." Adam's eyes darken.

A small flicker of shock registers on Mr. Quyền's face before he barrels ahead. "It's clear that this little dalliance will go nowhere. But Bông tells me that Miss Lang was seen exiting a room with you at an early hour. Too early an hour. Thankfully, it was Bông who found you. What might others say, if they caught you together?"

"I don't care what they say, Ba. It's no one's business. And frankly, it's not yours either."

"Ah, but it is, Bảo. What happens on this tour is my business. Am I not the chief investor? The financing keeping you all afloat—keeping *you* salaried and in that luxury apartment?"

A slow dawning overtakes Adam. Of course. Why would his father not use the most powerful tool at his disposal—his money—to beat his children into compliance? It has gone this way their whole lives. And it's worked—until now. Adam stands and makes his way to the door, puts his hand on the knob.

He says, "You can take your investment and shove it up your ass, Ba."

Mr. Quyền recoils, and to be honest, Adam does too. Vietnamese children, especially dutiful sons, do not speak to their patriarchs like this. Respect for elders has been the one value drummed into him from an early age. Respect for his *father*, in particular. The head of the household. The despot with the waistcoats.

A burble of regret emerges in Adam, but he quickly shuts it down when he thinks about how Mr. Quyền spoke about Evie. As if she were a problem to be solved, rather than the glorious, headstrong, absolute jewel of a woman she is. And that is one thing Adam will not allow.

As he opens the door to leave, Mr. Quyền shouts, "You think I'm bluffing, boy. But this is no card game. The stakes are higher than just you."

"I know that."

"If you do not do as I say and end things with Miss Lang, I will pull out my money. This company will be sunk before it's even left the ground. And you and your sister, along with it."

"You wouldn't do that."

"I would do anything to save this family's reputation, Bảo."

Jaw clenched so hard he thinks he might crack his own skull, Adam turns to leave. He has choice words for his father but chooses to cool off instead. To take a breath and strategize. It's what he does best.

Nevertheless, he can't help storming down the hall on his way to find his spare bike, parked in the garage of the estate along with his father's five luxury cars. As he turns a corner, he catches sight of Ruby pressed against the wall of the hallway, face totally still. She had been listening to his conversation with his father. She opens her mouth as if to say something to Adam, but he brushes past her before she can speak.

"BB," she calls faintly.

He doesn't answer. Just for a few hours, he wants a respite from his family and their endless requests. Just once, he wants a chance to think for himself without their voices filling his head, trying to influence his decisions.

EVIE

Hội An, Việt Nam

One little-known fact about Shanghainese actresses is that they are very light sleepers. As Evie sneaks into the room she shares with Fen after her knee-shaking, thrill-inducing night with Adam, she stubs her toe on an armchair. She cringes and swallows her cry of pain, but that doesn't stop Fen from shooting out of bed like a rocket.

"And where were you last night, my sneaky little hussy?" Fen asks with just a hint of bleariness.

"Bathroom," Evie answers, trying not to grin.

"For five hours?"

"I may have gotten waylaid."

Like that, Fen is up and grabbing Evie's arm. "By a certain grumpy CMO with rock-hard abs and a killer jawline?"

Evie doesn't answer, but Fen shrieks in delight anyway. Laughing, Evie tries to shush her roommate, but Fen's off, rambling about love dungeons and raining condoms. She throws a robe in the air, like it's a handful of confetti.

"I knew it, I knew it!" she crows. "You have the look of a very satisfied woman. But I'm not even a little surprised. I can predict these things."

"Like a sex prophet."

"Oracle of orgasms!"

"Soothsayer of seduction!" Evie pipes in, rummaging through her suitcase for an outfit that is casually cute yet subtly suggestive. Not enough to piss Adam's parents off, but enough to summon that wonderful intensity.

"Clairvoyant of climaxes!" Fen yawns. "Or should it be clairvoyant of clitorises?"

"Can you not."

"You have no appreciation for poetry."

"Right. I'm the problem here. Anyway, I'm starved, so hurry it up," Evie says, eventually landing on a black slip dress and a pair of nude-colored sandals. She ties her hair into a loose bun.

"A night of nonstop bonking will do that to a woman. Go on without me. I could use an hour or two of extra sleep. I was in the middle of a really good sex dream where Mei and I were on this Ferris wheel and—"

"*Bye*, Fen."

With a wave, Evie leaves Fen flopping back into her mess of sheets. This time, she finds her way without trouble to the dining room in the main house, where breakfast is being served. Talia is deep in conversation with Mrs. Quyền, who only wears half her usual number of diamonds, along with a pair of thick sunglasses drawn over her face, though it is a cloudy day and they are indoors. Talia gives Evie a quick wave as she passes, but Mrs. Quyền purses her lips and looks away.

O-o-kay. Perhaps last night's confrontation isn't quite forgiven yet. But no apologies before coffee. No apologies before talking to Adam.

The other couples mill around the room, reaching for glasses of freshly squeezed juice and banana-leaf plates topped with sticky rice in the shape of hearts. Evie takes a selection of fruit and a small portion of xôi with sugared peanuts. She can't help thinking that, in less than a week, she'll be back in her apartment in Midland, staring into an empty pantry. Wondering where the personal chef has gone. Has she gotten too caught up in this life? How does one conquer a romance hangover?

She tries not to think about the people she'll be leaving behind, but it's impossible not to dwell on the fact that she *is* leaving.

Evie notes with dismay that the last chair remaining is next to Ruby.

Ruby, who wears a massive frown as she scrolls with one delicate finger through her iPad. Ruby, who looks wound up enough to detonate into an explosion of designer scarves and ancestral disappointment.

Evie slides silently into the empty chair and begins picking at her papaya. Ruby looks up then and, to Evie's surprise, puts away the iPad.

"Evie," she says. Something in her voice makes Evie want to retreat, though Ruby is shooting her an approximation of a smile. A gesture of goodwill, at least, which is more than Ruby has given her so far on the tour. "How are you this morning?"

Thinking of Adam's lips last night, his fingers touching the soft, secret places of her, Evie begins to blush. "Pretty well, Ruby. And you?"

"A little restless. I was thinking of taking a walk, actually. The beach is very peaceful in the morning. Would you go with me?"

"Um. Me?"

"Yes, you," Ruby says patiently.

Ruby gives Evie a purposeful eyebrow raise. On another person, it could look like an invitation. On Ruby, it looks like a command. Evie shoves one last bite of papaya in her mouth and follows.

The sand is impossibly soft under their feet, and still slightly cool from the night air. Today, the water fades from turquoise to a deeper blue that mirrors the overcast sky. A gentle breeze lifts the hair off Evie's forehead. She sighs into it.

"Is it hard to believe you live here?" she asks. "In this incredible place?"

Ruby is surprised. "I don't live *here*. I live in Hồ Chí Minh City. With my husband."

Evie blinks. The first voluntary mention of her husband. "And will your husband be joining us?"

Ruby laughs bitterly. "No. He and I lead separate lives."

"That sounds . . . difficult."

"I suppose. I've been busy building the company, but it started even before that."

"I'm sorry."

She shrugs. "I'm not. Honestly, that's how it's always been for marriages in our family. And it works fine. No fuss. No dramatics. Just a partnership."

Evie watches the waves push against the sand. What a way to consider a marriage. Somehow, she doesn't entirely believe Ruby. The note of bitterness in the other woman's voice clues her in to the fact that things aren't nearly as drama-free as advertised.

Ruby goes on. "I heard you and my father exchanged some words last night."

"One could say that." Evie picks up a shell and palms it, feeling the grooves against her hand.

"Listen, Evie, I don't blame you," Ruby says, her voice taking on a confiding tone. "I know how frustrating my parents can be. And you were raised differently. Perhaps it's more comfortable for you to speak up. I'm not even saying you were wrong to say something. I think it's one of the reasons why my brother is drawn to you. Your fearlessness. But surely you must know it can't work. You and Adam?"

"What makes you so sure of that?" Evie furrows her brow. She wants to shut her ears against what comes next. Every step forward is met with another shove backward. Another obstacle. Shouldn't it be easier than this?

"Adam's intentions are often opaque, even to him. He's not one for sticking with a woman; before you, there were many, many flings."

"Many?" Evie flinches at the word.

"He's still in love with his ex, Lana. He pretends he's over it, but it's no coincidence that he picks women who are unavailable. Like the ones in Hồ Chí Minh City, careless party girls who'd never demand anything of him. Like you—destined to return to America soon."

Evie's face reddens. How can Ruby's perspective differ so wildly from Adam's? Perhaps Ruby is really that clueless. Or perhaps she sees something that Adam doesn't want to admit to himself.

How well do he and Evie really know each other? There was time for all that, she had thought. But now, listening to Ruby's pragmatic—if hurtful—words, she understands that the tour will come to a close soon. Too soon.

And they are no closer to knowing how to resolve the simmering tension between them. How to move forward without one person sacrificing their whole life for the other, the surest recipe for resentment.

"Perhaps you should let your brother make his own decisions," Evie says finally, her voice milder than she feels.

Ruby studies her. "But that's not how it works in our family. We are all tied together, whether we want to be or not. Did you know that our salaries are essentially paid by our father? That this whole company hinges on his approval?"

"I didn't know." Evie tries not to feel hurt that Adam has shared so little with her.

"Adam doesn't like to acknowledge it, but he—we—owe our whole lives to our father. And if he chooses, he can take it all away. This company. Our futures. He's threatened to do just that if Adam doesn't end things with you."

"That's ridiculous," Evie says, puzzled. "Because of one little argument? He'd be that petty?"

"He doesn't see it as petty. He sees it as protecting his children. His legacy. And I don't know if he's totally wrong. You're a nice person, Evie, but are you going to be Adam's forever person? His *wife*?"

"Say it with more disbelief, Ruby," Evie drawls, even though she's secretly hurt by the other woman's tone.

"Well, *do* you see it? Yourself going to the family events in Hồ Chí Minh City? Making conversation with all the people we grew up with? Finding a job here?"

When Evie tries to imagine it, she sees a big blank. But isn't that how she's always seen her future? Once, Auntie Hảo hired a palm reader to come to her house and read their palms. When the palm reader got to Evie's, she lifted her hand and dropped it as if it were burning. She tutted, *This one has no idea what she wants. Her path is unreadable.* Evie remembers this now, staring into Ruby's challenging expression. She has nothing to say to dissuade this woman.

Ruby says triumphantly, "I didn't think so. Isn't it better to let him go now, before anyone gets hurt?"

But I don't want to let him go. Evie thinks this, but doesn't say it aloud, because really, what good would it do? None of his family approves of her, which itself feels like a kind of rejection. How long can a relationship—a marriage—last, without the communal support of family and friends? Isn't that why she's always chosen men who orbit her world? It's simpler that way. But what more should she have to surrender in the name of simplicity?

The tour group lounges on the beach under a row of huge red-and-white-striped umbrellas dug into the sand. Servers pass around glasses of fresh coconut juice and salted lemonade, as well as smoothies crammed with tropical fruit. Everyone looks relaxed and happy, as they should. All their needs are taken care of.

Evie should be relaxed too, but she can't stop thinking about Ruby's words. Would Adam's father really take everything away, just because his son disobeyed him? Would it be worth it? Would *she* be worth it?

She's thinking of all this as Riley and Connor both stand at the same time. She adjusts her position to follow their gaze, thinking they've seen either a large shrimp platter or a shark circling in the water. But it's neither. A tall, gorgeous woman with masses of dark hair, wearing a white halter with a sarong, picks her way across the sand. Though she's graceful, her steps are hesitant.

The goddess passes the gaping men and stops by Evie. In a low, sonorous voice, she asks, "Can you tell me where to find Fen?"

Evie turns to point Fen out, swimming with her boogie board near the shoreline. Fen glances at the beach and, after one look at the mystery woman, drops her board onto the sand. She takes off like a dart toward them.

"Mei?" Fen calls, her voice shaking. Gaining speed. "My God, is that really you?"

"I couldn't stay away," Mei says softly. "Forgive me, Fen. I know we said we'd wait. But even a second without you is far too long."

She's holding Fen's gaze, as if it's just the two of them in this whole wide world. At first, silence falls when they are in front of one another. Mei plays with the edge of her sarong as she watches Fen's expression, a hint of worry on her face.

Then, with something like a sob, Fen launches herself into Mei's arms. They're both tearing up, planting soft kisses all over one another. Evie looks away to give them privacy, but she can't help the smile creeping onto her face at the sight of her friend's abundant joy. She feels like clapping.

The two walk away from the crowd, leaning close and ignoring the surrounding whispers. Breathing in the other's presence in the way that only two committed lovers can, with unhurried adoration.

"What the hell was that?" Connor asks, miffed, perhaps, that he never had a chance to practice his choicest lines on Mei.

"I think that was true love winning out," Evie says, a little damp-eyed herself.

Later, Evie helps the reunited couple pack Fen's bags. While Fen tosses everything inside her luggage haphazardly, Mei calmly removes each item and folds it into a precise square before adding it back into the suitcase. She picks up the vibrator and shakes her head, though she can't help giving Fen a wry smile. A squeeze of the hand. They are always touching in some way, whether Fen has her arm slung around Mei's waist or Mei is leaning to plant a soft kiss on her girlfriend's cheek. Their love for each other is so palpable that no one makes a fuss when they announce their desire to leave the tour early. Even Ruby with her keen eyes, her omnipresent frown, deigns to wish them good luck. *After* reminding Fen that her tour fee is nonrefundable.

Watching them, Evie feels a bittersweet joy. She's glad to be sending her friend off with her love, but despondent to lose her favorite companion on the tour. Yet she can't deny that the two women are a perfect match of opposites. While Fen is tumultuous energy and wild affection, Mei embodies a certain kind of steadiness, like a sweet breeze on a hot day. She's gentle yet firm, never letting Fen get away with anything.

"You'll text when you get back to Hồ Chí Minh City?" Evie asks Fen.

"Oh, no, honey, we're not going to Hồ Chí Minh City. Thailand awaits!"

"Let's just say: the destination is still a point of discussion," Mei says, putting a hand on Fen's arm.

"Oh, well, it doesn't really matter, does it? As long as we're together." Fen's expression is soft and unguarded. The kind of look one can give when love is so certain, so inevitable, that it makes little sense to try to hide it.

Mei plants a kiss on her girlfriend's cheek, grabs one of Fen's bags, then gives Evie a wave. "I'll put this in the car. It's nice to meet you, Evie. Thanks for keeping my girl out of trouble."

When the door closes behind Mei, Evie smiles at her friend. "No *wonder* you've been pining over her. She's probably the most gorgeous woman who's ever walked the earth."

"Duh," Fen says smugly.

"I'm happy for you," Evie says. "She's great. And you glow when she's nearby, like she's your own personal heat lamp. You're glowing so much that I have half a mind to be annoyed at you. But I can't."

"Because I'm adorable?"

"Because you're adorable." Evie squeezes Fen tightly. "Go get deliciously baked in Thailand or Australia or wherever. Defy your father and live out your dreams with your love, my soothsayer of seduction."

"What are you going to do without me?"

"It's not like you're going into the witness protection program."

Fen slings her remaining bag over her shoulder and gives Evie a wide, guileless smile. "Can I offer you some parting advice?"

"Why bother asking like you're not just going to steamroll me with it?"

Fen says sagely, "Do as the Asian aunties do."

"That was . . . not descriptive."

"I mean—act like every day is your last. Brandish the condoms. Break into the temples. Do the things. Say whatever it is you want to say, and don't let uptight fuckers like the Quyêns stop you."

"Easy for you to say. You're leaving in five minutes!"

"You ever think about why those aunties can do whatever the hell they want? It's because they've mastered something most of us spend our whole lives trying to learn. They've learned the art of not giving a fuck. They know that the only people they have to live with are themselves. And who wants to live with regret as a bedfellow?"

"Shakespearean of you."

Fen snaps her fingers loudly. "Pay attention, smart-ass. I'm saying, don't let yourself sink with regret, Evie Lang. You're a dynamo, and once you see it in yourself, it's only a matter of time before the whole world bows at your feet."

"I really love you, Fen." Evie pulls her friend close, bags and all.

"Back at you, my stealthy little hussy."

With that, Fen leaves, vacuuming a great deal of the joy out of the room. Abandoning Evie to her thoughts. Her regrets, yes, but also the memories of the best times on the trip. Memories crowded with Adam's presence. Memories that somehow feel as if they're fading by the moment without the momentum to sustain them.

Sure, she and Adam have had some good times. Some very good times, actually. But what kind of future could they have together? Evie needs to work. In the States. That's her bread and butter. Her way to independence. Just the previous week, her agent had emailed, saying that her invitation to a panel on grief and transference had been quietly rescinded. No explanation. Just that they had no room anymore to host her. Her agent's words were rough and brief, the kind you offer when you're about to drop a person. The world is forgetting about Evie. And that will not change if she decides to stay in Việt Nam.

Not that Adam has asked her to stay, of course. San Francisco has always been the goal. And now it's within reach. She just needs to make the logical decision for once, instead of following her own stubborn, reckless heart.

Where has all that passion gotten her in the end?

Do as the aunties do.

As in times when things get hard—like when her father and Auntie Hảo died—Evie decides to get away for a while. She packs her notebook and a granola bar in a messenger bag and finds the Quyèns' driver sleepily swinging in the hammock by one of the cars. It's late afternoon, the hour when many Vietnamese are taking their midday naps, shying away from the heat in the shade of their bedrooms. When the driver sees her, his feet hit the ground. He smiles toothily.

"Ready to go into town?"

"Not quite. Do you have time to drop me off at the Marble Mountains?"

ADAM

Hội An, Việt Nam

An outrageously large bouquet arrives at his parents' doorstep around dinnertime. There's a profusion of sickly-sweet honeysuckle, along with brilliant pink bougainvillea in a large glass vase. It must weigh at least ten pounds. He grunts and heaves it into the house.

"Subtle," he mutters.

"Someone has an admirer," Talia says.

She's on her way to dinner with the rest of the group but stops to help him wrestle the awkward arrangement onto the table.

"Who's it for?" she asks.

Adam takes the card, reading silently.

> *Darling Evie: London is not the same without you. Life is not the same without you. I've made the biggest, most boneheaded mistake in letting you go. Hurry home to me.—Atlas*

"Evie," he says shortly. "It's from her ex-boyfriend."

Talia watches his face sympathetically. Then she reaches over and squeezes his arm. "A woman like that is bound to have many admirers. But the people who pursue her hardest are not necessarily the ones she wants."

"No?"

"I don't have any insider knowledge. But all I can say is that love is an unpredictable thing. Just look at me—" And here Talia laughs. "I thought—Well, my attention was elsewhere at the beginning of this trip. But now I've found something with Pin. Something real. Lasting. I didn't expect to fall in love this quickly or this deeply. Yet here I am, ready to shift my whole life to be with him. It's kind of magical, if you think about it."

"It is," Adam says, his voice softening as he looks down at Talia fondly.

She glances over her shoulder to where Pin dawdles by the dining room, waiting for her. He's smiling, gentle adoration fully evident on his face. Talia, too, beams. Adam is glad for them. Who wouldn't want to find love like that? Then they walk in hand in hand, and Adam has no choice but to follow them like a third wheel.

The room is beautifully decorated for the night, with glass chandeliers and tall candles that cast dancing shadows on the walls. Individual salad plates are decorated with purple blossoms and candied nuts. The napkins are the smoothest mauve cotton. A quartet plays quietly in the corner.

And at the head of one of the tables are his parents, cool and sophisticated, the picture of graciousness. Asking questions, chattering about the weather and how much there is to see in Hạ Long Bay. Adam knows better, of course. Behind those rehearsed exteriors sits a well of ancestral snobbishness. They hold the lifelong desire to exclude, to protect themselves against outsiders. Outsiders like Evie. And Adam will be damned if anyone makes Evie feel like an outsider in his presence.

But then, sitting down to dinner, wishing for the umpteenth time for a glass of whiskey, he thinks about the obnoxious bouquet. What a gaudy gesture. And Atlas, what a ridiculous name. Couldn't he have one of those rugged, conventional American names like Tommy or Hudson or something? But maybe that's what Evie likes. A man doesn't send a bouquet like that without some encouragement.

The thought of Atlas—any man—touching Evie, murmuring in her ear, hell, even having a quiet conversation with her is enough to make Adam grind his teeth.

Ruby shoots him a questioning look, but he just shakes his head tersely. Where *is* Evie?

He heard about Fen and Mei leaving earlier this afternoon, though he hadn't been home in time to catch them. He'd been soaring through the countryside on his bike, thinking about his father's threat. How much was he willing to risk for Evie? At the end of the ride, he realized that he would be willing to risk *everything*. Even now, eyeing the corners of the room like a lovestruck idiot, Adam knows that he would put up with a thousand over-eager ex-lovers, a hundred more awkward dinners with his parents, if only for a chance at a future with her. He just needs to tell her.

When Riley plunks into the seat next to his, Adam asks, "Where's Evie?"

Riley shrugs. "Uh, not sure. Haven't seen her since this afternoon."

Usually, Fen would know, but she's long gone. On the other side of him, Connor speaks up. "I think she took the driver into town, like, four hours ago. He came back, but she didn't."

"And she didn't tell anyone where she was going?"

Connor shakes his head. Of course she didn't.

He texts her: Where are you?

There's no response. Then he calls, but the voicemail immediately springs a "full inbox" message.

Adam places a forefinger along the crease between his brows. A lot can happen in four hours. Should he be worried? Why is no one else worried? Is it too much to ask this woman to, for once, just stick to the same schedule as everyone else?

Adam moves past the group, smiling slightly at the oohing-and-aahing over the soup course: a thick seafood stew with curls of coconut cream laced through it. He greets guests as they beam up at him, tanned and happy.

Then, once he reaches the end of the table, he kneels next to Ruby and whispers, "Have you seen Evie?"

"No," she says, keeping her face still. "She's gone somewhere?"'

"Evidently. Where's the driver?"

"He's eating with the staff in the kitchen. But, BB—"

"What?"

"Don't get wrapped up in this mess. In *her*."

He glares at his sister. "One of our tour guests is missing and has been for hours. I think she's left her phone at home. It's our *job* to find her. And, aside from that, it's just what you do if you're not a raging sociopath, okay, Ruby?"

"I'm sure Evie is fine. Please sit. The main course is coming, and you're making a scene."

Though everyone is humming in satisfaction over their food, there are more than a few glances thrown his way, especially from his parents' end of the table. Outside, the sky darkens enough that they need to adjust the chandelier lights and add more candles. The thought of Evie being out in a strange city at night, without any way of contacting them, fills him with such anxiety that he doesn't stop to think. He shrugs Ruby's hand off and strides to the kitchen, past the stormy eyes of his father, until he's standing in front of the driver.

"What can I do for you, man?" the driver asks, mouth full of soup.

Adam tries to tone down the anger in his voice. "Did you take a woman into town? Dark hair? Pretty?"

"That's like everyone on this tour, man."

If he calls me "man" one more time, Adam thinks. Aloud he says, "It would have been this afternoon. She was probably wearing black."

The driver snaps his fingers. "Oh, yeah. Nap-time girl."

"What did you call her?"

He holds up his hands. "Sorry. No offense meant. She went to the Marble Mountains."

"Why?" Adam pins a glare onto the driver, who shrinks away.

"I don't know! I'm not paid to ask questions. Deliver them where they want to go, that's what Mr. Quyền told me. She said she didn't need me anymore, sent me back home. I'm sure she's there now after her climb. Want me to go get her?"

"No, thank you," Adam says gruffly. "I'll go."

"You're welcome. Anyone ever tell you you're terrifying as shit?"

Bypassing the dining room altogether, Adam hops onto his bike and coasts to the entrance of the Marble Mountains, past the restaurants starting to light their lanterns and the music piping from the nightclubs. When he arrives at the base of the mountains, he notices how utterly massive they are. The steps wind through a dark cave crowded with stone statues and altars. He tries not to think of the many implications of caves, where Evie is concerned.

The vendors are packing up their things for the night and the ticket booth is shuttered. Guests take their last pictures, streaming toward cabs and buses on the way back into town. Soon, no one is left except the employees. Adam heads over to an officious-looking man with a clipboard.

"The mountains are closed," the man says, without looking up.

"There's a woman still in there."

"Nope."

That one syllable makes Adam see red.

"What do you mean, *nope*? She went up into those mountains four hours ago, and she's not back."

"It's an hour-long walk at most."

"Well, she's not home."

"Anh, I don't know where your girl is, but I assure you, I've checked everyone off the list. There is no one left in there. Have you looked in town?"

Without answering, Adam hops back on his bike and drives to Ancient Town, through the winding roads, the bars crowded with lights and laughing young people. He nearly clips a vendor with a towering fruit cart, raising his hand in apology as he passes. What the hell is he even looking for? He has no clue where Evie could be. No idea what she's thinking. And that's the problem, isn't it? There's nothing straightforward about Evie Lang. It drives him crazy. In some ways, it's what keeps him panting after her, wondering about her next steps. But how sustainable is that in a relationship? When does excitement turn into full-throttle anxiety?

Right about now maybe.

He texts again: Can you just let me know you're okay? Or any of us?

Again, no response.

As he rides his bike up and down the streets, he feels his anger mounting again. A small part of him knows it's unfair. She doesn't owe him anything. She's likely used to behaving in exactly the way she likes and doesn't understand that even within the safe, luxurious confines of the Love Yêu tour, there will always be sketchy neighborhoods. There will always be dangers for a woman traveling alone. But of course she wouldn't register that. She's stubborn. Dreamy. A horrible combination.

He's just about to give up when he notices a woman in a slip dress standing in front of a bar, surrounded by American men in jeans and T-shirts. One of them has his hand on the woman's waist. She leans away from him, stumbling into the chest of another man, who laughs and whispers something in her ear. She's attempting to back away, but they've surrounded her now. When she wrenches her head away from the nearest man, glancing around her for an escape, he catches a glimpse of her face.

Goddammit.

In two seconds, he's off his bike and ramming through the crowd. When he arrives at her side, he takes her hand and shoves her behind him. Faces the men with clenched fists, glowering so darkly that they begin to back away.

"Hey, hey." One of them laughs. "It's okay, dude. Just having a conversation."

"She didn't *want* a conversation with you," he spits out.

The tallest man, wearing a gingham shirt with a ridiculous bandanna tied around his forehead, puts out a placating hand. "We had to try, right? How were we to know she had a man?"

She edges her way in front of Adam. "It doesn't *matter* if I had a man, you asshole. If I want to leave, you let me leave."

Gingham Guy shakes his head. "Okay, okay. Most women here are all too eager for some American dollars, you know?"

Adam takes a sharp breath, not just because of what he's implying about Evie, but what he's implying about Asian women as a whole. That old, tired stereotype. The one that dehumanizes women and assumes that all men must celebrate this level of chauvinism. It makes him sick.

He's stepping forward, ready to grab Gingham by the shirt collar, when Evie neatly cuts him off by drawing back her own fist and slamming it into Gingham's smug face. It's admittedly not a *hard* hit, but there is the audible sound of fist meeting flesh. Adam is equal parts impressed and furious, especially as Gingham begins making his way toward Evie.

"You little—" Gingham cries, holding his cheek.

Adam says, deadly quiet, "I'd watch what you say next, *dude*."

Gingham's friends whistle and hoot as Gingham pauses, then backs away, flicking them off with both hands. Evie blows him a kiss, which sends Adam's already shaken nerves into overdrive. His whole body is tense until the men disappear into a nearby bar.

Then he releases a breath—all the breaths—and turns to Evie, who's frowning and cradling her fist. The crowd around them disperses, disappointed by the anticlimactic ending.

"Ow. Hard head," she says. "I definitely need to take up kickboxing again."

Adam sighs heavily, hardly able to control his temper. "You could have just . . . not hit him, Evie."

"Right," she says sarcastically. "Like the way you were about to *not hit him*?"

He takes a calming breath and walks back to his bike. After a quick pause, she follows, lugging a bag behind her. Thankfully, she's changed her sandals into sneakers, and deftly avoids the mud puddles in the street.

"What's up your ass?" she asks finally.

"Where have you been?"

She holds up her bag. "I had to get my dress from the tailor. The Silken Peacock? I thought it would be rude to leave it. And Fen's too. Though she won't really need it, I guess. Did you hear that Mei came by to sweep her off her feet? It was pretty epic, as far as romantic gestures go. And I got a little distracted by the market. I wasn't too keen on facing your father's wrath for the second night in a row, you know."

Evie's smiling up at him placatingly, but he's still angry. Why can't he let it go? But then again, why can't she just stay out of trouble? Is this what a life with her would be like? Constantly chasing her, feeling like his heart is teetering on the precipice of a cliff when there's even a hint of danger around her? He blows a strand of hair off his forehead and hands her a helmet.

He asks, "Why didn't you answer your phone?"

"I left it at home."

"Can you *not* do that?"

"Can you *not* be so controlling?"

They're silent for a few long minutes, standing in front of the bike while the crowd streams around them. Adam notices everything from the windblown bun at the top of her head to the small scrape near her ankle. She has dark circles under her eyes, probably from not sleeping after their library rendezvous. The thought of it almost gets him hard again. But then he shakes the memory off. He's *angry* at her. Really angry.

"You were being selfish," he says at last. "You left without telling anyone where you were going. Do you know what could have happened to you? What if you'd fallen somewhere in the Marble Mountains and no one knew where you were?"

"I didn't! Those steps were a cinch."

"That is very much not the point. Everyone was worried sick."

"Everyone? Or just you?" There's a glint of challenge in her eye. As if she's daring him to say something.

"Okay, *yes*, I was worried, Evie. I've been roaming all over town for you. Is this a game to you? One of those stupid, reckless ways you try to show people you don't care?"

"It's not a game," she says in a small voice. "I care."

"You care," he repeats. Somehow, the word feels lukewarm to him, especially compared to the constant barrage of emotion he holds inside for her. "You know what? I *more* than care, Evie. I love you."

"You say it like a curse."

"Yeah, because I'm still mad," he says. His voice begins to soften. "But it doesn't mean it's not true."

"You do?"

"I do."

She steps closer to him, winding her hand up in his hair. Playing with the strands by his neck. He dips his head down to hers. Their breaths are tied together now, dancing in the night air. He smells something on her breath—orchid and a bit of mint. Then, she arches up on her tiptoes and presses her lips to his. And he's gone.

He lets himself luxuriate in the sensation of her soft lips, those hands wrapping around his middle, his own palms cupping her face. She nips his lower lip and he pulls her closer, his hands roving down to the small of her back. His tongue deep inside her. Thinking about all the other ways he wants to be inside her. A groan tears from him.

"So rude," a woman mutters nearby.

"Young people," another hisses, shoving against them as she walks by. "No decorum left in the world."

He feels Evie stiffening, then pulling away from him. He almost sighs with the loss of her touch, but then, with the effort no one should ever have to undertake, he instead rips himself away from her. Looks down into her eyes, which are now avoiding his, darting to the low plastic tables, the glowing white signs. All he wants to do is make her meet his gaze again, with that mix of lust and affection she showed him last night. But she steps away with a laugh.

"Aunties. Can't escape 'em."

He resists the urge to spin her back into his arms. He reminds himself that they're on the streets in a conservative country. That he's just told Evie he loves her. And that . . . she hasn't said it back. If he's not a complete and total jerk—which he hopes he's not—he'll honor her unspoken wishes and let her maintain the distance. Even if it kills him.

"Come on," he says, clasping the helmet under her chin. "Let's go home."

The night ride soothes the ruffled parts of him, bringing him back to his own logical thought patterns. Evie is safe. That adrenaline and worry can be shelved. They can figure this out rationally. What it means for him to love her. What it means that she doesn't appear to return his feelings.

Or *is* there a solution to that particular problem? All his life, he's dealt in numbers and equations that make perfect sense. The sum is correct, or it isn't. He does not comprehend this slippery gray area, where she is both with him and far away. For now, all he has is her arms wrapped around his middle, her thighs open around him. The faint smell of *her* mingling with the salt of the ocean, the faraway sweetness of flowering bougainvillea. For now, that's enough, because it has to be.

EVIE

Hội An, Việt Nam

After Adam drops her off at the estate, he disappears without another word. Not that she expects him to linger. He said that he loved her—and she said nothing back. She *wanted* to. Has thought the words privately since their time in the caves—probably before that. But how can she say anything now, knowing his future is so tenuous? He quit his high-paying job to help Ruby with Love Yêu. Without his father's money, could the business really fold? And will Adam be left without prospects?

He's more than his job to her, but does *he* know that? She can't make that decision for him.

She peeks out onto the patio, with its clusters of tea lights and a stone railing that looks over the water, now glowing with the moon's reflection. Pin winds his arm around Talia, who rests her head on his shoulder. Another couple strolls the beach, gesturing animatedly as they talk. Before this trip, Evie had scoffed at the thought of falling in love on the tour, thinking it another one of Auntie Hảo's outsized whims. A joke from beyond the grave. But now, having spent weeks here—weeks falling, no matter how reluctantly, for Adam Quyền—Evie understands it's no joke. The most surprising stories are the ones that sneak up on you, testing every preconceived notion of what you want and what you think you deserve.

Surprise. Adventure. All the romance she could possibly hold in her cold little heart. That's exactly what she got here, with Love Yêu.

But it's under threat. How long could LYT sustain themselves without Mr. Quyền's money? They are still a start-up, wedged in that dreadfully precarious make-or-break period when even the most minor financial setback could imperil everything they've built. The work is just beginning. Without the safety net of money from the investors, they could just as easily flounder, another passionate company taken down by their own ambition. Or in this case, the vindictiveness of one stony-faced investor.

How could she live with being the one who made these tours come to a screeching halt? Love Yêu isn't just a sound business idea. It's a chance for people to find the one thing missing from their lives. Before, Evie might have dismissed that notion as sentimental codependency. Empty marketing lingo. Now she thinks there's nothing more sacred.

Adam told her he wouldn't leave Việt Nam. And she can't leave America. So why not just end it here before the heartache starts? Save them both some pain. It hurt when things ended with Atlas, and she cares for Adam more after the few weeks they've spent in each other's company than the year she's known Atlas. The pain will be exponentially worse if she and Adam go much further.

She escapes to her room, plopping against one of the six fluffy pillows lining the headboard. Is it just her imagination or has the mattress gotten even softer and plusher? It feels like sinking into the downy bellies of a thousand swans. Say what you want about the Quyềns—and boy, could she—but they understand the value of quality bedding.

Once settled, she takes out her phone and scrolls to the last photo she has of Auntie Hảo. Perhaps it's nostalgia; perhaps it's something more pressing. She's overwhelmed with the longing to hear Auntie Hảo's voice. What she wouldn't give to sit across from her while they sip thimblefuls of vodka, gossiping about everyone and everything. She wants to rewind back to when things were light. When she wasn't so alone.

In her albums, she discovers a picture of her and Auntie Hảo grinning underneath a string of fairy lights. It makes her eyes spark with tears immediately. That night. That perfect night of love and hope and safety.

It had been last summer—before they learned about the cancer. Before Atlas, before the various failures. When her book had appeared on a couple most-anticipated lists, gaining tentative acclaim. Auntie Hảo had thrown a "little party" in her house in honor of Evie's fledgling success, but in true Auntie Hảo style, it had been far more lavish than the intimate soiree she initially promised. There was a bossa nova band. An executive chef from the Mission's most up-and-coming restaurant blowtorched individual ramekins of ube crème brûlée. (Later, he got so irritated that one of the guests hadn't finished his crème brûlée that he threatened to blowtorch the curtains, an act Evie hastily prevented with a liberal heaping of compliments and a very large absinthe drip.) Auntie Hảo's fabulous writer and artist friends feted Evie, dropping wet kisses on her cheeks and twirling her around the room like a proud little top. But Auntie Hảo had been proudest of all.

Toward the end of the night, Auntie Hảo stood on a long wooden table, stretching her arms up to the ceiling in her dramatic way. In one hand, she held a coupe glass of sloshing, sparkling champagne. Her snow-white hair curled artfully around her face while her silk caftan swished against a pair of embroidered red slippers. Evie would always remember the detail of those slippers. Phoenixes taking flight from an apricot bush.

"My niece is, in a few words . . ." Auntie Hảo announces, ". . . better than yours."

The room erupted into laughter while Evie blushed scarlet. Someone thumped her on the back.

"Evie Lang is a name you should memorize. She's going to be one of our greatest treasures in American letters. I'm sure many of you remember the summers she spent in San Francisco as a girl. Her gifts bloomed here. And mark my words, one day, she'll be back in our arms again. And we will welcome her with all our hearts."

"Hear, hear!" the crowd yelled, taking mighty glugs while beaming smiles toward Evie.

And amidst it all, Auntie Hảo's fond face, full of pride. *With all our hearts.*

As the echoes of that memory die away, wetness soaks onto Evie's cheeks. She misses Auntie Hảo in a way that's bigger than just the one loss—though it is in itself a momentous heartache. Losing Auntie Hảo has been like losing her father all over again. Without them, with only Evie's practical mother to guide her, she is adrift. Perhaps she has been adrift for longer than she's been able to admit.

In bed, she tosses and turns. It's midnight before her eyelids finally shut against the events of the day. She sleeps dreamlessly, though restlessly.

The next morning, the dense heat of the sun crowding against her eyelids, she reluctantly pulls herself from bed. Despite the swan-belly bedding, there's a crick in her neck. Her phone dings with countless text messages.

From Fen, a selfie of her and Mei in front of a tarmac with the message: Back to China, baby. Landed a big part. Mei's going to be my spoiled housecat. My father and his money can suck it.

Evie smiles at that and pulls a brush through her hair.

From Atlas: So? I'm waiting on tenterhooks for two answers now, my love. You really know how to keep a lad speculating.

. . . Forget I called myself a lad. Too much London. Too little Evie.

Hmm. That earns a frown from her. What the hell does he mean? And why can't he speak like a normal person if he wants an answer? (Or two, evidently.)

She pulls on a midi skirt with a tank top and espadrilles. Sooner or later, she'll have to brush her teeth and greet Adam's parents. Bid them goodbye and extend a heartfelt thank-you for hosting the lot of them. The tour group will be driving to Đà Nẵng, after which they'll hop on a private plane to Hải Phòng, then a final transfer to Hạ Long Bay, where they'll sail the gorgeous emerald waters and visit the floating villages. She's been looking forward to Hạ Long Bay. In part, she admits, because she wants to see the sights with Adam.

After last night, though, she doesn't know where they've landed. He said he *loves* her. That alone should have filled her completely. To be loved by a man like him should have been enough. More than enough.

But there's Ruby's conversation. The risk of all they would have to relinquish for an unsteady foundation for their relationship. Is it worth it? Is *love* worth it?

She glances down at a string of texts from Lillian: Holy effin' hell. Have you checked your email?!

E? I'm dying here.

You better be dead or in SERIOUS HARM. Literally the only excuses I will accept. Remember what I said about Liam Neeson?

Plus a cluster of skull emojis.

Mystified, Evie taps her mail icon and sees the flurry of unread emails. Hundreds; way, way more than she ever gets, even in the midst of grading season, when students are anxious to turn those D's into C's. Some of the emails are from her agent, some from a former editor; lots and lots from publicity teams. The subject lines are variations on "Congrats!!" Her agent sends her a link to a podcast with the words *LISTEN NOW*.

Puzzled, she clicks on the link. Within minutes, she learns that the former First Lady of the United States—a dignified and well-read woman Evie admires to no end and secretly wishes had run the country—mentioned one of *her* poems on a podcast. The one called "Lake's Last Hope," an old favorite. In the poem, there's an extended metaphor about breaking the ice to reveal racism in an increasingly fraught world. It had lightly but powerfully tackled issues of immigration and erasure. Her editor had questioned whether the poem needed to be included in a collection that was otherwise focused on personal narrative, but Evie insisted. It had felt timely. Politically prescient.

And now it had, apparently, become a very rare beast: a viral poem.

The First Lady's offhanded comment resulted in a renewed interest in her work. A resharing, retweeting, re-everythinging. Thousands of likes streamed into her dormant social media account. A wildly popular morning show began recommending her book as a top, buzzy read, even though it had been published a year ago. People were inviting her to speak on panels again—panels she had summarily been rejected from earlier in the year. Journalists wanted to know what it felt like to be quoted by the former First Lady.

Most important, her publisher wanted to know if she had another book in her. They were eager—nay, desperate—to see how soon they could get another volume of poetry out. And, peeking at her recent royalty statement, she can see why. The numbers are . . . startling. Never one to say no to a stray dollar or two in her account, Evie is now seeing figures that boggle her mind.

Then, most recently, there's an email from Atlas, using his official department head email and lingo. Midland College is offering her a bigger and better position than the one she has recently been fired from. He apologizes on behalf of the College of the Humanities for their oversight, says that there is money in the academic coffers again, should she choose to rejoin them for a reduced teaching load *and* a higher salary.

It is . . . the dream.

And it has all been happening in the past few days when she's been too caught up in cave-side trysts to contemplate her (usually flailing) career. But now, if she says the word, she can have it all, and for real this time. The fame, the kudos. The backstage catering table at the big-name talk shows. Plus, an actual professor title. She could ride this to the top.

But instead of shooting back a thousand "yes please!" emails, she sinks into a chair. Holds her phone away from her as if it's a serpent ready to spring. None of it makes sense. Isn't this what she wanted? What she'd have cut off her left arm for? Why, then, does this dull sense of resignation pound in her veins?

It's as if any semblance of choice has been taken from her. She wants everything offered—the book deals, the interviews, the *everything*. And she wants Adam. But she can't have both, and she *won't* be the woman who chooses a man over a career she's worked a decade to build.

Her life in America is calling her back, and even though she's dragging her feet, she knows it's only a matter of time before she answers.

It's nine p.m. in Ohio. Lillian picks up almost immediately. "Are you dead? Maimed?"

"I'm just not a *phone* person," Evie answers, her voice shaking with laughter.

"She's not a phone person. She says she's not a phone person!"

"Things have changed, huh?"

"Evie Lang, the queen of understatements. I could not *believe* when I heard the former First Lady talking about you. I was plucking my eyebrows, for God's sake! It shocked me so much that I plucked into my arch."

"I'm so sorry."

"You and me both; my brow girl will not be pleased. You can make it up to me once you collect your millions and pay for some eyebrow implants. Is that a thing?"

"It should be."

Lillian continues, "And then the next day, I couldn't go anywhere on Instagram without someone posting your words on some snowy background. Tagging that sorry excuse for an account that you have. *Then* Graham tells me that the department wants you back big-time. Atlas is spinning around campus, waiting for your answer."

When a light knock sounds on her door, Evie goes to answer it. "Hold on, Lillian."

"She says hold on!" Lillian replies sarcastically.

There's no one there. Instead, she nearly trips over a bouquet of flowers in a vase that's hardly large enough to contain them. They're pretty, if gaudy. There's a card attached. Atlas.

Evie sighs. "I think Atlas wants to get back together. Remember how he wanted to keep our thing a secret?"

"Some secret. I didn't tell Graham, but somehow he knew. The lunch ladies in the cafeteria knew. That guy at the Piggly Wiggly who you think is always giving you the stink eye? Pretty sure he was fully aware."

"Huh. Anyway, now Atlas seems to want to have a real relationship—out in the open, presumably sanctioned by the college HR gods!"

"Nothing like a mountain of paperwork to scream 'I want you back.' What are you going to say? To both questions?"

"No to getting back together. The man talks like Benedict Cumberbatch."

"Is that a bad thing?"

Evie rolls her eyes, even though she knows her cousin can't see her. "It's not a bad thing if you're Benedict Cumberbatch."

"Fair enough. And the other question?"

"The job. I would be insane to turn it down, right?"

"You know you would be. So why are you hesitating, fair cousin?"

Evie sighs. "You know that grumpy CMO I mentioned on the tour? Well, I might have, well, slept with him. A few times."

There's silence on the other end. Then Lillian repeats slowly, "A few times."

"In a cave. Outside a hut on the beach—well, that wasn't so much sex as heavy petting? And a library. *That* was sex."

"Well, well, well." Now there's a hint of amusement coming from the other end of the line. "And you thought the matchmaking tour wouldn't work."

"All right, Lawyer I-Told-You-So, not helpful. The problem is, it worked too well."

"Meaning?"

"Lill, I *love* him. I'm kind of, sort of, definitely head over heels for him. Would walk into an ocean for him. Would ride his motorbike with him until we're hot and sweaty and—"

"Oh, well, you didn't mention the motorbike," Lillian says playfully. "That changes everything."

"Unfortunately, nothing changes at all."

Evie describes her plight with Adam, leaving out no detail about her argument with Mr. Quyền and Ruby's aside. She talks about the constant push and pull. How nothing is simple with them. And yet, everything can be so *good*.

"My friend Fen—" Evie begins.

"You have a new friend? I'm trying not to be jealous."

"Fen says that sometimes you have to work to make your own riding-off-into-the-sunset situation. She's of the Auntie Hảo school of 'love bravely.'"

Lillian makes an understanding noise, but says, "I think it's easy to say that if you're someone like Auntie Hảo, who lived alone all her days and never risked a thing for anyone."

"So you're *not* of the love bravely school, I take it?"

"Oh, Evie," Lillian says. "I don't know. Love is like . . . a buffet."

"Come again?"

"I mean, imagine that there are all these different kinds of love on display, okay? Each one gets its own dish, all lined up for you to choose from. There's the passionate, heady, fuck-against-a-hut kind of love."

"I regret telling you that."

"Hut love is wild and sublime, but it tears you open. It's risky. It could give you indigestion."

"Lillian, please," Evie groans.

"Stay with me. Then there's the slow-burn kind of love, where you start out as friends and steadily become something more. It's comfortable, like a quilt on a really cold day. It's safe and dependable. That's what Graham and I have. You and Atlas had that too, at one point—"

"Until the plot twist where he fired me."

"Do I wish I'd had a peek at the hut love? Sure, maybe a little. But I think people who say that love is pain think there's only one kind of love out there to choose from. So just remember that. You get a choice."

"All I have to do now is choose, right?"

"Easier said than done, I know."

"I love you, Lill."

"Even after you get incredibly rich and famous? You'll still remember the little people?"

"Only if you never talk to me about hut love again."

"My word is my vow."

After they hang up, Evie opens the side door, the one leading to a balcony that looks out onto the sea. The room feels emptier without Fen's mess, her voice interrupting Evie's thoughts. Today, the water is calm, and the sky no longer overcast.

Yesterday, she climbed all 156 steps up the Thuy Son summit in the Marble Mountains to reach the very top. Some of the steps had been slippery, but she made it up there just in time to see the sun set over the rich green valley, highlighting the limestone surfaces of the other summits, along with the unraveling city with its flat roofs and ribbons of traffic.

She'd stood at the peak, feeling as if she had flown all the way up on wings. Knowing she did it on her own. Right then, she sat in the dying light and began to write, even as tourists streamed around her, clamoring for the best photo opportunity. She ignored them, in a world of her own. Words and images fell from her pen. She was able to sink into her imagination again, the way she had when she was writing *Auntie Hảo's Cabinet of Curiosities*. Only this time, there was an even deeper connection with her heritage. It was as if she'd been able to finally peel back all the onion-layers of her heart, to find her way to the beating center.

She loves Adam. She knows this. But she also loves poetry and the life she has in America. She's experienced love. She even learned to love bravely. But now? Now it's time to go home. To release Adam back to the life he's built, even if she won't be a part of it. Hot tears gather at the edges of her eyes. She brushes them away.

Beyond the ocean, the cry of a seabird rises, then falls in an elegy of heartbreak. It knows what's coming. She watches the bird dip into the ocean, brushing the water's surface with an angled wing. Then it's gone again, beyond the horizon. She goes back inside and composes an email to Atlas.

ADAM

Hội An, Việt Nam

"Your pants are too tight. And you are skinnier than a mantis during a famine."

"Yes, Bà Nội," Adam answers, placating his grandmother.

Bà Nội pinches the flesh along his neck as if he were a prize cow waiting for auction. It's not a light pinch. In fact, it hurts like a motherfucker. Adam grimaces and rubs the spot, which will bruise like a love bite. Except not at all like that. Of course it figures that his father's mother would have his same intense brand of physicality. Whereas his father is still hardy, if stout, Bà Nội looks like the crone that comes out of every fairy tale remake, blustering about thwarted fates and the end of the world. Well, she might if she weren't wearing a Chanel suit with a crocodile-skin bag squatting by her thin ankles.

Stooped form aside, Bà Nội remains a force. She holds most of the purse strings from her late husband's fortune and doles it out with what Adam has privately felt to be rather random methodology. He's never been the beneficiary of her financial support, which suits him just fine. He's learned that the Quyềns' brand of generosity comes with many, many conditions.

Despite her habitually harsh words, Bà Nội has a soft spot for Adam, for reasons unknown to anyone. She requests to see him every time he's in Hội An. Perhaps it's because he looks like his late grandfather, a stoic man who served in his share of wars and died only a decade earlier in his eighties. Or maybe it's because Adam never fails to bring Bà Nội her favorite brand of chocolate bonbons, the one thing she eats with any real abandon. Just now, there's a streak of chocolate on her cheek. Adam isn't sure whether to say anything, but then his mother reaches over with a wet handkerchief and wipes it off for her mother-in-law.

Bà Nội waves her away. "Do I look like I need a nursemaid, Sáng?"

"Oh, no, Mẹ, you're looking as youthful as ever. Really, I've always said you're in your prime—"

"Sáng, shut up. I'm here to talk to my grandson. If I wanted to talk to you, I have three hundred and sixty-four other days to be bored out of my wits. Now, Bảo, skinny boy, what trouble have you gotten yourself into?"

She gives him a fond look and pats his hand encouragingly. Her home isn't nearly as large or ostentatious as the Quyền estate, but there's a grandeur to it all the same. The salty breeze flows through the open windows, dancing with the drapes. All the furniture is antique, yet well-tended and timelessly elegant. Adam has always felt peaceful here.

When he was a child, and when his ông nội was alive, he'd often find excuses to visit his grandparents, scrambling underfoot even when they paid him no mind. He was the only grandchild who clamored to be around them as a kid—though now, as mercenary adults, all the cousins find excuses to see Bà Nội, claiming filial devotion, much to her shrewd-eyed dismay.

Adam answers, "Ruby's started a new company, and I'm working for her. A luxury matchmaking tour."

"Matchmaking! Why, that's how your ông nội and I met. Of course, he was madly in love after seeing my picture for just a few seconds. Ối giời ơi, was I a beauty. Things have changed since then. People got uglier for one. How's the tour going?"

"We're finishing our inaugural one now, and our guests are very pleased. It's gone off pretty well, all things considered. Ruby planned everything out meticulously. There's a ninety percent success rate."

"Only ninety percent?" Bà Nội asks curiously.

He hesitates. "Well, yes. We had a few . . . incidents. A tour guest left. And there was the thing with the police."

"The police!"

Mrs. Quyền speaks up. "It's nothing you need to hear about, Mẹ."

Bà Nội shoots Adam's mother a withering look. "Do I look like a child, Sáng? Should I cover my ears anytime an adult speaks? Go sit in the garden. You're bothering me."

"Mẹ—" Mrs. Quyền begins.

But, without another word, Bà Nội points at the French doors leading to the garden. With an aggrieved sigh, Mrs. Quyền obliges. Adam admires the hell out of that performance. If only he could command his parents— and a certain Anglophile ex-boyfriend—out of the picture with a mere gesture.

Bà Nội pours herself a cup of tea and hands Adam a piece of sesame candy. "Eat this, Bảo. You're too skinny. All due respect, but your mother is an idiot. Your father too. Of all my children, I have found no worthy heir. Foolish, superficial creatures. It's enough to make me wish for an early death."

"I wish you wouldn't."

"Well, you're the only one. Now, tell me more about this tour. Don't leave anything out because of my aged sensibilities."

"Or you'll send me to the garden to play?" He smiles.

After a severe look from Bà Nội, Adam acquiesces and gives her the non-PR-sanctioned version of the tour. He doesn't leave out a word about Connor's black eye and the police coming to take Đức away, Fen's girlfriend swooping into town to rescue her, even Evie's confrontation with his father. Bà Nội listens with her keen, watchful expression, snickering in some parts, asking him to repeat others.

When he finishes, she grabs his knee with one knobby hand.

"You are in love with this Evie woman," she says simply, a statement of fact.

He gapes at her. "How did—that is—"

She raises an eyebrow until he finally sighs and nods. "I'm in love with Evie."

"And your father doesn't approve."

"He has threatened to cut us off if I don't end it with her. He thinks she's too American."

"What the hell does that mean?" Bà Nội demands.

"Outspoken, I suppose. Disrespectful?"

He sees his mother wandering around the gardens, talking into her cell phone in what seems to be a very emphatic way. She kicks at a bench.

"What horseshit." Bà Nội snorts. "Your father *would* say that. He married the meekest little pigeon there ever was. Always had a type. Liked people he could boss around. But he can't boss your Evie around, can he?"

"No," Adam answers, grinning at the image of Evie standing up for him at dinner.

"And you like that, huh, my boy?" she asks slyly.

"Yes, I do."

Bà Nội slaps her legs with her hands and grabs her cane. With a hard thrust, she pokes him in the chest. Once, twice. He grimaces again, rubbing his pectoral. "Listen here, Bảo. Your father is a fool. What's more, he's a damn bully. I raised him—or someone did, I guess a nursemaid might have—so I know his flaws better than anyone. And we can all learn new tricks, even me at my old age, but he doesn't *want* to. So I'm here to tell you that his opinion doesn't matter. Do you hear me? You love this Evie? You go be with her. Marry her. Have babies with her."

"We're not there yet, Bà Nội," he protests.

"Well, get there. You're not getting any younger. My eyesight is going, and even I can see that gray hair starting to sprout around your ears. Did you know that sperm depreciates every year in quality, not to mention Evie's eggs?"

"Bà Nội, please don't discuss Evie's eggs. Or my sperm, for that matter."

Another jab in the chest. "My point, skinny Bảo, is that I will not let you walk away from someone you love enough to tell *me* about. Do you know that I had to hear about that Lana woman after you'd already proposed? I can hear it in your voice. Evie Lang is your mate. For every dollar your father withdraws from your sister's company, I will add twice as much of my own. So don't fret about the money."

"I wasn't planning on walking away from her because of the money, Bà Nội."

"Then what?"

Adam eyes the cane with a mixture of respect and consternation. "She lives in America. And I live here. It's just impossible."

"You know what's impossible, skinny Bảo? A man falling in love with a woman through a picture. Her feeling the same. The two of them, married for over sixty years, through more than half a century of war and overeager GIs and silly French coquettes and troublesome children who are still the plagues of my life. But that is what happened with your ông nội and me. What I mean to tell you is this: Don't be a coward."

Love bravely. Adam opens his mouth to speak, then closes it. What does loving bravely mean in this context? Moving across the world? Would it be so bad? Of course it wouldn't. Nothing would be bad with Evie by his side. He could start over, work at the very bottom rung of a company, grabbing coffee for supercilious businessmen, as long as he had *her* to come home to. If the only thing keeping him back is his ego, is that any excuse to walk away from this fascinating, infuriating woman who has needled right under his skin, into the very folds of his soul?

It is not. Nothing is worth walking away from Evie for.

Seeing the play of emotions across her grandson's face, Bà Nội gives a satisfied tut. "Thank God you're better at listening to sense than your father. Now that that's settled, go summon your mother, will you? She's going to melt out there in the heat. And you tell your sister, Ruby, to come see me. She's not a bad kid either. And I want to hear about this business of hers. I have a feeling she'll be looking for a new partner soon."

When they arrive back at the estate, Adam rushes to Evie's quarters. He doesn't see her anywhere in the halls. He pounds on her door, again and again. No one answers. Then he races outside and scans the beach. The usual suspects are lounging in the sand with their beach reads and SPF 70. But no Evie.

Just as he's getting on his motorbike to ride into town, he sees Ruby running toward him. For once, she has none of her usual self-satisfied aplomb. In fact, she looks rather ashen.

"BB, wait," she calls.

He idles the engine. "If you're going to talk me out of seeing Evie—"

"I don't have to," she says heavily. "Evie left this morning while you were at Bà Nội's house."

"She's gone ahead to Hạ Long Bay early?" He can hear the confusion in his own voice, but he doesn't understand the emotions racing across Ruby's face—a little fear, guilt, and disappointment.

His mind is crammed with questions. Why didn't she wait for the rest of the tour group? Does she know how to get around there without them? Will she be all right on her own?

And then Ruby says the words that make him hunch over his handlebars, as if he'd been punched in the chest.

"Bảo, Evie has gone back to America."

Adam turns the bike off. He stares at his sister. "What do you mean, she's gone back to America?"

She places a hand on his arm and says, "I don't know much. I saw that she got the flower arrangement from some man named Atlas. Then she told me that she was sorry, she had to go back earlier than anticipated. She said she wished us the best of luck. That she will leave a good review."

He laughs bitterly and without humor. "She'll leave us a good review."

"I know."

Ruby pulls him to her, and though at first he resists, he at last lets himself sink into his sister's arms. Not that he can feel them. He's numb. Utterly, irreversibly brokenhearted.

"She left," he repeats. If he says it often enough, maybe he'll believe it.

"It's for the best, Bảo," she says soothingly. "Soon we'll be sailing into the majestic bay, completing a successful tour. And you—you've proven yourself to be more than capable of being our CMO. I can't thank you enough. Don't you see? This is just the start for Love Yêu. The road ahead is lined in gold. And I want to travel it with you, my brother."

These words of approval and gratitude, the ones he's been chasing all his life, fall on deaf ears. It doesn't feel good to hear them. Truthfully, he can't feel anything, except the crushing loss. For Ruby, the future might look bright. But without Evie, he sees nothing but a string of endless, dark nights, in which his arms remain empty, and his heart cold. No amount of material success can soothe such a loss.

Why didn't she wait to say goodbye, at least? What could be more important than the question between them, that tremulous and beautiful gap, waiting to be filled by their story? He starts his bike again and rides away from his sister, his family, ignoring her pleas for him to stay. He doesn't know where he's going, but it doesn't matter now. He has no direction, no purpose, only the heaviness of certainty. It happened again. He's been betrayed and left behind, with nowhere to pour the love in his heart. He should have known better than to trust a stranger.

EVIE

San Francisco, California
two months later

Evie has never cleaned so much in her entire life. And not just swipe-at-a-couple-windows-and-call-it-a-day kind of cleaning. She's been engaged in a sweaty, all-day marathon that leaves her feeling like one of those crusted-over pieces of cheese at the bottom of a decades-old oven. Spent and disposable. But when you inherit a century-old Victorian bursting with decades of collected artwork and knickknacks from all over the world, there's bound to be a few pounds of dust. A spider or twenty-five.

Thankfully, Auntie Hảo's old friends haven't stopped dropping by with loaves of zucchini bread or bottles of zin. The most conscientious among them usually offer an extra hand for dusting and scrubbing. Of course, most of them prove less than helpful, easily distracted by trying on Auntie Hảo's clothes or reminiscing over said bottle of zin. Like Priya, who took a nap in the middle of the floor that Evie was in the midst of vacuuming. Or the screenwriter who curled into Auntie Hảo's claw-foot tub, sobbing because he'd received a rejection from a studio while he was supposed to be Windexing the mirrors.

Evie spends more time socializing than she does cleaning, but she doesn't mind one bit. It lifts her spirits to see the house teeming with life again, though there is a markedly somber tone, everyone remembering the force of life that departed too soon.

In between sobs, the screenwriter sniffled, "I love this house. It was my home, just as much as any other. Whenever I talk to anyone who knew Miss Hảo, they talk about the inspiration she gave them. She was the mother we never had; she was *magic*."

Evie agreed. In fact, something small and wonderful lit behind her mind when she heard his words, like a candle sputtering to life—an idea that only Auntie Hảo could have come up with. But driven by exhaustion and an overflow of emotion, Evie shuttled that idea away for the moment. There would be time. Years and years in this beautiful, boisterous place.

When she arrived back in the States, she went straight to Auntie Hảo's lawyer and got the keys to the San Francisco house. Her jet lag hadn't even faded before she collapsed into her old bedroom with the rosebud wallpaper and porcelain whale lamp. *Her house. Her life.*

There was no more talk of selling. With her newfound fame (well, as much fame as a poet might reasonably expect), she also has enough income to keep the house for a few years and leave teaching until she figures out what's next. Granted, it's much too big for one person. And the money won't last forever. But those are problems for another day.

Atlas took the news of her departure remarkably well. He asked if she might be open to a "long-distance, unlatched affair between kindreds," which she took to be a petition for an open relationship. She responded with a resounding no, not because of the open relationship part, but because of the Atlas part. Still, he'd had the generosity to arrange for movers to pack her few belongings in Midland and ship them to her in California.

Lillian had been equal parts dismayed and—once she realized that West Coast winery vacations were now on the horizon—overjoyed. Last Evie heard, Lancaster Small had taken over her old position. She sent him congratulations, which he did not respond to. Her old world moves steadily along without her, but there is a rightness to this.

She's exactly where she belongs.

After cleaning, Evie takes a long, hot shower, then dries her hair and puts on her favorite outfit. A Wednesday Addams–style dress that cinches at the waist, along with a pair of ankle boots and one of Auntie Hảo's long gold necklaces. She's attending another reading today, but this time, she's the headliner. There's a sign for her and everything.

After things took off with her last book, she decided that she would *live* bravely, if she couldn't love bravely. She says yes to any opportunity within reason, like speaking on podcasts, delivering speeches at conferences, and—most important for her career—signing a six-figure, two-book contract with her publisher for both another poetry collection and a memoir, something she has no experience with but is determined to learn by taking one of the many writing workshops in the Bay Area. Her classmates always gape a little when they recognize her name, but soon realize she is just as clueless as the rest of them.

The night of the reading, the small bookstore is crowded with people. At least half are already seated for her, she notes with a flutter of pride. At first, she felt guilty that she'd benefited so much from what she considered essentially a fluke. But soon, with coaching from Lillian and Fen, who's still gallivanting around the world with Mei between filming, Evie learned to take it in stride. To ride the wave for as long as she can. After all, that's the only thing you can do in an industry that changes like the tides.

Onstage at the bookstore, she reads her most popular poem, the one the former First Lady quoted, along with a few others, including the crowd favorite, a limerick about one of Auntie Hảo's raucous parties. Looking out onto the crowd, she sees listeners leaning forward, nodding, smiling.

A few are her neighbors, Auntie Hảo's old friends and now hers, beaming with such pride that Evie fights back a few tears. They're all clutching copies of *her* book. The validation feels fantastic, of course, but it's more than that. She feels at last as if she's come into the life she's always hoped for.

And yet.

There's a dull and insistent throbbing in her heart. A sense of having left something important behind. It had begun on the shores of Hội An, and months later, that feeling never, ever dissipates.

At the Q&A after the reading, a man in a fedora who reminds her of Đức asks, "What are you working on next?"

Evie takes a sip from her miniature water bottle. "I'm writing another poetry collection inspired by my recent travels in Việt Nam. I went on a matchmaking tour that my late aunt set up. Maybe you know of her."

The crowd chuckles.

Someone else asks, "What was the best thing you did in Việt Nam?"

She doesn't know what prompts her to say it, but she does, summoning all her honesty and vulnerability. "Falling in love. It was also the most surprising thing. But what I've learned is that the best moments are the ones that happen when you're fully in the moment. The best connections are the ones that happen in good faith, when two people allow each other to become radically vulnerable with each other. Love, friendship. Art. It's only possible when you allow yourself to leap."

There's a sigh around the room, an anticipation for a story with a happy ending, which most of us secretly want, even if we're not willing to admit it aloud.

Then a woman stands up at the back of the room. Evie squints through the glare of the lights, then recognizes the brush of blond hair. That dignified and rigid frame, a five-foot-seven steel rod. She gasps.

Grace Lang gives her a smile, one that's warm yet laced with regret. "Whatever happened with that love story, Evie?"

The way her mother says her name, heavy with affection, makes the audience wheel toward her. They take in Grace's cocked head, as well as Evie's visible shock. Their eyes ping-pong from mother to daughter.

Evie studies her mother. Her hair has grown a bit longer. Her clothes, more colorful. But it's Grace. In San Francisco. The woman who once vowed never to leave their tiny hometown got on a plane for *her*.

Pride swells in Evie, for both herself and her mother.

Evie takes a breath. "I wish I knew. There are no guarantees—even on a love tour."

The room sighs again, this time with a little sadness. People who read poetry know something about heartbreak.

Grace nods and slides back into her chair. Later, after the reading and the signings, the grateful handshakes, and that rush of exhausted triumph, Evie finds her mother standing near a display of *Auntie Hảo's Cabinet of Curiosities*.

"Want to see my house, Mom?" she asks.

And, as if they haven't spent years apart, communicating mostly through fragmented emails, Grace holds her hand out to her daughter. They walk out of the bookstore together.

On the narrow back patio, over glasses of pinot, they discuss Grace's lightly unpleasant plane ride ("A man *took his shoes off* next to me. I could see his toenails! They needed clipping, Evie!") and Evie's memoir. Grace is curious about everything, willing to fill in the gaps where she can. Evie is impressed by how much she remembers, but she shouldn't be. No one has marked Danh Lang's life with more love and attention than her mother.

"I wish Auntie Hảo had left journals or photos—something," Evie sighs. "She never spoke much of her childhood."

"Ah, you've reminded me."

Grace reaches into her bag and hands something to Evie. A photograph.

When Evie flips it over, she sees Auntie Hảo as a girl, her arm slung around the shoulders of another teen, a boy wearing a polo shirt and pants rolled up to the shins. Both are barefoot, standing on a boulder in front of a mountain. There's a picnic at their feet. The sun in the photo, plus the years of age, blows out all the shadows, so what remains are the wide smiles and dark heads, leaning toward each other. It's hard to make out their faces beyond that.

"Is that Dad?" Evie whispers.

Grace shakes her head. "This is Auntie Hảo's best friend and first love. They went to secondary school together. Their families were neighbors. In the eighties, though, your father's family had the chance to emigrate to the States. The man begged Auntie Hảo to stay with him, but she wanted to see the world. She wanted to go to college and make her way—which she did.

"She always meant to send back for him. For years, she would dream about having him by her side. But I think she was scared of what he would say. Whether he could forgive her. By the time she wrote, he'd already married another woman. Had a couple of children. It broke Auntie Hảo's heart. She refused to return to their hometown because it would mean having to face her heartbreak. All the regrets. She never spoke about him again. I think she always blamed herself for waiting too long to admit her feelings."

Love bravely.

So Auntie Hảo had a great love too, one so immense that it drowned out any longing for another person. She wasn't the example. She was the cautionary tale.

"How do you know all this?" Evie asks. It's hard to believe Auntie Hảo would have confided in Grace.

"Your father told me. He was concerned for his sister. Worried about her unprocessed pain, I suppose. If you muffle an emotion for too long— even a difficult one, like grief—it makes you hard. But now I know that if you let any emotion take over, like I did with my fear, it transforms you into a smaller version of yourself."

"I know, Mom. I understand."

Evie watches her mother wipe a tear away. She fidgets with her wedding ring, which she still wears, two decades later.

Grace says, "I found this photo in his papers after he died, though I never showed you."

"Why not?"

Grace presses her lips together. "It wasn't my secret to tell."

"I see."

Grace sighs. "But to be honest, I think I was jealous of your relationship with Auntie Hảo. And maybe even a little bit jealous of how close you and your dad were. I know Hảo was more adventurous and fun-loving. And she saw a side of you that I couldn't embrace at the time, I guess, in all my grief over your father."

"I was grieving too."

"Sweetie, I know. Evie, I'm so sorry. Seeing your name everywhere made me realize how little I understood you. How few attempts I made to connect. What you said in the bookstore about leaps? I was never ready for the leap. But I am now. I read everything you wrote. It was like seeing a curtain drawn back on your heart."

"I would have loved to share so much with you, Mom. And to get to know you. We were both so lonely."

"I wish I could do it all over again."

The night is descending, and Evie can only see shadows on her mother's face, flickering in the glow of the tea lights. Grace looks tired, but softer. Evie thinks that if she were to glance in the mirror, she might resemble her mother, even though everyone always said she took after her father's side of the family.

Evie reaches over and squeezes her mother's hand. "It's okay, Mom. We can get to know each other now."

Grace is surprised. "You think? It's not too late?"

"Sure," Evie answers with a crooked smile. "As long as we're alive, there's still enough time for everything."

"Even mothers who have years to make up for?"

"Especially those. Daughters too."

"And you'll tell me about the matchmaking tour?"

"I'll tell you everything."

They light a citronella candle and pour another glass of wine. Fireflies hum in the night. Somewhere nearby, a party starts up on someone's deck, music streaming into their ears. The city is waking up, like a child after a long sleep, raising her hands to stretch.

Looking at her mother, Evie reflects that maybe when Auntie Hảo talked about loving bravely, she wasn't just talking about romantic love. These days, Evie's found a way to love many people, in many ways. Lillian and Fen, Talia and the rest of the tour guests, even Atlas with his irrepressible curiosity and flamboyant zest for life. Her life is fuller than it's ever been. It's not the happily ever after Auntie Hảo likely imagined for her, but it isn't a miserable life. Far from it.

Still, Evie can't ignore the gnawing pain inside her, her desire to talk about Adam. How he appears in nearly every dream with his smile, his touch. How her longing for him is so acute that sometimes, even standing amid a crowd, she looks over her shoulder, as if he'll appear.

Among all the regrets of her life, she hates that she left him without saying goodbye. Perhaps she was scared he'd convince her to stay. Or perhaps she wasn't nearly as brave as she thought. Her decision to return to the States fills her with pride and shame in equal measure. She doesn't regret embracing her future—but she regrets that she never fully closed the door on the fleeting, breathtaking love story they could have had.

The night has just begun, and Evie, sitting across from Grace, finds another opening in her heart. She lets her mother in.

ADAM

Hồ Chí Minh City, Việt Nam

As Adam is jogging back to the LYT office for a virtual meeting, he bumps into someone passing in the opposite direction on the street. He begins to apologize, but then his gaze flicks downward, into his ex-girlfriend's perfectly made-up face. Lana blinks once, twice, before stepping back from him. As ever, she's gorgeously put together in a white blazer and silk trousers, as if she's come straight from Ibiza. The pungent note of amber in her perfume begins to give him a headache. Has her scent always been so strong?

He takes a moment to study Lana. What does he feel? A kind of distant goodwill? A brief dart of annoyance, like he's staring at an incomplete task? Not heartbreak. Never, he realizes, has it been heartbreak toward her. Wounded pride, sure, and betrayal, always. But heartbreak is reserved for another woman.

"Adam," she says, her hand touching her hair self-consciously. "God. It's been . . . ages. How are you?"

He tries to school his face into an expression of friendliness. Hồ Chí Minh City is still a small enough place that they might occasionally run into one another. In this society, you play nice. You don't make waves. But how can he pretend, when they've never had the Conversation? There was no closure, only a weird amnesia that seemed to spread over their mutual acquaintances, as if the relationship were a figment of his imagination.

Truth be told, Adam hasn't thought much about Lana in the months since the tour ended. Or since it began. His mind has been on other things. Other . . . people. What he feels toward Lana has been reduced to a dull, forgettable affection. He's surprised to find that his remaining hurt has little to do with their relationship and everything to do with how it ended.

He clears his throat. "Congratulations on your engagement."

She glances at her left hand, where a four-carat emerald-cut diamond crows up at him. "Thank you. We're very excited."

"Well, it was nice to see you." Adam tries to leave, really he does. But he can't help himself. He turns and asks, "Why did you let me propose, if you had someone else in the wings?"

She cringes, then hides her hand behind her back. "We're going to do this, then? Here?"

"I guess not." He begins walking away, shaking his head.

Then she calls, "I didn't know you were going to ask. I wasn't *planning* on it."

"*We* had a plan, Lana. You knew the engagement was the destination." He doesn't know why he's pushing so hard. What does it matter now? Still, he feels a sense of injustice. An unhealed blister.

She throws up her hands. "Who cares about the plan? You think there's an easy formula for life—plug and play, like one of your spreadsheets. But it's not like that. You idolized me as this perfect partner, but I wasn't. I made mistakes. We both did."

"I know that." And he does. He's reflected on his late nights, the way he'd often choose his friends or work over her. He's never been blameless. "I'm sorry for my part."

She blows a bit of hair off her forehead. "Anyway, this is all in the past, isn't it? Your father told us that you went on a matchmaking tour."

"My sister's company," he mutters.

She shoots him a sympathetic look. If anyone knows how much Adam has to prove to his family, it's Lana. She's been there since the beginning.

"It's unlike you. I didn't think you would ever agree to something like that."

"Things change."

The sun is dipping below the horizon, casting peachy hues over Hồ Chí Minh City. He's reminded of other sunsets. Of a brilliant smile to rival every unforgettable sight of the tour. Evie's face taunts him each day, even though he refuses to look at the photographs of her. Blocked her on his phone. None of it matters. He's memorized every square inch of her. She's inescapable.

Things do change. But sometimes, as much as it pains him, he wishes he could rewind to a time of possibility.

An alarm on his watch beeps. Lana studies the emotions shifting across his face, hesitating like she wants to ask a question. "I guess I'll see you later?"

He knows he'll be late, which will make Ruby irate, but there's something else he wants to say to Lana. One last thing. "Why didn't you just tell me you didn't want to be together anymore? It would have been cleaner. Kinder."

Her look is sad, resigned, as she changes shoulders with her new Prada bag. The real thing, likely, and not a factory knockoff. Lana, who'd only ever carried briefcases and utilitarian Swedish backpacks. "I'm sorry, Adam. I know I was in the wrong, the villain in your story. I accept that. But the truth is, I still had hope for a long time. I *wanted* to make it work. I waited for so long for you to feel the same way about me that I felt about you. Do you know what that's like? To live with someone who's only halfway there?"

Confusion crosses his face. "I was faithful."

"I know you were. But there's a difference between loyalty and passion. It was clear you could live without me, whereas for a long time, I felt I couldn't live without you. It was like watching you on a boat while I flailed in the ocean, waiting for a safety raft. Or waiting for you to join me in the sea. You were always keeping a part of yourself back. The gold nugget of who you were."

Was that true? Sure, maybe he was distracted sometimes during their relationship, but it was because they'd always been working together for the end goal. The high-rise. The perfect life. He didn't have time to hesitate, to dwell on his childhood traumas, and neither did she. Besides, the great thing about Lana was that she grew up in the same circumstances he did: wealthy, gifted, saddled with a conservative nuclear family with terrifically high expectations. She *got* him.

But there's a niggling truth under all this, pinching his rib cage. When has he ever given his whole self to someone else? Without ego, without fear of rejection? His family taught him to live life with dignity, to keep the walls so high that they would appear impenetrable to outsiders. It was a way to protect one's reputation. One's legacy. Along the way, loving at a distance became Adam's comfort zone.

But is that any reliable circumstance for love? Doesn't love require a measure of vulnerability? Even now, he can't forgive Evie for leaving him. But he would never humble himself to reach out to her first. It would mean letting all the walls down and standing unprotected in front of someone who'd destroyed him so completely.

And that is unthinkable.

Maybe Lana is right. Maybe he's not meant for love.

Lana puts a hand on his arm. "I'm the last person you want to hear this from, but trust me—when you feel it, you'll know. You won't hold back with the right woman. You'll let yourself be messy with her. Give her full access to your secret world. It'll be worth it, if you can manage to stop being so afraid."

She gives him a last, sad smile before she turns on her heel. He fights the urge to follow her, to argue. They've always been good at challenging one another, and in some ways, Adam thrived on the adrenaline of their shared ambition. But now here she is walking away, leaving behind something shimmering, uncertain. A question that he might know the answer to.

"So, Adam, what *is* the secret to a good match?"

He blinks at the computer screen, through which the podcast interviewer waits expectantly for his answer. He made his meeting just in the nick of time. She's recording him for her Vietnamese lifestyle channel, a project he booked before he went on the tour.

They, along with Ruby, are supposed to be discussing the app, due to launch in a few weeks. It's positioned as an alternative for those who don't have the time or resources to shell out a small fortune for the tour. The app focus is still on well-heeled clients, a decision Adam has increasingly begun to resist, and the membership remains exclusive. Vetted. Ruby says it's like Raya for affluent Vietnamese. Beta users have been raving about the ease of the user experience and the prime selection of candidates.

The secret to a good match. He repeats these words to himself.

If he knew, he wouldn't be sitting in Hồ Chí Minh City alone, staring at a screen in his blank cell of an office. He certainly wouldn't be spending his days thinking about a certain woman's long hair, the feel of her hands as she grips his waist on a motorbike. Wondering how she could have left without even saying goodbye.

The interviewer tries again. "Surely you must be an expert in love at this point."

She's a young woman with blue hair, yellow-painted nails, and a winning smile that veers onto the edge of flirtatious. Months ago, Adam might have flirted back, in the name of publicity for Love Yêu, if not personal inclination.

But now he can do little more than clear his throat. Why does he sound like a constipated frog?

Thankfully, Ruby—another square on the screen—laughs charmingly and answers for him. "I don't know that any of us would call ourselves experts in love. Love is still a mysterious phenomenon. What I will say is that we're experts in compatibility. We lean on a team of experts and a sophisticated algorithm in order to create the ideal circumstances for a love match."

"Doesn't a traditional matchmaker accomplish the same results? Why go to an app—or on a tour—for this?" the interviewer prods.

They've been talking for twenty minutes, and Adam has no idea what anyone has said. His head is fogged. His body is bone-tired from the six-mile runs he's taken up every morning to work off his emotions, along with the unexpected conversation with Lana. Every day since the tour has felt like a slog of epic proportions. This interview is the very least of his concerns.

But now, catching sight of Ruby's private chat—*SPEAK UP, BB*—he pastes a smile on his face.

He adds, "We have measurable success, in terms of both the tour and the app. Technology doesn't substitute for connection, of course. But it's a powerful tool we can't ignore. Plus, that's where many of our users are now. They're busy, they're sophisticated. They are eager for something a little more convenient than months of matchmaker meetings to yield one candidate."

"And how do you define measurable success?" the interviewer asks.

Again, he's at a loss. His own experience on the tour was no traditional success. Nothing for the books. His bed is still empty and his thoughts still full to the brim of *her*. He begins to shrug when Ruby again rescues the conversation.

She says brightly, "Well, let's take one couple from our tour: Talia and Pin. When we were choosing participants, I had a hunch that they would be suited for each other . . ."

Adam resists the urge to snort. Ruby had chosen Talia for *him*, and she could not have been more wrong about their chemistry. Of course, that would not have fit into the narrative, so Ruby ignores that little detail. Still, he's happy for Talia and Pin. On social media, Talia showed off a beautiful solitaire, with Pin beaming in the background.

Ruby goes on. "They are both cerebral and philanthropy-minded. In their questionnaires, they described similar wishes for their futures. There were other guests they could have chosen, but ultimately, they found each other."

"Against all odds," the interviewer says, a little dreamily.

"We just helped those odds along. They're engaged now. And they got to meet and fall in love among waterfalls, ancient temples, and flowering gardens in the most stunning parts of our country. How many other couples get to say that? It's a love story for the ages."

The interviewer sighs happily. "Well, now you're making me think I should apply for the next tour."

Ruby winks. "You should. There's still time to join. A fall tour would be a most romantic setting for your own story."

The interviewer laughs. "We'll see. And will you two be going on the next tour?"

"Hell, no," Adam says. The words fly from his mouth before he can stop them.

Ruby's glare singes the screen. She forces out a laugh. "I'm keeping him too busy here, doing his CMO duties."

Attempting to save himself, he puts in, "I wouldn't want to take up a spot that's reserved for another couple-in-the-making. Everyone deserves at least one fighting shot at love."

"Well said," the interviewer tells him.

The interview ends soon after. When he shuts his laptop, Adam thumps his head on the desk. Stupid, stupid. What's happening to him? He used to be able to do all this with aplomb. And now that Ruby hired a copywriter, he should have more time than ever to devote to Love Yêu. But all he really wants to do is curl up in his bed and reread his copy of *Auntie Hảo's Cabinet of Curiosities*, as if Evie's writing could bring her voice closer to him. He's picked up the phone endless times, only to remember that he blocked her. His email trash bin is full of dozens of drafts he never had the courage to send.

But truly, what is there to say? He's worried anything that comes out would be angry. Because he *is* angry. And he misses her.

Minutes after the interview ends, there's a knock on his door. Ruby enters, then studies his slumped form. The empty coffee cups lining his desk. His beaten-up running shoes, tossed below the windowsill. The lack of personal decoration in the office.

There's a long pause. He braces himself for the scolding, but then finds he doesn't care one way or another.

At last, her face softens. "Come on, BB, let me take you out to lunch."

"No, thanks. And stop calling me that." The words come out before he can halt them. And then he wonders: *Why haven't I said it sooner?* "I'm a grown man, Ruby, not your baby brother. It's disrespectful. Especially when you do it in front of our employees."

Ruby's eyes widen. "Oh, my God. Really? I . . . Well, I thought it was just an affectionate nickname. I never realized you felt that way."

"You never asked."

"I'm sorry. I really didn't know."

This is a new one. Ruby never admits fault. Adam nods in acknowledgment, though he doesn't fully allow his walls to come down. She never has time for conversation unless she needs something from him.

"Truly, I'll call you whatever you want. Come out with me, just for an hour or so. We never did anything for your birthday."

It came and went a week ago without any fanfare from his family, which was just fine. His friends had thrown him a party on a rooftop, and he drank himself silly but had gone home alone, despite the gorgeous women plying him with cocktails and compliments. He's honestly surprised that Ruby remembers his birthday, with everything going on.

In the months since the inaugural tour, she's hired a full staff for the tours, as well as a separate staff for the app. Bà Nội came through with a staggering investment that funded these growth initiatives, even though Mr. Quyền, ever astute to a good financial decision, didn't wind up pulling his. Adam suspects his grandmother likes lording her higher shareholder status over her son.

Cherie opted not to come back as a guide, but now she assists Ruby with office maintenance. Adam has heard through the grapevine that she's dating another Love Yêu employee, a tall and serious man who runs their finance department. At one point, Đức had stormed into the office to try to win her back, but Adam swiftly escorted him—and his fedora—out onto the pavement before he could sputter more than a few words of entreaty.

Ruby tries again. "I'll take you to Li Bai."

She names one of the most expensive restaurants in the city, clueing Adam in to her desperation.

"I have a gift for you," she says, a note of pleading creeping into her voice.

"I don't need a bribe, Ruby."

"Please, Adam."

There's something about the way she wrings her hands and stares into his eyes, as if willing him to agree, that makes him thaw.

Grabbing his wallet, he says, "Let's just go to the bún thịt nướng stand around the corner."

She makes a face. "You mean with the grumpy auntie who thinks it's her sacred duty to point out each new wrinkle that pops up on my face?"

"She tells me I get shorter every time I walk past," Adam admits. "It's like—a person doesn't get *shorter*. But tell that to Auntie. Who, by the way, hardly clears four feet herself."

"And yet—"

They intone together in resignation, "Best bún thịt nướng in the city."

Ten minutes later, they're seated at a low plastic table by the stand, cupping warm bowls of vermicelli with savory scallion-scented grilled pork that Grumpy Auntie prepared. She peppered her movements with scathing commentary about the Quyền siblings. Now they duck their heads, avoiding her scowls.

"That felt like going through a war," Adam says.

"Our parents think *they* had it hard."

The streets are muddy from the rain, but they tuck their legs away from the splash of motorcycles whizzing past. It's a cloudy day in Việt Nam, with just a hint of dropping temperatures. Around them, the usual bustle. A city as resilient as a mountain. Even in his moments of longing, Adam can appreciate the jumble of life and history in Hồ Chí Minh City.

With her mouth full, Ruby says, "I think she puts crack in her nước mắm."

Adam sets a cube of grilled pork on his tongue. As he often does, he wonders where Evie is now, mentally calculating her time zone. It's midnight in the Midwest. Is she in bed with Atlas? Talking about her poetry while he brings her a cup of tea—the things Adam desperately wants to do? The thought gives him a sharp jolt of pain, but now that feeling is so common that he tosses it back with the other locked-up emotions.

Ruby sets down her chopsticks. "Bảo. Adam. I said I had a gift for you."

"Okay?"

He's not paying attention. There's a little girl across the street throwing a pod of dried tamarind at her brother. The brother runs under his parents' legs, but he's laughing. Vowing revenge.

"My gift is firing you from Love Yêu."

His attention snaps back to her. "What the hell, Ruby? That's an awful gift."

"I'm not joking." She puts a placating hand on his arm. "You are so good at what you do, but you aren't really interested in doing *this*. It was bad enough seeing you mope around Hạ Long Bay. Your misery was heavy enough to sink our ship. You started nearly five different fights with Riley."

"That's an exaggeration," he mutters.

"Hardly. Now you're walking around in this state of permanent depression."

"I am not," he says indignantly, hearing how childish he sounds.

She continues as if he hadn't spoken. "A year ago, I begged you to quit your job and help me. You *have*. I would not have been able to manage the tour without you. But now we're fine. The company's doing great, and with the sign-ups predicted from the beta users of the app, we'll be rolling in cash and even more opportunities. Because of *you*."

"But—"

"You've done your job, and it's time for you to go on to bigger and better, whatever that means. Of course, you will still have shareholder status, and we're able to give you severance until you figure out what you want to do next. But there's no rush, Bảo. You've been doing what *we've* wanted for so long. Me, our parents, our employees, and our investors. It's time for you to find your own way. It's not really a gift, but something I should have told you a long time ago, as your sister. As someone who is always impressed by you."

Adam doesn't know what to say. There's a sheen of tears in his sister's eyes. She squeezes his hand.

"Ruby, I don't even know what I want to do next," he tells her finally.

"That's okay. You'll figure it out. You can make your way in unfamiliar places. I never had that sense of adventure, that ability to empathize with people. You forge real connections. Like the one you made with Evie."

He opens his mouth to protest, but she speaks over him. "I know you loved her. Do you still?"

He sighs. "I don't know that I'll ever stop."

Then Ruby's tears really fall. Adam, concerned, reaches over with a papery tissue. She takes it and dabs, whispering, "I was the reason she left."

"No, you weren't, Ruby. She did that all by herself." He'll never forget that feeling of looking for her, only to know she disappeared without a trace.

She shakes her head. "I'm so ashamed, Bảo. I see you every day, with this morose expression, looking like you want to fly across the world. And you do. You want to be with her."

"It's impossible."

"The day before she left, I told her that Ba was going to withdraw his investment if you got together with her. I said, essentially, that it would ruin your life if she stayed."

Adam's mind is racing. "What do you mean?"

"Don't you see? She left for *you*. To make things easier for you. Because the thought of hurting you and your future was too much. She left because she loves you too."

Adam lets his hands fall heavily in his lap. A thousand thoughts are crowding his mind. First there's the sting of Ruby's betrayal. Annoyance at her meddling. Then he's flooded by sadness, a well of longing. Somewhere in there, the old anger finds its way back to him.

"Even so, she should have said goodbye," he says fiercely. "Instead of leaving like a thief in the night without a word. I deserved more."

Ruby reaches into her purse with a small sniff and pulls out a sheet of paper folded into a tight square. She places it on the table between them.

She says guiltily, "That's not exactly how it happened. Evie asked me to give this to you before she left."

He stares at the paper as if it's drenched in poison. He sees his name in careful script. Evie's handwriting, which he's never seen. How could he be so in love with a woman he only knew for a few weeks? How can just the sight of her handwriting make his heart beat faster? Love is a cruel sorcerer.

Ruby brushes the remaining tears out of her eyes. "I'm so sorry, Adam. I never told you any of this because Love Yêu is *all* I have left. While I was on the tour, Thăng asked for a separation. It looks like it'll be permanent. A divorce. And I was adrift. Then I went crazy when Ba threatened to shut down the company. Really, severely out of my mind. I didn't know how to tell Ba and Mẹ—or you—about Thăng. I just wanted to pretend everything was okay. I needed you."

Adam takes a beat to process this. Ruby and Thăng have always seemed solid, despite the long-distance nature of their marriage. They were aligned in goals, the way he and Lana had been. It was as if Thăng was hand-selected by their parents. So what went wrong?

"You should have told me. I'm your family."

But even as he says it, he understands. Admitting weakness has never been part of the Quyền credo. Adam wouldn't have confided in Ruby about such matters. Even now, he's done exactly what was expected of him: he buries the heartbreak and continues to work.

Ruby replies, "I've always been Ba's dependable little soldier. I did everything without complaint. I guess I was just ashamed and scared of what the divorce would mean for my future, especially with the company. I mean, who could possibly trust an owner of a matchmaking service who couldn't keep her own marriage together?"

Adam is silent for a moment. Then he shrugs. "I never liked Thăng anyway. He always wanted to golf. What Vietnamese man *golfs*?"

Ruby laughs shakily. "Truly the worst of his sins."

"Are you all right, Ruby?"

"Surprisingly, not as bad as I thought I might be. I still haven't told Ba and Mẹ. You're the first person who knows. It's been a lonely few months, but I'll live."

Adam is at first unnerved to see the vulnerability in her face. But then he reaches over to hug his sister, taking her into his arms. He realizes that this is one of the only times in their adult lives that they've hugged. The Quyèns have never been known for being physically demonstrative. She holds him tightly in return.

"I'm here, Ruby," he says softly. "I'm just your dumb little brother, but I've never left."

"I know, Bảo," she sniffs.

A moment later, she releases him and says out of the corner of her mouth, "Watch out; Grumpy Auntie is shooting daggers at us. Thinks we're making a scene."

"Typical of you."

She laughs, then stands, pushing the note closer to him. "Just read it, Adam. I don't know what it says, but if I know anything about Evie, I know she's poured her heart into it. She's nothing if not honest."

A smile sketches across his face. "This is a fact."

"Just so you know: I liked her fine. I even secretly cheered her on when she and Ba got into it. But I was resentful that she got to be exactly who she wanted to be, without the constraints we had growing up. I was *jealous*. She's special."

"I know."

"I hope you can forgive me someday."

"We'll see. You were kind of an asshole, and you kind of screwed up my life."

Ruby hangs her head. "You're right."

Then he relents. "But I won't stop loving you, Ruby. Even if you piss me off sometimes. Even if you just fired me."

"It's for your own good." She gives him one last, sad smile. "Off to see my divorce lawyer now. Wish me luck."

As he watches his sister trudging down the street by herself, Adam is forced to acknowledge that, no matter how subconsciously, Ruby and Thăng were the blueprint for his own relationship with Lana. They seemed to be living in untroubled, uncomplicated harmony. And now the blueprint has been crumpled. Tossed aside.

Perhaps the measure of success in love is not through numbers or outward notions of compatibility—living in the same social circles, going to the same elite schools—as he indicated to the interviewer. Maybe the whole point is that love *isn't* logical. It is a night alone in a cave. It's traveling through the winding roads of life together, without a plan, but with the firm conviction that the journey is worth taking with the other person by your side.

Adam reaches for Evie's note and opens it, holding his breath against what he might find.

EVIE

San Francisco, California

It's a gorgeous fall day in Little Saigon, with shoppers streaming in and out of small businesses—the nail salons, sandwich shops, tailors, and acupuncturists. The breeze coming off the Bay is gentle yet insistent, prompting the aunties and uncles to unearth their hats and gloves, unaccustomed to the cold even after so many years away from Việt Nam.

The regular chess players, old men with their hands fisted into the pockets of their army jackets, gather around a card table perched perilously close to the road. They hover over every move, jostling each other to get a better view of the board. They are full of opinions about each play, pointing and cackling as the moment demands. Meanwhile, their wives frown from inside hair salons, watching the slide of money from one hand to the next.

"You better not be betting again, old man," one older, very short woman calls from the doorway of a salon. Her red nails drum against the frame.

"Chời ơi! Who bets on a game of chess?" another woman adds, from inside the salon.

One of the men on the street waves his hand dismissively. "Mind your own business, Bà."

"Your gambling *is* my business," the first lady returns, hands now moving to her hips.

The man reaches into his pocket for a lighter to light a cigar. "Isn't it time for your hair appointment? You look like phù thủy without it."

Evie hides a smile. He'd called his wife a witch.

A huff of indignation from the wife. "What's it say that you married me, then, asshole?"

"That I like charity work." He hoots, slapping his knee.

There's a long pause. Then, like fireworks, bursts of laughter erupt from the street and the salon. Just before the salon door slams, the wife shakes her head, a tiny upward tick of her mouth hinting at her own amusement. The chess play goes on.

It's a world unto itself, full of activity and loud conversation, right here in the Tenderloin. A mix of English and Vietnamese, though the ratio is more firmly weighted toward Việt. The sound of the language fills Evie with a longing so intense that she bites her lip to keep from shivering. She pulls her trench closer.

That morning, she woke up with an urge for a bowl of hủ tiếu, and knew she had to go to the closest source. She missed the sound of Vietnamese voices, the smell of cinnamon-laced broth and fresh, baking bread. She missed *Việt Nam*. Here, among the crowd of people, she's easily taken back to her days on the tour—days that changed her forever. She finds herself thinking about mornings looking out at the South China Sea past the roil of waves and the smoldering sunrise. Stone steps winding up ancient temples full of her father's heritage—*her* heritage.

That she's here today, in Little Saigon, tells her that Auntie Hảo's plan worked in at least one way. Perhaps Evie didn't walk away with a relationship. But she came back to the States feeling a sense of dual citizenship to both America and Việt Nam in her heart, if not in the legal sense. For that, she sends up another burst of gratitude to Auntie Hảo. Like a kiss, a brief breeze touches her cheek. She can't help thinking it's a celestial reply.

After her breakfast of tapioca noodles in a deep, porky broth, she finds herself lingering on the street. She loves the row house, but it often feels like an echo chamber. It's *much* too big for one person, though she has promises of visitors from Midland and beyond. Fen and Mei have vowed to come around the winter holidays. Lillian has booked a trip over Thanksgiving, already planning their itinerary around the food spots she wants to introduce Evie to.

Despite the richness of her life, Evie is uncertain about the future. Her newest book ekes out of her word by word. She spends three times as long editing a poem as she does writing it. Her editor is happy with the work in progress, already excited about the memoir that will come next. Usually, the pressure would have incapacitated Evie, but not this time. Perhaps it's because she's already known what it feels like to lose everything, as she did earlier in the summer when she lost her job, and the year before, when she lost her beloved aunt. When you've sunk to your lowest, every step forward feels like an ascension.

Evie remains busy through readings and conferences, and even a weekly workshop for teens at the local community center where fifteen- and sixteen-year-olds troop into the carpet-tiled room with undisguised excitement, all energy and voice and big ideas. They inspire Evie. She spends more time than she should preparing for each class. She takes them to poetry slam readings and introduces them to her newly acquired West Coast poet friends. Throughout this experience, she finds that she does have an aptitude for teaching—just not within the confines of academia. Plus, teens are *fun*.

And yet. Her heart hasn't fully healed. The *next* part of her future is one she's not quite equipped to handle.

Maybe that's why when she passes a tiny woman standing in front of a dark shop, Evie pauses, a question in her eyes. There's something about the woman that catches Evie's attention. She wears round glasses low on her nose, her cheeks rosy-red and plump as a child's, though she looks to be at least in her sixties. Her hair is that gorgeous silvery color perfected by Asian grannies, waving around her face in a fluffy blowout. She looks nothing like Auntie Hảo, but she exudes a mischievous warmth that immediately makes Evie feel at home.

"Come in for a reading?" the woman asks. She steps closer to Evie and looks deep into her eyes.

"Well—"

"Fifty percent off for the lost girl."

The lost girl. Something about her phrasing makes Evie want to cry.

She notices the cardboard sign hanging inside the window. *BEST PSYCHIC IN LITTLE SAIGON.* Evie's never been a superstitious sort. She opens her mouth to decline politely, but then the woman gives her a nod that feels at once so reassuring and promising that Evie follows her into the building.

The furniture sits low to the ground—a coffee table with cushions surrounding it, knock-off Tiffany-style table lamps that emit a murky golden light, a plastic swivel-headed fan placed in the corner of the room. Evie smells joss sticks and oranges and mint oil, a beautiful mélange of home. She takes a second to adjust to the dim light, but then she settles on one of the cushions.

"You can call me Bà Oanh. Tarot, palm, or clairvoyance?" the woman asks.

"A buffet of the supernatural!" Evie tries to joke. But on catching Bà Oanh's impatient glance, she answers quickly, "Regular old clairvoyance."

There's a long silence as Bà Oanh takes Evie in. She notices Evie's dangling earrings, her fuchsia lipstick. The way her boots tap nervously. Her bitten-down nails. It makes Evie fidget to be observed so closely. It's almost as if the sound of the street has died down, making way for this ominous silence that feels nearly suffocating. This world fading into another.

Finally, Bà Oanh pronounces, "You are in deep denial. You have absolutely everything you've ever wanted, but you cannot open yourself to the only thing you've ever needed."

"Love?" she whispers.

Bà Oanh says scornfully, "No, dummy. Courage. Love does not happen without—"

"Bravery," Evie says quietly.

"Exactly. Now you understand. You left a great love behind, didn't you, child?"

Evie nods. Bà Oanh continues, "And now you regret it. I feel it coming from every pore in your body. Love lost is a difficult trauma to overcome. I think it is an ancestral trauma with you."

Evie thinks about Auntie Hảo and her childhood love. Her mother losing her father. Yes, perhaps the map of grief has always been inside her, etching through her life until she believes it to be the only destiny for a love story.

"But you understand now that the loving is worth the losing?" Bà Oanh asks, peering closely. "Think of it. Think of him."

Evie swallows. As if every moment of her life isn't consumed by thoughts of careening through the hills with Adam on his bike. Hiking through the jungle. Witnessing that tender heart of his, encased in metal—a cage whose bars it seemed only she could melt. And hadn't he done the same for her? Freed her? Shifted her life in tiny increments, until it felt like she could never go back to the way it was before?

Loving him taught her to love herself. Maybe that is the whole point of loving bravely. To shine that adoration inward, so that you can accept whatever happens outside the self.

And these days, it's easier than ever for Evie to love herself. Auntie Hảo's unruly coterie—who've fully adopted her into their fold—value her exactly as she is. Her mother, Lillian, and her friends *see* her. And the literary world has finally acknowledged her. But even before that public recognition, she'd been proud of herself for going on an adventure by herself. She'd tested her limits—on her own—and had come out triumphant, even if she hadn't fully completed the tour.

Bà Oanh says, leaning back in satisfaction, "You see. Now it will all work out."

"But it's not that simple," Evie protests. "I *left* him. I wasn't brave at all. How can I move forward with this regret?"

"You wonder if he will forgive you." Evie nods. Bà Oanh continues, "My child, he will forgive you. He already has. Just tell him."

"How will—"

"You American children, always spinning yourselves in circles about the plans for the future. Leave it up to fate for once."

"What if—"

"Time's up!"

With an abrupt yet agile leap, Bà Oanh gets to her tiny feet and begins fiddling with her tea collection. She hands over a sachet. "That's for later. Your man will like it. On the house!"

It's an orchid-scented oolong blend, labeled Triumph Tea. *Hmm*. Evie hands over the bills to Bà Oanh, who counts, squinting in the dark. Then she nods and shuffles Evie out the door.

"Nice doing business with you! Tell your friends."

The mysterious aura Bà Oanh had manifested during the reading fades, replaced by the brisk, businesslike air of an auntie late for her next appointment. Evie blinks into the sunlight of the street. It feels a little like stepping through a portal. Back to real life. She half expects the little psychic shop to disappear behind her, but it doesn't.

As Evie begins to walk back to her apartment, Bà Oanh calls, "Hey! Lost girl."

Evie turns. Bà Oanh gives her a big, toothy smile under her glasses. "You know what to do with that big house, right?"

A slow grin creeps onto Evie's face at the sight of the other woman's knowing expression.

She does know, has since the first moment she stepped through the doors of the row house this summer, though she didn't want to admit it to herself at first.

Now a line from Auntie Hảo's letter floats up toward her, almost as if the words were written in the air, silvery and insistent: *set up a crazy artists' commune*. Auntie Hảo knew too.

The row house is meant to be a retreat for writers and artists, a place for them to work and dream, building that community Auntie Hảo had always tried to create. Evie can see it so clearly. There'd be big dinners in the evening with bottles of wine, buns from the pastry shop down the street. Conversations by the hearth. Connections that would carry them all through the lonely minefield of creative work. She'd offer scholarships to anyone who needed one. Maybe she could raise money through grants or donations from patrons. It could work.

Of course, she has no business acumen at all. No understanding of spreadsheets or marketing or publicity. But she knows someone who does.

Bà Oanh winks at the sight of Evie's dawning excitement. "It'll be gangbusters, girl."

Then suddenly, Evie laughs, a wild and free sound that travels through Little Saigon, drawing the attention of those on the street, who crane their necks to watch her. A woman in a trench coat and boots, gleefully dancing in a circle, as if she has no care in the world. Nothing to lose at all. Rather than the looks of disapproval she expects, most give her indulgent smiles. They make room for her joy.

That joy carries her all the way back to Auntie Hảo's house—her house. She's deep in thought, considering the ways she might turn the upper floors into studios. Does she have time for this? How could she not? She almost hears Auntie Hảo's echo. *You can do anything you dream, my darling girl.*

"Now, that is a smile worth getting on a twenty-hour flight for."

She stops. Her breath escapes.

She knows that voice. Deep and tender and full of affection. Edged with humor, brimming with challenge. The voice she dreams about every night.

Evie slowly raises her head.

There, sitting on her front steps, is Adam Quyền, wearing a pair of gray slacks and a cream-colored sweater pushed up to his elbows, offsetting the golden cast of his tan. His hair is mussed, a small duffel bag by his feet. He stands and walks toward her, each step so deliciously full of promise. As a smile spreads across his face, one meant for just her, she feels that heat licking at the center of her—mixed with something even more precious than the lust he's always able to summon. He's different, somehow. His shoulders are relaxed, his expression open and unguarded. He is *radiating* love.

She swallows. "You. Here?"

"So monosyllabic today, sweetheart."

"How? Why?"

He reaches over and strokes a strand of hair from her face. "You sure you work with words for a living?"

His thumb lingers near her jawline, and his touch is gentle, yet firm. As if it's meant to be on her. She can't help leaning into his palm. Staring at him like he's a mirage. She resists the urge to paw at him, to make sure he's really in front of her.

She tries again. "How did you get here? I mean, I know a flight, but why and . . . You're *here*, Adam. Don't you believe in calling first?"

"I predicted the chances of you running away to the nearest mountain to be around seventy percent. And that was generous. Couldn't risk it."

"Again with the data sets. My grumpy CMO."

"Wait, you call me that?" His eyes light up with suppressed laughter.

"Um." She averts her gaze guiltily. "Only at first. After the rooster."

"And now?"

"I just call you Adam."

"Well, good. Because I'm no longer a CMO. Ruby fired me."

"I think we have to sit down for this."

She drags them down to sit on the front stoop, and immediately, Adam wraps his arm around her shoulders and tucks her in tightly to his side. He emits so much body heat that she wants to shrug off her coat, needing only his warmth. But his grip is firm, his thumb rubbing circles on her arm that are entirely distracting. She's studying his jawline, those strong shoulders, daydreaming about a certain kiss outside a hut in Nha Trang, when his voice cuts through.

"Is this okay?" he asks, bending to look at her.

In reply, she snuggles closer. "This will always be okay."

He brushes his lips on her hair. "Ruby fired me, but only because she wants me to find something I am truly passionate about. It wasn't Love Yêu, as much as I came to admire what Ruby was trying to do. My last day was on Friday. And I walked around my apartment, thinking and planning. Maybe I would travel? I could start my own company? But then, every time, I'd see you in my mind. Or I'd be out at a restaurant and wonder what you'd think of a dish. Once, I saw an antique mandarin's writing desk, and I could picture you leaning over it, working on your poetry. You're kind of a big deal now, did you know?"

She groans. "Only in very small circles. Like, my living room."

He continues, ignoring her, "And I'd think of us lying in bed together, talking into the night."

"That's what you thought of us doing in your bed?" she says archly.

"Among other, infinitely naughtier things."

"Oh." She shivers, biting her lip.

"Evie, what I'm saying is that anywhere I want to go, anything I want to do, will never be fully satisfying without *you*. You give me the joy that was missing from my life. That spark that never caught until you came along. When I think about what's next for me, I think of *you*. And only you."

"Adam," she says. There's a wetness on her cheeks now. She reaches over and takes his hand. "I missed you so much. And I am so, so sorry for how I left. I was scared. I thought it would be easier for us both . . . but it really, really wasn't. Not for me, anyway."

"Not for me either, sweetheart."

He runs a hand through his hair and releases her so he can face her fully. He pulls a folded piece of paper from his pocket and smooths it out on his knee.

"I didn't see your letter until last week. Ruby—well, she had her reasons, but she never gave it to me. I'd been so angry at you for leaving. I thought that you were going back to that ex of yours. Map or whatever."

"Atlas." She hides a smile.

"Okay, whatever," he says, a small tick in his jaw. "But when I read the letter, I knew you felt the same way about me as I do about you."

"And how's that?" She's about to put him out of his misery, to confess her feelings, when he cuts in without hesitation.

"I love you, Evie Lang," he says, his face now inches from hers. "I'll say it as often as you need me to. I love you the way you love others. The way you will fight so fiercely for your friends—for me. My father's never been put in his place a day in his life; even Ruby is a little scared of you. But honestly? I just love your creative, spontaneous, incredibly irritating self. If you never published another poem, never left our bed, I would still be wildly infatuated with you. Nothing matters but your soul. It's goodness and light and beauty. You're the thrill I never want to stop chasing."

The wind whooshes in her ears. Happiness floods her veins.

"Oh." Her tongue is heavy. The smile on her face is *stupidly* dreamy.

This. This is her person. He flew across the world for her. He leapt past every obstacle in his way. He's fearless, and she wants nothing more than to jump with him into their beautiful, utterly unpredictable future.

"I love you too, my Adam," she says. She brings her hand up to reach for him. Gazing into those dark eyes, which remain fixated on her.

"That wasn't so hard, was it?" he asks.

When their lips meet, it's with the pure sweetness of a long-awaited pleasure. Like the first lick of ice cream amid the scorch of a tropical beach. Or a rush of air after a long underwater dive. They marvel at the way their mouths fit together, how their tongues understand just when to push, when to tease and retreat. Adam's hands move to Evie's waist, pulling her against him, so she's nearly sitting in his lap. Her fingers wind through the softness of his hair.

It could go on forever, this kiss. But then there's a hooting from down the street, some of Evie's teen workshop students whooping, "Get it, Miss Lang!" until they pull back and begin laughing.

"Those kids belong to you?" Adam asks, amusement dancing across his face. He raises his hand to them as they bop by, smirking and high-fiving Evie as they pass.

"Pretty much," she sighs. "I'm supposed to be teaching them, but—well, you know the saying. Teacher becomes the student and all that."

"More like 'teacher becomes the hopeless softie.'"

"You're not wrong. Speaking of softies, Adam."

"Yeah, Evie?"

Their names belong together. It shouldn't have taken her so long to fight fate.

She tells him, "You said so many nice things to me. And they are all true, I am great. But I also want you to know that you are the dream I've never felt worthy enough to reach for."

"Baby—" he begins.

"Let me finish. After Auntie Hảo's and Dad's deaths, I thought my heart should stay shut for a while; maybe I never said that to myself consciously, but I sure never let anyone in. Then there were all the failures of my career. The breakup that won't be mentioned. I went to Việt Nam for an escape from reality. It was just supposed to be a simple vacation. And then I met you. Nothing was simple. I saw beautiful beaches, epic mountains—"

"Connor's puke on a karaoke stage—"

Evie laughs. "Don't remind me. But the point is that I had to go through all that to clear away the other voices. The ones telling me that I'm not good enough. *Your* voice cut through the rest, always assuring me that you would never leave, even if I did. Now I know we're *both* enough." She pauses here and takes his hands for emphasis. "Together, we're everything."

"When did you get so wise?" he murmurs.

She says airily, "When I started seeing a psychic."

"Um?"

"I'm also opening a retreat for creatives in my house."

"Wow, okay. That sounds—"

"And you're going to help run it."

Adam raises an eyebrow. "I have questions. Many questions."

She laughs and pulls him up along with her, standing on her toes to plant another warm, delicious kiss right on his lips. This time, there's a new urgency to the kiss. A desperate wanting, accumulated through months apart, through dreams in which their mouths always find each other again.

And yet—the reality has always been better than anything they can imagine. As they move together, Evie's letter, long forgotten, wafts out of Adam's lap, into the deepening afternoon light, now transformed into a golden color that hints at new beginnings. The letter floats, as if on wings, past buildings lined with recycling bins, past the bodegas, right out to the bay where sailboats skim along the fogged shoreline.

On the piece of paper, one part is faintly visible amid the others, just for a second: *come find me.*

Evie sighs happily, her lips still touching his, and mumbles, "Your questions must wait. We have more urgent destinations."

With that, they're both running up the steps, laughing as Evie fumbles with her keys, then finally lets them into her home. There, in the threshold of the house Auntie Hảo had gifted, they decide to finish everything they started, a whole world away.

ADAM

Huế, Việt Nam
one year later

"I can feel you staring at my ass," Evie mutters out of the side of her mouth.

Surprised, Adam stumbles, then laughs. She's not wrong. There's a delicious tightness to it as she climbs the rough terrain in the rainforest, her calf muscles tensing, the sweat running down her calves. The temperature in Huế is marginally cooler than when they were last here, but it's still difficult to get used to the subtropical climate after all their time in Northern California. Adam never thought he'd get used to the chill in San Francisco, but it turns out, he enjoys the brush with seasons. Of course, it's easy to enjoy anything with Evie by his side.

At the moment, they're a world away from their row house, on their way to the Phong Nha caves again. This time, they have a full tour with them. There will be no getting marooned on a deserted beach. No skinny-dipping in a dark pool of water or making love on the sand, as much as Adam would like that. This time, they opted for a hotel for the night, after which they'll meet Ruby and—shock of all shocks—his parents for lunch the next day.

"Better I look than grab, right?" he whispers darkly in her ear.

"Pervert."

"You're acting like you don't want it just as much as me."

She flushes tellingly and swats at him. "Get all this out of the way before we see your parents, Quyền."

He makes a dismissive gesture, then corrects her. "Quyền-Lang, thank you very much. They won't care. We're married, and with Ruby now single, we are the surest path to perpetuating their dynasty."

"Perpetuating their dynasty," she groans. "There it is. Killed my hard-on."

Evie walks ahead of him through the rainforest, her steps sure in her well-worn boots, now a regular hiker after their time near the redwoods. Every time he sees her, he can't help thinking of her beaming face as she turned to him in San Francisco's City Hall, ready to make it official. Though they'd married quietly, Evie in a white slip dress and Adam wearing a navy suit, they'd had a large party afterward at Auntie Hảo's house—their house.

Lillian, Graham, and their baby daughter were there, along with the rowdy band of creatives that Adam reluctantly accepted as their adopted children, if adopted children got roaring drunk and composed arias in claw-foot tubs at midnight and observed absolutely zero boundaries when it came to bedroom doors. The first thing he'd done after he moved into the house was change out all the locks, so they'd actually work. Evie had laughed at him, but she soon saw the wisdom after he pulled her into their room, soundly turning the lock for hours—and hours—of blissful privacy.

"Speaking of dynasties," Evie calls behind her. "Do you think the Cabinet of Curiosities is in good shape for the winter retreat?"

Adam puts on his operations officer hat, a role he'd been all too glad to accept. "Enrollment was pretty high; we actually had to waitlist a few. There's never enough room for the potters. They require so much *space*."

"They're the nicest, though! Half our dishware is made by the potters. Including that penis-shaped chalice that you always wind up using for the Saturday salons."

"The one you *thrust* into my hand every time, because you think it's hilarious?"

"Yeah, that one." Evie giggles.

"The potters are all right," he admits. "More useful than the poets, of course."

"Hey." She sticks her tongue out at him. "We *bleed on the page*. Not like you soulless marketing robots, who only bleed buzzwords."

He laughs. "I make it a personal mission to bleed as little as possible, metaphorically or otherwise. I hear you have an aversion to blood. But, Evie, winning that city grant meant we were able to offer a couple of full scholarships. One of them was awarded to a young woman from Kansas. Tori Sanchez."

"I saw her application," Evie says, her voice softening. "In her admissions essay, she wrote that her mom died earlier this year. She needs a new start."

"I thought you'd appreciate that. If the money holds out, there will be a recurring scholarship in your father's name."

Evie reaches back to squeeze his hand. They've run a few other retreats and each unfolded so successfully that the social accounts for Cabinet of Curiosities buzzed with tagged photos, DMs, and requests for interviews from local press outlets. The formula for Cabinet of Curiosities is a simple one: The nonprofit gives creative people space away from their normal routines to create and find community. But the magic is in the details, like the beautiful, fresh meals served family-style every night and the in-home masseuse services offered each Friday, and the Saturday night salons where everyone can share a work in progress and receive gentle, nurturing feedback.

Adam reflects proudly that it's actually *Evie* who's the magic. She brings everything she loves about community into one place, always selecting participants who are generous and (generally) ego-free. It's a kind of matchmaking, she says, picking the right mix of characters for a retreat. Sometimes she consults her psychic, Bà Oanh, whose fees she's tried multiple times—to Adam's chagrin—to write off as a tax-deductible expense.

Nowadays, Ruby will often call Evie for business advice, and Adam doesn't blame her. Evie manages conflict with such wisdom and calm that Adam can scarcely recognize the scattered woman who initially arrived on the tour. She's the one who can coax inspiration from even the most deadlocked artists, often sitting with them in silence until they find their way out of the darkness together. She tells them that she's been there, in that hopeless place. And they believe her. They trust her because she's one of them.

But despite the fact that they could be holding these retreats consistently, they only run them twice a year. For one, they don't need the income.

Love Yêu was recently acquired by a huge, international dating conglomerate, and Adam sold his shares for a hefty fee, channeling much of it into Cabinet of Curiosities and reserving the rest for their pet hobby—travel. Ruby is still the CEO of Love Yêu for the time being, but knowing her, she's itching for another business venture.

So far, they've held off on opening more retreat sessions, because Evie needs the time and space for her own work. Her second book of poetry comes out soon, already flush with rave reviews, and she's been head down on her memoir, a rewarding if emotional feat that has taken a lot out of her. She and Grace often talk on the phone, rehashing the old memories and crying over Evie's father. Adam regrets that he never met him or Auntie Hảo, but Evie assures him that they would have been nearly as in love with him as she is.

Now, standing at the entrance to the cave, Evie shoots him a brilliant smile, and his heart clenches at the audacity of its own luck. *His wife.* For years, he searched for a way to check off that last box, a way to finally make his parents happy. But it was only in daring to flout their expectations that he could find his own path—earned and sincere—to joy. At the end of that path will always be *her*.

And his parents have come around, in their own haughty, grudging way. It helped that Ruby supports their relationship entirely—and that her own divorce offered a kind of distraction. Adam was relieved to see that after the initial turmoil died out, Ruby was eager to start anew. She has always deserved better than Thăng (those tribal tattoos!), and now she recognizes that. She jokes about going on the tour for her own purposes this time around.

Adam joins Evie in the cave, taking in the cooling temperature and jagged fossils along the edge. The shadowy cavern is still and quiet, with a distant twinkling of lights from the headlamps of another tour group.

"They call this the Dark Cave," he whispers, wrapping his arms around her from behind.

"A bit on the nose."

The tour guide tells them they can take in a mud bath if they choose.

Everyone else peels down to their swimsuits, then hops into the earth-toned pool, sinking up to their necks in warm mud. Usually, Evie would be game too, but she shakes her head and leads him away from the group, threading her fingers through his.

"No mud for you, sweetheart?" he whispers into her neck.

"My thoughts are dirty enough without it." She spins to face him, then wiggles her eyebrows. "Besides, I have a proposition for you."

"Yes. The answer is always yes." He kisses her on the nose, moving down her face to reach her lips. But she ducks away.

"Focus! I was thinking . . ."

"Dangerous."

"You have no idea. What if we buy a house here? In Việt Nam? I know you miss it. You gave up so much for me. You shouldn't have to give up your home too."

He shakes his head. "Home is where *you* are."

She grins and swats at him. "Put it on a doily, mister. I'm serious. We can afford it, and I would like to be able to think about hosting international retreats someday. I miss it here. It's my heritage too. Ruby and I were talking about combining a writing workshop with a tour—can you see it? Marrying inspiration with travel and the best instructors? We could offer fellowships from donors. Your parents' hoity-toity friends would jump at the chance to appear in a bestselling book dedication. And we'll need some headquarters overseas if we're going to make it happen."

He groans. "You and Ruby are going to empty our bank accounts." But his brain begins to add up numbers. He knows he could get some of his friends on board. And they could build on the highly successful formula that he and Ruby created. Plus, he and Evie could travel on the tours themselves, as hosts. She could write, and at night, they could make love on the balconies overlooking a private beach . . .

A smile spreads across his face. He admits, "I can see it."

"I knew you'd come around," she crows.

"That took all of five seconds."

She winks. "Longer than I expected, honestly. And—who knows?

Maybe someday, we'll fill our Việt Nam home up with more than just irascible artists."

When she bites her lip, looking through her lashes at him in a silent question, he sees that too. A future filled with miniature, sleepy-eyed versions of her and vacations up the coast of the South China Sea and sticky fingers reaching into the barrels of saltwater taffy on Pier 39. The two of them, heads bent together after a long day, sighing with satisfaction about their full, complicated, always surprising life.

He says without hesitation, "Yes. Yes to all of it."

When he meets her mouth, it's with a crushing heat, a desperate will for her to see what's in his heart. He wants her to feel, with no doubt in her mind, the jubilant, overflowing love he holds for her—and for their blooming future. Into the kiss, he presses his confidence that they will make a life together, one step at a time, filling each busy hour with even more joy than they ever thought possible.

But as her lips meet his, hungry and answering, he realizes that she already knows what he's thinking. They have always been able to speak without words. Theirs is the language of stars and heat and overwhelming possibility. Theirs is the result of an existence lived bravely. Lived together.

And maybe somewhere far away, there's an old woman clucking in satisfaction, knowing that her greatest wish for her niece has come to pass, though not without the dips and pivots and wild turns that accompany every life worth living.

Every wise woman knows this truth: a joyful life is never simple. If anything, those wild turns are the point of it all. One only has to remain faithful to the destination.

The wise woman in the clouds blows a kiss down to her niece, which Evie feels as a shiver that fades as quickly as it arrives.

Hand in hand, Adam and Evie slip away into the sunshine, leaving the silence and darkness of the cave. Turning the page for a new couple to make their own brave, unforgettable leap into the radiant unknown.

AUTHOR'S NOTE

Many great love stories start with longing. And when I wrote Adam and Evie's story, I longed for nothing more than the slosh of waves on my skin on the shores of Nha Trang. The flurry of a night market in the starry hours. The soul-shaking awe of standing at the threshold of a centuries-old temple. For a time during the pandemic, Vietnamese borders were closed to visitors. Some of my family were waylaid in Việt Nam, while the rest of us waited for their return in America. During those uncertain months, I felt a great yearning to be back home—or, a version of home I'd remembered. This longing is, perhaps, the challenge and blessing for many diasporic artists. We'll forever chase an evaporating dream.

The inspiration for the matchmaking tour in this novel comes from my own experience on a whirlwind tour through Việt Nam (not a matchmaking one, though!). I experienced many of the sights in the book firsthand, and still think about them today. Some of the locations are but peeks into a dream itinerary I hope to complete with my husband and daughter one day. A handful are imagined for the book. Thank you to all the wonderful Vietnamese tourism sites and travel content creators who brought these remarkable places to life for me. Any errors or deviations are my own.

Books let our imaginations travel where our feet cannot. My heartfelt thanks go to you readers for taking this journey with me. May we all love and live as bravely as Auntie Hảo would have wished.

ACKNOWLEDGMENTS

Such gratitude to my agent, Abby Walters, who immediately went all in when I expressed a desire to write romance novels. Your resourcefulness and keen-eyed vision for my work have transformed my life. Equal thanks to my editor, Molly Gendell, who leapt with me into the genre and used her vast editorial skills to draw out the best in Adam and Evie's love story. I felt your enthusiasm every step of the way! A special thanks to Priyanka Krishnan for shepherding this book to the finish line.

Thank you, Ploy Siripant, for another unforgettable cover, and for always bringing stories to life with such verve. Thank you to talented Decue Wu for an illustration that perfectly captures the scope and swoon of this novel. Undying gratitude to the dream team, Rachel Berquist and Jessica Cozzi—how lucky I am to work with you again! Thanks to DJ DeSmyter, Jackie Alvarado, Grace Vainisi, and Amanda Hong.

All my gratitude to the Ohio Arts Council and the Sustainable Arts Foundation, not only for your financial support that has allowed me the time to continue writing, but for your belief in my work.

Heart-eyes and crushing hugs to my beautiful friends who let me share my favorite jokes in my novels. You make an otherwise lonely writer's life so rich in joy.

My lifelong gratitude to my most beloved grandparents for gifting me a tour of a lifetime to Việt Nam, and to my mother, for going on the adventure with me (and for sneaking out past curfew to chase late-night food cravings with me). I'll prize those memories forever. I desperately hope you skipped the hut, cave, and library scenes while reading.

Thank you to my sweet Ellie for designing the first cover sketch for *Adam & Evie*, and for your infectious enthusiasm for all things romance. No one believes in love more sincerely than you! I hope that never changes. And to Dan, who reads my drafts with excitement and never bats an eye when I spring another wild idea on you. Celebrating the wins (and mourning the losses) feels so much more profound with you.

Lastly, to all the passionate readers, reviewers, librarians, and booksellers: Thank you for making books cool, in the way only you can. Every message of support, every recounting of your favorite scenes, every IRL meeting makes me absolutely giddy. I couldn't do any of this without you!

Nora Nguyen is a romance novelist with a yen for quick banter and breathtaking travel destinations. As a lifelong romance enthusiast (lookin' at you, bonnet-rippers), she fully believes in the healing power of a transportive love story. Her work has been published in the *Los Angeles Review of Books*, *Wired*, *Elle*, and other publications. A recipient of an Individual Excellence Award in Fiction from the Ohio Arts Council, Nora lives in central Ohio with her husband and daughter. She writes literary fiction under the name Thao Thai, where her debut novel, *Banyan Moon*, was a Read with Jenna and Barnes & Noble Discover pick.

More Asian American Fiction from HarperCollins

"A riveting mother-daughter tale."
—*Elle*

"Radiant.... An intimate account of one family's planting of roots in American soil and the sacrifices great and small that each member makes along the way."
—*Washington Post*

A sweeping, evocative debut novel following three generations of Vietnamese American women reeling from the death of their matriarch, revealing the family's inherited burdens, buried secrets, and unlikely love stories.